Race Point

For
Kevin John Snyder, Esq.
All yours, little brother.
Really miss you.

"Hate is a bottomless cup; I will pour and pour."

Euripides, *Medea*

Chapter 1
Boston, Massachusetts
Present Day

Standing alone on the 52nd floor of the Prudential Tower, Klaryssa watches the women's champion cross the finish line of the Boston Marathon, taking no notice of the spot where, five years ago, her life nearly ended.

Having braved horizontal sheets of wind-driven rain in temperatures that at times dropped below freezing, the winner of the women's division is the first to hail from the United States in over three decades. This same competitor posted strong performances in previous marathons, including the race in Chicago a few years earlier when she finished a close second. Klaryssa also competed in the Chicago Marathon that year, and although she crossed the finish line every bit of an hour and a half after the winner had broken through the tape, she was proud of having clocked her best personal time ever in marathon competition.

In the months that followed, Klaryssa trained harder than ever, preparing for her next contest: the 2013 Boston Marathon. Klaryssa had every confidence that she could top her personal best in that race, and when the time finally came and she passed the 26-mile mark, all she needed was one final surge of adrenaline to get her across the finish line in front of the Boston Public Library on Boylston Street. It was 2:49 PM on Monday, April 15, 2013.

Seconds later, Klaryssa's world went silent.

When she finally awoke four days later, surrounded by intensive care monitors, flashing lights, and a huddle of long white coats, Klaryssa was unable to speak due to the ventilator tube that was still in her airway. When her eyes opened, all she saw—and all she cared about—was the face of her then-13-year-old daughter, Yeva, whose tears were raining down onto Klaryssa's forehead.

Klaryssa spent 15 days in the Brigham and Women's Hospital in Boston and another three weeks in a rehabilitation center. A month and a half after the incident, she was walking on her own, without crutches and without assistance. Six months after that, she was walking without a limp, and a year after that, she was running again—running through parks, along abandoned rail lines, and along lonely back roads. But there have been no more races for her, and no more marathons. Not yet, anyway.

Three people were killed in the marathon bombing that day. Three nights after the bombing, the two terrorists, Tamerlan and Dzhokhar Tsarnacv, shot a 27-year-old police officer to death.

Besides the four people who died at the hands of those two terrorists, 270 people on Boylston Street were seriously injured, many losing one or more of their limbs. Klaryssa's doctors told her that she came within a millimeter of losing her life, and, at one point, they were certain that she would lose her right leg. But, now she is walking—and running—with neither pain nor limitation. She thinks that her only visible scar, a pinpoint dot on her left cheek from a tiny piece of shrapnel, actually looks like a dimple. So, apparently, does everyone else. Two terrorists brought death and mutilation to the city of Boston, and Klaryssa Mahr ended up with a speck on her face. When she looks in the mirror, she doesn't even notice the scar. All she sees is the luckiest person on earth.

Today, five years later, Klaryssa is the guest of honor at a reception at the Top of the Hub, a landmark panoramic penthouse restaurant on the 52nd floor of the Prudential Tower, two blocks from the marathon finish line. Klaryssa is an associate professor in the School of Arts and Sciences at Tufts University, and, earlier in the day, she signed several hundred copies of her bestselling book, *Medici's Hand*, at Barnes & Noble, the bookstore located on the first floor of Prudential Center. *Medici's Hand* traces the origin and patronage of the Renaissance art of Italy, and Klaryssa dedicated her book, along with all of its proceeds, to the victims of the marathon bombing. Critics and readers alike laud the book, and the unexpected volume of sales make it the only "academically oriented text" on anyone's bestseller list. Klaryssa is left to wonder if it is the book's content and research qualities that have made it so popular or if it is instead her unique link to the events that took place immediately following the terrorist attack on that Monday afternoon in April of 2013.

On a 42-second-long segment of videotape recorded from a nearby security camera on the day of the marathon bombing, Klaryssa can be seen being catapulted off the ground as if she is wired to the strings of some invisible puppeteer. After slamming back down onto the pavement like a sack of rocks, she quickly stands up and limps to the aid of a runner who is spread eagle along the side of the street, blood visibly gushing from his neck. Klaryssa compresses the man's wound with her bare hand until a police officer arrives with a first aid unit. In the next frame, she is seen standing up once again but then immediately collapsing back down onto the asphalt, her body limp and sprawled. The last frame of the film shows a gusher of blood erupting from Klaryssa's right inner thigh. A two-inch-long bolt from the Tsarnaev brothers' improvised explosive device had ripped through Klaryssa's femoral artery, and the release of the bolt caused such a massive hemorrhage that Klaryssa nearly bled to death in the middle of the street.

After 11 units of emergency blood transfusion and a seven-hour-long operation, the lacerated vessel was grafted, and the vascular flow to Klaryssa's leg was restored.

The man with the neck wound survived.

Klaryssa, comatose and feared brain dead, saw none of the media replays of her actions undertaken between 2:49 and 2:50 PM that day.

In the 24 hours that followed the marathon bombing, at least two billion people in 130 countries did see it.

Klaryssa remembers none of it.

**

Klaryssa is still staring out the window at the street far below when she is jolted by a tap on her shoulder from behind. Unintentionally, Klaryssa drifted away from the crowd assembled in the rooftop restaurant, somewhat lost in her own memories—or, more likely, her lack of any memory whatsoever.

"Professor Mahr," says an elegantly dressed woman, the one tapping Klaryssa lightly on the shoulder. "I am sorry to interrupt, but please, if I may introduce myself. My name is Eleanor Picard, and I've so wanted to meet you."

"Good afternoon, Mrs. Picard," Klaryssa says, extending her hand, somewhat embarrassed by her overreaction to a simple tap on the shoulder. "Please, it's Klaryssa. A pleasure."

"I had every intention of being here earlier for your book signing, but, well, I underestimated the traffic on a day like today and foolishly took a

7

flight in this morning instead of last night," Mrs. Picard says. "And likewise, please, all my friends call me Elle."

Elle speaks with what Klaryssa assumes to be a slight British accent, and she stands out in an informal gathering such as this for all the right reasons, wearing a perfectly tailored designer suit and a pair of Christian Louboutin high heels. Klaryssa guesses her age to be 60 or so, but she might be older, for the woman has every appearance of someone who takes exceptional care of herself.

"Loved it, really just loved it from start to finish," Elle says, producing a copy of *Medici's Hand* she has stashed in her satchel. "Can't say I ever knew a terrible lot about this part of early Renaissance history, but I certainly do now. Bravo to you."

Klaryssa feels the crimson rise in her cheeks, and not for the first time today. Elle hands her the book, and Klaryssa writes a personal note to Elle on the title page, signing the initials *KDM* as she always does, and hands the book back to Elle. "That means a lot to me, Mrs... Elle," she says, her one-sided dimple indenting a bit. "It's my first attempt at this sort of thing, and you never know what kind of reaction you will receive when it's finally in print. Thank you very much."

Klaryssa, while flattered and appreciative, senses a certain unease and a heaviness in the air. Elle surely didn't fly all the way to Boston—from wherever she's from—just to have her book signed.

"Long flight?" Klaryssa asks, as casually as she can.

"Not really. From Kentucky," Elle says, shaking her head slightly. "There are no direct flights, so it's a bit of an irregular mishmash of a route getting here."

"Patriots' Day," Klaryssa blurts out. "If you've never been before, it more or less serves as our yearly Spring coming-out party. Some years, it is also opening day at Fenway Park, and when you throw in the marathon, you've got quite the city festival. Do you have family here, maybe someone who's competing?" Klaryssa asks, her unease growing.

"No, nothing like that," Elle says. Klaryssa notices Elle's hand trembling a bit as she again reaches into her satchel. "I really came to find you, Klaryssa…to find you and show you this."

Elle hands Klaryssa a tome, a book that is clearly quite old with a very worn cover and frayed binding. The book's title reads, *HISTORY and PROCEEDINGS OF THE HOUSE OF LORDS*, stamped with the date 1759.

Klaryssa runs her hand over the book without opening it. "I didn't see one of these on the bookstore shelves earlier today," Klaryssa says, setting the book on a nearby table, wondering why Elle, or anyone, would go through so much trouble just to show her some old book. "But I'm afraid I can't tell you much about the House of Lords, or, for that matter, British law from that era. But I have colleagues in our history department who would be happy to…"

"It's not the book itself that brought me here," Elle says, her hand still shaking as she opens the book to a marked page. "It's what I found inside. I came here to show you this."

When Klaryssa looks down at the open book, her heart goes still. She is unable to utter a sound.

Chapter 2

Saratoga, New York

August 1946

Roscoe was likely the only person in the world—or at least the only person in *his* world—who was blind to the fact that he was a loser.

How different it all might have been if Roscoe had just stuck to card games—any card game: hearts, spades, Oklahoma gin, pinochle, five-card stud, low Chicago, blackjack—it's your call, just deal the cards.

To Roscoe, the thrill of the ever-changing winning and losing permutations involved in just about any card game imaginable became ingrained at an early age. To him, those permutations, that lust for the unknown, became second nature during the early years of his youth. Roscoe's youth consisted of endless miles on the road with his father, Spike, a journeyman trucker and pilot who spent his days bootlegging crates of moonshine and his nights seated behind the first card table he could find.

Somewhere along those cragged highways, Roscoe began to throw what precious few spare coins he had into the game, learning in a hurry what it meant to be in the school of hard knocks, that place where no one—not even your old man—cared a lick about how much lighter your hip pocket might be at the end of the night. He was on his own, and he knew it.

It was Spike's sometimes friend and more-than-sometimes adversary Herman, a gangly, hunched-over Nevadan, who taught Roscoe all he ever needed to know about beating the competition at the poker table. "You don't care," he would say in a low, grave voice, staring down at 12-year-old Roscoe, a stream of Camel non-filtered soot trailing behind his every word. "See these cards? They's just like women. They's just as fine and just as dang'rus. Ignore 'em boy, and before you know it, that top gem is seated in your lap. You don't want to act like the guy who don't give a shit, you want to *be* the guy who don't give a shit."

After that, Roscoe's shtick was decided. It didn't matter whether the game was dealt on a tailgate or on a barrelhead, at the far end of a schoolyard or in the backroom of a whorehouse. Roscoe's eyes, forever at half-mast, revealed nothing. His mannerisms never gave anything away, because he didn't *have* any mannerisms. Roscoe had a rangy build, a mop of wiry hair, a pallid complexion, and a hangdog expression, all of which helped him cloak whatever hand he held, be it meek or mighty.

Forever slumped on the edge of his chair, Roscoe appeared, at times, near comatose, toying with the foes who, on occasion, had to elbow him back into the hand. He was a master at treading water, never yielding to the take-it-and-run demon that had undone a legion of hustlers before him and would continue to undo many after him.

His favorite gambling prey were the college blue bloods who fancied themselves seasoned card sharps. Roscoe knew that the talent of this parade of silver spooners was nothing short of laughable, pathetic even. The only challenge was finding a somewhat graceful exit after he emptied their pockets. There was always the threat of one of the brawnier ones taking a quick but thunderous swing at Roscoe's jaw and tossing him out into the back alley with a broken face.

But in truth, Roscoe never *liked* card games very much. To him, they became all too easy, every last one of them. It was more about the opponents he faced for hours on end than the games themselves. All those vacuous dolts, he'd think—every one of them as witless as the four suits of queens, kings, and johnnies packed inside each deck. Roscoe didn't want to win against his opponents, because he was never outmatched. He wanted to win against *them*—the games themselves.

***

Roscoe was drafted into the army two days after the attack on Pearl Harbor, and after being shuttled between a string of Pacific outposts, he was assigned to the desolate islands of Western Alaska. He and his fellow GIs had ample time to let their thoughts—and their money—run wild. The number wheel, dice, roulette, bingo, chicken fights, and dog fights were only the beginning. They would bet on anything: the day's lowest temperature, the total snow accumulation, when it would start snowing, when it would stop snowing, changes in wind direction, the number of minke whales they would see surface while out on patrol—the list was endless. With every dawn came a new, ever more inventive and esoteric game of chance. The Americans' penchant for gambling was so well-known that Russian soldiers stationed in the Aleutians Islands would goad their American allies into betting on how many busted bottles of vodka they would find when they opened the next shipment container.

But, no matter how many bunkhouse card games he tried to scare up to cover his mounting losses, there were never enough games to save Roscoe's financial hide. Having placed his fingers into every game-of-chance pie, the only thing Roscoe left the military with—besides an honorable discharge—was an arm's-length list of creditors. He ducked all the Russians he owed by hopping on an early transport plane out of the Aleutians, bribing another copilot out of his seat with five stolen bottles of rotgut rye whiskey.

While on the transport plane, Roscoe began to suffer from intractable vomiting. His illness was presumed to be caused by the toxins he was exposed to during his single episode of active combat: the retaking of the island of Kiska from the Japanese. But Roscoe wasn't puking his guts up because of some toxic gas he inhaled in the line of duty; rather, his illness was the result of an emetic medication that he kept on hand—and consumed—for just such a situation: when he was deeply in debt and had to flee. Two nights later, once his self-induced vomiting had subsided, Roscoe escaped his domestic debt via a one-way trip down the fire escape at a GI hospital.

Roscoe was free. And Roscoe needed a new game.

Roscoe's dream was every high-roller's dream: he wanted to make his mark—his fortune—by bringing the ultimate foe to its knees. And, as Roscoe saw it, the foe that was about to eat his dust had four knees and weighed in at well over half a ton.

The Saratoga Racecourse in upstate New York, shuttered for most of the war, had sprung back to life in the summer of 1946. During July and August, there were nine races a day, six days a week, and Roscoe knew full well of the vast plunder that beckoned at the start of every race.

After a stint of honest work with a cross-country transport company, Roscoe had some cash to work with at the start of the racing season. That cash would serve as the seed money that every horseplayer needs to jumpstart his next conquest. But that cash didn't last long. With Roscoe, it never lasted very long. As the end of the 1946 season in Saratoga neared, Roscoe was in Dutch with a frightening list of local loan sharks.

But, on that day—the last day of the racing season—that didn't matter much to Roscoe. He was like a boxer, a boxer who had taken a few hard hits in the early rounds; maybe he'd even smelled canvas once or twice. But he was still standing well into the late rounds, waiting for the perfect time to make his move. Patience, he constantly reminded himself. It was all about patience and timing. Roscoe was biding his time, playing possum with the phantom he was chasing. He was right there, lurking in the darkness, a coiled rattler poised to strike. He was not *losing* all his bets those past many weeks. He was *investing* in this line of champion racers all along. He wasn't a chaser looking for that string of luck to save the day—he was meticulous, calculating, persevering. To Roscoe, gambling was a science, every move computed to the last decimal. Today would be his day, he was sure; the finale he had choreographed right from the start was about to unfold.

The last race of the season was due to start in less than a minute. Roscoe knew that as soon as the horses crossed the finish line, he could cash in and waltz out the front gate with a couple stacks of crisp new bills. It had already been a stellar day for Roscoe, as he had—for the first time in his life— correctly called the winner in six of the previous eight races. He parlayed everything he had on the last race, betting it all on two horses: Sal's Rev and Tyrant's Throne.

Sal's Rev was a jet-black four-year-old colt —and a powerful finisher. Roscoe had previously watched Sal's Rev work out from behind one of the training barns, and this nag, he knew, was ready to fly. Roscoe had even met the horse's trainer late one night at a local watering hole. The trainer had told Roscoe that the owner of Sal's Rev—a miserly prick from a filthy rich Canadian family—had named the horse after a man who'd cheated him out of a winner's purse just before the outset of the War. *Sal's Rev*, the trainer had told him, was short for *Salvador's Revenge*. But Roscoe didn't give a damn about the horse's name or its history. All he was looking for was a tip on a hot horse, and, before the night was over, he had gotten one. And he had gotten it for free, no less.

Tyrant's Throne was an entirely different story. He was a long shot, but his jockey was a strong, young apprentice, hungry for a season-ending victory. Tyrant's Throne was ready to shoot out like a cannonball at the start, and it was in this horse that Roscoe had his ace in the hole.

The night before, the track had been soaked through in a torrential downpour, and, although the upper surface had largely dried out in the early morning sun, the lower layers were dense and still holding on to a lot of moisture. Roscoe knew the track well, and he was certain that early speed would prevail and that no one would be able to catch up to Tyrant's Throne—except for the formidable Sal's Rev, that is. It was going to be a two-horse race, he was certain. The other seven nags were window dressing. They all had hardly a snowball's chance in hell of winning. Roscoe knew the right trainers. He knew the right jockeys. He knew the track, and, most important of all, he knew the stallions. Roscoe, ever the cagey blood-horse savant, was about to see his big, summer-long "investment" pay off.

Or so he thought.

Roscoe always watched the race from the top of the stretch run, a good 400 yards from the finish line. That was where the real horsemen stood, far away from the clubhouse box seats where the moneyed snobs sipped champagne in between cheers for the horses they'd purchased and trained with Daddy's inheritance. Those people had no real stake in the enterprise, Roscoe thought. They were neither horsemen nor "investors." They were hangers-on, and they never knew what it was like to be a master handicapper, a handicapper who had already picked six winners in eight races.

The start of the last race went off cleanly. The first quarter-mile was run only a second off the track record. But Roscoe, with a clear vantage point from the top of the stretch run, didn't like what he saw. Tyrant's Throne's rider was holding the horse back, and Sal's Rev was running second to last, a good 11 lengths off the lead. A quarter mile later, neither of Roscoe's horses showed any signs of life. Around the far turn, it seemed that all was lost. Roscoe could only stand there and watch as three horses he had written off as worthless vied for the lead.

And then—in the span of no more than two or three seconds—everything changed. Over his shoulder, Roscoe saw a sudden flash of light, which was followed by another flash even brighter and more expansive than the first. At that same instant, the horses who were out in front staggered, and one of them even reared up in fright. The horses farther back suddenly surged forward, bumping their way through the muddle at the front of the pack. As they rounded for home, Tyrant's Throne found himself charging into the lead, and Sal's Rev was moving through the pack like a freight train on the inside rail. It was a two-horse race after all—somehow. At the finish line, Tyrant's Throne held on to win over Sal's Rev by no more than half a length.

Roscoe had bet all he was worth on that race, putting down every dime he had on the horses who had just finished first and second. As soon as the results were made official, Roscoe would hit the jackpot. He was the vindicated, in-the-clutch handicapper he knew he could be, and his next move was to make a beeline to the cashier's kiosk and collect his winnings.

But something was seriously and suddenly amiss. At the end of the race, from where he was standing, Roscoe saw one of the field judges—the track official who essentially served as a referee for a designated section of the racetrack—jump down from his viewing stand and unlock the secure phone line that connected him directly to the stewards, who were the highest-ranking racing officers. Roscoe had no idea what the field judge was saying, but he was sure that the field judge was reporting on whether or not the intense flashes of light in the sky near the end of the race had in any way affected the race's outcome. And what was that light? Was it lightning? It had to be, Roscoe figured.

He turned and looked again at the western sky, where the flashes had appeared. He saw a bank of faint dark clouds but nothing that appeared too threatening. And, at no time was there even a hint of a thunderclap. The sudden uncertainty about the outcome of the race created a growing murmur in the crowd, and, a moment later, that murmur turned into a collective gasp as three red flags were hoisted upward, just beyond the finish line. A single red flag signaled that the stewards—who had ultimate authority over every aspect of the race—believed that one of the jockeys had interfered with his competitors during the course of the race. Seeing one red flag occurred a couple of times each season. It wasn't terribly unusual. Roscoe had even heard of an occurrence, many years earlier, when two flags were flown simultaneously, meaning that the horses in first and second had run uncleanly. But three hoisted red flags indicated that the horses who had finished first, second, and third might *all* be disqualified. No one could fathom such a result.

Roscoe could not take his eyes off of the field judge. That was the man who was calling the shots—Roscoe was sure of it. The race had had every appearance of being completely clean until the three-second span of chaos that occurred just before the horses rounded for home. Roscoe had watched this same field judge before and after every race over the course of the entire summer, and never once had he seen him use the phone line to the stewards. Most of the time, the man stood as motionless as a statue, devoid of all emotion, and he seemed to barely pay attention to the race in progress. But now the man was shouting into the phone, gesticulating wildly, pointing to the western edge of the track, where the flashes of light had appeared.

The sky, Roscoe thought. It wasn't the track, and it wasn't the jockeys. It was lightning in the sky. That's what caused the fracas, not the jockeys. There wasn't any cheating. The riders weren't running roughshod. It was a force of nature; can't you see that? You can't disqualify the winners because of a freak occurrence? You can't cheat them like that.

You can't cheat *me* like that.

But they did. Moments later, it was announced that the horses who had finished first, second, and third had all been disqualified for interfering with the horses who were at the front of the pack just before the top of the stretch run.

Only minutes earlier, the old racetrack had exuded a celebratory atmosphere. Saratoga, which until recently had been a boarded up, has-been establishment, had reached the end of a successful postwar season. And now the place was a madhouse. Patrons charged toward the bookmakers and pari-mutuel clerks, unsure of who had won and who had lost, who was owed money and who was screwed. There were shouts of anger directed toward the racing officials, the jockeys, the trainers, the owners—even toward the horses and the track itself. Roscoe stood frozen, dumbstruck at what was unfolding around him, but he shook himself back into the moment and looked back at the spot where the instigating field judge had been standing. The man was gone.

Vanished.

Roscoe looked all the way across the track. He thought he saw the field judge ducking behind one of the barns in the backstretch. Was it him? And, if so, Roscoe wondered, how did he get all the way over there so fast? Before all this, the guy had barely ever moved an inch, let alone several hundred yards.

Roscoe's first instinct was to chase after the field judge. Although he might have stood no chance of catching up with him, such a hot pursuit might have also served as a convenient moment of exit. And more than anything, Roscoe needed an exit.

"You!" a man said, jabbing a stiff finger behind Roscoe's shirt collar. "Just the fella I was hoping to bump into."

Roscoe was sure that a knife blade was about to pierce through his skin, through the back of his chest, and into his heart. Roscoe knew this had to be about money, which meant he was a dead man. Yet that voice was not one he knew. It was not the voice of any of the bookies who took his bets, nor was it the voice of any of the "loan specialists" he was in deep with nor any of the ruffians who specialized in "debt collection." It was a cool, civil voice. When Roscoe slowly turned around, he saw a young, tall gentleman who was wearing a spotless three-piece suit and a dark fedora.

"You're the one who was outside that club, outside the Piping Rock, a few nights ago," the man said, seemingly oblivious to the melee around him. "You were mouthing off about how if this or that has a motor you can run it, ride it, fix it, or fly it. Is that about right?"

That's exactly right, Roscoe thought. That was one of the standard lines Roscoe used on the rare occasion when he was in search of genuine employment.

Roscoe nodded and said nothing.

"Were you drunk?" the man asked, staring at Roscoe with a tight grin.

"What?" Roscoe asked, distracted by the charge of state police and Pinkerton officers who had left their security posts to assist the local police with crowd control.

"That night last week at the Piping Rock Lake House," the man said, cool as ice amidst the bedlam, "I know you were drinking. I could see that. But were you drunk?"

"No," Roscoe said, shaking his head nervously. "A few beers, nothing more."

The man nodded without expression. "Still in need of work?" he asked, jerking his head in the direction of the front gate.

Roscoe looked over the man's shoulder and saw a beaten-up Mayflower moving truck idling about 50 yards from the main entrance of the track. Roscoe's eyes shot back and forth between the parked truck and the exit. There wasn't a single security guard or police officer in sight.

There was not a trace of Roscoe's legendary poker face when he looked at the man and nodded in the affirmative.

"Two bills now, and two more once we arrive," the man said, taking off his hat and showing Roscoe the two $100 bills tucked inside. "We had a driver lined up, but, unfortunately, he's been…inconvenienced," the man went on, his top lip hooding upward as he spoke.

This was a godsend, Roscoe thought. It didn't matter who this guy was, what he was hauling, or where he was going. This was Roscoe's ticket out of town, and the ticket actually came with money.

Normally, every commercial vehicle exiting the facilities was visually inspected, inside and out, with all papers and IDs verified. But the furor near the finish line was, at that moment, reaching riot status, and all law enforcement had been urgently summoned to that side of the track. There would be no questions asked because there was no one there to ask any questions. Roscoe could ride off into the sunset without a care in the world.

"Roscoe, right?" the man asked, slipping Roscoe the $200 and putting his fedora back on in one smooth, slick motion.

"That's right," Roscoe said, resisting the urge to offer a handshake under such bizarre circumstances. "And you are?"

"Let's stay on your side of the street, shall we? For now, I'll be the one asking the questions. So it's Roscoe. Got a last name?"

"Fowler," Roscoe said, looking back out toward the parked truck. Roscoe's given surname was Haller, but he had changed it to Fowler after his midnight bolt from that GI hospital, a simple move to thwart any of the Alaska-based GIs who might have tried to search him out for the green he owed them.

"Don't follow me," the man said as he turned away. "Walk down toward the gate, get behind the wheel of that truck, and drive."

"Drive where?" Roscoe asked. "Where are we going?"

"Away from here," the man said without turning around or breaking stride. "Far away from here."

Chapter 3
Boston, Massachusetts
Present Day

Klaryssa's heart pounds in her chest. As calmly as she can, she gestures for Elle to follow her to the far side of an adjoining room, away from the crowd and clamor.

Pressed between the pages of Elle's book is a charcoal sketch of a middle-aged man whose head is turned sharply to the right. His neck muscles are taut and strained to their limit. The man's features are chiseled and strong and undeniably attractive, with a sculpted Roman nose, deep-set eyes, and an angular jaw. He has a trimmed beard, and his face imparts a peaceful, almost forlorn look. The man is wearing no jewelry, only a heavy cloth or leather headband that circles the crown of his head at least three times. The sketch is drawn on thick, dry parchment and is no more than 12 by 18 inches in size. The margins of the piece are sharp and spotless, and the image itself shows no sign of wear, water damage, or soiling of any kind.

Although the drawing's condition is so pristine that it appears practically new, Klaryssa is certain that the work is at least 500 years old.

She is also certain that the sketch was drawn by Michelangelo.

"My God," Klaryssa says once she is able to muster the words. "Where…where on earth did you get *this*?"

"Let me start over, if you will allow me," Elle says, looking relieved and more at ease than she did a minute earlier. "My grandfather—my father's father—was a career military man. He lived to a ripe old age, with many years of both work and travel after he retired, as a colonel, from the army. Well, he did a lot of both—work and travel, that is. His business endeavors were almost always successful, and he was a shrewd investor. He was able to buy a large tract of land near Keene, Kentucky—very rural at the time, and, remarkably, it remains so today. He built a lovely horse farm there, which was, and still is, our family home.

"My grandfather's travels actually brought him even more good fortune than his businesses did, at least in my estimation," Elle continues, her dark eyes glinting in the rays of the afternoon sun that fleetingly pierce through the gloomy sky. "He saw so much of the world in his later years, and what he came to realize was just how indelibly the fine arts define and enlighten our world. He spent so much of his earlier years fighting battles and seeing bloodshed. Only later did he see the force and permanence of great art.

"It was his dream to start a scholarship fund for budding artists, and it was a dream he worked to achieve to his last day. 'Place an artist's tool in a young hand, and you'll find no room for a weapon.' He used to say that all the time, and this from a much-decorated army officer, mind you.

"So, the colonel collected art wherever he traveled," Elle continues, watching Klaryssa fold a couple of book pages over the sketch to protect the drawing. "And a lot of it. When my grandfather passed away, my father took up the mantle: collecting, investing, and building a financial base for the scholarship fund.

"But, after the Second World War, when all should have been rosy, their collective dream took a fatal blow. My father's investments did not blossom like my grandfather's, and in the latter part of 1946 and into the next year, there was a drastic downturn in the stock market. I was just a little girl at the time and had no knowledge of such things, but I learned later that many of my father's investments—in particular mining and railroads—went bust. It was all very sad because he was such a big-hearted, kind man. Prior to the '46 crash, he had even given away many of the family's paintings to museums all over the country. He didn't want these works to hide, gathering dust, in our home. He wanted to share them with the public, particularly with art students, who could learn from—and even imitate the style and techniques of—artists from past generations.

"One lot of paintings, all of which featured old English horse farms and horse racing champions, was stolen. The lot was destined for a national museum of horse racing that was going to be built in upstate New York, and, thankfully, the artworks were recovered undamaged. My father was that kind of man, always trying to spread the wealth. While he had it, anyway."

Hearing these details, Klaryssa now knows that Elle is at least in her early to mid-seventies, quite possibly closer to 80. To Klaryssa, Elle has an almost regal glamor about her, with a beauty that appears to have kept an easy lead over Father Time.

"My father passed away many years ago, and through the years, our family has grown considerably, and we all remain very close. Close for the most part, anyway," Elle continues. " O n e of the reasons we all stay connected is the farmhouse in Keene. It is our gathering point, our center. We had to sell nearly all of the surrounding land many years back, but the house is plenty big enough for all of us, which is both a blessing and a burden. The place is in dire need of repairs, so we —my four surviving siblings and I—decided to sell whatever we could live without to finance the home's rehabilitation.

"The place has one of those oversized two-story libraries, with volumes of books that have served as little more than dust magnets since my childhood. We were about to have an appraiser give us a price for the whole lot of them, but we thought it might be best to go through the books ourselves first. You never know when an old family letter or heirloom might tumble out."

"While checking in with the House of Lords, this is what tumbled out," Klaryssa says, tapping at the pages that are covering the sketch.

"Yes," Elle says, an anxious smile appearing.

36

"The ironic thing about all this is that none of us are artists, or art students, or even inclined towards the fine arts. I have no misgivings about speaking for all my family in that regard. When I found this drawing, I hadn't the slightest idea as to what it was. It was the paper, really, that gave me some hint as to its age…so thick and sturdy. Printed works are all made so cheaply these days, so it just struck me as being very old.

"My brother Kendrick was there with me that day, just last week, when I found the piece. Kendrick knows even less about art than I do. He ran an accounting firm for over 40 years, for God's sake! So we did what one should never do, but what at times we all succumb to doing. I took to the Internet to investigate more Renaissance websites than you can name. But, you are the expert. So, that's why I'm here. Can you tell me—"

"It is," Klaryssa says, without apologizing for interrupting. "I can't read minds, but I don't have to read yours to know why you're here. It's real. It's *exactly* what you think it is."

"Reproductions," Elle says hesitantly, her hands trembling, "I understand they flood the market, regardless of the subject matter. Is that not true?"

37

"It's very true," Klaryssa says.

"Is there any chance then?"

"None. At some point in his life, likely in his early years, Michelangelo drew this sketch. For all we know, it's the only work of its kind anywhere. It's authentic, drawn by his hand, and I cannot even begin to estimate its value."

"Heavens," Elle says as she takes a seat in a nearby chair. She stares out across the cityscape. "Heavens."

Klaryssa takes a moment to let all she has just been shown sink in before she sits down next to Elle.

"Elle, besides yourself, and now me, only your brother knows about this?"

"No one else," Elle answers quickly, her eyes still fixed out into the distance.

"And neither you nor your brother have any idea where the drawing came from? No link you can find to your father's or grandfather's art purchases? No records at all?"

"Oh, it was so long ago...no idea at all. There are scattered records, but nothing of any relevance that we could find."

"It's safe to say that the sketch and the book it was found in have no real relationship," Klaryssa says as she picks up the tome. "I doubt whoever placed the drawing in here had any idea what he or she was holding in their hands. Probably just a place to keep it safe—or hidden."

"Or flat," Elle says, dabbing her eyes. "Do you know what I found in the volume next to this one? A pressed water lily."

They both laugh, and the reveling crowd takes no notice.

"At least something good came out of Parliament," Elle says, still laughing. "I'm American-born, but most of my education, all the way through my graduate studies, was in London. So I know full well that body's depth of dysfunction."

Klaryssa, her mind now racing as fast as her heart was a few minutes earlier, waves a waiter in their direction and asks for two bottles of water. She can't help but wonder what Elle's next move will be. Bring in an appraiser, who might have all kinds of motivations and be less than discreet? Go to the press and chance this becoming a media sensation? Try to keep it all a secret? Is that even possible? Perhaps Elle herself even has doubts about sharing this finding with the rest of her family, considering all of the acrimony such a discovery might engender.

But most of all, Klaryssa wonders if the sketch in question might be linked to one of history's greatest lost masterpieces.

"Have you seen anything like this appear out of nowhere before? Does this sort of thing just *happen* sometimes?" Elle asks, now looking at Klaryssa.

"No to both, I can safely say," Klaryssa says, unable to suppress a smile. "This is *extraordinarily* rare, and, from your reaction, I think you knew that before we met. There are, of course, stories and fables of great pieces being unearthed, but most prove to be forgeries or a case of someone letting their fantasies run wild. Rumors abound that many of the greatest artists of all time have works that remain undiscovered, but the odds of ever finding them at this point are next to none.

"One of the most notable bits of lore actually concerns Michelangelo, if you can believe it. Supposedly, one winter, he drew a portrait of a snowman. No one knows where the work ended up, but more than one biographer mentions the great missing snowman portrait. Can you picture that: 'This whole Sistine Chapel thing is beginning to bore me. But look, there's a snowman!' Ridiculous, really.

"I can only imagine how overwhelming all this must be," Klaryssa says warmly. "But, tell me, is there some other way I can help? I have no question whatsoever as to this work's authenticity, but besides verification, is there anything else I can do?"

"To be perfectly honest, there is," Elle says after taking a sip of water. "I see no reason not to be straightforward with you; God knows you've been on the level with me, which I so appreciate.

"I want to see a rebirth of the aspirations that my father and grandfather held so dear, and to do so, only one thing is necessary: money, plain and simple. If the origin of this work can be traced—establishing that there is no doubt as to my family's rightful ownership—then I'll have no trouble convincing my sister and brothers that the piece *must* be auctioned and the proceeds used as seed money for a fine arts scholarship fund. I want to see a fund dedicated in perpetuity to my father and grandfather. I can think of no greater calling, truth be told.

"I have seen my children and grandchildren apply to schools—top universities with huge endowments—where the lack of available scholarships is an atrocity. I'm fortunate, having had the means to pay for my family's education. But I can only imagine how often brilliant students with creative minds are stunted because of woefully inadequate scholarship money. Totally senseless, and I've seen enough.

"I well realize just how intrusive all this is," Elle says, leaning in closer, "barging in on the celebration of your much-deserved literary success. But any light you could shed on all this, any historical traces that illustrate a clear path…it would just mean so much to my family and me, and, quite possibly, to many others."

"There isn't the least concern there," Klaryssa says. "I was never much for this sort of gathering anyway. As you can see, the revelry is going on full steam without me. And I'm on sabbatical leave until late August, so, with my book already on the market, I have time to do some digging. This does, of course, leave the problem of the much needed new roof."

Elle narrows her eyes, tilting her head curiously.

"Sounds like this odyssey started with your family looking for ways to fund the old homestead's renovation," Klaryssa says after taking a drink of water. "You could re-roof a pretty big building with the proceeds from auctioning a work like this."

"All that has changed," Elle says, her voice soft and her tone thoughtful. "In the past few minutes, *everything* has changed. Now, I see the world and its many possibilities in a new light."

Klaryssa gazes out across Boston harbor, watching one of the hundreds of flights that will take off from Logan Airport today arch skyward and fade into the dark cloud cover. She once considered the outgoing flights on marathon day as being loaded down with an untold number of broken dreams. All the training and anticipation of thousands of runners, yet each year, only a handful of wreaths are bestowed. But all she thinks of now is how the marathon today proceeded without incident, and how every marathoner on every flight leaves Boston a winner.

"There is another matter, new roofs and kitchens and all that aside," Klaryssa says, clearing her throat and pulling herself back into the moment. "For the immediate future, what are you going to do with the sketch?"

"I've already done it," Elle says without the slightest hesitation. "It's sitting right in front of you for a reason. You're going to keep it."

"Me!" Klaryssa says, nearly jumping out of her seat. "That's the last answer I expected. Why on earth would you leave this with me? You don't even *know* me."

"Well, you're part of a renowned academic department and institution," Elle says, standing and straightening her suit jacket. "No doubt you have access to safe-deposit boxes and such. I've every confidence that it's in the best of hands."

"But this is *priceless*," Klaryssa says, standing up and holding the book between them. "We met just minutes ago. You don't even know me."

Elle glances up at a nearby TV monitor, seeing the beaming smiles of the two newly crowned marathon winners being pelleted by icy specks of drizzle that are falling from the slate-gray sky that blankets the city: men's and women's champions, one from Japan and the other an American, now arm in arm, the twisted green fronds of the victor's wreath wrapped around each of their heads.

Elle looks back at Klaryssa, noticing for a brief moment the dimple-like indent in the middle of her left cheek.

"My dear," Elle says, clasping Klaryssa's hand in hers, "I know you plenty well."

Chapter 4
Boston, Massachusetts
Two Days Later

Through four years of college and five years of graduate school, Klaryssa's favorite running route was along the Charles River Esplanade in Boston's Back Bay neighborhood. From the eastern edge of the Esplanade, she could traverse the Longfellow Bridge into Cambridge, or wind through the streets and alleyways of Beacon Hill and the West End. The extended routes were usually contingent on Klaryssa's time allotment or, more often than she would care to admit, on how much her Achilles tendon was burning. But Klaryssa's favorite run through the city changed once the last section of Boston's Central Artery highway was demolished. The Central Artery, a 50-year-old elevated highway that was the scourge of the cityscape and a national eyesore, was replaced by the Rose Kennedy

Greenway, a 15-acre garden promenade that now sits over the city's $20 billion tunnel system.

To Klaryssa, this creation of public space was more than an urban landscape facelift that was two generations overdue. This public space was where Klaryssa reclaimed her life and her vitality. It was where she reclaimed her legs—first with a walker and then crutches, next with small steps and then bigger steps, and finally with jogging and running—running *fast*.

Now, she is counting laps.

As Klaryssa runs, it is no more than 40 degrees Fahrenheit. A stiff breeze wafts onto land from the harbor; a sideways drizzle soaks the air and the ground. Such dreary conditions mean that no one crosses into her running line.

While cutting through Christopher Columbus Park on her way to her favorite North End café, Klaryssa hears a rustle in the stand of trees that separate the park from the Long Wharf waterfront. Someone is charging through the trees in her direction, and, seeing no one else in the park, she picks up her pace, knowing that once she gets to the North End neighborhood there will be others on the street.

A moment later, a tall, broad-shouldered man wearing sweatpants and a black hoodie jumps from the tree line and into Klaryssa's path. The man extends his arm straight in front of her.

Klaryssa doesn't blink or break her stride.

"You're late," she says without looking at the man.

"Overslept," the man shoots back, now running alongside Klaryssa.

"So you're lazy," Klaryssa says as they exit the park and head up Atlantic Avenue.

"Hey, rude. Long night at the shop."

"So you're late *and* lazy," Klaryssa says with a smile, flicking raindrops from her brow in the man's direction. "Best espresso in the land a mile ahead. And the most expensive, so thanks in advance. Maybe I'll get one of those chichi double lattes instead. Oh, and, by the way, they only take cash."

***

Klaryssa Mahr, born Klaryssa Dasha Marchenko, is the last of six children born into a family in the northwest Ukrainian city of Chervonohrad. Klaryssa's father died of alcoholism when she was

48

three-years-old, and in the years that followed, her family's financial means went from meager to dire. She and her sibling next closest to her in age, Sergey, were sent to live with a maternal aunt in the town of Hunter in New York's Catskill Mountains. To assimilate into her new American surroundings, her surname was cut down, and with a single letter accidentally added to the end of her middle name, she became Klaryssa Dashan Mahr.

In school, Klaryssa excelled in the humanities: languages, philosophy, and the arts. With financial aid and a stack of long-term loans, she enrolled at Harvard after being accepted via early admission. During the summer between her freshman and sophomore years of college, Klaryssa went on an extended backpacking trip in Scandinavia, and, upon returning to Boston, she chose to take a year's leave from her studies. Her decision was not the result of illness, injury, or getting lost in the northern wilds of Sweden. It was because of the brief time she spent with a man she met in the final weeks of her backpacking trip: a man she knew only as Isak.

Yeva was born seven months after Klaryssa returned home from her backpacking trip, which further distanced Klaryssa from both her mother in

Ukraine and her aunt in the Catskills. After returning to the States, Klaryssa never again heard from Isak, and despite her every effort, she was never able to locate him.

While on a rafting trip along the Penobscot River in Maine, Klaryssa met Ian Sterne, one of the rafting guides. About four hours into the river trip, Klaryssa came to the realization that her then-boyfriend—who was sitting next to her in the raft—was in fact a childish whiner and, at best, lousy company. That was also the first time Klaryssa had been away from Yeva for more than half a day, and although the rafting trip was only for a weekend, she missed her two-year-old daughter more than she thought possible.

Ian, a recent graduate from Virginia Tech, had worked as a white-water kayaking guide during previous summer breaks. He was bored beyond measure with his work as a rafting guide in Maine; he longed for the waters of the Colorado and its Class-V rapids. At the time, he was also disenchanted with his significant other. He and his then-fiancée regularly got into heated and nasty arguments, and it was becoming clear to Ian that marriage would never happen.

Neither Klaryssa nor Ian recall the exact nature of their first conversation, but they instantly hit it off. The day after they met, they took off together so Klaryssa could introduce Ian to the light of her life, Yeva.

In the years that followed, nobody familiar with either Klaryssa or Ian ever quite believed the truth about their relationship, and the truth was, they never dated. Their relationship has always been joyfully platonic, which is even harder to believe for onlookers who take even a casual glance at either of them. Such glances are, more often than not, wide-eyed stares.

Klaryssa's long, light brown hair drapes off to one side of her face just above her arched eyebrows and roundish blue-grey eyes. She has a naturally lithe build, and with more than 40 road miles run every week, she's as fit as any cross country competitor half her age.

Ian, measuring in at 6'4" and at least a foot taller than Klaryssa, has the frame of a Pro Bowl wide receiver. As strapping as he may be, Klaryssa has never once given a second thought about the nature of their relationship. And neither has Ian.

***

"So the Croat is getting iced, that's what you're telling me?" Klaryssa says, Ian having just given a rambling explanation of his current romantic situation, which, as always, sounds dire.

"That is not *quite* what I said, KD," Ian says. He's the only person in the world who calls Klaryssa by her initials. Looking at her over the top of a menu, he continues. "We're just slowing it down—a break from each other, if you will. Maybe we're both feeling a little, I don't know, cramped."

"Uh-huh," Klaryssa grunts with an I've-heard-all-this-before air.

"And her name is *Elena*," Ian says as he peruses the coffee selections on the menu. "I thought you liked her?"

"I like her OK," Klaryssa says. "I mean, what's not to like? I'd put her ahead of the one before her. Or before *her*. Or before *her*. Well, maybe not that one. Or was it the other one?"

Without looking at Klaryssa, Ian puts up a hand. "All right, all right, enough already. This is all for another day. More importantly, it seems like forever since I saw my Yeva. C'mon, a photo for her Uncle Ian."

Klaryssa pulls out her iPhone and shows Ian a short video of Yeva dancing at her most recent ballet performance at the Berklee College of Music. "She's loving it over there," Klaryssa says, replaying the video one more time. "Finals are soon, so there's not too much dancing at the moment.

"You know I had my doubts when she started last August, but there's no rewinding the tape now. She seems to have found her element, which I never thought would happen. Don't you think? Even though she's right here in the city, it's best she gets the dorm life experience, you know? But as close as she is, I still don't get to see her enough."

"Show me someone who gets to see their 18-year-old college kid often enough," Ian says, watching Yeva's final pirouette. "She looks really happy. I was so worried, almost as much as you were, after...after it all."

Yeva has a lengthy history of anorexia and childhood depression. She became so thin after the 2013 marathon attack that she required inpatient psychiatric care for several weeks. Klaryssa actually made it home from the hospital before her daughter did, and spending nights in her South End condominium without Yeva was even more painful than her inpatient recovery after the marathon bombing. Klaryssa's nights alone at home were agonizing; her pain was amplified by her awareness of how desolate Yeva's world must have been while she lay in an intensive care unit, clinging to life by no more than a thread. Her life had been given back to her, but her existence was barren without Yeva, her world a bottomless void without their trudges through the snow or their walks along the beach, their bedtime stories or the songs Klaryssa would sing to Yeva while cuddling her before she faded off to sleep.

The loss Klaryssa felt was so complete that she actually pined for the nights when Yeva awakened her with the same piercing questions—at times asked with a whisper, at times with a scream, at times through a gusher of tears—about the father who didn't care about her. Since before her first birthday, Yeva had asked time and time again about her daddy—the father she had never met nor would ever meet. The father who would never hold her or smile at her or comfort her or tell her that she means more to him than anything in the world.

"Who was there with her, every day, like clockwork, while I was wrapped in tubes and wires and then in rehab?" Klaryssa says. "She's close to very few people, and there is no one in her life like you. Sergey tried his best to help out when I was in the hospital, but he teeters on sanity's edge on the best of days, and he has his own issues to worry about. After what happened at...at the marathon, Yeva just imploded. You pulled her back to life. Back to me."

The two of them sit in silence, Klaryssa turning away from Ian's gaze. When she finally looks back across the table, she sees Ian peering above the menu at the passersby on Hanover Street.

"Why are you pretending to read that menu?" Klaryssa asks, holding up both palms. "It's almost eight o'clock, and no matter how much you say you overslept, there is no way you didn't down either a stack of Johnnycakes or one of those mega-omelets before trying to jump me in the park. So hand that prop you're holding back to the wait staff, will you please?"

"So I had a *little* something in preparation for trying to keep up with you. Just order me coffee while you get your double latte revenge for my tardiness today. And don't forget to order some water over there, sister. You're the one who just clocked six miles. Or was it seven?"

Klaryssa sends Ian a dismissive wave. "While we await our waiter, why don't you give me some of your sage advice on what this year's marathon brought my way," she says, getting to the most important business at hand. She had called Ian after the marathon, as soon as she parted ways with Elle, explaining all the details she could about Elle Picard and the surprise she brought with her.

"The whole thing is just so hard to take in. This total stranger just waltzes up and drags you away from your party and hands you this...this *thing*. You couldn't make up a story so screwy. And seeing how that was two whole days ago, tell me what you've dug up since then, you being a lady of sabbatical leisure."

"First off, everything Elle told me checks out," Klaryssa says, stretching one leg under the table. "Her family, the address in Kentucky, all that basic stuff. I even pulled some articles on this '46 stock market crash, so there is no reason not to believe that her family's fortune hit the skids way back then."

"OK, but you could have accomplished all that with two spare minutes on your iPhone," Ian says, his impatience leaking through slightly.

"C'mon, KD. I'm sure you unearthed a lot more than that about this Mrs. Picard."

"Elle. That's her name, if I may remind you," Klaryssa begins, raising her eyebrows. "She mentioned that her father gave away all kinds of artwork to various museums, and that checks out as well. Elle didn't give a lot of specifics, like which pieces went to which museum, but she did have a list of cities where the donations were made: Philadelphia, Chicago, New York, Sacramento, and a number of others. A lot of the particulars concerning the holdings these different museums have are available online, so I spoke to the respective curators, and there were no surprises. All the artworks donated years ago by the Picard family are catalogued and appropriately marked wherever the pieces are on display. And none of the donated paintings have even the remotest relationship to the Renaissance masters, let alone Michelangelo. Elle promised she'd ship me any old records she can scour up at the family home in Keene, so maybe they will be of some use. It sounds like their family's archive is, at best, a jumble of old papers, so I'm not holding out a lot of hope on that end."

"And the end game of all this cloak-and-dagger business is?" Ian asks.

"Well, Elle came up here for two reasons," Klaryssa says, pausing to thank the waiter for the coffee and latte. "First, to verify the authenticity of the drawing, and there is no question on that point. It's as real as the Sistine frescoes. Second, she wants to establish provenance, and here, I have to really admire this woman. A piece like this coming into the market, say at Sotheby's or Christie's, will undoubtedly create a firestorm. You'll have European families and museums and American institutions asking all kinds of questions about proprietorship. People will come out of the woodwork for a piece like this, for the publicity alone. Remember, this is an incredibly hot topic now, with so much controversy over stolen works and establishing origin and producing a clean title for any work of art.

"The auction houses will cast a wary eye on a piece like this, because the world is casting a wary eye at *them*. If Elle and her family just go out and try to sell this straight up and valid objections arise, they could end up in the courts for years. They want to start a scholarship fund, and if all that legal stuff drags on for four or five or who knows how many years, Elle and her siblings might all be gone. And then other family members take their place, all of them with different agendas, different priorities. Suddenly it's 'scholarships...what scholarships?'"

Ian lightly flicks his wrist, watching the foam of his coffee twirl in the cup. He's unsure of what to ask next.

"You're the eBay guru, for shit's sake," Klaryssa goes on, trying to jolt the man a bit. "You must've seen stuff like this before. It's an auction website, after all, is it not?"

Ian Sterne is, by any measure, a bona fide eBay guru. After graduating from Virginia Tech and earning a master's degree in engineering a year later, Ian had his sights set on a handful of doctorate programs. But a lifelong history of irregular sleep patterns led to an enterprise that proved far more profitable. Instead of staring at his bedroom ceiling for hours every night, Ian chose to stare at the eBay website and follow the patterns of listings, sales, and purchases. His observations include the sales and purchases of everything imaginable: vintage barbecue pits, suits of armor for your pet, unopened cans of 30-year-old ravioli, camping gear from the original *Friday the 13th*, and hair clippings from an assortment of pop stars.

Ian's tastes aren't solely eccentric; he also keeps an eye out for more conventional wares, such as household furniture, car parts, used bicycles, and less-than-fine china. More often than not, he buys and sells items without ever seeing or holding the product. His shipping company agent serves as a middleman and claims a small percentage of each transaction. Since the start of his eBay enterprise, the transactions haven't shown the first sign of slowing down. Ian has no warehouse, no inventory, no production costs, and no surplus product—and no need for a PhD.

"It's not at all the same," Ian says, taking a sip of coffee. "Yes, sure, it's an auction site in many regards, and I guess there can be a dogfight over the de facto ownership of a given item, but that sort of controversy just doesn't come up on a regular basis. It's a *volume*-driven business, which is how I make a living. Even though the number of items sold seems to border on infinite, it's still relatively manageable to keep a record of every vendor and customer. Rogue elements never get any traction, because at the end of the day, it's all exposed for the world to see online. This isn't a business model where valuable or priceless artifacts drive the machine. It's all the junk we have stashed during our lives being shaken out of the trees and finding refuge on an electronic shelf. There is nothing you can't find or sell, but valuable items like what we're talking about, things that might draw controversy, are a *very* tiny percentage. What we're talking about is in a completely different stratosphere. It's a different universe altogether."

Klaryssa sits in silence, staring into her coffee, mulling over the entirety of what she knows about the piece in question.

"When you called me yesterday, with that KD's-kinda-fretting-well-maybe-just-a-little voice, I had the strange sense that you thought I might be able to put a second oar in the water on whatever you are working on. I see those wheels turning over there."

Klaryssa waves for the waiter and jumps from her seat.

"Pay the man," she says to Ian as she walks out the front door and waves at an idle cabbie at the end of the street.

"Do what?" Ian says, his words chasing after her.

"Throw down some cash; I've got something to show you."

61

"What? Where?" he asks as he puts $20 on the table.

"You'll see."

"We can't run there?" Ian asks, grabbing his hoodie.

"I can. But we…just get in," Klaryssa says, hopping in the cab. "And don't bitch about the leg room again."

"How can I?" Ian says in a huff, slamming the door shut. "There isn't any."

Chapter 5
Boston, Massachusetts

Fifteen minutes later, the red-light-running Jamaican cab driver drops Klaryssa and Ian off on a side street bordering Boston's Museum of Fine Arts. Klaryssa uses the electronic keypad and fingerprint reader to enter the museum through a doorway reserved for staff members. The waddling on-duty security guard inspects Ian's driver's license face to face and winks at Klaryssa, gesturing that the two may enter.

"Must be nice, having such influence and access," Ian says as he gives Klaryssa a slight bow. "Getting in here, right past security, outside business hours. Just look at you, Mrs. Bigshot."

"I worked odd hours here all throughout college and grad school, remember?" Klaryssa says, motioning Ian to move along. "That's 10 years worth of weekends, and I'm not the only faculty member at Tufts with the same perk. We've been sending students here to assist the curators for years and years, so access to our workspace during off hours is never a problem."

"Being a renowned author doesn't hurt either, eh?" Ian says, admiring the sculptures in the middle of an adjacent room that is sealed off by a metal barricade.

"Enough from you," Klaryssa says, now charging down a set of stairs to the basement level. "This way, please. You can admire Rodin's work another time."

"Rodin, eh? Huh."

***

Klaryssa unlocks the door of a small windowless room and turns on the lights. She opens a safe deposit box and removes the tome Elle left with her two days earlier; she opens the book to a marked page. After putting on a pair of latex-free gloves, she removes the thin, clear protective barrier that was covering the Michelangelo sketch.

"What do you see?" Klaryssa asks Ian, looking intently at the lone figure in the 500-year-old drawing. "The lights in here protect against UV damage, so take your time."

Ian takes a minute or so to inspect the sketch. "If this guy was turning his head to look at the same blonde in the bar that I was looking at, I don't think I'd stand a chance," he says.

"Try again," she says, slamming her heel onto Ian's foot. "I didn't bring you here for your frat-boy humor."

"Look, KD," Ian says, now leaning in closer, "I am seriously out of my league here. If this is a bona fide Michelangelo work, and I believe you when you say it is, then my inclinations are to be awestruck and silent. I've got the first one covered; now I'm working on the second."

Klaryssa gazes down at the sketch, letting her fingertip run lightly along the margins of the fragile paper, barely touching the edges of the artwork. Klaryssa's pale blue eyes shimmer in the soft light. When Ian looks at her, he sees the facial expression one might see on a cloistered monk who, out of nowhere, is handed an original Gutenberg Bible.

"The minute Elle and I parted ways on marathon day, I immediately came here. I felt like I was carrying the contents of a Brink's armored truck with me. I guess I was, in a sense. Thankfully, when I got here, I was alone. The grad students had the day off. I just sat here for who knows how long, just gripped by this piece, completely unable to pull myself away. Half of me wanted to tell the whole world what I was holding in my hands; the other half wanted it to stay a secret forever. You're the only one I've shared this with. And believe me, it is going to stay that way for now.

"This is a strong, vigorous man," Klaryssa continues, using her finger to draw slow circles over the drawing. "A strong, vigorous man who has a look of peace and solitude on his face, don't you think? But there's something larger and more imminent going on. Look, it's as if he's alarmed, startled, suddenly jolting his head in one direction. This is a moment of urgency; there's a sudden transformation in his surroundings. I think Michelangelo is showing us a man at the very instant of being caught off guard, and he wants us to know that this is a singularly vital moment in this man's life."

"All joking aside, you really see all that?" Ian asks.

Klaryssa looks at Ian with a crooked grin. "You sound like one of my students. I always see doubt written across their faces. Some students come right out and ask, 'Where and how do you see that?' or 'Is it really that complex?' It's got a lot to do with knowing the artist, of course, knowing his or her previous works and orientations, and in this case, we're talking about arguably the most brilliant artist the world has ever known. In the first part of the 16th century, when this work was definitely completed, Michelangelo's artistic prowess, and his renown, were in full bloom. He was a consummate student of anatomy; he spent his entire life studying the human form. He believed that the body was the physical representation of the soul.

"There's restiveness in this work," Klaryssa says. "Michelangelo's intent here must've been to send a powerful message. Just look at his use of charcoal in this work—the flawless form of the neck and facial musculature, the perfect curves, every outline and every diagonal as sharp as glass. Each aspect of this man's features shows hundreds of strokes that vary in pressure, direction, depth, intent. Michelangelo had a peerless eye for light and shadow and used them often to delineate volume and shape in his characters. He was also compulsive when it came to anatomical exactness in his sketch work, and this drawing is a perfect example. To Michelangelo, muscular precision was its own lyrical beauty. That's what I noticed first the minute Elle showed this sketch to me; that's what I've been looking at ever since. "

"I'm trying to see all that, m'lady, I swear I am," Ian says, looking back and forth between Klaryssa and the sketch. "But what I'm seeing here is the guy that every other guy on earth wants to be."

"You might change your mind when you hear more about where he was and what was happening around him," Klaryssa says, cocking one eyebrow. "So just follow along with me here.

"In the middle part of the 14th century, long before Michelangelo's time, a series of battles took place between the cities of Florence and Pisa. One skirmish, which occurred in Tuscany, is known as the Battle of Cascina, and, in this instance, the city of Florence prevailed."

Klaryssa pulls up an image on her iPad. "In 1504, Michelangelo was commissioned to paint a rendition of that battle on the wall of the Palazzo Vecchio in Florence. And if you can possibly believe it, Leonardo da Vinci was commissioned that very same year to paint a scene from another medieval battle to be placed on another wall in the exact same room in the Palazzo.

"It's never been determined whether either painting was actually ever completed, but what is known with absolute certainty is that the overlords of Florence made what is without question the most tragic decision any group of civic fathers has ever made. The Palazzo chamber was remodeled, and both works, one from the hand of Michelangelo and the other from da Vinci's, were reportedly destroyed."

"And my older brother and I still weep over our mom trashing our baseball card collection," Ian says, deadpan.

"OK, take a look at this," Klaryssa says while pointing to her iPad screen, which displays an image of a painting of 20 or so men along a riverbank. Some of the men are young, others are middle-aged, and others are older with scraggly beards and wrinkled features. A few of the men are partially clothed, others are naked, and some are in full military garb with weapons in their hands. One of the men, in addition to holding a spear or a long knife, also carries a shield. There is no evidence of bloodshed, although in the foreground, a pair of hands is seen sinking into the water along the river's edge, presumably the hands of a mortally wounded warrior.

"This painting is the work of Bastiano de Sangallo, who was a student of Michelangelo," Klaryssa says, pointing out various details of the painting. "He based this piece on a cartoon sketch Michelangelo drew of the Battle of Cascina, but that Michelangelo drawing was also destroyed, almost certainly by a jealous rival. As you might imagine, he had no shortage of those.

"There is no blood or gore in Sangallo's work because it depicts the precise moment when the men of Pisa initiated their assault on the Florentine army, and it takes place while the men of Florence are bathing along the riverbed. Historians record that the Cascina battle took place in the middle of the summer, and it's not hard to imagine that there was a searing hot sun in the sky. Every soldier was outfitted with heavy metal armor, and presumably they were all cooling off in the waters of the Arno River. Sangallo used the Michelangelo cartoon sketch as the basis for this work, and in it, he captures Michelangelo's original intent—that is, to render an image of the battle scene at the very moment the fighting commences. And again, it's a historical fact that the battle began with a surprise attack along the Arno River. You see weapons in hand, poised to strike. A viewer has full knowledge when looking at this piece that in the next moment there will be bloodshed."

"Back to the dude in the sketch for a moment, if I may," Ian interjects. "I take it he has something to do with what you're seeing in the Sangallo painting?"

"There are a number of surviving sketches drawn by Michelangelo that are believed to be renderings of characters he intended to portray in the Cascina painting," Klaryssa says as she shows Ian several of the sketches. "But you can see as plain as I can that none of these drawings show any facial features. You see moving limbs, twisting torsos, and taut musculature, but you get no faces."

Klaryssa again shows Ian the drawing that Elle brought to her. "Look at this again, and now look at the man in the middle left of the Sangallo painting here on the screen. What do you see?"

Ian looks back and forth between the two images. "Same guy, yeah? That's him."

"That's *him*," Klaryssa says, a swagger in her voice. "This is a militiaman, a warrior. His army brigade is under attack, and the impact of this image is the shock of *mo*tion, not the shock of *emo*tion. He's a veteran soldier, a seasoned warrior. At the sound of battle, he reflexively turns to his right, but his face expresses what one might expect in someone who is at peace, in a reflective mood, or someone who is relaxing, having just taken a swim in the refreshing waters of the river."

"Conjecture, all of this?" Ian asks after letting a long beat pass.

"You better believe it," Klaryssa says. "But the reason why authenticated Michelangelo sketches are so rare is that the vast majority were destroyed during his lifetime, usually by Michelangelo himself. He said his drawings were the 'font and body' of his work, the vehicle he used to achieve technical perfection in his sculptures and paintings. He saw no need to keep an archive of his sketches, and of the few that did survive, many have informal notes written on them. There was a scatterbrain wire somewhere in there, because he actually used his working sketches as notepads, jotting down casual daily observations or his scheduled appointments or even his shopping list— anything. But not Elle's Michelangelo sketch, right? This one is all business, no stray notes or doodles. You only see a few mathematical notations in one of the margins, because this sketch was a prelude to a bigger work. The master kept *this* drawing because he needed it to complete his *Battle of Cascina* masterpiece."

"How much of all this have you explained to Elle?" Ian asks. "I needn't remind you that this sketch belongs to her and her family. Does she know just how significant it is?"

Klaryssa looks up toward the ceiling and slowly shakes her head. "In a word, no. I made it clear that this is an astounding find, an incredibly valuable find, but I couldn't make a true estimation of its value. One of the Michelangelo sketches that I just showed you on my iPad is being auctioned later this year, in London, and conservative estimates predict a $12-15 million price tag when the hammer falls. That piece has created a huge sensation, but the drawing that belongs to the Picard family would be...well, it would be something more than a sensation, whatever that is."

"Now I understand the urgency in your voice over the phone yesterday." Ian looks back at the image on Klaryssa's iPad. "For once, that stolid Ukrainian center of yours seemed to be wobbling just a bit."

"Well, I haven't even gotten to the reason I called you."

Klaryssa carefully covers the sketch and locks it in the safe deposit box. She sits down at one of the small work tables and motions for Ian to have a seat opposite her.

"There's more?" Ian asks, cocking his head. "You can't be serious."

"Plenty serious," Klaryssa says, her eyes wide. "There's a lot more that I haven't told Elle, and here the fog gets even thicker."

***

"You have, I'm sure, heard of many great masters who never achieved notoriety or fame during their lifetime," Klaryssa begins. "But Michelangelo, obviously, was not one of them. He was known throughout all of Europe at an early age. He died just short of his 89th birthday, which was extraordinarily old for the time. He had, and in fact still has, plenty of biographers. Some are reputable, some less so. One biographer, a contemporary of Michelangelo, was a man named Bruno Abbiati. Now, very little is known about Abbiati, so the accuracy of his surviving writings can always be called into question. That said, he gives details of the interior renovation of the Palazzo Vecchio that we find nowhere else—specifically, the arrest of one of the carpenters during the building's refurbishing.

"Abbiati says that one of the on-site workers was jailed for stealing two panes of glass, and while the thief was locked up and awaiting trial, he told his jailer that there was no trace of the Michelangelo painting on the night he stole the panes of glass. The painting was gone. The theft of the glass panes took place the night before the chamber's demolition began, and the thief was recorded as saying he saw another man in the Palazzo that night. He believed he recognized the man as a local art student. That night had a particularly bright full moon, so he saw this man scurrying down a stairwell and out onto the street. As I said, the unspeakable tragedy was the destruction of both the da Vinci and Michelangelo works during the chamber's renovation, both masterpieces supposedly either just completed or nearing completion at the time."

"He was making it up, yeah?" Ian interjects. "The thief, that is. He was lying. He was doing anything he could to bargain his way out."

Klaryssa lets out a long sigh. "Well, you're *probably* right," she says. "But the thief, according to Abbiati anyway, told his jailers that only the Michelangelo was missing. Why not the da Vinci? Why not both? And why not tell the police that he witnessed the painting being stolen and give them an exact description of the thief he never saw, sending them off in a different direction and maybe setting himself free as a reward for all his vital assistance? But he didn't do any of that—not that we know of, anyway. He was vague and uncertain. He told his jailer that Michelangelo's *Battle of Cascina* was no longer hanging on the chamber wall and that he thought he knew who made off with the painting."

"So what happened to this guy, the window glass thief?" Ian asks. "Convicted and sent away?"

"Lost to history," Klaryssa says with a resigned look. "Abbiati never again mentions the man, and neither does anyone else. Little surprise, though. Few historians have ever even heard of Abbiati, let alone the criminals he quotes in his writings."

"But you have," Ian says, tapping Klaryssa's forehead with his finger. "Sounds to me like this Abbiati fellow has you sold."

Klaryssa opens her shoulder bag and thumbs through a large envelope until she finds a folder stuffed with a scattering of yellowed papers.

"You might say that," she says with a grin. She pulls out several stacks of paper. "One of our retired professors spent her life studying the greats of the Renaissance; when she passed away a couple of years ago, she donated all of her papers to Tufts. She'd amassed volumes and volumes of material on Michelangelo, so that's how I found out about Abbiati's writings.

"During her long career, this same professor also solicited a number of universities in Italy in search of any information on the last days of Michelangelo's life. Oddly enough, she wasn't looking for any lost masterpieces but rather any writings or notes he may have left while he lay dying in some distant corner of Rome. Most medical experts have concluded that he was probably in a coma for some time before he died, and so there is very little known about anything he said or wrote in his final days. But these papers hold a treasure trove of material, none of which I have ever seen or heard mentioned anywhere else," Klaryssa continues, spreading out the sheets of paper in front of Ian. "Michelangelo wasn't alone when he passed away, and the only person known to be with him was a 20-year-old apprentice named Alessio Sartori. These are pages from young Sartori's personal journal."

Ian looks over the pages without touching any of them. To his eye, the papers appear as ancient as the Dead Sea Scrolls. "They sent that professor this kid's actual diary?" Ian asks, waving a finger in front of the tattered pages.

"No, no, not at all," Klaryssa says. "This is a reproduction of the young man's journal. Years back, well before my time, you would see copies made in this fashion whenever you made contact with serious art historians in a place like Italy. Reproductions were made to look like the real thing: parchment-like paper, dipped in tea for effect. Italians and their flair for the dramatic, you know."

"Believe me, I know. I've been dumped by an Italian before, and the *arrivederci* I received—and some might say deserved—had not a trace of subtlety. Now, anyway, what does all this say?"

"Quite a lot," Klaryssa says. "I can't read Italian, but somewhere along the line, these excerpts were translated by a graduate student from Venice. As I mentioned before, Michelangelo lived a life plenty long enough to accumulate enemies and jealous rivals, and that was not lost on the students he mentored, including Sartori. Sartori recorded Michelangelo's final hours in graphic detail: his master's tormented breathing, fetid odor, and 'mottled, increasingly chilly, slowly greying skin.'

"Knowing Michelangelo would soon die, Sartori remarked on the 'heathen vultures' who he feared would ransack his master's belongings and 'abscond with any treasure they can lay their grease-soaked hands upon.' And, like the artist Sangallo that I mentioned earlier, Alessio Sartori painted his own rendering of the Battle of Cascina many years later. The difference is that Sartori, in his journal, tells us that he used Michelangelo's original *Battle of Cascina* masterpiece to paint his own adaptation of the medieval battle scene, recounting how he was able to complete the work by spending 'two nights and as many days, without the thought of sleep, applying the last brush to this grand battle, with both my eyes on his every stroke.' When Sartori uses the word 'his,' he is referring to Michelangelo, and he gives every indication that the original painting had indeed been saved from its scheduled destruction, just as Abbiati contends. But his last entry is the most remarkable of all.

"Sartori tells us that he hid the authentic Michelangelo *Battle of Cascina* painting by wrapping the original canvas inside his own rendition of the *Battle of Cascina*.

"Sartori then placed both canvases in the hollowed-out leg of an oak table—I'm serious— that for years had been used by Michelangelo's students. After Michelangelo died, Sartori tells of his deep despair and 'throttled soul,' making him unable to work at all for several months. He then took up residence in a small apartment outside of Florence, 'far from the vermin that stalk Rome's alleys,' and casually mentions that he took the oak table with him as one of his 'precious few' earthly possessions."

"Are you gonna make me ask about the fate of that table?" Ian asks, tilting his head toward Klaryssa. "I don't suppose it showed up at a flea market somewhere a couple hundred years later, huh?"

"If it did, no one's telling," Klaryssa says. "And Sartori certainly didn't spill any secrets, because he never got the chance. Within two years of Michelangelo's death, he contracted an illness that was almost certainly tuberculosis, and in short order he died a lonely pauper.

"From there, the trail of the original Michelangelo *Battle of Cascina* goes stone cold. Both the historian Abbiati, who was an old man, and Sartori, who was barely out of his teen years, died within a few months of each other. If there are any other threads that follow the fate of the painting, they've remained buried for over four and a half centuries."

"And this Sartori fellow and his journal entries—no one's ever taken notice of what you just dug up over the past two days?" Ian asks, again pointing at the handwritten pages sprawled on the table in front of him. "Something this profound, and translated into English no less, went unnoticed by everyone else? Including, and no offense here, the professor who found this material?"

"This happens all the time," Klaryssa says, flipping through some of the pages in Sartori's journal. "The translator was probably plowing through thousands of pages, and he or she was only doing what they were hired to do, and that's translate. The professor who hired the translator was looking for something else entirely, and I'm sure she never even read through these particular entries."

"So you really think this painting still exists, spirited out of that celestial chamber under the moonlight?" Ian says, now leaning all the way across the table.

Klaryssa allows a hint of a grin to creep across her face.

"Why didn't Michelangelo just take the damn thing right off the wall himself?" Ian asks. "It was right there, the product of his hand, and it was about to get the ax."

"Because it wasn't his to take," Klaryssa says. "He was commissioned to do that particular painting, so the work was, in fact, the property of the city of Florence. If he walked away with the piece, then *he* would've been the thief. If he wanted to save the painting, he would've needed someone to sneak into the Palazzo at night and pull the work off the wall. He could then apply all his finishing touches and hide the work."

"Talk about conjecture," Ian says, sitting back. "Now I know why you didn't share any of this with Elle Picard. She might've dropped dead from a heart attack right on the spot."

"Of course I couldn't tell her any of this," Klaryssa says emphatically. "That would have been very premature. But, for the first time in over 500 years, there's a scent in the air, and this is more than just smoke in the mountains. The Michelangelo sketch Elle brought to me is unlike any other, and her grandfather bought that drawing, along with a pile of paintings, when he was traveling through Italy all those many years ago. There's an old adage that says that in the artist's hand the painting follows the sketch, and in history's hand, the sketch follows the painting. I never really believed that; it always sounded like an old wives' tale to me. But now...now, I'm not sure what to believe. So that's where you come in."

"Me?" Ian says, half choking on the word. "There's no hound dog sitting over here. I know absolutely nothing about medieval art and even less about tracking down lost antiquities. Remember, I do the opposite, which is sell people stuff that's sitting right in front of them."

Klaryssa leans forward, her elbows on the table. "What do you know about horse racing?" she asks.

"Horse racing? Thankfully, not too much. For a couple of years after graduation, I'd get together with the guys from college every summer and we'd all watch each other lose money. What's that got to do with any of this?"

"Elle told me that many years ago, her father gave away a collection of paintings to an organization in upstate New York, a foundation run by a group of high-minded men and women who were in the initial stages of building the National Museum of Racing. Elle briefly mentioned that the donated paintings were stolen, but she didn't provide much in the way of details except to say that all of the paintings were recovered within a few days. The museum was completed, and from what I gather, it's been a big success. It's in Saratoga."

Ian lets out a nervous laugh, slapping a palm on the table. "Yep, that's the place that took our money, me and my buds. The track, that is. The museum is right across the street. I've never been inside, but I'll bet it's cheaper than spending the day betting on those horses."

Klaryssa nods slowly. "I'm sure—all those shadowy horse-racing savants you gamblers envy. You know, the ones who live in the rotted-out trailer, their '73 Pinto in the front yard, up on blocks. Plenty to be envious of there, obviously."

"OK, OK, there's no need for this sass," Ian says, stretching out his words. "Now, back to your delusion that I can help locate a 500-year-old work of art."

"I looked into this art theft, the Picard art theft that is, and the circumstances are a step or two beyond bizarre," Klaryssa says. "It was in 1946, and the Picard collection was being stored in a locked area on the racetrack premises. In the final race on the last day of the races that year, there was a riot because the racing judges disqualified three horses, the ones who finished first, second, and third. There was a big hullabaloo, according to news reports I dug up, because none of the patrons knew what was happening at the time.

"Naturally, as this was and still is a gambling endeavor, the fracas that day was over who actually won and who actually lost—who made money and who was in the hole. And in the commotion, of all things, the paintings were stolen. That's quite a coincidence, don't you think? Last race, last day, the racing officials jumble the winners and losers, and then, 'Oh, by the way, something happened to the paintings we had stashed in the basement.'"

"Now I know what you've been up to these past couple of days," Ian says with a slow nod. "But again, I don't know where and how I can possibly help. I hate to break the news to you, but I wasn't around in 1946."

"But you can find someone who *was*," Klaryssa says, wagging a finger at Ian. "The same family who, out of nowhere, walks into my life with a treasure of untold value was also the victim of an art theft years ago—an art theft that, on its face, appears to have coincided with some freakish event that occurred during a horse race. Now, I'm no champion of coincidences, but even if I was, you could never sell me this one.

"You're going to find me a person who was there that day, at that track, in 1946. What have you told me from day one about all this eBay business? That it's the largest market in the free world, right? You can find someone who sells racing memorabilia, like jockey silks or antique bridles or losing betting stubs or any other crap related to people throwing their money away by watching a line of horses run in a circle."

"Oval," Ian says meekly, drawing an oblong image in the air with his finger. "They don't run in a circle. They run around an oval."

87

"Fine, fine," Klaryssa says, waving away Ian's finger drawing. "Circle, oval, ellipse, octagon, whatever. All you have to do is find someone, or some thread, that leads back to that race all those years ago. Then, you're going to get that person to tell you about *another* person who knows *another* person whose great uncle was there that day. In the next 30 seconds, you could buy some piece of racing history, repackage it, and resell it as you always do, and by lunchtime, the piranhas will be circling. You just find me the piranha that can connect you—me—us—with someone who witnessed whatever the hell happened on that August afternoon.

"Oh, and just as an aside," Klaryssa adds, stretching her legs, "what we're talking about here is the greatest lost treasure in the past thousand years of Western civilization. So keep that in mind."

Chapter 6
Provincetown, Massachusetts
August 1946

Roscoe shimmied himself under the truck's front axle, slamming the crown of his head against a piece of driftwood that had jammed its way into the underside of the chassis. About an hour earlier, Roscoe had turned off the main road, known locally as the Old King's Highway, and since then, he had been driving at a snail's pace through a large expanse of steep sand dunes and puddles filled with knee-deep brackish water. Roscoe didn't have a handsaw, but he did have a flashlight, so at least he was able to see what had brought the truck to a sudden halt in the soft, foul-smelling muck.

After 10 minutes of inhaling clouds of diesel fumes and exhaling every cuss word he could think of, Roscoe finally managed to twist the half-buried tree branch enough to free the truck's undercarriage. They were off, once more, to God knows where.

At the beginning of the driving job, Roscoe was sitting alone in the truck's cab, having been instructed to pull away from the Saratoga Racetrack and head east along a two-lane road that connected them with Route 20. The man giving Roscoe orders was seated in the back of the truck. Roscoe followed Route 20 east, crossing over the state border and into Massachusetts. About an hour after darkness fell, Roscoe was told to divert north along a winding dirt road, eventually coming to a halt at the top of a steep hill. From the hilltop, Roscoe saw a scattering of faint lights to the west, which he figured must be from the town of Windsor. A couple of miles back, he had seen a rusted, vine-covered sign that advertised for a hotel called the Windsor Lodge. But Roscoe saw no sign of a lodge or hotel or dwelling of any sort along the rutted dirt road. The only sign of life nearby was the chorus of crickets emanating from the surrounding woods.

As ordered, Roscoe brought the truck to a halt atop the hill. At the time, there was enough light shining through the spider-web cracks in the side mirror for Roscoe to see three men emerge from the back of the vehicle, each carrying a stack of black rectangular slats. A minute later, a somewhat larger truck pulled up along the same road from the opposite direction, and the three men then loaded the slats into the back of the second truck and jumped in. The driver of the second truck handed Roscoe the keys to the second truck and gave him explicit instructions: "Here's your new ride. Get in, go down the hill and back to Route 20, and head east toward Boston. Don't look back. Drive slowly, and stop only when you are told to stop. If you have to take a piss, hold it. Same if you have to take a shit. You'll get fed, and you'll get paid. And ask no questions. None. Ever."

Some of the stops along Route 20 lasted a couple of hours or more, generally during daylight hours and always a bit off the main highway. Eventually, they headed south, away from Boston, toward the Cape Cod Canal. Once they were over the canal, the same routine of going seemingly nowhere for hours on end continued until they left Old King's Highway and began the overland trek in the dark of night through an endless chain of sand dunes.

Roscoe, covered with gluey muck and with the taste of salt water in his mouth, returned back behind the wheel. He began to wonder when, and even if, the odyssey would ever end. "Nice going," one of the three man in the back of the truck said with a sneer, talking to Roscoe through the small grate that connected the cab with the back of the vehicle. "You're one fine wheel man, yessiree. You're a little smelly, but no matter. Ain't my truck. Ain't my upholstery," he said with an uproarious cackle.

The man's name was Merle, and he was the only one of the three men in the back of the truck who ever spoke to Roscoe. The only thing Roscoe knew about Merle was that his greatest pleasure in life appeared to be laughing at his own jokes.

Roscoe hated Merle.

"See that pool of water up ahead a little ways, about the size of the one you just went for a swim in?" Merle asked. "Pull over to the right, but don't cut the engine."

A minute later, Roscoe got his first look at Merle, who jumped into the passenger side of the cab the instant the truck came to a halt. Merle was a squat, bulbous man with thick, salt-and-pepper eyebrows that nearly met in the middle of his forehead. The man had the roundest face Roscoe had ever seen.

"You any relation to Lenny Fowler?" Merle asked without introduction. "You look a little like him, ya know? He was a friend of my old man's, but now that I think about it, you couldn't be from the same family. This guy was a wimpy sort of fella, a real worm, and it seems to me you've got a set of cubes on you. Hey, you know what my old man used to say to this guy Lenny? I musta heard it a hundred times. 'There are leaders, and there are Fowlers.'" Again, he finished with a cackle.

"Lookie here," Merle continued without breaking stride, pointing at a picture in the newspaper he was holding. "Look familiar?" Merle asked, holding the photo a couple of inches from Roscoe's face. The picture, published in a Boston newspaper a day earlier, showed a burned-out moving truck at the top of a hill somewhere in the countryside. Roscoe didn't need a news article to tell him what had happened to the first truck he was driving. Two nights earlier, through his rear-view mirror, he had watched the rig go up in flames, not more than ten seconds after he started driving back down the hill in the truck they were all now riding in.

"Vaguely," Roscoe said, rearing back in his seat.

"Vaguely?" Merle roared, specks of food firing from his mouth and splashing against the windshield. "Hey guys, this one's a real card!" Merle went on, banging on the divider between the cab and the back of the truck. "Vaguely," he repeated in a slow, mocking tone. "I don't know about you, Mr. Fowler, but I didn't like that old truck to begin with. Nope, don't miss her even the tiniest bit."

Merle cut off the engine and stuffed the key into his shirt pocket. He then jumped out of the cab, popped open the hood, pulled at a couple of wires, and slammed the hood shut.

"So you're staying here for a spell, Mr. Roscoe Fowler," Merle said, sticking his beefy head through the driver's side window. "Sit tight, don't even think of leaving your seat, and when we get back, you'll be $200 heavier and we'll all ride out like we was never here. You can drive us all up to Boston, we'll get us some sauce and some grub, and then you're on your own. Meanwhile, just try and stay out of all these nasty mud puddles, will ya?"

Merle pointed at a nearby pool of standing water, laughing and shaking his head at Roscoe. He then walked to the back of the truck and signaled the other two men to follow him. They all trudging off into the distance, each one holding a flashlight. A couple of minutes later, all three men disappeared over a sand dune.

Whether traveling with his father or as an enlisted soldier in the US Army, Roscoe had spent nearly every day of his life either on the road or on the run. All too often, he was doing both simultaneously. Ditching his ride and seeing it set ablaze was nothing new to him, because he had helped his father with that task more times than he cared to count. But Roscoe's present circumstances were new even to him.

He kept asking himself how the man at the racetrack had ever recognized him. And how had this man found him amidst all the bedlam that was breaking loose? The man had said that he knew that Roscoe was a transport driver, so obviously, Roscoe reasoned, he had been following him. And what had happened to the original driver? And the convenience of it all: a near riot breaking out at the very moment this stranger wanted to have his truck driven out the front gate, a suddenly unguarded front gate. And why had it taken more than two days to drive a little over 200 miles to the end of Cape Cod? What was going on in the back of the truck while they sat motionless for hours along the side of abandoned farm roads? And the biggest question of all: what is, or was, in the back of the truck?

Roscoe saw the three flashlights move in and out of sight along the stretch of sand dunes that extended eastward toward the shoreline, so he figured that the three men were at least a couple hundred yards from the parked truck. Roscoe felt as though he was watching the men sojourn across the sand as if they were Egyptians submitting to a royal decree from Pharaoh. This made no sense, he thought. None whatsoever.

But then it occurred to Roscoe: The rectangular slats, whatever they were, were still in the back of the truck. They had to be. He watched the men walk away, and they certainly didn't have a load like that strapped to their backs.

The flickering flashlights, dimmer with each passing minute, moved farther to the east.

Roscoe grabbed a pair of dusty binoculars that sat on the dashboard and jumped out of the cab. He walked to the top of a nearby sand dune, crouching low amongst the matted reeds so Merle and his boys wouldn't spot him should they look back in the direction of the truck. Spying through the binoculars, Roscoe got a good look at the three men, their flashlights ablaze. He noticed that one of the men was carrying what looked like a rolled-up canvas. Could this be a ship's sail, one to be rigged onto the mast of a small boat they have stashed along the shoreline? They couldn't possibly have plans to take to the sea at this hour. That would be madness, he thought.

As Roscoe crawled away from the top of the small sand hill, he suddenly realized that this place seemed familiar to him. Glancing in the opposite direction, he recognized the lights of Provincetown and the Pilgrim Monument, the town's unmistakable hilltop landmark, which towered far above everything else. There was enough light from the third-quarter moon for Roscoe to see all the way to the tip of Cape Cod. While looking out across the vast kingdom of rolling sand dunes, a distant, hazy memory came rushing back to life. He had been here before, he was sure of it. Roscoe recalled the summer when he and his father had spent a couple of weeks in a dune shack out there, in the middle of nowhere, and he remembered the place being as desolate as the surface of an uninhabited planet. The huge boomerang-shaped beach was called Race

Point, and he remembered how much he hated the time they spent here.

His father had probably been hiding out from someone and, if that had been the case, he had chosen wisely, because what Roscoe saw through his then 10- or 11-year-old eyes was a godforsaken expanse of wind-whipped sand where there was no one to play with and nothing to do.

When Roscoe got back to the truck, he noticed that Merle had locked the back door, which was hardly a surprise. Even less of a surprise was how fast Roscoe picked the lock, another skill he had honed years earlier while aiding dear old Dad in any number of ventures.

Once he had opened the door, Roscoe jumped inside the truck and turned on his flashlight. In front of him were rows of framed oil paintings, each depicting a different scene related to horse racing: horses with their trainers, horses with their jockeys, steeplechase races, match races, and a number of renderings of European royalty riding their mounts.

To Roscoe, there was not much question that the cargo before him had been offloaded from the first truck and packed into this truck. In a corner of the truck, Roscoe found a simple tool set and two folded-up newspapers, one an issue of the *New York Times* and the other an issue of the *Boston Evening Globe*. Roscoe had seen one of the men buy the newspapers, along with food and cigarettes, at a delicatessen the previous evening.

Roscoe took another quick look out across the vast expanse of sand. He thumbed through the two newspapers until he found a couple of articles that had been circled in pen by one of the men, and, as he expected, the marked articles told of an art theft from the Saratoga Racetrack the previous day.

Both journalists detailed the approximate age of the stolen paintings, and listed the names of the artists but made no mention of the estimated value of the artwork. Only the *Times* article made brief mention of the three-horse disqualification, citing the "highly irregular and disputed last race finish" that was believed to be "coincident and after the fact" with regard to the art heist. Both articles quoted racetrack and law enforcement officials who reference 14 "prized and highly sought after" works of art.

Roscoe made a closer inspection of the paintings, noting that the largest was about five feet by six feet in size, and, like the others, it was housed in a heavy, ornate wooden frame. To

Roscoe's thoroughly untrained eye, each of the works appeared to be completely intact. Roscoe counted the paintings. Then he counted them again. And again.

Fourteen.

There were 14 framed antique paintings lined up against the inside walls of the truck. In the previous day's newspaper articles, the president of the Saratoga Racecourse and the chief of the New York State Police were each quoted as saying that 14 paintings had been stolen from the race track premises, and, at that moment, Roscoe was staring at all 14 of them.

Roscoe scanned the news articles again, confirming that he had not misread the number of missing paintings. The authorities could not have been clearer or more explicit. Before tossing the papers back into the corner, Roscoe spotted two other articles that had been circled, both from the *Boston Evening Globe*. One of the articles showed the same picture Merle had just shown Roscoe, the one of a burned-out truck found along a rural western Massachusetts roadway. The article quoted a local sheriff who said that he found the vehicle "charred beyond recognition," so there was no mention of any relationship between the scorched vehicle and the Saratoga art theft.

The second article was a short piece about a dead body found behind one of the lake houses in Saratoga two days earlier. The deceased was a man named Emmett Elry, and he had been stabbed in the chest by an unknown assailant. The article stated that Mr. Elry had no known family, and all that was known about him was that he had worked as a freelance long-haul trucker for many years.

Roscoe threw the newspapers into the corner, jumped out, and slammed shut the back door of the truck. He knew that if he did as instructed and stayed where he was, Roscoe Fowler would be the focus of the next news article about a dead body being found in some ditch. He realized beyond any doubt that the man who had been stabbed to death in Saratoga was the original getaway driver. The "inconvenienced" original getaway driver. Why else would Merle or one of the other ruffians draw a circle of pride around such an article?

Roscoe looked out across the maze of sand dunes and saw nothing. His first instinct was to run for his life in the opposite direction, toward Provincetown, where he could hide out for a few days until the killers were long gone. He still had no earthly idea why Merle and his boys had set out like Bedouins across the sands toward the ocean shore, but that was the least of his concerns. He knew that once they returned from whatever caper they were on, they would kill him and take off with the truckload of stolen art. Roscoe couldn't have cared less about the pile of hot paintings stashed in the back of the truck. He was out to save his own hide and nothing else.

But wait a minute, Roscoe thought to himself. The paintings, they're all there, all 14 of them. The theft had garnered coverage in big city newspapers, and if Roscoe had been allowed to put on the radio in the truck's cab, he no doubt would have heard coverage over the airwaves as well. The theft of the paintings was big stuff, big news. Such a high-profile robbery meant a reward would have been offered for recovering the stolen property, and more likely than not, it was a big reward.

Roscoe turned on his flashlight, popped open the hood, and reconnected the wires that Merle had ripped apart before he took off into the distance. Roscoe knew that Merle was not only a fat slob and an asshole but also a moron, because Roscoe knew more about engines than anyone anywhere. Merle probably thought he knew nothing more than how to drive through ruts and swamps and sandpits and dicey places like that. Merle, that ignorant, worthless piece of shit, had no idea that Roscoe could pick a lock and patch up wiring with his eyes closed.

It took no time at all for Roscoe to hot-wire the truck, crank the engine, and get the truck moving again. He headed back out toward Old King's Highway, for the most part following the same tracks he had made a little earlier. The headlights and taillights had already been dimmed, and Roscoe had previously lowered the tire pressure to ease their passage over the sand dunes. He planned to stop at the first service station he found and pump the pressure back up on all four tires, refilling the gas tank while he was there.

Then he would drive up toward Boston, ditch the truck outside the city, and call the local police to report the abandoned truck he happened to stumble upon. But first, he had to find out about the reward money for the stolen art. That was his number one imperative. He knew he would end up being the hero in all this, but all the better if he remained a silent hero. No one knew who he was, and no one of any importance—like the execs who ran the Saratoga Racetrack—knew that he had ever been to Saratoga. He would get full credit for finding and returning the stolen art, and he would be handed, ever so quietly, a handsome reward.

Once again a winner, Roscoe would then pay off his debts and head out for more action, more plunder, more cash. He had no interest in Boston or the scenic beaches that were only a short distance outside the city. Sure, there was nightlife and there were beautiful girls and maybe a card game here and there, but that just wouldn't cut it for Roscoe. He needed a city like New York or L.A. or Reno. Those were the places where it all really moved.

Roscoe, once again, was on the move.

Chapter 7
Boston, Massachusetts
Present Day

It took Ian less than 20 minutes of online searching to find the star he was looking for, and his name was Assault.

In 1945, the colossal King Ranch of South Texas debuted a dark chestnut colt named Assault, and, in his first outing, the horse managed to outrun only one of the other 12 entries he ran against. The horse fared somewhat better over the next few months, but in a trial race before the 1946 Kentucky Derby, he came within a few yards of finishing dead last. For reasons that no one could explain at the time, Assault's trainer convinced the King family hierarchy not to scratch the colt from running in the Kentucky Derby. Written off by both sportswriters and patrons, Assault was seen as a second-class entry who would show a game effort for a half-mile or so before being run over by the heavy hitters. It would likely be his last romp before moving on to the retirement pasture.

Two minutes after the starter's bell sounded, Assault was an astounding eight lengths clear of the rest of the Derby field, an unmatched feat in any of the event's 71 previous races. By early June, the colt had also laid claim to both the Preakness and Belmont Stakes, leaving the King Ranch flooded in Triple Crown Champagne.

Once Ian secured an authentic racing program printed on the day of Assault's Derby victory, he was able to post a unique piece of American sports history on one of his eBay sites.

Ian was offering diehard racing aficionados the chance to own a framed set of original racing programs from each of Assault's Triple Crown races. A certificate of authenticity was included, and, as an added bonus, one of the three programs had an autograph, albeit a bit faded, signed by the jockey who rode the winning colt in all three races.

Once Ian announced this "once-in-a-lifetime chance to own a historic thoroughbred racing treasure," bidders started jumping in fast and furious. If Klaryssa wanted the attention of anyone even remotely connected to the events of summer 1946 in Saratoga, this was her best shot.

Bidders' messages, discussion boards, Facebook posts, random inquiries—Ian and Klaryssa had to cull the wheat from the chaff, and, to no surprise, the former was sparse and the latter abundant. One Oklahoma rancher was even offering to sell his prized stallion, a certified bloodline descendant of the Triple Crown champion himself. This was contingent, of course, on someone out there meeting his outrageous asking price.

Klaryssa combed through hundreds of leads, and out of them all, only two showed promise. The first was an eBay forum posting from a man named Harvey Mangold, who lived alone at his home in Bolton Landing, New York. Bolton Landing sits along the western shore of Lake George, and Harvey, long retired from 50 years of working in and around Saratoga, called the immediate post-World War II years "the best a man could ever dream of." Harvey welcomed phone calls, Internet chat, and even visits to his home, which Klaryssa found particularly impressive for a man who had to be within sight of his 90th birthday. This was too fine an offer to let pass, so Klaryssa made plans to drive out to Lake George and pay Mr. Mangold a visit.

The second lead was an email from the executor of the estate of a man whose name was Robert Lancet. Mr. Lancet had been a fourth-generation Saratoga resident, and his hobby, prior to his premature death in a car accident several years earlier, was collecting a series of oral history recordings from those who spent their lives involved in any facet of horse racing.

The executor was certain that Mr. Lancet would have wanted his oral history project to continue, and since nobody else had expressed any interest, he sent Klaryssa an electronic copy of the recordings free of charge. When Klaryssa received the recordings, she was surprised that they were well organized. She planned to listen to various segments during her five-hour drive to Harvey Mangold's home on Lake George. She would leave Boston before dawn, listen to all she could while driving, and arrive at Lake George with plenty of time to spare, so she could make use of the trail bike she had strapped to the roof of her car. After a couple of hours cycling along the lake's scenic bike trails, she would knock on Mr. Mangold's door and see what, if anything, she could learn.

All that changed when, by way of a long-buried audio clip, Klaryssa met Mr. Blass Sarren.

Chapter 8

On the Road

Klaryssa left Boston a little before four in the morning, packing only her bike, a change of clothes, a thermos of black coffee, and the audio recordings that were made several years earlier by the now deceased historian Robert Lancet. She had downloaded all of Lancet's oral history clips onto her iPhone the previous evening, and while heading west along Interstate 90 en route to Lake George, Klaryssa began to wonder how long the thermos of coffee might last her.

Lancet was clearly a dedicated amateur historian who had a true fondness for horse racing, but to Klaryssa's ear, the recorded conversations were painfully predictable: fast horses, slow horses, winners, losers, good times, and not so good times. She heard a couple of hours worth of plodding dialogue between Lancet and a parade of jockeys, breeders, grooms, barkeeps, gamblers, and members of the racetrack maintenance crew. Much of it was repetitive, and, so far, all of it blasé and humdrum.

Klaryssa was close to silencing Mr. Lancet and putting on some of her favorite jazz when she stumbled upon the reminiscences of a man named Blass Sarren.

LANCET: "So, there is no question in your mind that Man O'War was the champion of all champions?"

SARREN: "Oh, he was mighty. Just mighty. Ya know, the one race he done lost was a mess at the start, a real mess. Nags wasn't even lined up straight, n'even close. Signal to start was given, and old Man O'War wasn't even turned straight. Everyone who wuz standin' out there saw it. But Man O'War, he nearly pulled it off anyway, don't y'know. Horse that beat him named Upset. E'ry one knows that, but man what a dinger that was. Upset by Upset. But yeah, Man O'War was best of all. Secretariat, I saw him too, yeah I did. He's a close second for best I saw."

LANCET: "And when did you start working at Saratoga?"

SARREN: "Ha, no one believes it now, I was ten year old. No joke there. Happ'n all the time back then. We's lucky, all us, m'pals and me. Work, cash, work mo', your pocket fills."

LANCET: "And working there, at Saratoga, was the only job you ever had?"

SARREN: "Well, it was *all* kindsa jobs, friend. All kinds. Helped groom, hot walk the racers, cool 'em down after. Then when I wuz older, I was really mostly buildin' and fixin', ya know. Put new roofs on more'n once. Gold steeples—how ya think they got fixed'n polished? Track rail, ya know, there's miles of 'em. Miles. Never seen one wobble or collapse. Know why? Friend, yous lookin' at why. No, it was all kinds a jobs, just only one place. Only place I 'er needed."

LANCET: "So there was enough work off season, all those lonely cold months between the summer excitement?"

SARREN: "Plenty. N'er a lack of tasks in a place that size."

LANCET: "You must miss it all, after so many years—the crowd, the action, famous people milling about every summer."

SARREN: "I's old, you know. And a little sick, I'm 'fraid. Got my fill, f'sure. Though I do miss all them Hollywood folk and pols, ya know. They lit the whole place up, e'ry time."

112

LANCET: "You mean movie stars? And did you ever see one of our presidents there?"

SARREN: "Shit yeah! Oh, sorry. Forgot we's recordin' all this. Yeah sure, movie stars. Gable, Wayne, Audrey Hepburn, Rita Hayworth, even Brando—once anyway. Ne'er seen a president there, though heard Roosevelt paid a visit one time. Probably a secret sorta thing, security and all. Gov'ners for sure, senators, all that. And Hoover, oh yeah, all the while."

LANCET: "You mean J. Edgar Hoover, the FBI chief?"

SARREN: "For certain, all the time. Yessir, e'ry year, for sure. Loved them horses, and he'd lay down bets. Yup. I always said 'hi' when I saw'm, and he always said 'hi' back. Real nice fella, nice to e'ry one. Well, to those that d'serve it. There's bad apples about back then, and he had no use for that sort, no sir."

LANCET: "You saw him in action there, in Saratoga? J. Edgar Hoover, our FBI Director, actively involved in law enforcement?"

SARREN: "Didn't have to. I mean, he's there, all in a fancy suit, never a ruffle or mix'n it up with any mob in plain sight. But my brother—my lil'st brother—he heard it all. Seen plenty too, but heard e'ry thing. See, my li'l brother, he went t'school, had smarts f'sure, and he did the transcribin' for the FBI office in Albany. Hoover made sure plenty agents wuz there, and when they run inta some mob or dirty sort, my li'l brother, Rees his name, wrote down e'ry word. He was always suppo to be hush hush, but sometime, well, take Rees out for whiskey and such, he'd tend to, you know, loosen up."

LANCET: "So your brother, Rees, he worked at the FBI field office in Albany?

SARREN: "That's a fact."

LANCET: "Mr. Sarren, if you don't mind me asking, is your brother still alive?"

SARREN: "Don't mind 'bit. Dead 21 years. Cancer. Worse than the one I got now, guess. And no cause to say sorry f'any a this. He had a fine life, just like me. But yeah, oh yeah, he heard all kinds a back and forth down there in Albany. Biggest one, y'know. a'least the biggest bad sort of fella he talked 'bout, he really got the business from those FBI boys. Bet you heard of the guy. Name's Lansky."

LANCET: "Meyer Lansky! Your brother sat in on the FBI's interrogation of Meyer Lansky?"

To Klaryssa's ear, Lancet's voice had moved up at least two octaves.

SARREN: "You heard me right, friend. Rees, he was right there when they was puttin' the heat on that fella, and more'n once. You know, the only time in 'is life that crook Lansky e're spent in lockup was in this tiny jail near Saratoga. You know dat? But that was years later. Now I'm talkin' 1940s, after the big war. Lansky was there all the while, in Saratoga, that is. Lake houses where there was gamblin' and all that. And at the racetrack, sure. All the big mob was. But this time was different. Big stuff. The FBI boys, they was talkin' to Lansky 'bout this art that went missin'. Hoover was steamin', these Feds told Lansky, cuz these paintings were pinched right outta the track. And Hoover, he loved dat track. Took it all personal, and those Fed boys, they was pressin' this Lansky, cuz they figured he had to have a hand in this one. Where'er there's money, there's a mob, right?"

LANCET: "What happened with all this, in the end? Did they catch him in the act?"

SARREN: "Not a chance, not w'this fella. These guys with Fed badges, they pushed Lansky real hard, what my li'l brother tol' me. The badges say these paintings and such, they stolen, and whoever swiped 'em, they's stupid 'nough to cross the state line. FBI located a torched truck over in Mass'chusetts, know what'm sayin'? Cross the border, FBI in charge. And they's hot, and they's pushin' Lansky, big time. My brother, he say Lansky actin' scared, but not scared of FBI. Seemed to Rees that Lansky scared of who'er pulled off this job. Even sounded like he mighta known who did the job, this big art theft and all. Lansky say something like 'instead of pushin' me round, maybe you should look in your own backyard.' Who e're heard of a big mob boss being scared? Not me, man."

The recording breaks off for about 20 seconds as Sarren begins to cough.

LANCET: "Did Lansky say anything else?"

SARREN: "Hoover, guess he was always real big on not missin' anything said in these interrogations. Rees tol' me FBI boss never missed nothin'. Y'know my brother wasn't even s'pose to make eye contact with anyone in the room, let alone tell anyone outside the room what all was said. He be fired on the spot, maybe even jail time. All he s'pose to do is transcribe, know what I mean? Not another damn thing. Oh, sorry again, this on tape and all. But Rees, he sneaks a look at

Lansky, and like I tol' you, this big shot mob fella is lookin' tight. Jumpy. Maybe even sweatin'. But then Lansky narrows his eyes and says ta those Fed badges something like 'I got nothing in this, hear me? Nothin'. You can run back and tell Mr. Hoover that, and then you can tell him somethin' else. Tell him when he finds the guys that pulled this off, I'll do the rest of his job for him. I'll save him and you all kinds of time and trouble. And same for your courts down there in DC. Once I'm finished, you won't be needin' any courts.'

"Rees say this Lansky fella was trying to leave the room sound-in tough and all, but Rees, well, he say the man seemed pretty rattled. Shaky through the whole interview."

Klaryssa played the recording again and again, pulling into a rest area at 6:30 in the morning to replay this one segment of the Lancet interviews. Out from this small town's underbelly steps a man named Blass Sarren and his fantastic tale about J. Edgar Hoover, an off- the-wall art heist, and the enigmatic mobster Meyer Lansky. Could this possibly be for real, this man's brother and the FBI and Hoover and Lansky? Could any or all of this narrative be substantiated? Did Blass Sarren just invent all this? Was he a neglected and obviously

117

sick old man looking for one last hurrah, a final moment in the limelight?

Lancet was clearly out of his element when, instead of spinning the warm, folksy saga that he wanted to record, he was suddenly flattened by this chronicle of high crime and skullduggery. Blass Sarren sounded both sincere and confident. He sounded for real, Klaryssa thought. After he quoted Meyer Lansky's statement to the FBI agents, Blass went into a convulsion of coughing for at least a minute or so, and when he recovered, Lancet launched into a driveling monologue about how sad it must have been to see the racetrack shuttered during World War II. For Klaryssa, this change of topic was as painful to hear as it was tragic. It was a cardinal sin for an interviewer like Mr. Lancet to have let a trail that was so hot just fizzle and die. But what really mattered was that Mr. Lancet had somehow found Blass Sarren and recorded his recollections, and his stories gave credence to Klaryssa's growing sense that the bizarre events that had occurred on that August day in 1946 were very much related to each other. Unnerved as he may have been by the story he was hearing, Mr. Lancet had nevertheless recorded a voice that told of matters that no one else knew anything about—a voice that told Klaryssa that the Picard art heist had drawn the immediate attention of authorities at the highest level. The biggest question of all, of course, remained unanswered.

What, exactly, had been stolen?

Chapter 9

Lake George, New York

After spending more than an hour listening to multiple replays of Lancet's interview with Blass Sarren, Klaryssa's Lake George bike tour had to be slimmed down to a quick roundabout along the lake's western shore at Silver Bay. She had never been to Lake George before, and while cycling the narrow two-lane road that hugs the lakefront's western border, she quickly realized why so many of her friends made this their summer getaway. The lake itself, 30 plus miles long and dotted with tiny islands and rocky inlets, was framed by rolling, untouched Adirondack peaks three miles to the east along the far shore. Klaryssa wished she had driven here the night before and had the chance to bike up to Ticonderoga at the northern tip of the lake, but she was, after all, not here for a spring cycling trek, so that would have to be for another time.

She stopped and ordered a quick breakfast at a vintage 1950s diner. The interior walls of the diner were lined with black-and-white photos of the *Minne-Ha-Ha* and the *Mohican*, the two longest serving vessels in what is said to be the country's oldest paddle wheeler/steamboat tour company. As with her Lake George biking trip, any thought of taking a sunset steamboat cruise would have to be put aside. She had come out here for one reason. After the oral history recording she had just heard, that reason seemed suddenly real and all the more pressing. Klaryssa fastened her trail bike onto the roof rack of her car and drove south along the lakeshore toward Bolton Landing.

Harvey Mangold's home was situated on a small hilltop lot three blocks above the town center, with an unobstructed view of Green Island and Braley Point farther to the north. Mr. Mangold greeted Klaryssa at the front door and showed her into a small sunroom while he went into the kitchen for the tray of tea and shortbread cakes he had prepared. He insisted that Klaryssa call him Harvey because "there's no one who doesn't."

"That devil Assault was meaner than a razorback," Harvey Mangold says, wasting no time in picking up on the historical thread that brought

121

the two of them together via an eBay forum. "Trust me, if ever there was a perfect name for a horse, or for that matter any animal that ever called a barn his home, that was it: Assault. And that's exactly what he'd do to you, faster than you could blink."

Harvey rocks back in his chair. "I seen him throw exercise riders right onto their ass. Saw it more than once, with my own eyes. If some cocky greenhorn from that King Ranch thought he might take the champ out for a sprint, he found out in a hurry that the champ had different thoughts on the matter. The minute that kid got comfortable in the saddle, distracted as he showed off for his cute little girlfriend, old Assault—you know he wasn't that old—he'd toss that boy into the dirt. He might even try and kick the kid once or twice while the lad was trying to scramble to his feet.

"I don't believe the horse was really that ill-tempered," Harvey goes on, still rocking slowly. "It's more that he didn't like being anything other than the center of attention. He wasn't anybody's toy, if you know what I mean. He was just all business, and if you weren't, you were going to hit the deck, and you were going to hit it hard."

"You saw him race, I take it," Klaryssa says, realizing immediately that she was stating the obvious.

"Couple times," Harvey says with a wistful smile as he stirs his tea. "Fact of the matter is he wasn't really a great horse. He was a *good* horse, a very good horse, who *did* something great. After he took that Triple Crown, he won here and there, but he was beat more often than he won."

Klaryssa turns toward the lake after she hears a quick series of loud squawks from just off the shoreline.

"Blue herons," Harvey says without looking. "All kinds of birds to watch up here. You hear them plenty, too. Peregrines, loons. The mallards are everywhere. Can see the bald eagle too, even in the wintertime. They're all my neighbors, and I wouldn't live anywhere else."

"You've lived here your whole life?" Klaryssa asks, sticking to small talk. "This is my first time here, and it's a lovely area. The lake is stunning in the sunlight."

"Never tire of looking out at that lake, even after all these years. But I wasn't born here. I'm from the South, in case you couldn't tell by my accent that has never quite faded away. My daddy moved us here when I was a little lad, into this very house. You know, when I started finding work down in Saratoga, back when I was a teenager, I rode there in a friend's pickup truck every day, to and from. My family, we didn't have a car, and up here, I got around on a horse of my own. A mixed-breed Warlander, had him for years. Horse is long gone, but still the same house. And when I leave through that front door for good, it's going to be feet first."

"So you worked around horses your whole life, not to mention raising and riding one yourself," Klaryssa says, still trying to stay on script. "You must miss them, I'm sure."

"Every day," Harvey answers, taking a sip of tea. "Love them. Always did. Worked till I was 75; that's 11 years ago. Might of retired when I was younger if I didn't love them so much. In case you didn't know, you can bet money when they run."

Klaryssa smiles, looking back out toward the two blue herons perched on a rock just off shore.

Harvey cuts a piece of the shortbread and places it on a plate in front of Klaryssa.

"So you're an artist?" Harvey asks. "And you're a writer too, if I'm not mistaken."

"Thank you," Klaryssa says, eyeing the shortbread. "Well, I'm not quite an artist myself. I'm on the faculty at Tufts University, in the art department. And I did publish a book recently, yes. My first one."

"Try some," Harvey says, pointing at the plate in front of Klaryssa. "It's homemade, but not from this home. Lady friend of mine made it for me. For us, that is. She can bake, oh yeah. Get to be my age, lady friends are a lot easier to find. If I'd known that before, I'd have tried to get old sooner.

"Tell me, if you don't mind," Harvey continues while cutting himself another slice of shortbread. "Boston is five hours from here, a lot longer if you're dealing with traffic and bad roads and all that. That's a 10-hour round trip, maybe more. So, I asked myself, why would a young professor, an author, come all this way to talk with some geezer about a cantankerous horse who near everyone else had long forgot about? So, since that's what I've been asking myself, I'll ask you that same question."

Harvey's dark green eyes hold Klaryssa's gaze for a moment.

"Harvey," Klaryssa says, letting out a deep breath, "I know nothing about horses or the races they run or the tracks they run on. I rode a pony a few times when I was a little girl in Ukraine, where I was born, but that's it. And if you can bear with me, you'll soon know why I drove out here to meet with you, because I need your help with something. From what you mentioned on eBay, you were working at the Saratoga track that summer, in 1946. Is that correct?"

"That was me," Harvey says, giving Klaryssa a slow nod. "My second year there; I was 15 years old."

"Do you remember the last day of that summer season, in 1946?"

"No one who was there ever forgot *that* day. If they stayed all the way to the end, that is. Not sure there are many of us left, though."

"I asked a friend of mine, a very close friend who knows a lot more about eBay than I do, to help me find someone who was there that day and witnessed first-hand what happened. One thing led to another, which led me to you, thankfully. So I have to ask, what did you see during that last race? Is there anything you can tell me about what happened during that race and immediately after? And believe me, any questions you have for me, I'll answer. Just say the word."

126

Harvey stares into his teacup before he takes another sip. "You know, in all my years working in that town, out of all the wacky things that I saw, that might have been the wackiest of them all. And no one, and I mean no one, ever, has really asked me about it. Until now, that is.

"All us boys working there, we was all fixing to pack up, you know," Harvey now leans back in his chair, looking up at the ceiling. "Last day, last run. A lotta pieces to break down, and it was going to be a long night. More hours, more pay, so we were a happy bunch, oh yeah. Tired, but happy. I ran one of the tractors, smoothing out the running surface between races. So at the time that last race came around, I wasn't much paying attention. I was just thinking of what I had to get done once the race was over. Then all of a sudden, at the turn in the track near where we had the tractors parked, this horse rears up, and, for an instant, it looks like they all might tumble like dominos. Thank God, nothing like that happened. I'd seen that before, and it's just an awful sight. So there's a shuffling of the horses at the front of the pack, and half a minute or so later, it's over. But, as I guess you know, it wasn't really over."

Klaryssa sits in silence. She does not want to derail the story and make the same mistake that Lancet made when he interviewed Blass Sarren.

"A few minutes later, it was a nuthouse," Harvey goes on, taking off his glasses and setting them on the table. "Three flags go up, and there's a ruckus like I never seen before or since. Then the order of finish, meaning the winners and the losers, all changes. So fast, all of it was so fast. Us boys, we just looked at each other, not saying much because we were all sort of shell-shocked."

Klaryssa lets a long moment pass before asking, "Harvey, while you worked there, did you ever meet a man named Blass Sarren?"

"Good Lord, you can find anything on that eBay!" Harvey says, leaning forward and tipping over his empty teacup. "Now *there* is a name I never thought I'd hear again. I take it the same friend that brought us together also stumbled upon the great Blass along the way."

"That's exactly what happened. There was a link to someone who had audiotaped—"

"That Lancet guy. Sorry for interrupting, Klaryssa," Harvey says, as giddy as a schoolboy. "That Lancet, he would talk to anyone who had put in a bunch of years at the racetrack. I spoke to him once or twice, briefly. He said something once like, 'Mr. Mangold, you must be a fixture around here.' Well, if I was a fixture at that place, Blass was an institution. Everyone knew Blass, I mean everyone. See, I worked at the track during the summer and fall each year, otherwise I worked odd jobs here and there. You know, bartending, kitchen help. Made pizza that people couldn't get enough of, but that place is long gone. But Blass, he was at the track for many years before I got there. It was the only place he ever knew, and that is no lie. The man never went to school a day in his life, but he had enough street sense to fill the brains of 10 people. He and his brother, you'd see him around in the summer too, they could speak perfect French. Better than their English, particularly Blass. I think they learned it at home, their momma I guess. She was born in Paris, I believe."

"I take it he passed away," Klaryssa asks while Harvey pours more tea.

"Yeah, 'bout 15 or so years ago. One of those lymph cancers. Slowly ate him up. What do you expect, though? He was 94 or 95, no one knew his age exactly. Even him. Miracle he made it half that far, with the life he led. For years he smoked like it was some sort of contest, but he quit that.

Drank heavy on and off, but he quit that, too. Gambled forever…not sure he ever quit that habit. And you know, odd thing was, he was a quiet guy when I knew him. He seemed to me kind of a silent sort, working with his nose to the grindstone. It was only after he retired that he started spouting like a broken faucet. And once he started, good gravy, you couldn't shut him up."

Mr. Lancet found a way to shut him up, Klaryssa laments to herself.

"Some of the boys thought it was the cancer drugs they were feeding to old Blass," Harvey continues. "Maybe that's what made him talk so much. The doctors, they gave him pills for the lymph tumor, and I guess they worked, because he lived a bunch more years. And along the way, he turned into a motor mouth."

"Finding out about Blass Sarren, it happened just as you said a minute ago," Klaryssa says once she is sure Harvey is done speaking. "A series of audiotapes were given to me, and I was listening to them on my way here today. Blass started to talk about some of the luminaries he had seen come and go over the years, and then he mentioned the art theft that took place at the racetrack on the same day, and apparently at the same time, as the uproar that occurred during and after that last race in 1946.

"On the audiotapes, Blass does more than just mention the incident. He, in fact, goes into the nuts and bolts of the investigation that took place immediately afterwards. He talks about the FBI running in a mobster for interrogation, and all the heat that the FBI director was applying to find the stolen art. And he identifies the mobster by name, claiming it was actually Meyer Lansky. A lot of what he talks about is from what his brother told him, so the details are second hand, and that always raises more doubt than an eyewitness account. But, hearing this man talk, you just have the sense he's being straight."

"Like I said, when Blass started speaking, he just kept going," Harvey says, still looking intently at Klaryssa. "And let me tell you, there were mobsters around there, all right. Including that Lansky fella. He was at the track. At the nightclubs, too. Wanna follow the mob, just follow the dough, you know what I mean? So, why not steal art, you know, paintings and all that? It's money, right? So, is that why you're so keen on all that happened that day…an art historian and writer maybe writing about an old art theft. Am I close?"

"Well, not exactly," Klaryssa says. "Very recently, I was approached by someone who is trying to trace the origin of a piece of artwork that she and her family own. I offered to help, and, in short order, I happened upon a news article about the art theft in Saratoga all those years ago. The stolen artwork and the piece I am investigating have a common origin. They're somehow related, I just don't know exactly how."

"You know, at the end of it all, nothing was *really* stolen," Harvey says, standing up from his chair. "Hold on a sec, I wanna show you something."

Harvey shuffles off into an adjoining room and, a minute later, walks back into the sunporch carrying two large plastic bins.

"No problem, I'm fine," Harvey says after Klaryssa stands and offers to take one of the bins. "No worries here. I'll find it."

Harvey opens one bin, and then the other, thumbing through piles of paper and eventually pulling out a stack of yellowed newspaper clippings.

"These are from the Albany paper," he says, handing the stack to Klaryssa. "Take a look."

Klaryssa reads through three news articles, all from late August and early September 1946. Each of the pieces includes detailed photographs of various paintings from the Picard art collection. Scanning through the articles quickly, she notices that each of the photographs has the words "Courtesy of the Picard family" printed underneath, meaning the photographs of the paintings were taken by the Picards prior to the collection being shipped to Saratoga. The articles were all printed after the paintings were recovered, the journalists lauding the efforts of local law enforcement and FBI investigators in recovering the stolen art collection.

"Nothing taken," Harvey says, pointing back and forth between the various news photographs. "Permanently, anyway. From what the authorities had to say, nothing really went missing."

Klaryssa studies the pictures for another minute or so before looking up at Harvey.

"Guess you don't believe everything you read?" he asks, grinning slightly.

"No," Klaryssa says, setting the news articles on the table. "No, I don't. It's all just a little too...too—"

"Convenient?" Harvey adds, his expression revealing his long-held misgivings about the published reports.

Klaryssa grins, nodding slowly.

"There was this guy I worked with out there, name was Buster," Harvey says, breaking the brief silence. "Biggest guy you ever saw in your life. Drove a tractor, just like me. When he sat down on that machine, I swear, it sank an inch or more into the dirt, that's how big he was. So same day we're talking about here, end of August 1946, Buster—I forget his last name—he's parked a ways away from where the rest of us boys were. See, it was his day to be on the backup tractor in case any one of the other tractors broke down. He's parked just off Union Avenue, which is right next to the racetrack, and that's the part of the track where the horses head for the stretch run. So before the last race that day, he turns around and happens to notice this big photography setup near the main entrance. He said later it was like some type of Hollywood scene and all—reflectors, big cameras, the whole deal. Buster said he figured it was all there so they could get a big glory shot. You know, war is over, people celebrating, last day of summer season and such.

"When the horses were running a few minutes later, and then reached the part of the track where Buster was sitting, Buster sees this big flash from behind him. He said it was like lightning firing up from the ground, that's how bright it was. He turns that way again, and he sees another flash of light. Blinding, at least as bright as the first one. That's when the horses got spooked, no question. Buster, he's sitting up high on his tractor, so he's seeing things others there can't. So, no sooner does he turn around one more time, he sees that one of the cameramen is gone, and the other one is taking down the photography setup and scurrying away too. They were gone as quick as they came, and Buster, who was right there, said it didn't look to him like they were there to take no picture."

"'When you want to know the facts, you rely on the press. When you want to know what happened, you rely on the irregulars,'" Klaryssa says after letting Harvey's words sink in. "That's a line from a Ukrainian movie, talking about the 'irregulars,' or kids on the street. They know, and more often than not, they're the only ones who know. So, what do you think happened?"

"Fix," Harvey says without a breath's hesitation. "Not a question in my mind. Not a question in *anyone's* mind. Any of us boys out there, anyway. I mean, damn, we all saw it. Never seen anything like it again. But the truth is, the thing never made any sense. Even though the top three finishers were disqualified, remember, for every person who thought they won but lost, there's another who thought they lost but won. So I can't begin to tell you who gained in all this. And what were we going to do? We were just a bunch of kids, no one would believe anything we said. What could we prove anyway? But the boys and I, we knew whatever happened was staged like a Broadway play. And we had the best view in the house. Best view, that is, except for one."

Klaryssa is looking straight into Harvey's eyes, and she's certain that the man has plenty more to say.

"Harold *Melcher*," Harvey says, with more than a hint of distaste in his voice. "Melcher was the patrol judge who watched every race from an elevated platform along the inside rail. He's the referee, if you will, for that side of the track. Most of the track officials were real nice to us fellas, knowing we worked hard, and they'd say thanks here and there. But not this Melcher guy. He was as sour as a vine of stale grapes. And he was a slouch, too. Day after day, he'd lumber up onto that platform like he was on his way to the gallows. It was like he couldn't have cared less. Yeah, just plain lazy. Lazy up to that day, anyway. I'm here to tell you, he was the one who put the fix in."

"Do you mind?" Klaryssa asks, taking out a pen and pad to take some notes. "I really need to–"

"Not a bit," Harvey says, leaning back. "Melcher, when the race ended, charged over to call the boss men, the stewards. There was this private phone line, and he was having this long conversation. And then, after he hangs up, the man is off and running the opposite direction, toward the backstretch area of the track, where the horse barns are located. And that's where we were located, too. I see that miserable SOB come right past me and sort of disappear behind one of the barns.

"Word was that Melcher was having heart attack-type pain, and he was heading into one of the medical aid stations. It's a fact that there was a doctor and nurse back there to care for anyone who was sick or injured, which in those days was most often due to heat stroke. But there was no way to know if this guy fell sick or not. Have to remember, within a couple of hours, everything was going to be packed up and on its way to New York City, and

137

that included the doctor and nurse. They'd be heading off to the big city, too."

"Like I said from the start, I know nothing about this sport," Klaryssa says, scribbling down notes. "But it seems to me that it would take more than one person to pull off a deception on this scale. How can you be so sure it was this Harold Melcher, that he acted alone in all this?"

"Need you to look at this, too" Harvey says, rummaging through the bin of old papers and pulling out one photograph.

"This is an aerial view of the racetrack. I'm sure you can find a better one on some website, but this shot will do. This is the far turn, or farthest point from the finish line," Harvey says, pointing to a spot at the upper-left of the photo. "We'll call it 10:00. That's where I was at the time. Buster is down here at 8:00, and Melcher's viewing post is between us, say 9:00, and the incident we are talking about occurred right in front of him. Now look how far that is from where the boss men, the stewards, are standing. It's almost half a mile away. The racing stewards can't see anything that happens out on that side of the track. There was no tape recording or any of that sort of thing back then. The racing stewards depended completely on the field judge, in this case Melcher, to tell them about any mishap or sloppy riding by any of the jockeys. He had at least as much authority as the stewards, and in this case, maybe more so. He was not only the judge; he was the jury, too. All 12 members, in fact, packaged into one sleaze ball."

"But the jockeys, they would have to be part of this…" Klaryssa starts to ask, but she cuts herself off when she sees Harvey shaking his head vigorously.

"Not at all. I'm not saying there was never a bad actor out there, but let me tell you somethin', those jocks ride their hearts out on those mounts. They're as competitive as any athlete in any sport, and I'll never believe one or more had anything to do with this. These horses, they may be powerful and as fast as the wind, but they're super skittish and can get spooked by a shadow or even a flicker of light. That avenue is right next to the track, and with the giant camera bulbs and those reflectors, they'll all start jumping when the sky lights up. Can't prove it, but I'm telling you that the jocks had not a thing to do with it. Nor did the other racing boss men. One man only, and that's Melcher. All he had to do was hire a camera crew to fire off the lights a couple of times to create a commotion out there. Maybe he signaled them, who knows. But those camera boys were outta there like scared rabbits, and soon enough, so was Melcher.

"I know what happened, but I never knew why," Harvey goes on, putting away the photograph. "Until today, maybe. Just a hint, anyway, from what you've told me. Never in a million years would I have thought that last race fiasco had anything to do with some stolen art. Nobody did. You know, these horses, it's all about gambling and money. By the next day, it's still all about the horses and gambling and money, only in a different place. So the whole incident was forgotten in a hurry. And the stolen art collection…a couple days later, it's back where it belongs, too. So since there was nothing much to be suspicious about, there really wasn't any story left."

"Except yours," Klaryssa says, feeling herself blush a bit after the words came out. Harvey looks across the table at Klaryssa, a kind grin creeping across his face.

"When the next season opened down in Saratoga, July 1947, there was a new field judge out where Melcher was stationed. Don't recall the man's name, but that's no matter. Word was, Melcher was hired to be a racing official at Hialeah

Park in Miami. But this friend of mine I met somewhere along the way, he was a cook at the Hialeah track. He and I, we'd see each other in the summer, and I asked him about Melcher because I just had this knot inside me about the guy and I wanted to see if there was any trace of him. And what does my friend tell me? Never heard of him, never seen him, and didn't know of anyone that had."

"So he was gone, just like that," Klaryssa says, a resigned look on her face. "Disappeared."

"Yep. He disappeared," Harvey says, his words slow and emphatic. "For a spell, anyway."

Klaryssa leans forward, her spirits suddenly rekindled.

"Nine or 10 years pass, and I'm working off season at this Italian place out on Saratoga Lake. This guy comes in—I didn't know who he was, because, being wintertime, he's wearing this big wool jacket and hat and all that—and he recognizes me first. It's a fella named Charlie, and he was one of the boys I worked with for a while during the summers at Saratoga. Charlie—everyone called him Chas—he asks me if I want to get a beer at a local club after I got out of work, and I said sure.

141

Seemed to me at the time there was something he wanted to talk about.

"Well, there was," Harvey continues. "Chas didn't much like our boss at the racetrack, so he quit and eventually opened up a bar out in Provincetown at the end of Cape Cod. The town was an artist community even back then, so it was filled with spenders and drinkers. Partiers, I guess is what we'd call 'em now. So there was money to be made, you know. Chas says his place was hopping most nights, and he's doing real well. Then he tells me that one evening, the previous summer, this guy comes in and he's sure it's Melcher. He can't ask, of course, and he doesn't stare the guy down or anything. The guy has something to drink then takes off. Chas figures he was probably wrong. You know, he was just a fella that looked like Melcher.

"Next week though, the same guy shows up, and Chas has the same suspicions. This time, the guy meets two other fellas, and they're talking in the corner. Long, serious conversation, it seems. And it's a hot day, too. The guy is only wearing a thin t-shirt, and Chas can see the tattoo on both of the man's forearms. A black cross, just below the elbows. Of course, when Melcher worked at

Saratoga, he had to wear a jacket and tie. All the bigwigs did. Except one day, when it was hotter than blazes out there, Melcher took off his jacket and rolled up his sleeves. And that's when Chas knew the guy in his bar was Melcher. Two arms, two black crosses. It was him, no question.

"So Chas did something stupid," Harvey continues, laughing. "So stupid even *he* said it was stupid. Chas follows the guy. Said he couldn't hold back, because all us boys at the track knew that this Melcher was dirtier than a pen of pigs, and he just couldn't let it all go. Chas tells me he bides his time, and when Melcher leaves the bar, Chas comes up with some excuse why he has to leave and so he shadows Melcher, keeping a safe distance. Chas had a motorcycle, which helped plenty, because a lot of people out there rode them, so it was easier to follow him, you know, inconspicuous and all. But it was the middle of the day, so he still had to be real careful. He tailed Melcher out to a place called Race Point, which is this big lonely stretch of beach, kinda at the end of the world out there.

"Chas stays way back but sees that Melcher and these other two guys are walking around this old lifesaving station that's been out there forever. They don't stay very long, and after a few minutes,

143

they part ways. Chas keeps following Melcher, who's now alone, and five minutes later, Melcher pulls up to a place called Ocean Bluffs. Chas wisely takes off, but later that week he does some snooping around and finds out that Melcher had bought this Ocean Bluffs property in 1945. It's this enormous tract of land sprawling across a 200-foot high sand dune. And check this out: the property had been in the same family since the late 17th century, and Melcher purchased it in one of those sales that's done real quiet like, if you know what I mean. He paid them their full asking price. In cash."

Klaryssa is now listening with her head tipped toward the floor and her eyes closed, wondering how on earth Ian had ever found this man.

"I keep hearing Blass Sarren's voice in my head," Klaryssa says eventually, "talking about the FBI questioning that mobster, Lansky. Lansky denied having anything to do with the art theft, but does anyone dare believe anything a known career criminal like that tells you? It sounded like Lansky knew who pulled off the art heist, and that he was actually scared of him. Or them, whoever *they* may have been. But you've connected so many dots,

Harvey. Truly, you have. Melcher was part of something big enough to intimidate even the crime bosses, and whatever that something was, they went to an awful lot of trouble to create a diversion. Now, what they were after, I still don't know. But if I ever figure it out I'll know who to thank."

Harvey walks around the small table and embraces Klaryssa.

"What next?" he asks.

"A trip to this racing museum everyone keeps talking about," she says, pointing southward. "Right down the road. I want to get a look at those paintings that were, well, sort of stolen. Need to see them for myself—count them for myself."

"Do you mind if I borrow these?" Klaryssa asks, holding up the pile of news clippings. "They might come in handy."

"They're yours to keep. You have any idea how long they've been sitting in there?" Harvey says, pointing to the plastic bin. "You've already made better use of them than I ever did."

Klaryssa thanks Harvey again and promises to let him know where it all leads. After starting up her car and turning around in the driveway, she offers Harvey a broad smile, waves goodbye, and drives away.

Chapter 10

Saratoga, New York

Klaryssa counts the framed, wall-mounted paintings for a third time, and the result is the same.

Fourteen.

The 14 paintings donated by the Picard family to the National Museum of Racing and Hall of Fame in Saratoga are scattered throughout the various exhibition halls within the facility, including the Colonial Gallery, the Pre-Civil War Gallery, the Post-Civil War Gallery, and the 20th Century Gallery. In advance of her arrival, Klaryssa made an appointment to meet with the museum's director in hopes of gaining access to some of the museum's historical files. On the manifest she was given, she read that each piece from the Picard collection had been painted by a different European artist, with two of the works completed in the first half of the 17th century.

"I so wish we knew more about these pieces," Oliver Rainey, the museum's director, tells Klaryssa as he points to two paintings hanging side by side in the Colonial Gallery. "These are the two oldest works donated by the Picard family, and all we know is, well, that they're really old."

Klaryssa looks at Oliver and smiles. "You've got plenty of company on that count," she says. "I'm asked to weigh in on pieces in both publicly and privately held collections. So often there's no discernible signature in the corners, no particular pattern seen in the work that suggests a known painter, and just no reliable trail to follow. It's particularly difficult with older works, such as these."

Klaryssa again inspects the two paintings, this time with her face just above the canvases. One of the pieces shows three men dressed in garish, resplendent outfits and mounted on dark chestnut stallions, each with a stable hand at his side. An immense country estate is visible in the background, and, in Klaryssa's mind, it is hard to envision anyone other than members of the British royal family posing for such a formal portrait. The second painting, in somewhat better condition than the first, portrays a group of hat-waving young

147

men, some on foot and others on horseback, corralling a small herd of lively yearlings and guiding them toward a hillside pasture.

"I don't see any initials or remnants of a signature anywhere," Klaryssa says, moving in even closer and inspecting the lower margins of the two paintings. "I take it the artist of each of these pieces remains unknown."

"We haven't a clue," Oliver says, shaking his head. "These are the oldest paintings in the entire museum collection, and although the two works were without question done by different artists, their exact origin remain a conundrum.

"The title of the work on the left is *Viscount Campden with Journeymen*, but the original title of the second is not known for certain. Records from the Picard family refer to this work by the title *Morning Frolic Near Bisenzio*, but there is no way to trace this title beyond the family who sold the work to Colonel Picard. So, in all likelihood, someone along the way simply attached an endearing name to the piece. These two works, along with the other dozen paintings from the Picard family, were part of the original collection of antiquities placed within the galleries when the museum first opened in 1950.

"Except for renovations here and there, none of the paintings have been moved an inch since their arrival. You are the only person in recent memory to ask about the '46 art heist, so I'm very happy to share any information I have with you.

"Most fortunately, the theft is just a footnote in the museum's history, as all the paintings were recovered in short order. But since the Picard pieces have a particularly colorful history, not to mention a noteworthy route to their new home here at our museum, not one has ever been moved or allowed to be taken out on loan to another institution. They've seen enough excitement, in our opinion, and these pieces add so much to the history of horse racing here in America. The sport can be traced to countries all throughout Western Europe and parts of the Middle East."

As they continue throughout the museum, Oliver points out sculptures of several world-class racehorses, the trophies those champions claimed during their celebrated careers, and recorded footage of historic races where the winner's margin of victory was as much as 200 yards or as little as half an inch. Klaryssa had walked through these same galleries earlier, when she was alone, and, as she had then, she finds it hard to feign interest in any of the exhibits unrelated to her particular curiosity.

Oliver had done some research into Klaryssa's professional history prior to her visit, so he is aware of her acumen as an academic in the world of fine arts, as well as her very recent success as an author. What he also knows about her is that she is quite distracted.

"Can't help but wonder if you are working on another book, perhaps one that examines art and how it relates to the history of sports in America?" Oliver asks, trying to act only casually interested. "Just a guess on my part, of course."

Klaryssa knew from the beginning that she would almost certainly get hit with a question such as that, and she also knew for certain how she would handle it.

She would lie.

"Your guess is closer than you might think," Klaryssa says, slowly nodding at Oliver, her one-sided dimple indenting slightly. "I've just taken an interest in post-Renaissance art and how it shaped early American painters. I sort of ran into all this... you know, artwork depicting sports legends, paintings of racehorses. Not sure where I'll end up going with this topic, but the Picard collection, in particular, has piqued my curiosity. The paintings they donated cover so many years; they're from such diverse cultures and display quite an array of artistic styles. And then, of course, I happened upon the theft that occurred all those years ago. My understanding is that the museum had yet to be constructed and the works were all in what was thought to be safe storage and, the next thing you know, poof!"

Oliver straightens his back and looks across the room to one of the Picard paintings from the late 19th century. "Absconded with, the entire collection," Oliver says gravely, pointing to the portrait hanging on the opposite wall. "As with that historic piece, every last painting found its way to what will forever be its home."

"I can only imagine what that day was like. For the museum founders, that is," Klaryssa says, doing all she can to sound genuinely giddy. "I can envision, you know, the founding fathers reveling in the return of the recovered artwork. Almost like a group of renowned archeologists holding up a priceless, long-lost artifact for all the world to see."

"Follow me, Professor Mahr," Oliver says, a broad grin spreading across his face. "I've something you may find most illuminating."

Oliver's office, which doubles as the museum's archive and registry, is so far below street level that Klaryssa figures it must have served as a large vault at one point.

"A bomb shelter," Oliver says when Klaryssa asks about the subbasement room. "1950s paranoia and all that. As if the world is any better now. Please, have a look here."

Oliver produces a folder from a lower cabinet drawer and opens it. Piles of photographs spill across his crowded desk.

"The exact day you just spoke of," Oliver says with pride. "1946, of course, and we had no physical location at that point. These pictures were all taken at the local police station by a well-known professional photographer."

After asking permission to use a magnifying glass sitting on Oliver's desk, Klaryssa studies each of the photographs in great detail. The pictures show charter members of the museum posing next to each of the 14 recovered Picard paintings, and, to no surprise, each of the museum executives is beaming with delight. Although each of the photos is of exceptionally high resolution, there is something about these photographs that immediately strikes Klaryssa as being distinct from the pictures Harvey Mangold gave to her. However, she resists the overwhelming urge to place Harvey's photos side by side with the photos strewn across Oliver's desk.

"I realize this may be asking far too much," Klaryssa begins, tapping on the edges of several of the pictures with her fingertip, "but with all the research needed before one begins to write, and these shots telling so much about—"

"Say no more," Oliver says, putting up his hand. "I cannot ever allow original documents to leave the premises, but your request is not without precedent. Prior to our golden anniversary celebration in 2000, a local writer of some notoriety was working on a history of our museum, and our board granted his request to use these and other photos in his articles. Sadly, but in my opinion, not unexpectedly, his project went nowhere. Accomplished journalist or not, such an endeavor has little chance of coming to fruition when the writer starts his day with a pen in one hand and a bottle of Wild Turkey in the other. Anyway, if these photos can be of aid in your research, it is within my authority to have reproductions made for you. If you stop by our front desk anytime after 3:30 today, my staff will hand you a flash drive that contains a copy of each of these photographs."

Klaryssa expresses her deep appreciation. She assures Oliver that the museum, and, in particular, its very helpful staff, will be fully credited, wherever appropriate, in her future publications. And that, Klaryssa knows, is no lie.

Chapter 11
Saratoga, New York

Klaryssa squeezes her eyes shut, unable to look at the photos any longer.

Her day had started 15 hours earlier, when she left Boston and headed for Lake George to meet with Harvey Mangold. Her long talk with Harvey—along with the Blass Sarren interview recordings—had convinced Klaryssa all the more that Elle's charcoal sketch and the 1946 Picard art collection theft were both, somehow, linked to an epic five-century-old Michelangelo masterpiece that was thought to have been either destroyed or lost forever.

Klaryssa returned to the museum and picked up the flash drive that contained the collection of old black-and-white photographs that no one had otherwise ever really cared about. She thanked Mr. Rainey's staff for all of their assistance, and she even gifted them a box of chocolates as a token of her appreciation. She then changed into her running clothes and headed toward the main entrance of Saratoga's famed racetrack, which was just two blocks away from the museum.

With no one else anywhere in sight, she slid herself through a gap between the wrought iron fence that fronted the property and a twisted chain link post at the far end of the grandstand section. At worst, Klaryssa figured she would hear a distant scream telling her how much trouble she was in for trespassing on private property and how the police were on their way to drag her off to the slammer. Fine, shout your lungs out, she thought to herself. Your words might reach me, but your legs won't.

Having drawn no one's attention, Klaryssa found a bench near the outside rail of the track and opened the downloaded file of photos from the flash drive. The file contained detailed photos of all 14 of the recovered paintings, with one or more of the museum's founding fathers appearing alongside the artwork in each of the images. The paintings themselves appeared to be completely intact, with no signs of having been defaced or handled carelessly. She then placed the pictures Harvey Mangold gave her next to the downloaded images from the museum for comparison.

157

All of the pictures before her had been taken in the summer of 1946. As best as Klaryssa could tell, Harvey's photos were probably taken by way of an order from the insurance company that covered the paintings' shipment to Saratoga, and they were taken no more than a week or two before the photos from the museum. Klaryssa studied each of the images, again and again seeing the exact same paintings in the two sets of photographs. Each of the photographs has outstanding resolution, and, after inspecting the images one more time, her eyes boring holes into each brushstroke, she still can't tell the difference. She is stumped. Beyond any question, the paintings in each of the two sets of photographs are identical. There are no signs of forgery, and no sign that one or more of the paintings was switched out for another.

Klaryssa knows she is no closer to establishing the provenance of Elle Picard's Michelangelo drawing than she was on the day she first met Elle at the marathon. Although two of the museum's Picard family paintings are considerably older than the others—both dating from the early 1600s—there is no evidence that either of those pieces has any relationship to Michelangelo or even to any of his understudies. Klaryssa has no idea when or how Elle's grandfather took possession of the Michelangelo sketch, and, what's more, Klaryssa can find no direct link between this same sketch and the *Battle of Cascina* masterpiece.

The supposedly sage aphorism that tells of the painting following the sketch and the sketch following the painting is nothing short of driveling nonsense, she thinks. Michelangelo's *Battle of Cascina* doesn't exist, and Klaryssa now knows that the only place the painting will ever be seen is in the head of delusional academics like herself. Any perceived connection between some bizarre 1940s horse race and an art heist is pure folly, because, in the end, there was *no* art heist. Klaryssa knows she has been a fool, a fool who embarked on a fool's errand of her own making, and it is time to end this merry chase and return home. If Elle Picard magically appears in front of her, Klaryssa will hoist a white flag and admit defeat.

Klaryssa looks along the length of the racetrack's grandstand and clubhouse seating areas, eyeing the immense, steeply pitched slate roof that covers both sections. A series of even steeper gables, topped by the golden spires that Blass Sarren spoke of, are visible along the length of the roofline. The setting sun, to the west of the

159

grandstand, casts a broad shadow across the track's sprawling infield. Even in the evening's faint light, the infield has the look of an enormous garden poised to explode into full bloom. To Klaryssa's eye, the entire place looks like it could be open for business by the next afternoon. All that's missing, besides the racehorses and their jockeys, are the 40,000 or so patrons who would soon part ways with the rolls of money that line their pockets.

But something is drilling a hole through Klaryssa's mind. When Oliver Rainey scattered that collection of old photos across his desk in the museum basement, Klaryssa spotted some subtle difference between those pictures and the ones Harvey had given her earlier in the day. But what had she seen? After staring at the two groups of photos for well over an hour, how could she not identify this one, crucial, distinguishing quality that she had spotted in a flash of an instant back in Oliver's office?

She leans against the track's outside rail, giving herself a clear view of the observation platform where Harold Melcher stood all those years ago. Farther to the left, she sees the broad avenue that borders the racetrack, and she imagines Buster the Giant being nearly knocked off his tractor by the freakish sparks of light that supposedly brought down the house on that August day in 1946. Her eyes then follow the freshly painted red and white rails that border the inside and outside periphery of the racetrack—the track that Buster and Harvey and the other boys of summer took care of all those years ago.

Klaryssa's eyes, like her thoughts, are wandering. No matter how many times she looks at the photos, she cannot figure out what she is missing. Her mind is a jumble. Worse yet, she feels beaten.

As she often does when her writing projects reach a dead end, Klaryssa begins to tap her fists lightly against whatever surface is in front of her, which, at this moment, is the wooden rail she is leaning against. She looks toward the far turn of the track and then the other way toward the finish line, banging on the rail as if she is playing the bongo drums.

"Come on, think," Klaryssa says to herself through gritted teeth, lifting her fists higher and thudding the rail harder. "Just…think."

After several minutes pass, with her fists still banging against the rail boards, Klaryssa looks up at the sky and slowly shakes her head. No, she thinks. Don't think. Forget it. Just forget it all and go home. Call Elle and tell her…

"Bloody hell," she says, having cut the inside of her hand on a twisted nailhead jutting out from the underside of one of the wooden boards. "Nice going. Perfect end to a perfect—"

Klaryssa stops herself, looking down at the wooden rail and the droplets of blood dripping from its edge.

The rail. The border. The frame. The nail.

The nail.

Klaryssa rolls her shirt cuff over her cut hand, and again she opens the photo file and places the pictures next to Harvey's photos, scanning through the images one more time. This time, however, she examines the photos as if the paintings themselves are not even there. What she had spotted earlier was not a difference in the artwork, but a difference in the frames holding the artwork.

She compares every detail of the frames in each set of photos, including the upper and lower edges of the frames of the two oldest paintings, *Viscount Campden with Journeymen* and *Morning Frolic Near Bisenzio*. *Viscount Campden with Journeymen* appears in every way exactly the same in both sets of photos. But in the four corners of the frame of the *Morning Frolic Near Bisenzio* painting, one set of photos shows the original wooden pegs holding the frame corners together, and in the second set of pictures, taken no more than a few days later, the circular outline of the wooden pegs is missing. The frame in the second set of photos is held together by copper nails, which shine like punctate stars in the night sky. Klaryssa knows that the copper nails had to have been placed sometime between the day the paintings were stolen and the day they were recovered.

This is all Klaryssa needs to see.

"Harold Melcher, you thieving son of a bitch," Klaryssa says to herself, looking out toward the field judge's viewing platform along the inside edge of the track. "I don't know who you were or where you came from, but I know what you did. Cracking open the frames of the paintings, and, by God, I know what you—"

"Hey!"

A voice bellows in her direction from the upper section of grandstand seats. A security guard is pointing at her, and the man's overlapping rolls of abdominal fat are leading his charge down the long flight of cement stairs.

"Who the hell are you? And what do you think you're doing here?" the man screams, a hand gripping each side rail as he lumbers down the stairs. "You're trespassing!"

Klaryssa pockets her phone, grabs the file of photos, and looks for the same break in the fence that she used earlier to sneak onto the property.

"You're in deep shit, lady," the man yells, fumbling for his walkie-talkie.

Klaryssa sees the gap at the end of the rusting iron fence and heads that direction in a full sprint.

You pulled it off, Harold Melcher, she thinks to herself.

The theft of the century, and no one ever knew it happened.

"Do you hear me?"

You did it, Harold Melcher, you son of a bitch.

"Get back here!"

You did it.

Chapter 12
Queens, New York
September 1946

What a fucking moron, Roscoe thought to himself, spitting on the ground.

That jockey—a *seasoned pro*—had sent his mount charging to the front like he was leading Sherman's cavalry. The track was as hot and dry as Death Valley, and speed never holds up under such arid conditions. Another 50 bills down the drain, thanks to some Kentucky farm boy who thought he could outrun the field from the front. The jockey should have been patient, biding his time and making his big move well into the stretch run. Damned idiot.

Roscoe just had to take it. He had to get bent over the barrel, once again, because some buckaroo jockey didn't know the track. Roscoe, as always, did know the track.

Two weeks earlier, when Roscoe had called the police to report the ditched truck he had simply "stumbled upon," his short-term plans had been worked out to the last detail. He would collect his loot, pay off his creditors in Saratoga, and then head to Reno, where all the games of chance would lean in his favor. But the Massachusetts State Police, those bastards, worked him over pretty good. They had all kinds of questions.

"How'd you ever come across this vehicle?"

"How'd you ever get here?"

"You walked here?"

"From where?"

"Where exactly were you heading?"

"Where the hell are you from, Mr. Fowler?"

And the Saratoga racing execs hadn't been any kinder to him. As with the police, they had a pile of questions. Asshole ingrates, the whole lot of them, he thought. He was sure the police had had a little chat with the racing bigwigs, telling them they had their suspicions, their doubts, the whole story sounding a bit too contrived. But, in the end, he had been begrudgingly handed the reward he richly deserved, albeit only a fraction of what he had expected. Roscoe thought a $1,250 recompense for safely returning every last painting was a pretty damn paltry reward, less than $100 per painting. But, when they had finally handed him the cash, he had taken it and ran.

No matter now, though, he thought. I'm a free man.

He was free from the cops, free from the high and mighty Saratoga chieftains, and, most of all, free from Merle and his two minions. Let Merle and his boys wander through the wilderness out there at Race Point. With a little luck, the deep blue surf would wash the three of them out to sea.

Twelve hundred and something dollars hadn't been enough for Roscoe to start anew out in Reno, so he had hopped a train to New York City. He still had some of the reward money packed inside his wallet. He wasn't exactly sure how much, but he was still in the game. He had all the knowledge and experience a man would ever need, and, given enough time, the odds would work in his favor, he thought. All he needed was a little more time.

Reno would have to wait, just like the Saratoga bookies who held a pile of his chits would have to wait. They couldn't expect payment now, not after Roscoe got shafted out of the big reward he rightfully deserved. They'd get their money, once he parlayed his way back into the big time. Besides, Roscoe had been hitting Aqueduct Racetrack every day, and despite a few early setbacks, he knew it was only a matter of time before his winning ways kicked in.

***

"Just took a ramrod straight up my backside," the man standing next to Roscoe said as he balled up a fistful of betting stubs and threw them to the wind. "I know that jockey. He's been riding one place or another since he quit junior high. The kid's solid, and he's got all the moves, but sometimes he's just too much of a damn cowboy. I hope that trainer is slapping his sorry ass around right now."

The man was referring to the same jockey, and the same horse, that Roscoe had wagered on.

"The six? You bet on the six horse, too?" Roscoe asked, eyeing the man warily.

"Liked him," the man said, jabbing his index finger at the horse's name in the program he was holding. "Liked him plenty. Bet on him about a year ago. Different track but same kind of day, you know. Dry, with a decent tail wind through the stretch. Same jockey, and he rode that horse like he was driving him home to save his momma's life. Horse hasn't been worth a lick since then, but I got a good look at him coming out of the stable about an hour ago and he seemed as calm as a monk. He seemed confident. You know what I mean: head high, staring straight ahead. He looked like a bargain at nine to one. But hey, what the hell do I know?"

Roscoe watched the man flip the pages of his racing program to the seventh race, which was due to go off in about 20 minutes. The man's eyes scanned down the line of entries in the upcoming race. He checked off this and that, crossing out the name of one entry and circling the trainer's name of another. This guy is a horseplayer, no question about it, Roscoe thought. But is he a winner?

For years, Roscoe had known that you never sought out the guys who were winners. There are so few of them, although many horseplayers fancy themselves as such. Few actually are. Seek out the losers, he always reminded himself, for once you know which horse the loser is betting on, you simply steer clear. Rubbing elbows with a loser was a priceless gift; your odds only improved, and it was all free of charge. Such people were like manna from heaven for Roscoe.

"Name's Roscoe, Roscoe Fowler," Roscoe said, extending his hand. The man shook Roscoe's hand, firm and quick, his face without expression. The man then went straight back to his racing card. "Karl Blythe," the man said without looking up at Roscoe, still zoned in on the next race. "Everyone calls me Bly. Good to know you."

This might be the one guy out here who knows more about racing than I do, Roscoe thought.

"You said nine to one," Roscoe asked as casually as he could. "Last race, you got nine to one on the six horse?"

"Mmm, yeah," Bly grunted, still staring intently at his racing program.

"Best I could get was seven to one," Roscoe said after a long pause, still trying his best to seem indifferent. "I waited it out but never saw better than eight to one. So I laid it down at seven to one, a minute before they went off."

"Where you put down the bet?" Bly asked, giving Roscoe a quick glance over the top of his glasses.

"Inside, with one of the pari-mutuel clerks," Roscoe said, pointing over his shoulder.

171

"There's your difference," Bly said with a resigned nod. "Don't like laying down my wagers in there. It's you against the house. Got no quarrel with that, but you never get the best odds. Me, whenever I'm going deep, I'm doing it over at barn 33."

Roscoe knew he had a keeper. He had heard talk of a bookmaker who took action near one of the barns in the backstretch, but no one had ever spilt much in the way of particulars. Most gamblers out there didn't know about barn 33, and Roscoe figured that if he stayed close to Bly, he'd wind up meeting the man who could give his betting odds the boost they needed.

"Mind you, it's not every horse, not even every race," Bly said, jamming the racing card into his back pocket. "Far from it. But you'll do better with my man than wagering with the clowns inside, that's for damn sure. Not much time, so I'm heading toward the other side to get my bets in. My man will take your action just as fast as he'll take mine, so you're welcome to join. No commission coming my way, so it's no skin off my ass either way."

Bly continued to make notes in his racing program while he walked onto the backstretch

172

toward barn 33, Roscoe following close behind without breaking the man's concentration. Roscoe knew why so many veterans took every opportunity they had to cruise the track's backstretch for an enlightened perspective on the upcoming races. The backstretch was where you could size up the horses well before the race, spying out which ones looked jumpy or too lathered up, maybe overheated or just plain worn out. More to the point, you found out which mounts looked like champs and which ones looked like pigs.

Bly started to wander off to speak to someone, but, first, he looked at Roscoe and pointed at the door where the bookmaker had set up shop. Roscoe walked in like he owned the place.

"Welcome to New York, Roscoe," Merle said from the far side of the cramped, dark, musty room. "Was so hoping we'd have the chance to meet again. You know, a chance to reminisce about old times."

The door behind Roscoe bolted shut, but he didn't turn around. It wouldn't do any good, and he knew it. He knew all he needed to know. He knew he was a dead man.

Chapter 13

Queens, New York

"Would have done the same thing as you," Merle said in an almost reassuring tone, with no trace of the backwoods twang Roscoe remembered from a couple of weeks earlier. "I tell you the truth, I would have," Merle said, speaking with a crisp, distinctly continental accent.

"We didn't treat you very well or give you any hint as to what our mission was. And you, with all your mechanical knowledge—it was by far your easiest way out. Stealing my truck and deserting us, that is. And I'm so grateful for your returning those lovely paintings to their rightful owner. You were rewarded for your heroism, yes?"

Roscoe nodded meekly.

"Somewhere north of a thousand dollars, I believe?"

Again, a weak nod.

"Tell me, how much of that is left?" Merle asked, slowly emerging from the darkness.

"I don't...I don't..."

"You don't know. Yes, yes, of course you don't. Neither do I. Neither do the gentlemen standing behind you," Merle said, now gesturing to the space between the door and Roscoe's back. "In fact, I believe you've met Karl Blythe. That is *Karl* with a *K*, Roscoe, and I want you to remember that. I also want you to remember his formal title, which is Captain Karl W. Blythe."

Karl came out from behind Roscoe, and, at the same moment, Merle took another step forward. Roscoe could now see that both men were wearing thick red armbands. The middle of each armband was emblazoned with a stark white circle surrounding a black swastika.

"Allow me to also introduce Captain Otello Kappel," Merle said with a broad hand gesture as the third man moved into the light. "As you did Captain Blythe and I, you abandoned Captain Kappel in the wilds of your outer beaches a couple of weeks ago. Clearly, he also somehow managed to survive your impudence. And if I may at last formally introduce myself, I am Colonel Merle Huber, SS Commander.

"Now, Herr Fowler," he continued, "back to your bankroll, or lack thereof. Hand whatever you have over to Captain Blythe," Merle ordered, reaching into his pocket.

Roscoe never learned how to pray, so all he could do was squeeze his eyes shut, tip his head down slightly, and await the bullet that would blow his brains all over the floor. But as his last mortal seconds ticked past, Roscoe did not feel any pain or hear the sound of a gunshot. He opened one eye just enough to glance up at Merle, looking for the pistol that would end his life.

Roscoe watched Merle bite the end off a fresh cigar. Merle clicked open the heavy gunmetal lighter that he had just pulled out from his pocket and hold it to the cigar until a bright glow appeared.

Roscoe thrust a hand into the bottom of each pocket, grabbing every last dollar he had. He handed two small fists of bills to Captain Blythe.

"Two hundred and three US," Captain Blythe reported after counting the cash.

Through the smoke of the cigar, Roscoe could see Merle's eyes boring into him. He could feel the man's contempt, his hatred. He could feel the man's power. Along with a stream of cigar smoke, Merle let out a baleful laugh. It was the same vile cackle Roscoe had heard from the cab of the truck he was hired to drive.

"Roscoe, Roscoe," Merle said, sending another plume of cigar smoke up toward the ceiling. "You know, you really should avoid these games of chance, the horses and all that. Seems to me you could make a better living driving through swamps and jimmying locks. And, of course, hot-wiring trucks. Not to mention stealing them."

All Roscoe knew was that he was still alive. Standing in the middle of the dank room, he felt both legs trembling beneath the knees. He uttered not a sound.

"Clearly you have had some interaction with the police and other authorities over these past many days," Merle went on. "You must have, to collect all that loot and become the art world's savior. Tell me, besides inventing a bullshit fable about you finding a stolen truck and convincing them all of what a fine citizen you are, what else did you have to say?"

"Nothing, not a thing, Colonel," Roscoe said in an instant, sensing a flicker of hope in his heart. "Not one word to anyone, about anything. On my mother's grave, I give you my oath, absolutely nothing. Why would I? How could I? To mention anything else…I would be the one who ended up in jail for stealing the truck. Stealing it twice, no less. No one outside this room knows anything."

Merle began to pace, casting a slow glance in the direction of both his underlings. He then looked back at Roscoe. "When you broke into the back of the van, you saw the newspaper articles, didn't you? And do not lie to me."

Roscoe nodded.

"So, you know what happened to the driver we had hired before we found you?"

Again, Roscoe nodded.

"I believe here you refer to this as a man 'getting cold feet,'" Merle said, an amused look on his face. "Besides, this fellow knew too much, and, well, you were in the military, right? You understand there are times when extreme measures must be called upon, do you not?"

Roscoe again nodded, this time with more vigor.

"Your surname is Haller, am I correct?" Merle asked, putting up a hand. "No need to answer, we both know it is true. Unlike the first driver we hired, whose name I cannot even recall, you have street smarts and you have balls.

"Karl, give our friend here his money back. Perhaps we can call upon him in the future to assist in our cause, although I do wonder what he might do when he runs out of money. And you will run out of money, Roscoe. You will lose all of it, of that I have no doubt. Who's to say you won't resume your thieving ways, end up jailed, and then sing like a lark about all you know so you can free yourself?"

Captain Blythe reached into his pocket and handed Roscoe the money. Roscoe sifted through the bills as quickly as he could. It was all there, every last dollar.

Roscoe let out a laugh, not really hearing anything Merle had just said to him. He had no idea how and why he might have found humor in any of that, but he suddenly had the sense that everything going on around him was all part of some deranged joke.

He laughed again, his face feeling flushed and hot, and, for reasons that made no sense, he counted out his money one more time. The bills seemed to be flowing in the breeze, flowing in a breeze that was nowhere to be found in the airless room. Roscoe squeezed down tight, so the wad of cash wouldn't fly out of his hand. Then, suddenly, he noticed a strange, bitter smell. A minute ago, the room had been full of Merle's pungent cigar smoke, but this was different. This smell was organic and earthy, acrid and wholly unfamiliar.

Roscoe looked around him as if he was in a trance, watching the three other men in the room move from one corner to the other. The headache he was experiencing didn't bother him all that much, but the spasms of nausea he felt began to magnify, and, a second later, Roscoe doubled over onto the floor in wrenching pain. In an instant, his gut became a volcano, vomit and feces being sent in opposite directions as if fired from twin cannons.

Roscoe heard someone call his name, and, when he looked up, he saw a monster leaning over him. And that monster's name was Colonel Merle Huber.

"They really know how to build these horse barns, don't they?" Merle said, his voice maniacal, deeply muted through the grotesque-looking leather and metal gas mask he was wearing. "These horses, they are their owner's prized possessions, and they require such exquisite care. The walls and ceilings in these stalls are lined with the most durable wood they can find. Perhaps hickory, or hard maple. They construct these barns in that fashion so that in the event one stallion has a rotting sleeve of intestine, or perhaps a mare is giving birth, the other horses are minimally disturbed by the screams that accompany such unimaginable pain."

Roscoe simply could not find air. His face was as blue as cobalt, and he began to convulse, his head slamming like a hammer against the floorboards.

"Prussic acid," Merle said, holding up a small glass vial and leaning in closer, the slimy film coating his gas mask's metal filter nearly touching Roscoe's face. "You may have heard this synthetic referred to by its other name, hydrogen cyanide. Its action is so simple, really. It merely disconnects normal bodily functions. That is all it does. Such a simple compound, yet so effective. So efficient. So tidy. So...*proven*."

Roscoe's eyes bulged violently, blood streaming from the sides of both sockets. He began to choke on his own vomit, making a faint guttural sound with each shallow breath. Merle waved his Nazi armband in front of Roscoe's pulsing eyeballs.

"Herr Fowler, may this be your last sight, your last earthly memory," he said, using one hand to grip Roscoe by the neck, slowly squeezing shut his airway. "You and your nation thought you put us all in our graves, relegating our cause and our creed to history. Once again, you lose, Roscoe. You all lose, because our history will merely be played out on another shore. This shore, your shore. We are here *now*, Roscoe. And we are everywhere."

Chapter 14
Boston, Massachusetts
Present Day

While driving back to Boston from Saratoga, Klaryssa updated Ian on all she had learned from the Blass Sarren tapes, from her talk with Harvey Mangold, and from her visits to the museum and the racetrack. After hearing all Klaryssa had to say, Ian took a day trip to Cape Cod to see if he could uncover any more details about Harold Melcher from the town records. Ian then took a long walk along Race Point Beach before driving back to Boston to meet up with Klaryssa at her condo in the South End neighborhood.

"What happened to your hand?" Ian asks, pointing at the Band-Aids just above Klaryssa's right wrist.

"My latest D-minus in anger management," Klaryssa answers, without looking at her hand. "At least I evaded an arrest for trespassing."

"*Trespassing*?" Ian asks, trying to sound surprised. "Evading *arrest*? Slicing a chunk out for your hand? Compared to you, my adventures at that racetrack many moons ago were pretty mundane. All I ever did was lose money."

"I'll elaborate another time," Klaryssa says as she hands Ian a magnifying glass and ushers him toward a table where she has lined up the two sets of photographs that she had been staring at over much of the previous 12 hours. "Like I told you over the phone, all these pictures were taken within a week or so of each other in the summer of 1946. The pictures of the 14 paintings on the left all have frames that are held together by wooden pegs, but eight of the 14 paintings in the photos on the right have frames with copper nails holding each of the four corners together.

"Whoever stole the artworks knew that one of the paintings from the Picard collection had a canvas cover, or a canvas over a canvas. In other words, the artwork on display, as in the painting you were looking at, was used to conceal another artwork hidden beneath it. The thieves knew that one of the paintings in the collection was covering the canvas that they really wanted, so they disassembled the frames, one by one, until they found what they were after.

"If this whole smokescreen created during that horse race is true, with the artificial lightning and multiple disqualifications and all that, then the thieves went to astounding lengths to get their hands on this entire art collection so they could find the one painting they wanted. And they certainly knew a lot more about the artwork than the Picard family, because Colonel Picard could not have possibly known that one of the paintings that he was giving away to the museum was actually covering a...a..."

"A Michelangelo masterpiece," Ian says in a low voice, finishing with what he knows Klaryssa really wants to say. "That is where this is all heading, right? You haven't quite said it, either now or earlier over the phone, but you didn't call me over here at this hour to tell me about one horse picture covering another horse picture.

"Am I close with any of this?" Ian asks, after pausing for a long beat.

"Yes, you are," Klaryssa says, showing Ian blown-up images of the *Viscount Campden with Journeymen* and *Morning Frolic Near Bisenzio* paintings. "These are the two oldest works from the

186

Picard collection, and, according to the museum's director, Colonel Picard acquired both of them from the same family while he was traveling through Italy. If you look at this," Klaryssa continues, now pointing to the four corners of the *Viscount Campden with Journeymen* painting in both sets of photos, "it's obvious that this is one very old frame, and, in all likelihood, it's the only frame that has ever housed this artwork. In each of the corners, you can see thick wooden pegs holding the joints together. There's no sign of any metal anywhere.

"Now, look at the other photos, the ones of the *Morning Frolic Near Bisenzio* work. This painting is just as old, and, as with the other painting, its frame is likely the original one. But, if you look carefully at the four corners of the frame, you can see small copper nailheads in the second set of pictures. Somebody put them there, trying to hide any trace of having tampered with this artwork. And they succeeded, whoever *they* are. Or were."

"I see what you see," Ian says, going up and down the photos with the magnifying glass. "But, if the thieves went to such great lengths to cover their tracks, why didn't they just reuse the original wooden screws?"

"Wasn't going to happen," Klaryssa says, shaking her head. "Those wooden pegs were ancient, and they frayed and fragmented whenever you messed with them. Once the thieves found what they came for, they nailed the frames back together, and, in the end, they made it look like the art collection was reclaimed without a scratch. And, like I said, it worked, for more than seventy years."

"Up until a few hours ago," Ian says, the skepticism in his voice unmistakable. "I mean, you've dug up something that no one else has even thought of for all these years. But what does any of this prove, KD? You have a bunch of pieces that you're jamming together and then saying to the world, 'Look, it all fits! It's all here!'"

"Look back here for a minute," Klaryssa says, again pointing at one of the photos. "See this?"

"Sure," Ian says, looking at the picture of the *Morning Frolic Near Bisenzio* painting that Klaryssa is holding. "It's one of the paintings that the thieves cracked open, for whatever reason, right?"

"Right," Klaryssa says. "Colonel Picard bought this from the same family that he bought the

Viscount Campden with Journeymen painting from, right?"

"Right, that's what you said."

Klaryssa points to three overstuffed file folders on a nearby table. "The day after I met Elle Picard at the marathon, she FedEx'd me that giant stack of papers. An absolute mess, and I'm less than half way through. But, I did find a bill of sale for the two paintings we're talking about, and there are two signatures on the document. One is that of Colonel Picard, the buyer, and the other is from the seller, but the ink is so worn and the paper so moth-eaten you can't make out the name.

"The address, to the extent that there ever was one printed on the bill of sale, is also smeared, but you can make out the name of the city where Colonel Picard purchased the two paintings. The whole thing is written in Italian, which is little wonder given where the purchase took place. Now, do you remember the name of the painting I just showed you?"

"This one? Yeah, sure," Ian says, pointing at *Morning Frolic Near Bisenzio*. "It's *Someone Frolicking Near Somewhere*, right?"

"*Morning Frolic Near Bisenzio*," Klaryssa says, tapping on the photograph. "The museum

189

director in Saratoga came right out and told me that this painting's original name is lost to history, so the family who owned the work for generations likely gave it the name that's etched into the molding. They named it after an area they knew well...an area near their ancestral home of Prato, which is a city next to Florence. And Prato borders the Bisenzio.

"Bisenzio, Ian. *Bisenzio*. Bisenzio is a river that flows through the city of Prato, and it's a tributary of the Arno River. As in *that* Arno River," Klaryssa says as she points to the image of the *Battle of Cascina* painting on her laptop. "The Bisenzio River flows into the Arno River, and the Arno River happens to be in the foreground of the Michelangelo masterpiece that was supposedly destroyed all those centuries ago.

"Don't you see?" Klaryssa says without breaking stride, more wired than Ian has ever before seen her. "These aren't just a bunch of pieces being forced together to complete some neat and tidy puzzle. You've got a crime so perfectly orchestrated that no one ever knew it actually happened. It was so slick that the true intent of the Saratoga art theft was missed by everyone, including the FBI, who took such a keen interest in the caper that they dragged in the head of the mob for questioning. And, out of nowhere, all these years later, a stranger walks up and hands someone —unfortunately me—a Michelangelo sketch that was long buried in the home of a family that owned, unbeknownst to them, a painting that for centuries hid one very big secret.

"Colonel Picard thought he was purchasing a portrait of some pastoral scene near an Italian horse ranch. He never remotely knew that what he actually bought was the greatest lost treasure in the history of Western art. And, even more mind-boggling, is the number of years—number of centuries—that a family in a small Italian town had the Michelangelo painting hanging on their living room wall and never knew it. But *someone* did, and that someone knew exactly where the masterpiece was, and he figured out a way to steal it. And that someone's name was Harold Melcher.

"So, that's what I have," Klaryssa says, letting out a long sigh and dropping herself onto the sofa. "Now, what did you learn about that lonely house out on Cape Cod while I was on the road?"

Ian reaches into his leather gym bag and pulls out two small glass tumblers and a sealed bottle filled with a clear liquid that is spotted with tiny red flakes. The distilled spirit in the bottle is known as horilka, and Ian knows that the fastest way to raise the ire of a native Ukrainian is to refer to their national drink as vodka. Vodka is from Russia; horilka is from Ukraine. And this particular brand of horilka, called Pertsivka, is distilled from honey and contains flakes of hot chili peppers.

"Damn. Talk about top shelf," Klaryssa says, grabbing the bottle out of Ian's hand. "I'm buzzing enough right now as it is. I'm not sure I need this."

Ian takes back the bottle, twists off the cap, and sends a generous pour into the bottom of each glass.

"You'll think otherwise when you hear what I've got to tell you. That lonely house you were told about, the one Harold Melcher bought way out there at the end of Cape Cod?" Ian says as he empties his shot glass in one throw and then pours himself another. "It's not so lonely."

"The family that Melcher bought that Cape Cod property from," Ian begins, having downed his second shot of horilka, "bought it, or were granted it, for use as farmland when Massachusetts was just a colony—way before the Revolutionary War. This one family owned the land for over 250 years, until 1945, when Melcher purchased the property for an unlisted and undisclosed sum. The place is located in the town of Truro, and I got a quick look at the area when I was out there, along with getting a chance to peek at the town hall property records. And, sure enough, everything that old fella in Lake George told you—"

"Harvey," Klaryssa says, throwing back the shot of horilka that Ian had poured for her. "Harvey Mangold."

"Him, right. Well, it all checks out," Ian says. "When Melcher bought the place, it was 60 some odd acres, with a single dwelling in the middle of the lot. But the updated plot plan on file shows the property to now be a bit less that 55 acres. The same house is still there, although it's been renovated once or twice since the 1940s."

"So Melcher sold some of the land along the way? Klaryssa asks. "Five acres, more or less?"

"Nope," Ian says, shaking his head.

"So what then?" Klaryssa asks, shrugging he shoulders. "The place just shrank?"

"Exactly right," Ian says, nodding in a dramatic fashion.

Klaryssa gives Ian a dazed look. "Is this place out of a Harry Potter story or something, where things like the laws of physics and fixed dimensions just don't apply?"

"Oh, the laws of physics very much apply. And you'll know what I mean when you see the place."

Klaryssa cocks her head slightly, saying nothing.

"You just have to see where this place is located," Ian says, pulling up an image on his iPad. "The property is situated on this immense sand dune, over 200 feet above the ocean, and every year, tidal surges erode slices of the property from the base of the sand dune. From there, the top edge just shears off into the sea. I guess it's the tax Mother Nature charges for getting to call a place like that home.

"There aren't many houses out there, but the ones that you can see here," Ian says, now pointing to a scattering of small beach houses as seen on the aerial view displayed on his iPad. "These places, according to town records, have at most an acre or so of land. But Melcher, all those years ago, found a place that at the time was over *60* acres in size."

"You weren't kidding when you said isolated," Klaryssa says, looking at the bird's-eye image of the property. "None of these other houses are anywhere close to Melcher's place. If he wanted privacy, this place was ideal, and no doubt it came at a premium.

"If Melcher found a way to buy this lot of land from a family that had owned it for seven or eight generations, he probably told the owners that they could name their price. But, if he pulled off that art heist in Saratoga and then succeeded in disappearing from the scene, why in the world would he want to be stranded out there? Just to see the sunrise each morning and watch the gulls fly past? If Melcher managed to fence the

196

Michelangelo painting, you'd think he would have sought refuge offshore. But, for whatever reason, he wanted to be alone in that specific location. And, from what you told me over the phone, his descendants, all these years later, are of the same mind."

"Apparently so," Ian says, now pacing slowly. "From what I know, Harold Melcher had no family of his own, but a sister and two of his bothers lived out there for many years. His sister's grandson is listed as the present owner. His name is Matthias Huber, and he's 57 years old and has no visible means of support. All I had to go by was his name off the property records, but I had a friend do a little search to see what he could dig up about the guy."

"One of your chums from college?" Klaryssa asks, unable to suppress a grin. "Some egghead you met along the way, this one perhaps deft in intelligence work and the like?"

"You don't know the half of it," Ian says, pressing on his temples. "And he's still at it, as we speak. As in, he's still digging up anything he can about Harold Melcher, Matthias Huber, and the rest of their clan."

Klaryssa starts to get up from the sofa but then startles when she hears the apartment door swing open. Yeva, her hair pulled in a long ponytail and wearing an oversized jet-black sweater, runs to the far side of the room and vaults into Ian's arms.

"Hey, kiddo!" Ian says, smothering Yeva in a bear hug. "A little late on a school night, don't you think? You should be in a sound slumber, rehearsing ballet moves in that dreamy head of yours."

"Or studying for your exams," Klaryssa says, closing the door that Yeva left wide open. "And hello to you, too. Glad you could make it."

Yeva patters across the room and gives Klaryssa a peck on the cheek. "Hi, Mommy," she says, her face flushed and traces of sweat around her brow line. "I studied for three hours tonight. No, three and a *half*. And you told me to come over and surprise Ian. So, check it out…I'm here."

"And I suppose you ran over here, alone, after midnight, all dressed up in basic Yeva black. Why do you think I offered to cover all your Uber fees?"

"Mom, it's only a few blocks," Yeva says with an edge. "And some of those Uber drivers really creep me out. The last guy I had looked like

198

he was from Mars or something. Besides, I brought a flashlight and pepper spray with me, and I needed to run a little before practicing."

"Practicing what?" Ian asks as Yeva bumps past him and moves out onto the roof-deck.

"My ballet moves, silly man," she says, chasséing along the length of the deck. "Don't let me interrupt; you two just pretend I'm not here."

"Ninety-five pounds, and it'd be easier to ignore a hippopotamus in the room," Klaryssa says, Ian spotting a glint of pride in Klaryssa's eyes. "She's got that college night owl thing going, I guess. I just wanted her here when you arrived, maybe jumping out of the pantry and knocking you off your feet."

"She nearly did that anyway," Ian says, watching Yeva stretch her legs against the outside railing of the roof-deck. "She always does. Just seeing her doing so well…"

"It's five floors down to the concrete, little lady," Klaryssa says to Yeva in a firm voice, knowing Yeva will still ignore her warning. "I've got the broom out, just to clean up the mess after you land head first."

Yeva lets out a line of giggles, moving her leg up onto the upper rail.

"She did say to pretend she's not here," Ian says, Yeva suddenly reappearing and yanking off her sweater and throwing it at Ian. "But, I must tell you, she doesn't make it easy. Anyway, where did we leave off?"

"We left off at Harold Melcher and this college buddy of yours doing some snooping around. Now, what is the deal with this guy Melcher?" Klaryssa asks, jabbing Ian in the middle of the chest with her finger. "What was he a part of? Melcher must have been working with some seriously enterprising and savvy people to get away with such an elaborate theft, because he actually found a way to fix a horse race in order to steal the Picard paintings, knowing that one of the paintings he was making off with had a Michelangelo hidden behind it. The theft was so brilliantly orchestrated that the entire Picard collection, minus the hidden Michelangelo, of course, was returned a few days after the theft by a man named Roscoe Fowler. So by all appearances, there was a proverbial happily-ever-after ending."

"This Fowler guy," Ian asks, his eyes still on Yeva out on the roof-deck. "Were you able to learn anything about him? Any trail to follow, from the museum archive maybe? Was he in on this theft in any way?"

"Negative on all counts," Klaryssa says with a resigned shake of her head. "The museum handed Mr. Fowler a cash reward, and then the man took off. There were apparently suspicions about the guy right from the start, but nothing could be proven. The Massachusetts State Police never bought Fowler's story about 'stumbling upon' the truck that had the stolen paintings stashed in the back, and the Racing Museum's hierarchy even went on record as calling the man 'shifty' and having 'every appearance of a vagrant,' or something along those lines.

"But the interesting thing is that a few years after the theft, a major magazine wanted to run a story on the incident and went looking for one Roscoe Fowler. A small team of investigative reporters sent out feelers all over the place, visiting the museum a number of times and offering to pay Roscoe handsomely for an interview. Nothing. The guy had disappeared."

"So much for him, then," Ian says, shrugging his shoulders. "So that brings us back to Harold Melcher."

"Right, Harold Melcher," Klaryssa says, looking intently at Ian. "Who *was* this guy, and what the hell did he do with the Michelangelo painting? You told me a few minutes ago that you had a lot to spill, and I know it's not just about the winter storms that slam into Cape Cod and eat up the shoreline."

Ian draws in a slow, deep breath. "My college classmate, the one I just mentioned, his name is Zorn Maryn. Yes, that's really his name, and we met first semester freshman year. He, in fact, does do intel work for a private firm—a *very* private firm, with very private clients from all over the world. I'm always there whenever he needs a hand, and vice versa, and it's been that way since college. So, after you called me from Lake George, I called him, and man, did he jump on it—Melcher and Blass Sarren and the art theft and the FBI investigation and all that. Zorn has access to a level of resources and surveillance that is nothing short of scary. And let me tell you, he's all over this.

"First off, Harold Melcher died of a stroke in 1972." Ian continues. "And, in the years between his purchase of the Truro property and his death, the guy never left the country, was never arrested, and basically succeeded in living a life of near complete anonymity. The only place the man was ever seen was at a beach called Race Point, which is in Provincetown, located just to the northwest of his home in Truro. He would—"

"Hold it, wait," Klaryssa says, waving her hand in the air. "If this guy lived in the shadows for the rest of his life, how do you know he frequented this place in Provincetown?"

"Well, that's easy," Ian says, his eyes wide. "A one-word answer: Zorn. Zorn makes one hell of a living spying on billionaires, their wives, their husbands, their business associates, their concubines, and their palm readers, not to mention listening in on their 'private' conversations and reading the contents of their paper shredders. As he describes it, his life is the prefect mix of monotony, madness, and money. So, like I said, when I told him everything that you told me, old Zorn sprang to life. This is the type of cyber playground he dreams about. He found pictures of Melcher from the 1940s, because, remember, Melcher was hired by the State of New York as a racing judge, so all Zorn had to do was access his employment records from the state offices in Albany. These are old records for sure, but for him it was a breeze. Once he had Melcher's mug shot, he used facial recognition software and a search program he developed to cross that photo with every known photo taken from the outer reaches of Cape Cod in the 1950s and '60s. And he's 99% sure that Melcher showed up at Race Point Beach, time and time again, all year long, year after year."

"So, Zorn found the dude's favorite place to swim," Klaryssa says, unmoved. "Don't get me wrong, what your pal Zorn did to get more info on Melcher is damn impressive, but so what? All we know now is where Melcher splashed around in the surf."

"In late October, or early March, off the tip of Cape Cod?" Ian asks, waggling both eyebrows. "A 60-something-year-old man, swimming out there every fall and winter? I don't think so."

"So what do you think? Or, more to the point, what do you and Zorn think?"

Yeva reappears, rehearsing her brisé jumps in both directions through the doorway that leads to the roof-deck.

"Will you come to my performance next month?" she asks, batting her eyes dramatically at Ian as she moves rhythmically in and out of the living room.

Ian feels like he's sitting mid-court at a tennis match

"Wouldn't miss it, love," he says. "Front row, that'll be me."

"Yeah, me too," Klaryssa adds, trying to sound annoyed. "Front row—easier to throw tomatoes."

Yeva flits in and out of the room a couple more times before returning to her stretching exercises along the deck's outer rail.

"From what Zorn told me earlier, Harold Melcher spent the rest of his days on Cape Cod so he could have direct access to the shoreline, including Race Point Beach. There's an old lifesaving station out there, one of a dozen or so that sprang up ages ago because of all the shipwrecks. The storms and hidden shoals and riptides make for brutal conditions, and there are volumes of stories that tell of dramatic rescues being launched from those lifesaving stations.

"Melcher was able to run all the rescue drills and training exercises he wanted, because he was a member of the Coast Guard Reserve. Same for his grandnephew Matthias and Matthias's son Stephan. Across multiple generations, every one of them managed to get assigned to the Reserve's

Cape Cod stations for at least part of their careers, primarily because they all know, or knew, the manifold hidden dangers in the waters in and around Cape Cod. It's one unforgiving shipping lane, and I can tell you first-hand that the sea doesn't care if you're working or playing out there. Things can get dire in a hurry, and you can die in a hurry. So there are a lot of good reasons to run rescue drills and engage recruits in training exercises out in the middle of nowhere, and, by all appearances, the middle of nowhere is Race Point Beach."

"Something tells me that you and Zorn have more to say about this family that's been living on that big sand dune all these years," Klaryssa now taping her empty shot glass on the table.

"Zorn ran a search on the rest of Harold Melcher's family," Ian goes on, again pacing the room. "That includes Melcher's brother-in-law, a man by the name of Merle Huber, who was Matthias's grandfather. Merle…" Ian's voice quivering slightly, "Merle was a Nazi SS Colonel who found his way into the United States a couple of months before Germany surrendered. In all likelihood, Merle got through immigration with falsified papers, and he didn't come here just to escape capture as a defeated military commander. Merle came here as a man on a mission. The Huber family came from Austria originally, as did the Melcher family, and Colonel Merle Huber, before becoming part of the Nazi's world conquest machine, was an honors student at the Academy of Fine Arts in Vienna. No doubt Merle's glowing academic resumé was instrumental in his securing a position as an art officer in the Hermann Göring Division, where he oversaw the organized looting of priceless art throughout Europe during World War II."

Klaryssa stands motionless in the middle of the room. She starts to say something but then stops herself, motioning for Ian to continue.

"Now, I know you know far more about the Göring Division than I ever will," Ian says as calmly as he can. "Zorn gave me a stark rundown on Hermann Göring and the unspeakable atrocities he carried out during World War II. He told me about Göring's ultimate authority over the plunder of gold, precious gems, paintings, manuscripts, books, and religious treasures. And, to compound this travesty, Göring planted members of his inner circle on this side of the Atlantic once Nazi defeat became inevitable. This was all done through aliases and falsified papers. The extent of this penetration into the United States, Canada, and South America remains unknown.

"But SS Colonel Merle Huber and other Göring henchmen passed through immigration by claiming to be war refugees, with all traces of their past as perpetrators of war whitewashed by counterfeit documents. Huber was an educated man who spoke multiple languages, and, along with an untold number of other Nazis, he left behind his war-ravaged country and stepped into a new life on this side of the Atlantic."

"And I thought *I* had a day full of surprises," Klaryssa says, a dumbfounded look on her face. "All this from Zorn, right? You met the right people in college—did anyone ever tell you that?"

"You just did, and I'd have to agree," Ian says, pouring Klaryssa another shot of Ukrainian firewater. "And Zorn found out more about Colonel Merle Huber and his grandson Matthias than just the location of their favorite beach. Merle, it turns out, was hauled in by the FBI for questioning about a robbery at a private home in the Berkshires in the 1950s. Zorn sifted through the transcripts from FBI files, and apparently Merle's fingerprints were found in the home of a very wealthy family that owned a collection of Egyptian antiquities that had been stolen on a winter night when no one was at the house. Merle explained it all away by telling the Feds that he had toured the home with several other 'amateur Egyptologists' a few weeks prior to the robbery. So they let him walk.

"He walked, all right. But not for very long," Ian goes on, swirling his shot glass. "A little over a year later, an arrest warrant was issued with Merle's name on it, this time in connection with the theft of three priceless medieval prayer books from a display case in a church outside Providence, Rhode Island. Somehow, Merle was tipped off about his impending arrest, so he was able to stay ahead of the cops for a short while. But, within a few days, the police had him cornered at some fleabag hotel in Boston's Combat Zone. When they broke down the door, the authorities found no sign of the stolen prayer books."

"Merle didn't talk?" Klaryssa asks, watching Yeva perform a series of ballotté jumps across the deck, knowing that any warning against such moves would fall on deaf ears. "He didn't spill it all to save his skin?"

"Merle didn't have much to say," Ian says, watching Yeva's ballet moves and pulling in a deep breath of the cool night air. "He was dead."

Klaryssa whips around, saying nothing.

"By all indications, he bit down on a cyanide pill," Ian says, mustering the most matter-of-fact tone he can.

"A *cyanide* pill?" Klaryssa asks, trying to suppress a shriek. "Was any of this ever made public?"

"Not a bit of it, as far as Zorn could find," Ian says, shaking his head. "The FBI put a lid on it. The only thing the news services reported were quotes from the Feds about an 'ongoing investigation' and all that. There was apparently no suspicion that Merle Huber had any accomplices in his crimes, so his family was never investigated. And, just so you know, none of the stolen antiquities, either the Egyptian artifacts or the medieval prayer books, were ever recovered."

Klaryssa gives Ian a long, unblinking stare.

"Zorn has a particular interest in Matthias Huber," Ian says eventually, "because Matthias, unlike Merle Huber and Harold Melcher, is very much alive. Through the years, Matthias has taken out a number of loans against the Truro property, so

Zorn had no problem securing photo images of the man from bank records. With the high-res headshots he found, Zorn used the same facial recognition software to cross those images with literally millions of public and not-so-public pictures taken over the past 10 to 20 years. Nothing came up at first, as in flat, zero, nada. He ran it all again, and still no hits. So just for the hell of it, Zorn extended his search to 30 years. He waited, and then waited some more, and after a couple of hours, he got a match."

"From where?" Klaryssa asks, holding out both hands. "Where else did he find a trace of this guy?"

"Not from where, but from *when*," Ian answers. "The authenticated profile photographs of Matthias Huber match a black-and-white security camera image that was taken just before 1:00 AM on March 17, 1990."

Klaryssa arches her head back and closes her eyes. "Holy shit," she mumbles, feeling the blood drain away from her face.

"Holy shit."

Chapter 16
Boston, Massachusetts

Just after midnight on Sunday, March 18, 1990, a
St. Patrick's Day party was beginning to break up at
a rooftop apartment on Palace Road, near Boston's
Fenway Park. Less than a block away, Richard
Abath, one of two security guards on duty at the
Isabella Stewart Gardner Museum, couldn't ignore
the drunken war cries that were echoing up and
down the avenue. To secure the museum's side door
from any wayward party guests and, in particular,
those who had been quaffing green beer since
lunchtime, Abath opened, slammed shut, and
immediately dead-bolted the heavy metal door.

At 1:24 AM, two men in police uniforms
rang the side door buzzer and told Abath that they
had heard a disturbance in the museum's courtyard.
Abath took a quick look at the officers' police
badges, noticing that one of the two policemen was

turning down the volume on his walkie-talkie as a dispatcher's voice came squawking through.

Although he was unsure of the admittance protocol for on duty patrolmen, Abath allowed the two officers access so they could inspect the courtyard for armed intruders. Once they were inside the museum, the police officers placed Abath and the second security guard in handcuffs and told them that they both had outstanding arrest warrants and would be taken to the precinct station for processing.

Abath, who became suspicious when he realized that he had not been frisked before being placed in handcuffs, asked the officers what charges were pending against him. One of the police officers then told Abath and the other security guard that in fact there were no pending charges, and they were not under arrest. He also told them that they would be taken to the basement and locked in a storage room with their limbs wrapped in duct tape, for this was not a police investigation. This was a robbery.

A little over an hour later, a rusted-out Dodge Daytona pulled away from the Gardner Museum and headed north along Palace Road, its trunk loaded down with two used Army Surplus

213

police uniforms, half a roll of duct tape, a worn-out buck knife, and at least half a billion dollars in stolen art.

The theft of 13 irreplaceable works of art from the Gardner Museum, characterized as "mind-numbing in its simplicity, audacity, and scale" by a renowned criminologist, remains the largest private property theft in world history. Despite ceaseless investigations by the FBI, Scotland Yard, and a long list of international anticrime organizations, the robbery remains unsolved. Given the crudeness with which the theft was carried out—the masterpieces were cut from their frames with a hunting knife—many crime experts have theorized that the thieves were rank amateurs. The contrary view is that these were true professional criminals who went to considerable length trying to look like rank amateurs.

The very motive for the theft remains an enigma. Why would the thieves, who spent nearly an hour and a half in the museum, simply walk past two works by Raphael and one by Botticelli? Why was the museum's most celebrated and valuable painting of all, Titian's *The Rape of Europa*, left untouched?

Most criminologist see these oddities as a confirmation of their theory that the robbery was carried out by a pair of brutish bush-leaguers, while others, distinctly in the minority, see this as more evidence that the thieves knew exactly what they wanted because the people who hired them knew exactly what *they* wanted. But, whatever the reason for looting certain treasures while leaving others behind, this was a crime that stole the soul out of the Gardner museum—a crime in which vacant frames that once housed epic masterpieces such as Rembrandt's *Storm on the Sea of Galilee* and Vermeer's *The Concert* serve as heart-wrenching reminders of the sublime beauty that was torn from the gallery walls that night.

The list of suspects in the Gardner heist includes mobsters from greater Boston; mobsters from Philadelphia; mobsters from the mid-Atlantic; local thugs who likely had little, if any, idea as to what they were actually stealing; and professional thieves who, essentially, served as mercenaries at the behest of either Russian oligarchs or any number of shadowy Middle Eastern billionaires.

In the years that followed the robbery, scattered reports of "a potentially stunning breakthrough" all proved to be less than stunning until the release of a surveillance video taken the night before the infamous theft. In August 2015, federal investigators, acting on an anonymous tip from a former graduate school classmate of security guard Richard Abath, reviewed security camera footage from the Gardner Museum taken on March 17, 1990. The video, recorded between 12:50 and 1:00 AM that morning, shows a grainy image of a young man gaining access to the museum through the same side door that Abath opened for the two policemen imposters approximately 24 hours later.

With this stark revelation, federal investigators, Gardner Museum officials, and fine art aficionados the world over were left asking the same unanswered questions: Why was an apparent total stranger allowed entrance into the museum in the middle of the night? Was Richard Abath an accomplice in the plotting and execution of the museum heist, or was he just a hapless stooge caught off guard? Did the security camera from the night before the robbery capture a staged rehearsal of the theft that was to take place 24 hours later?

Every viewer of the video footage is left to wonder if the man seen on the surveillance camera is the one responsible for the hollow frames that now serve as grim, haunting reminders of the works of artistic genius that vanished into the darkness all those years ago.

***

Klaryssa and Ian, both standing stock-still at opposite sides of the living room, are left staring at one another.

"Are you two practicing to be statues in the park or something?" Yeva asks, peeking her head around the corner. "Mommy, you look like one of those frozen people in the subway station who leave out the can for spare change."

Klaryssa shoots Yeva enough of a look to send her back out to the far end of the roof-deck.

"This match—the one between Matthias Huber's headshot and the guy on the Gardner security camera," Klaryssa begins, "how confident is Zorn on this? Does this kind of thing come with a percentage or grading system or something along those lines?"

"It actually does, I guess," Ian says, giving a slight nod. "It's not a perfect match, according to Zorn. The headshots Zorn has of Matthias are high-resolution, but you've seen the video image from the Gardner at least as many times as I have. It's

217

security camera technology from the 1980s, and there's a snowstorm element on the screen that you can't get past.

"On the plus side though, one of Matthias's bank record pictures taken within a year of the Gardner video shows what Zorn calls 'multiple points of positive intersect' when compared to the shots of the man who was allowed inside the museum the night before the Gardner robbery.

"Remember, this is what Zorn does, day and night, and he likes what he sees. He's plenty confident, but there's a strong subjective element in all this, and he says there's not nearly enough to serve as stand-alone evidence in a criminal trial."

"That answers my next question," Klaryssa says. "Obviously, if there was enough there to charge this guy, the whole world would now know the name Matthias Huber. But do the police or FBI have any of this? Is Huber under suspicion for the Gardner theft? Is he a person of interest, or whatever?"

"All very good questions, none of which Zorn can answer right now," Ian says. "He figures there's a good chance the Feds have very little, if anything, on this guy. And, remember, Matthias was in the Coast Guard Reserve for years, with no

218

suspicions being raised. Even though Merle Huber, Matthias's granddad, likely committed grand larceny on at least two occasions, he exited the stage for good before he could be arrested and charged. And there's no link between his crimes and Matthias, who has managed to remain squeaky clean.

"Federal authorities use facial recognition programs all the time, but even if they found the same match as Zorn did, it would be essentially worthless because there's not so much as a speck of dust on Matthias's goody-two-shoes record."

"All this according to Zorn, I take it," Klaryssa says, this time with more than just a hint of sarcasm.

Ian nods his head.

"So, now what?" Klaryssa asks, distracted by something she hears outside on her deck, figuring that Yeva is, as usual, moving around the chairs so she can practice her series of fouettés.

"You know what I know, and now I know what you know, but it's not like we can walk up and ring the FBI's doorbell and tell them all about a horse race scam and a hidden Michelangelo piece and Nazis in the backyard and oh yes by the way we solved the Gardner heist. We can't go anywhere with this, because even though you and I might see a firestorm, the authorities won't even see a spark, right? And we really have no idea what is going on at the house out on Cape Cod. Just theories."

"That's correct," Ian answers matter-of-factly. "So, I guess we'll just have to knock on Matthias's door and find out for ourselves."

"Should we bring him a little of this, just to loosen him up?" Klaryssa asks, holding up the bottle of horilka.

Ian looks at the horilka bottle for a brief moment and smiles.

"Like I said, Zorn is all in on this. And you'll see that for yourself tomorrow. Or should I say," Ian says, looking at his watch, "later today. He has access to his company's private plane, and we can meet him at the airport in a few hours."

"He's actually coming here?" Klaryssa asks, giving Ian a slanted look. "Like, here, later today?" Klaryssa suddenly stops herself when she hears a sharp flapping noise outside, on her roof-deck.

"What's all the racket out here?" Klaryssa shouts to Yeva, walking out onto the roof-deck and looking in every direction. "If you insist on dancing along the edge, at least do it without waking up the neighborhood. It's late, in case you haven't noticed.

And believe it or not, some people have to work in the morning."

"It's not me, Mom," Yeva says, leaning over the railing in a full stretch, pointing at an American flag mounted on the upper-level balcony of an adjoining building. "That guy's flag is banging all over the place. I'm as quiet as a little church mouse out here."

Klaryssa looks out in the direction of the flag whipping in the freshening gusts of wind. She stares at the flag, closing her eyes for a minute or two, letting a flurry of random images race through her mind.

Something's wrong, she thinks to herself.

She looks again at Yeva, her daughter's leg and torso muscles tensing to their outer limits with a Crescent Lunge stretch. Then she looks back at the flag. The noisy, rustling flag.

Something's wrong. She knows something's wrong.

"What's the deal?" Ian asks, now standing in the doorway. "What are you looking at that's so important?"

Something is missing.

"Do you see what I see?" Klaryssa asks, pointing to the lit flag on the top floor of a nearby

221

brownstone. Ian looks at the flag twisting in the stiff breeze, watching it snap against an open window.

"OK, your neighbor likes to fly the American flag," Ian says, shrugging his shoulders. "So whoever lives under that roof is more patriotic than you."

"Yeah, Mom, it's just a stupid flag," Yeva says, again practicing her brisé jumps. "It's not like it will keep you awake or anything. You could probably sleep through an earthquake."

Klaryssa brushes past Ian and walks into her study. She pulls the *Atlas of Military History* off one of the bookshelves.

"I'm not talking about the *flag*, and I'm not talking about the flagpole," Klaryssa says, rifling through the pages of the atlas. "I'm talking about what's on *top* of the flagpole. Or, more to the point, what is supposed to be on top of the flagpole. Think for a minute—go back to the Gardner theft, the photos of all that was looted that night. What do you remember about the pieces that were stolen?"

"A handful of big-time paintings, some drawings, and a vase or something like that," Ian says, sounding befuddled and looking back and forth between the swirling flag and the open art atlas.

"Eleven paintings and drawings, an ancient Chinese vase, and *this*," Klaryssa says, jabbing her finger at a page in the art atlas that shows a color photo of a 10-inch-high gilded bronze eagle. "This is the finial, or ornamental topping, that originally sat at the apex of the pole support of a silk Napoleonic flag. The gilded eagle was Napoleon's war emblem, and it's the symbol his *Grande Armée* carried into battle.

"This is a photo of the same exact bronze statue that was stolen from the Gardner, and the reason behind the thieves stealing this particular statue has mystified crime investigators since day one. It was by far the most obscure and least valuable of the stolen items, and many criminologists saw this as evidence that the theft was carried out by a couple of bozos who thought the statue was made of pure gold and was thus worth millions. But that never made any sense to me, and now you and Zorn have shown me why it never made any sense."

Klaryssa thumbs through the pages of the atlas until she finds a two-page black-and-white photo spread of the Nazi Army on parade through central Berlin in the late 1930s. "Look at the banners the soldiers are carrying, and the insignias along the staging on both sides of the parade route. That's the *Reichsadler*, or Imperial Eagle, and, as you can see, it's *everywhere*. It's virtually the same rendering of an open-winged eagle as the Napoleonic emblem that was stolen from the Gardner. Napoleon's *Grande Armée*, like the warring legions of ancient Rome, used the eagle as a symbol of military prowess. It was Hitler himself who chose the *Reichsadler* as an insignia of Nazi power because it was used by the glorious military leader he sought to emulate above all."

"Napoleon," Ian says slowly. "Hitler was Napoleon's greatest admirer."

"That's why the eagle finial statue was stolen from the museum," Klaryssa says, slamming the atlas shut. "They didn't steal it because they thought the thing was made of gold. They stole it because to a collector of Nazi memorabilia, it would be a trophy of immeasurable value. The thieves knew what they wanted when they talked their way into that museum.

"They were after Napoleon's winged eagle finial because *that* is the ultimate Nazi war machine trophy. And consider now the masterpieces that

224

were swiped the night the Gardner heist took place. Of all the great Renaissance painters the Nazis revered, none were held in higher esteem than the Dutch Masters—"

"Rembrandt and Vermeer," Ian says immediately. "The guys who took down the Gardner Museum were mercenaries who were hired on somebody's order.

"Whoever *somebody* is," Ian adds, he and Klaryssa once again left staring at one another.

"You two are doing that statue thing again," Yeva says, putting on her sweater and running shoes before tiptoeing over to Klaryssa and kissing her on both cheeks.

"Ian, can you drive me back to my dorm?" Yeva asks, still hugging her mother. "I'm too tired to walk, and if I get an Uber, I'm afraid I'll get that Martian guy again."

"You got it, kiddo," Ian says. "We'll be out of here in a flash."

"Love you, baby," Klaryssa says, embracing Yeva so hard that she nearly lifts her off the ground, pulling away just enough to see a slanted grin appear across her daughter's face. No matter how often she tries to will it away, Klaryssa sees Isak in Yeva's facial expressions—especially on the occasions when a wry smile suddenly appears, and when a sullen pout immediately precedes bolts of flash fire temper. All shades of the man Klaryssa last saw on a howling night in the wilds of northern Scandinavia when she was 19 years old.

"Want me to cook for you and your friends this Sunday night? You can bring over all the hungry dancers you can find."

"Yeah, yeah," Yeva says. "Pierogies and borscht and horilka for everyone!"

"That'll be lemonade for everyone," Klaryssa says with a smile. Yeva lets out a melodramatically long groan from the other room.

"Ian," Klaryssa says in as low a whisper as possible, her eyes still on Yeva. "What the hell are we into here?"

227

Chapter 17
Provincetown, Massachusetts
Present Day

Stephan Huber scans the northeast horizon with his binoculars, the water's surface in the distance as flat as a glass tabletop. He takes the last drag of the joint he's been working on, the burning ash singeing the tips of two fingers and the final plume of smoke from his favorite Moroccan hash rising up past the binocular lenses. When the haze clears, Stephan looks farther to the east. The only vessel anywhere in sight is a battered lobster boat steaming in the direction of Provincetown Harbor.

Once again, Soto is making him wait.

Stephan has never actually met Luis Soto, but, through the years, he's had more rendezvous with his men than he can count. Stephan has been left to imagine the scale of Soto's wealth, hearing legends of the man's stash of gold bullion, his vast hills of rolling vineyards in the highlands of

Argentina, his castle overlooking the highest peak in all the Andes, and the parade of young talent that he has at his immediate disposal.

Apparently, Soto has everything a man could ever dream of at his immediate disposal, including the oceangoing yacht that recently weighed anchor at a port along the west coast of South America and headed north to the Panama Canal, weaving through the Caribbean and then traveled along the Atlantic Coast all the way to the waters north of Race Point. Race Point is in Stephan's backyard, so close to his own home that he can almost see his front door from the water when out on patrol.

Soto's men are coming to him because Soto, as always, is on the buying end of this transaction. Soto is sending his personal envoy to seal this deal, for this deal is another step in the man's inexorable expansion of his greatest treasure of all: his collection of priceless art. And to consummate this deal, Soto will have to come to him. He always has to come to him.

But Stephan, seated in the stern of a Coast Guard rescue raft, sees no trace of any other incoming vessel on the horizon and is left to wait. Soto always makes him wait.

I've got two more rolls of Moroccan in my pocket, Stephan thinks to himself. Don't make me finish both of them, Soto.

***

When viewed counterclockwise on a map or nautical chart, Race Point's immense expanse of sand is seen facing to the northeast, then directly to the north, then to the northwest, then directly west at the Race Point Lighthouse, then oriented in a southwesterly direction at an area known as Herring Cove. The beach then becomes a narrow strip of sand surrounded by water on all sides, curling like an arthritic finger into Provincetown Harbor.

As always, Stephan launched his raft from the Old Harbor Lifesaving Station, located in a field of waving dune grass on Race Point Beach about four miles east of where he is now moored. The station itself, a decommissioned rescue outpost with a wooden four-story observation turret, is now a historical site with scheduled tours and rescue reenactments during the summer months. The summer season tours, however, only allow limited access to this historic outpost, with the remainder of the property closed to the public.

230

Stephan has never once considered himself part of the public.

When it comes to the dangers and vagaries of maneuvering light craft on the waters around Race Point, Stephan learned all he would ever need to know long before he joined the Coast Guard Reserve. By the time he entered high school, Stephan had memorized the coordinates of every surrounding landmark and the precise locations of the deadly shoals that have claimed over a thousand ships throughout recorded history.

At an early age, he learned that the only way to navigate the waters of Race Point is to know the patterns of the shifting sand—the hidden shallows and narrow lengths of submerged sandbars that, at low tide, can appear more than half a mile offshore. The peril lurking just below the surface is compounded by gales that can whip up without warning, and a storm-driven grounding has the potential to send thousands of tons of water into a shattered hull. A ship's cargo, and, at times, its crew, can be sent spilling into the merciless surf in the blink of an eye.

But Stephan did not become a skilled mariner out of any intrepid sense of altruism, nor did he join the Coast Guard Reserve to defend the nation's borders and protect the maritime environment. Like his great-grandfather and his father before him, Stephan has spent his life navigating the waters around Race Point to maintain and perpetuate a conduit for the trafficking of stolen art.

Stephan never knew his great-grandfather, Merle Huber, or his great-granduncle, Harold Melcher. All Stephan knows of them is that they were heroes, martyrs in a sacred cause that has claimed millions of lives. These were men of vision, unbending resolve, and enduring conviction. Both were part of the Nazi intelligentsia during the Second World War, and both were sent across the Atlantic as envoys in the waning days of the war, their charge being to plant and nurture the seeds of their Führer's divinely decreed precepts of national and racial unity. The New Order would be established on America's shore by any and all means necessary. All activities would be carried out by a burgeoning group of activists and local militias, and all would be financed in perpetuity through a stream of commerce set in motion by Herr Merle Huber and Herr Harold Melcher.

As with any means of commerce, there must be a product, a seller, and a buyer. Merle Huber and

Harold Melcher, the sellers, procured their product by entering the United States as war refugees and successfully smuggling an archive of Nazi records in with them. These records, culled together both before and during World War II, held information on the location of tens of thousands of invaluable works of art. They then quickly recruited other members of the decimated Nazi regime to assist in their nascent enterprise of looting antiquities from every corner of the United States and Canada. All of their recruits were, like themselves, refugees who crossed the border by purging themselves of their fascist ideology, renouncing the ways of their native land's war-mongering leader, and "swearing allegiance to their new nation."

"The land of the free?" Herr Huber once brazenly asked his fellow thieves after a successful haul. "I know nothing about your land, but your art is certainly free!"

Potential buyers proved even more plentiful, many of them "war refugees" who stepped into their new lives as freedom-loving citizens of Argentina, Chile, Brazil, and other South American countries. These were members of the Nazi intelligentsia who, both literally and figuratively, struck gold once they found their way to their new home on the other side of the Atlantic.

Pallets of gold bullion and foreign currency, along with chest loads of precious gems and jewelry, accompanied these fascists across the ocean via a route that became known as the Spanish Ratline, a clandestine passage that allowed unimpeded transit from the ports of Spain to the welcoming shores of Latin America. The wealth these men accrued was as fabulous and as overflowing as it was hidden, and their appetite for master works of art was nothing short of rapacious.

Precious metals and gems were seen as means to an end, mere products of the natural world that could be found anywhere. These men, defeated in war but in possession of endless wealth, considered themselves stewards of the incomparable work produced by medieval and Renaissance artists.

The biggest challenge, linking the buyer and the seller, proved to be little challenge at all once Herr Harold Melcher became a member of the Coast Guard Reserve. His immigration papers were, like those of many who crossed over the United States border at the end of World Was II, forgeries that made no mention whatsoever of his

Nazi past. Being an accomplished seaman since his youth, Harold Melcher proved to be an ideal candidate to serve in the Reserves, receiving one or two brief assignments before being stationed along the shores of Cape Cod. In his capacity as a reservist, he had easy access to the Coast Guard facility at Race Point, and, from there, Harold merely connected the dots.

With the help of a small army of seasoned thieves, now citizens of the United States and all self-proclaimed Sons of Liberty, despisers of fascism and all its dictums, Harold and his brother-in-law Merle built a criminal empire from the home they purchased in the town of Truro, just to the south of Race Point. The property itself, isolated on the top of an immense sand dune with a commanding view of the Cape Cod shoreline, provided an ideal location to direct the trafficking of stolen antiquities offshore.

Any piece of stolen artwork, once procured, was sealed inside an airtight container and stashed behind false wall panels in the observation tower at Race Point Beach. Drop-offs, exchanges, and rendezvous points were arranged through an elaborate system of coded communication sent via telegraph, with covert operatives stationed all along the Atlantic coast. There was little, if any, fear of interference from the authorities, because members of the operation's inner-circle, having sworn an oath of complete silence, had near total control of the shoreline and, in essence, were the authorities. The transfer of funds was completed through accounts opened in South America and Switzerland, with money funneled back into the United States via backchannels that, in the words of Harold Melcher, worked like the finest watch you ever saw.

Over generations, this same enterprise flourished and became far more sophisticated, all of it hidden in plain sight at Race Point and other locations along the Atlantic Coast. Millions of dollars of stolen art was sold offshore every year to buyers in South America, Russia, and the Middle East. Throughout his life, Harold Melcher would liken the syndicate he built to that of the Italian Mafia, boldly telling his legion of minions that the word *mafia* is Sicilian for *enterprising*.

But in the mind of Stephan Huber, much of the verve of the operation has eroded since those glorious days when the first-generation members of the New Order, such as Herr Huber and Herr Melcher, first came across the Atlantic. Stephan has poured over every page of the personal journals of these two men, reading account after account of how they lived a life centered on one and only one goal: the conquest of the masses by imposing their doctrine by any and all means necessary.

A fascist soldier is not hatched, they both wrote. He is made. Fashioned. Molded. And, with an army of trained, single-minded soldiers, their Reich would be victorious here, on the American shore. Their charge was to forge a nation founded on racial and national purity, and any means to that end was justified and righteous. They knew theirs would be a war fought over many years, perhaps for generations, but to rule supreme, there must always be war.

Herr Huber and Herr Melcher reveled in the war they waged, and, in equal measure, they reveled in that war's spoils. And how Stephan delighted in the journal entries that spoke of those spoils, the Reich's hierarchy sipping Champagne while dining on the most succulent Caspian caviar, their all-night orgies replete with a fountain of aged cognac and a cortège of teenage schoolgirls.

But in reading through these journals, Stephan learned that, above all else, lay loyalty—an unfaltering allegiance to the Fatherland and to the father of Nazism. Disloyalty was an unspeakable disgrace. As such, every member of their movement was compelled to follow an unbreakable code of silence. Throughout his life, Herr Merle Huber indoctrinated new recruits with the creed that they would "tell no more tales while alive than they will when dead."

Matthias Huber, Stephan's father, eventually assumed the helm of the operation and has been in complete control since Stephan was a small child. Matthias was a skilled sailor at a young age, and seafaring came naturally to him. After graduating high school, he too joined the ranks of the Coast Guard Reserves. This gave Matthias unlimited access to the Race Point facility and all the other stations along the shores of Cape Cod, and he taught Stephan everything he knew about sailing and handling light watercraft. Stephan has always respected his father's unbending resolve to their cause, Matthias instilling in his son the precepts that are "bound by the blood of the soldiers before us" and assuring Stephan that the millions they appropriated through their enterprise would "allow the tentacles of hundreds of organizations to reach out further, setting this land on its righteous path."

But through the years, Stephan has harbored an ever-deepening animus toward his father. He has learned to live with Matthias's excessive caution, his deliberation over absurdly minute details, and his reluctance to include him in confidential meetings. Stephan also manages to ignore how the man disavows the enrapture of their spoils, with no trace of alcohol or other intoxicants in his life, choosing instead a monastic existence where afternoon tea is served and poetry is read aloud on a daily basis. But the secret life his father leads has never been a secret to Stephan. Stephan knows the reason his mother and his little sister left their home for good when he was in the seventh grade, and the reason he has never once seen his father pursue, or even look at, another woman.

Those Provincetown boys, father. You're suppose to hate them. You're suppose to despise them.

You're suppose to annihilate them.

***

At long last, Stephan spots the vessel he's been waiting to see.

"Two miles out and closing at 20 knots," Stephan says to Earl, his reservist crewmate and partner in clandestine ops for many years. Stephan takes off his shirt in the early afternoon heat, stretching his ripped shoulder muscles and biceps, knowing that there's no one around to file a complaint about his being seen out of uniform.

"Love to know how much money that Soto has in his sock," Stephan says, flicking the last of another joint into a shallow wave. "Get a load of that launch he's sending our way. That piece alone must have cost him a million or more. One of these days, I've got to get a look at Soto's mother ship, maybe even hitch a ride to Argentina and spend a few weeks at the man's pleasure palace down there in the Andes. Just imagine the life that lucky fucking dog leads, Earl. Day and night, wandering through those mountain vineyards, sipping all that fine wine and chasing all that tight Latin ass."

"What's the play?" Earl asks, staying on task and taking a long look at the approaching boat launch through his own set of binoculars.

"The plan is for them to make a sudden stop about 300 yards out," Stephan says, massaging his neck muscles. "Make that a not-so-sudden stop. Don't want it to look like they're about to flip their launch like that asshole helmsman tried to pull a while back. We're just supposed to do a quick check, and they'll motor off after we make the drop."

When Stephan leans forward to give the anchor line a tug, Earl sees the perfectly square chessboard tattoo that is etched into the center of his back. The original tattoo, inked into the skin below his shoulder blades when Stephan was a senior in high school, was a series of jet-black swastikas. Prior to applying to the Coast Guard Reserve, Stephan had all the right angle lines connected, creating a chessboard that forever erased any evidence of his adherence to a doctrine of racism and hatred.

"Maybe Soto's boys brought some chess pieces; we can have us a quick match," Earl says, pointing a finger at the chessboard tattoo and then taking another look at the approaching boat launch.

"Yeah, sure. I'm game," Stephan mutters. "If they forgot the black knight, I'll call my old man. He probably has one stashed up his ass."

"Shit Steph, we got trouble," Earl says, feeling a sudden yank in the center of his stomach. "Real trouble. Check out port bow."

Stephan pulls the field glasses up to his eyes and sees what Earl sees. Instead of the usual three men manning the boat launch, he sees four, one of

241

them just a kid, college aged, who's sitting on the port side rail and bouncing up and down like an excited little puppy. Stephan looks the kid up and down a couple of times, sensing not the slightest hint of concern or emotion.

"We're moving up along the starboard side," Stephan says through a deep drag of hashish, starting up the engine without taking his eyes off the cocky kid sitting on the rail.

Stephan motors off in the direction of the boat launch, his thoughts wandering back to the time when he was locked up in a Bahamian jail after getting caught red-handed stealing two cases of beer. Stephan will never in his life forget his cellmate during those brutally hot days, a squalid, muscle-bound martial arts master named Derth.

Spending 24 hours a day within the confines of an eight foot by ten foot cage was plenty enough time for Derth to teach Stephan a few of life's most valuable lessons, the most indelible of which were delivered while Derth was pummeling the pretty American boy senseless.

Anything can be a weapon, little man. Anything. Just depends on your situation.

Those were Derth's prophetic words while he stood smiling at Stephan through his greasy goatee, watching the squirrelly 16-year-old cower in a corner of their cell, where liquefied excrement bubbled up between the floorboards by way of a rotting sewage pipe. He repeated them again and again.

Just depends on your situation.

Matthias let his son stay in that jail for three full weeks before securing his release and returning him home. While Stephan's arrest ended up permanently expunged from his record, the schooling he received from Derth was forever seared into the deepest corners of his mind.

Stephan has packed on 70 pounds of pure brawn since he left that Bahamian lockup, pumping iron for two and a half hours every day and downing a handful of androgens after every workout.

"*Buenas tardes, mis amigos,*" says Simon, one of Soto's trusted envoys, tipping his cap and smiling at Stephan and Earl when they approach along the starboard side of the launch. "We were merely stopping for a brief moment to take some photos. The vista from here… *estupenda*!"

With only a scattering of high clouds to the north, the view might almost be worth the trip, Stephan muses to himself. Just to humor Simon, he does a 360-degree spin, making out Provincetown Harbor and the Pilgrim Monument a few miles to the east, then eyeing the length of Race Point Beach and the beach's lone lighthouse directly behind them. In the distance, Stephan can barely make out two or three of the buildings that make up Boston's skyline, along with a trace of flickering light from one of the Cape Ann lighthouses at the tip of the North Shore.

"So we're safe here, as in the past?" Simon asks, subtly pointing a finger skyward. "I take it there will be no surprises overhead."

Through his sunglasses, Stephan eyes Simon's three crewmates, including the college boy, who is still seated on the bow's port rail. All three remain silent, because whenever Simon and Stephan rendezvous, no one else ever speaks.

"How can there be?" Stephan asks, knowing that Simon is referring to the possibility of any sudden attention from a passing helicopter. "I *am* the police out here, so if there was a chopper deployed, I'd either know about it in advance and we wouldn't be here, or it would be because *I* called one out for support, which would be stupidest fucking thing I ever did in my life. You know the routine, Simon. I have a package for you, and as soon as you take it, I'll signal Matthias. Then you can do the same for *el padrino*, and we'll go our separate ways."

"Of course," Simon says with a curt nod, moving aside slightly to give Stephan room to board the vessel.

Without hesitation, Stephan unfastens the sealed plastic tube he has strapped to the floor of the raft and jumps onto the boat launch. He tucks the tube under one of the boat's unoccupied seat cushions, and he then takes a step toward the ice chest that is sitting in the far corner of the boat.

Anything can be a weapon.

Derth's words pound their way through Stephan's head.

Pen, glasses, newspaper, sock, bottle. No need to pack a weapon. There's always one right in front of you.

"What's in this container?" Simon asks, a question that he knows will stir the fires of indignation that Stephan feels toward his father. Simon knows that whenever Matthias is moving a given piece of art, the only other person who knows the particulars about the sale is the buyer. Although tempted on many occasions, Simon has resisted using the words "delivery boy" whenever he meets up with Stephan.

"Can't tell you that I know," Stephan says, his words icy calm but his glare as stern as granite. "All I know is that this little chat is over once we send that signal to our respective parties. As with every time we're together, Simon, *mi amigo*, the culmination of this deal is my only concern."

Well, almost my only concern, Stephan thinks to himself, flipping open the ice chest.

The teeth, Derth taught him. *If you use a bottle, gotta strike them teeth first. Sends those shards in the exact direction necessary.*

"You boys planning a little celebration on your way back to the big ship?" Stephan asks, picking through the stock of beer, wine, and Champagne that is on ice.

"But of course," Simon says, now looking at his three mates with a broad smile. "How could we not, after such a long and fruitful voyage. If only you could join—"

Angle it upwards. Remember, little man, gotta get them teeth first. If you miss them teeth, bottle might not break. You'll carve off his face for sure, but that scumbag might still be alive.

In one motion, Stephan grabs the neck of the unopened Champagne bottle and roundhouses the college boy with a full-throttle swing to the upper jaw. The impact sends an explosion of arrowhead-sized glass shards ripping into the frontal lobe of the boy's brain, sending him windmilling off the side of the launch. A gusher of blood, spinal fluid, and dental fragments follows a trail of facial skin and severed bone down into the surf.

"Wish I could, Simon, but I'm on the clock out here," Stephan says, throwing the stem of the Champagne bottle straight into Simon's crotch and jumping back onto the raft.

"*Madre de Dios*!" Simon yells so loud that a small flock of cormorants takes flight off a nearby sandbar. Simon and one of the other crewmates leap to their feet and cross themselves, the third man falling to his knees and praying aloud in Spanish.

"Do not try and tell me who he was, Simon. *Do not*. Because I can tell you exactly who he was and exactly what he was. He was a mouth, *hombre*. A very, very big mouth. He was a rat, a fucking tenderfoot, you stupid piece of shit. There are no apprentices allowed, Simon. *Never*. How do you know he wasn't a cop? What if he was being greased by a cop or by someone on your side or on my side who's getting wise to all this? Of course you don't know, you ignorant motherfucker!

"Signal Soto, and I'll signal Matthias, and we're done here," Stephan goes on, still shouting, his face red with fury. Simon's two terror-stricken mates begin to pull the dead body onto the boat launch.

"And leave him in the water," Stephan says, restarting the engine. "That's where all the mess is anyway. There isn't a drop of evidence on your boat, which doesn't matter now because the only inspection you'll get out here is the one I just gave you. Weigh him down into the water and head east until you see that pod of seals. Follow them, because that's what the sharks do. Those seals are the best friends we've ever had out here, and you might even see the sharks munching on a couple of them well before dusk. Then untie homeboy here and let him loose. The dorsal fins will make what's left of him disappear.

"Sloppy," Stephan says, spitting into the water. He then takes off his sunglasses and eyes Simon and the two remaining crewmates disdainfully. "Really, really fucking sloppy. My guess is Soto would have your nuts roped up on the yardarm if he knew how careless you were out here. All of this works because we make it work, Simon, and that means no window-shoppers allowed. Next time, and there will be a next time, it's just going to be you and your two douchebags here who let you do something so stupid. There will be no goddamn hitchhikers. And be on time when we next meet, *amigo*. The signals we arrange, all the backchannels and walls to keep this silent, it's all for a reason. We rendezvous as *planned*, not when it fits your fucking pleasure.

"Get us away from this pile of shit," Stephan says to Earl without looking back. "At least I still have a clean shirt, with none of that little weasel's brains splattered all over the front.

"Problem solved, without need of blade or pistol. Nothing to report, this never happened," Stephan says to Earl a couple of minutes later, lighting up his last Moroccan joint as they head back toward their launch site at the top of Race Point Beach. "And those great whites, they've made my life one hell of a lot easier out here. That kid back there, whoever the fuck he was," Stephan continues, taking a full drag and then handing the joint to Earl, "he'll be telling just as many tales as a dead man as he did while alive."

249

Chapter 18
Truro, Massachusetts
Present Day

Along the top edge of the Ocean Bluff sand dune, Matthias Huber sits alone in a weathered beach chair, taking in the deep blue hues of the Atlantic that extend to the horizon in three directions. Lines of frothy waves break onto the narrow shoreline far below. The only sign of life along the beach is two teenage boys who are making every effort to launch a kite that will take the shape of a menacing dragon should they ever manage to get the thing airborne.

Matthias takes a sip of his favorite Chinese tea, watching the two boys charge up and down the beach and recalling, for a moment, how thoroughly bored he was with the box kite his father gave him when he was 10 years old. Matthias remembers running along that same stretch of beach all those years ago, trying desperately to hoist that worthless square of balsa wood and torn fabric into the sky, while his old man, seated on a craggy driftwood log, pontificated with men Matthias later learned were "business liaisons," all of whom invariably proved to be worthless buffoons.

But what Matthias remembers most about that late July morning was the nine-foot-long bluefin tuna he saw hanging from the center of a passing fishing boat, with a trail of blood bubbling out of the gaping harpoon wound on the underside of the enormous fish. He spotted the boat after a thunderous wave swallowed up the last of his box kite, and, as the boat was only a hundred or so yards off shore, Matthias jogged along the shoreline to keep pace with the vessel.

One of the three fishermen saw Matthias running along the beach and waved to the child, but before Matthias had the chance to wave back, he felt the familiar searing crack of his father's belt between his shoulder blades. Matthias was facedown in the sand, his father whipping him several times as he babbled about his useless chicken-shit-of-an-only-child and about how humiliated he felt now that his friends had seen his wimpy little boy crash his new kite into the water.

But Matthias ignored the high-pitched spits of scorn that followed the waft of stale alcohol in his father's breath, just like he ignored his father's two friends who were now pointing down at him and snorting with laughter. Matthias didn't moan, and he didn't cry, and when his father was done hitting him, Matthias lifted his head out of the sand and waved back at the fisherman whose clothes were covered with the blood of the mammoth catch that was strung up by its tail in the middle of the small boat.

Ocean Bluff is the only home Matthias has ever known. The oceanfront cottage is just as isolated as it was on the day when his great-uncle Harold Melcher purchased the property. The sand dunes along the eastern shore of Truro are the highest of any in New England, with views so commanding that Matthias's front yard shares a border with both Cape Cod's oldest lighthouse and a surveillance radar station that was operated by the Air Defense Command during the Cold War.

Today, the sky over Cape Cod is spectacularly clear, without a trace of the dense fog that shrouded the shoreline just after dawn. Matthias stands up and looks through his binoculars at a pod of gray seals heading northward through the surf, counting the heads that pop up between the waves. When Matthias hears footsteps, he puts one hand into the air, signaling the two men who are now standing next to him to be silent while he continues to count the seals as they break through the ocean's surface.

"Yesterday I spotted 19 of them," Matthias says, looking through the eyepiece of the binoculars and watching the seals frolic in the waves. "Now I'm quite sure there are only 17 of the cute little fellas and gals. And it's the same bunch, no question there. They each have such distinct markings, and I fear the two missing pups are, at this moment, churning their way through the belly of one of those opportunistic sharks that have been patrolling the waters this season. Those great whites always appear so well fed, don't they? I myself have never seen one that had the look of a wanting predator."

"This is the man I told you about, Father," Stephan Huber says, pointing his thumb at the man standing next to him. "His name is Brooks, Brooks Wagner. And he's the one making inroads in the Mid-Atlantic states, in the schools and universities."

"Yes, just 17," Matthias says as he again counts the seals, adding a layer of elegance to his already genteel voice. "Playful sort, aren't they?

Playful right up to that first ring of the dinner bell, when those big dorsal fins start to close in. Sit, both of you." Matthias commands, still staring at the seals through his binoculars.

Brooks immediately takes one of the two beach chairs that faces opposite the chair Matthias always sits in. Stephan flicks his cigarette butt down the sandy path and then slowly sits down in the other chair. Matthias, who despises even the slightest form of litter, chooses to ignore Stephan's contemptuous disregard of his pristine surroundings.

"Well maybe those two little seal pups are still out there somewhere," Matthias says, now looking down at Brooks, his eyes flickering in the sunlight. "Though I fear the next time either of them surfaces, it will be in the center of a shark turd."

Brooks stands up out of his chair and starts to extend his hand. Matthias ignores the gesture and drops himself back down into his own beach chair.

"So, you lads take care down there in that water," Matthias says with a churlish tone, signaling for Brooks to sit back down. "Apparently, this world needs the both of you, and my son here is about to tell me why."

"We've got the right man here, Father," Stephan says, his massive neck and shoulder muscles twitching slightly as he speaks. Even through his sunglasses, Stephan can feel the weight of his father's gaze bear down on him. Matthias, as always, senses his son's unease. And, as always, he is thoroughly enjoying it.

"Tell me, Brooks," Matthias says, still looking at Stephan. "Is Wagner your real surname?"

"Sir, yes, it is," Brooks replies, giving Matthias a single sharp nod. "And my family—"

"Simple question, simple answer," Matthias interrupts, still staring at Stephan, his signature pure-white linen suit gleaming in the late morning sun. "My son here has told me about you, about your stealth and resolve and patience. But a word of caution, if I may," Matthias goes on, now turning away from Stephan and looking at Brooks, his eyes again shimmering.

"Never be too patient when it comes to these college newbies. They arrive already brainwashed by their parents and teachers and ministers, high on the praise heaped on them for being open-minded and tolerant in their social and political views. Even the most right-leaning have been largely hardwired to fall in line somewhere along the politically correct spectrum. Otherwise, the academic record required of these students would be unobtainable. Any young mind that espouses the truths we know will be forever shunned from higher education.

"Virtually every freshman you will encounter has been programmed in the scripted American dictate, where the reality of our oneness —the oneness that you and your kin and Stephan and his kin share—has been blotted out. You know, you cannot accomplish anything alone. So, tell me, how many others are in league with you?"

"Several dozen, sir," Brooks answers forcefully, "at least 50 or 60. I'm still vetting some, and this takes time and resources, as you well know."

"You mean money," Matthias says after taking another sip of tea. "This is neither the place nor the time for pitter-patter, so just come out and say it. We go nowhere without our bankroll, and Stephan here will see to it that all the funds needed are quietly transferred. So, I ask you what I have been asking our ranks for more years than I care to count: how and where will you reach these young minds before they are completely beyond our grasp?"

"The darknet remains our most powerful inroad," Brooks says emphatically. "Its capacity and potential grow by the day. Our footprint is everywhere, and I can assure you, sir, that we remain anonymous. Our message boards and websites serve as simple reality checks on the perverse orientation and twisted reality of the elected and religious leaders that our society empowers. We expose those who are hell-bent on equality for Jews and mud races and ragheads and those poor *disabled* persons. And we ally with college students of both genders and all ages and walks of life. All the programming that has been internalized since their early childhood, compliments of their family members and other asinine role models, can be unwound. We set them on the righteous path, and from then on, there is no turning back."

"For a moment there, I was wondering where you hid the teleprompter," Matthias says after letting a long beat pass, a shade of a grin appearing beneath one side of his pencil mustache. "Command performance, Herr Wagner. But, tell me, do you actually get to see any of your budding proselytes, or is all your work performed through the darknet's dark vapor?"

257

"The darknet is just that, a net," Brooks says, Stephan looking on and nodding his head like a schoolboy who's about to spit out the correct answer in class. "We merely make these young minds aware of how many people, just like themselves, are unwittingly suffering the indignity of servitude by the laws and accepted social norms of our nation. We show them just how close we are to the realm of righteous order, where they can be a cog in building a world where not a morsel of their natural talent nor a penny from their hard-earned paycheck goes to the millions of entitled urchins that soil this great land.

"And the venues to further influence these students, face to face, are everywhere, such as after-hours bars, dorm lounges, meetings before a volleyball match at a sports club, and lecture halls after the last class of the day. Some settings are right out in the open, like the back row of a lecture hall. Many so-called all-American undergrads troll the dark pages of the web, and after they find us, they realize just how hungry they are. And they are plenty hungry."

"As hungry as those who took to the streets down there in Virginia, near the grounds of a school founded by that slave owner Thomas Jefferson?

When I see the replays of that day, I almost feel the man's watchful eye upon the marchers," Matthias says with a barely suppressed sneer. "Glorious irony, if you ask me. Tickled my fancy almost as much as those boys out in California who used flagpoles as instruments of impalement. These are all very fine people, and we all know I'm not the first person to recognize them as such. And I believe it was one of our brethren who spoke of the 'honesty and courage' of those actions."

"Exactly, sir!" Brooks says, his eyes darting in all directions. "I believe our movement gave birth to these righteous expressions, and we must parlay this success."

"And how do you propose to do that?" Matthias says quickly, again glaring at Stephan. "My son here tells me your specialty is the shepherding of young bloods into our mix. He has sat here before, heaping praise on other touted powerhouses intent on creating a critical mass of like-minded Americans. And, well…I'm still waiting."

"We must walk these young minds through the process," Brooks says, now looking between Matthias and Stephan. "When we meet, for the first half hour or so, we're only throwing out softballs.

Where did you grow up? What sports did you play? Who did you hang with? All that sort of thing. But before long, they come to realize how much they have been conditioned to the scripted social order of our nation, and then they begin digging deeper and want to know more.

"We like to see these meetings as a venue for indoctrination, but, in truth, there's a little bit of indoctrination and a lot of nodding with attentive approval. In short order, some come right out and talk about the lazy blacks and the Hispanics they know and, of course, the self-righteous papists and long-suffering Jews and now even the refugees from every corner of the earth who are pushing their way into our land. So many young minds sing from the same song sheet. By all that is right on God's green earth, they've been waiting for us. They *want* us. We spread around a few dollars at a bar, and, before long, our weekend retreats have full rosters. And it's there that the social order we aspire to has its podium. One by one, we expose all the base elements that pollute our world, including the gays and lesbians and now the transgenders who demand to be treated as equals instead of being recognized as the scourge that they are."

"Look at those who took to the streets in Charlottesville," Stephan says, detecting no unease in his father's demeanor and almost admiring the man's dead calm as their guest rails against those who share Matthias's sexual orientation. "Many of the marchers traveled several hundred miles, some a thousand miles or more. We have a hand in every white nationalist movement you can name, Father. Brooks has a small army by his side; give any one of them an audience, and soon enough, everyone in that crowd will pay attention to *us*."

"It appears that my son is reading from the same teleprompter, Brooks," Matthias says in a sour tone, dramatically whipping his head from side to side.

"At the schools we infiltrate," Brooks continues, still at full steam, "we search out the students who will make it in this world, and the decisions they make in their lives will be as forthright as they are subtle. They will decide who gets hired and fired at the workplace. They will determine who gets promoted and who doesn't and, of course, who really pulls the strings.

"Perhaps most vital of all, they will decide who gets on the local election ballot and who, tragically, of course, *just* misses out. And, naturally,

261

they will decide who gets elected. Their *commitment* to society's downtrodden will amount to nothing more than lip service. It will never be enough to satisfy the bleeding hearts of this world, but, with time, such people will be sent to the margins where they belong. Members of our legion will always keep their true loyalties below the radar screen, including their commitment to keep our borders locked shut and impervious to yet more undesirables."

Brooks stops talking when Marta, Matthias's housekeeper, approaches with a pot of steaming tea. Both Brooks and Stephan eye Marta up and down as she leans forward and pours Matthias a fresh cup of tea. Marta sets down the teapot and walks away without saying a word.

"Bless you, Marta," Matthias calls out, looking back and forth between his two companions who are both watching Marta's long dress twist in the late morning breeze.

"My apologies, gentlemen, how very thoughtless of me," Matthias says, gesturing towards the teacup he is holding. "Would either of you care for some tea? It's known as Da Hong Pao, or the Big Red Robe, and the brew dates back to the early Ming Dynasty. Its benefits to your health and vitality are nearly innumerable."

"I appreciate your kind offer, sir, but no, I am fine. Thank you," Brooks says, nodding his head slightly.

Stephan shows no response, knowing that his father, as always, is being a rude prick who had told Marta earlier not to bring out any extra teacups.

"Stephan here will see to it that you receive all the necessary funds," Matthias says, again picking up his binoculars so he can follow the pod of seals swimming north through the rising tide. "That will be all for today."

Brooks offers his thanks to Matthias and walks away quickly, leaving Stephan alone with his father at the edge of the sea cliff.

"Still two missing," Matthias says, feigning concern over the two seal pups that were likely eaten by sharks earlier that morning. "Tomorrow, sadly, there may be yet two or three fewer. But you and I will be here rooting the rest of them on, won't we now. And if someday you decide to drain your system of all those chemicals you regularly infuse, you might learn to enjoy the bounty we're blessed with here.

263

"Why, just yesterday, while following my favorite family of seals, I spotted two finback whales in the distance. And if you look at the top of the lighthouse over there, you'll see a pair of storm petrels perched on the catwalk just below the lantern. Take it all in while you can, my son, and just try to ignore the Hitchcockian flock of flying rats that have a bad habit of clouding our skies.

"He'll do," Matthias says after an uncomfortable silence passes, giving Stephan another dead stare. "Brooks, that is, as if we're here to discuss anything else. I checked out his family tree, and, more to the point, that family's collective mind and resolve. Like I said, he'll do. Let's just hope he doesn't start tossing gutter balls like that last moron you brought out here. See to it that he has access to all the money he needs for our websites and beer hall blasts and mountain retreats and all that.

"Just make sure none of this ends up on the front page like it did a few months ago. When are you going to learn that it's not about publicity but subtlety? Subtlety must be the medium of our message. And that means no screaming banners on the six o'clock news. Let's see if Brooks can plant some seeds into Southern minds. Let them see just how powerful they can be, so we can get closer to setting our country on its destined path.

"This Brooks is certainly reading from the right script. Let's just see if he sticks to it and delivers. If he does, I'll make all his dreams come true, perhaps even starting off with a romp with little Marta. That alone should keep your friend Brooks enthused, so don't you go getting greedy and defile this housekeeper like you did the last one. Yes, poor Liesel. Dear, dear Liesel. How could you ever forget a pair of legs like that? And you didn't take no for an answer, did you now? I believe that's why she disappeared and left me all alone, high and dry up here on top of the world, with no one to prepare this delectable tea I so enjoy. I believe that once you treated the reluctant and barely legal Liesel to a date in the sand with that androgen-fed limp wanker of yours, you scared her away forever."

That beats being someone's squealing, gray-ponytailed bitch, Stephan silently muses, sending his father a brief, icy stare.

"If we bankroll him, the sky isn't even the limit," Stephan says flippantly, his granite eyes still wide, as a knifing blast of cold air cuts between him and his father. "Brooks and company will fan out over several states between now and the end of the year, and he'll account for everything we send him. You just have to make the transfers from the Caribbean account, and the rest is as good as done."

"You just worry about the next rendezvous with Soto's men, as the deal I have arranged with Soto is notably bigger than the last one. I'm still working out the particulars with him, and he has been delaying more than usual, and that alone is a concern. It makes me wonder if the man is as financially flush as he leads us to believe, so we are in a dicey place here.

"And I'm sure you recall your last meeting with Soto's envoy just a couple of weeks ago, when you polluted these clean waters with a young lad's facial skin, not to mention half of his brain. There will be no more making a mess like you did last time. Test my limits, *dear boy*, and you will soon find your own."

Matthias knows that nothing rattles Stephan more than hearing his own father refer to him as *dear boy*. Stephan feels his blood boiling, and, when he begins to speak, he sees Matthias shoot up out of his chair.

"Quiet," Matthias says, spotting two park rangers walking along an abandoned fire road a

266

couple hundred yards to the north. "Who the hell are they?" he asks without pointing in the direction of the two rangers. "Have you ever seen them out here before?"

"No, never," Stephan says, still seated. "But they're with the Park Service, so what's your worry? Can't you tell by that daffy getup they all wear?"

"Park Service, yes, but what's their business up here?" Matthias goes on, looking in the opposite direction as he speaks. "The rangers walk that old fire road from time to time, but I've never seen either of those two before. It's usually that slob with the pendulous gut whose face turns purple if he takes more than ten steps from that truck the taxpayers provide for him. These two look like they're from the Lilliputian division. There can't be 200 pounds between the both of them combined."

"Just ignore the little weasels," Stephan says. "They measure water runoff and erosion and wind currents and bullshit like that. They can't get a real job, so they jot a few notes in their spiral scratchpad and then lick their paycheck off the bottom of the public trough every two weeks. Fuck 'em."

"Can't get a real job," Matthias repeats Stephan's words with a surly tone, staring off into the distance. "A real job...like taking things that don't belong to you and selling it all to the highest bidder. Those poor, poor, lost pathetic souls."

Klaryssa and Zorn make their way up an abandoned
fire road that runs along the Ocean Bluff sand dune,
with Ian staying in his car near the Cape Cod
Lighthouse, less than a mile away. The fire road is
only used by National Seashore park officials, and,
to help prevent any undue attention, Zorn and
Klaryssa are wearing official-looking uniforms that
Ian found on eBay. They   also have on wide-
brimmed hats and ID badges that, from a distance,
look real enough. As a further precaution, Zorn
gave Ian a GPS tracking device that follows the
movements of the vehicles used by the real
National Seashore personnel, and, if necessary, Ian
would send Zorn and Klaryssa a signal that they
needed to duck out of sight should the bona fide
authorities access the fire road.

      "His name is Drago," Zorn tells Klaryssa,
after having pulled out from his shirt pocket what,

by all appearances, is a lifeless grasshopper. "He is the latest in micro-avionics. He's modeled after the pallid-winged grasshopper of our western deserts, and he can fly and land in as many directions and in as many places as we choose to direct him to. Once Drago is inside Huber's house over there, we'll have ears and eyes in any room we'd like. We can control his movements with my phone, and we can gain entrance to the cottage by guiding him through that open second-floor window. Everything he sees, we see, and everything he hears, we hear."

Zorn adjusts Drago's tiny metallic wings, and, with the aid of a smartphone app, the tiny drone springs to life. "See you soon," Zorn says after Drago takes flight, and he watches the mechanical insect flutter its wings and make a sinuous path toward Matthias Huber's bedroom window.

"Fly, fly, fly," Zorn says in a soft voice, showing Klaryssa the drone's flight path on the screen of his smartphone.

***

Douglas Zorn Maryn and Ian Sterne met at a campus-wide holiday party held during the first

271

semester of their freshman year at Virginia Tech. It was some time after two in the morning when Zorn, who at the time was barely five feet tall and weighed in at less than 100 pounds fully clothed, stumbled upon a drinking contest hosted by the crew team. One of Ian's teammates, fresh off his eighth shot of bourbon, spotted Zorn in the crowd and boisterously asked him if he would consider being their team's fourth-string coxswain. When Zorn responded by asking this same teammate if he would consider going out to the parking lot and fucking himself to death, Ian knew he had met a friend for life. Three years later, at the age of 20, Zorn graduated second in his class with degrees in computer science and electrical engineering, and the first of his two doctorate degrees followed a couple of years later.

After a stint in the corporate world, with all of its Department of Defense contracts, Zorn signed on with a private surveillance firm that is so private it doesn't even have a public name. Zorn's specialty, to nobody's surprise, is gadgets—his latest and greatest being Drago, the tiny insect spy drone that is now at the center of Zorn's covert surveillance.

Klaryssa cannot help but wonder just how Elle Picard's simple request to establish the provenance of a Renaissance sketch ended up leading her to the edge of an immense sea cliff, where she'd be spying on a family of Nazi thieves with a wisp of a man who appears to have walked straight out of central casting, complete with a nasal voice and shaded John Lennon eyeglasses.

"Check it out. Now there are three of them standing out there," Klaryssa says, nodding in the direction of Huber's property a hundred or so yards to the south of where she and Zorn are positioned. Klaryssa bends down and picks up a piece of shale, inspecting the rock with feigned interest.

"That basically triples the chances that we'll be spotted. The guy with the binoculars has to be Matthias Huber—he's the right age and body build, as best I can tell. I think the burly dude with the sandy blond hair and sunglasses is Stephan, Matthias's son, but I have no idea who the third guy is. I've never seen any member of their family before in person, just the photographs you sent Ian, but there's no question that that's their house. And I'm guessing they don't rent the place out very often."

"Just keep doing what you're doing," Zorn intones, facing away from Klaryssa and maneuvering Drago's flight path on his phone. "You know, park ranger stuff, whatever that might be. Just keep inspecting the pebbles and shells and all that. And take a look along the beach every now and again, and remind me to do the same."

"How's it going with your magic bug?" Klaryssa asks, looking down at the beach and watching two boys with their now airborne kite run in and out of the surf.

"It's a little windy, but we've only got a few feet to…ah, damn. Might be a minute before we gain access."

"What?" Klaryssa asks without looking at Zorn. "What's happening?"

"Someone just closed the bedroom window. Doors, historically, are a far more reliable avenue. We'll just have Drago twitter about while we wait for the right moment."

"The rocks I'm looking at all look alike," Klaryssa says in as calm a voice as she can. "You're supposed to be a park ranger, too, so look out across the water and point. Don't worry about what you're pointing at, just point, real official like. If we blow our cover out here, we are so dea—"

"Some girl just came out of the house," Zorn interrupts, briefly pointing toward the horizon with his index finger while watching the images Drago is sending back to his smartphone screen. "She's heading out to serve the three men coffee or whatever. That means she'll probably re-enter the house in another couple of minutes, and, by the looks of things, she'll be alone when she does so. That works in our favor, although not to the degree that you might anticipate. Although two or more sets of eyes increase the chance of our drone being spotted, a single set of eyes is more attentive, so conversation and banter between multiple parties entering a dwelling oftentimes works to our advantage."

"The girl serving the refreshments," Klaryssa says, the pressure in her voice building. "What's the latest?"

"She left a steaming hot container of something or other with the three musketeers over there, and she's heading toward the back door of the cottage."

"I'm gonna pick up another rock," Klaryssa says, reaching down to the ground. "So look at me for a second and act like you're telling me something. We can't afford to arouse any suspicion, and all that matters is that you get that bug through the back door."

"We're in," Zorn quickly responds. "The screen door has just slammed behind the lass holding the serving tray and our favorite mechanical grasshopper."

"Awesome, Zorn. Seriously. Now, take a look down along the beach and you'll see two young boys flying a kite. Don't wave or anything like that, just look intently in that direction and then we can wander around a bit before we head back down the fire road to meet Ian. I'll text him in a few minutes, but we have to linger for a short while. It can't look like we're charging out of here all of a sudden."

"It's a dragon!" Zorn says, looking down at the beach far below and watching the electric green kite gyrate through the swirling wind currents. "As if from the *Epic of Gilgamesh*, he rules both land and sky."

"Shit, Zorn, don't *point* at the *dragon*," Klaryssa says, gritting her teeth and nearly shouting to be heard over a sharp gust of wind while she ushers Zorn down the fire road. "Just keep moving along with me. Remember, we are *park rangers*, and park rangers have no interest in *dragons*."

***

Once back inside Ian's SUV, Klaryssa and Zorn remove their ranger hats and fake ID badges and change into sweatshirts, covering what is left of their barely passable disguises.

"Great going, pal," Ian says, placing a firm hand on Zorn's shoulder while giving Klaryssa a wide-eyed look. "Great going to both of you. Now what's showing up on that screen you're holding?" Ian asks, pointing to the images being transmitted from the drone's electronic eye to Zorn's iPad.

"He's currently resting on the top shelf of a bookcase," Zorn says, adjusting the brightness on the iPad screen. "Ian, look. You can clearly see two of the three characters that Klaryssa and I saw out along the edge of the sea cliff. There was a third man with them while we were standing at the end of the fire road, but there is no sign of him anywhere now. Wait though, yes. That's the girl we saw bringing the men something to drink. Now she's cleaning up in the kitchen."

"OK, so who are these people?" Ian asks, looking at Klaryssa. "Are we even sure that this is the right place, with the right family? We need to nail that down first."

"We all know this is where Matthias Huber lives," Klaryssa answers, pointing at the images running across the screen. "The thin guy with the pencil mustache—that has to be Matthias. He matches up with the other pictures that Zorn sent you. And the twitchy, muscle-bound dude you see pacing around, he's the one we saw in those photos from Race Point. That's Stephan Huber, I'm sure of it."

"And the girl?" Ian asks, pointing at Marta, who is seen moving in and out of the kitchen. "Any idea who she is?"

"None," Klaryssa says, tilting her head at the image now on the screen. "I don't think Matthias has a daughter. Maybe she's a niece? Hired help? From what I'm seeing here, she and Stephan are not interacting in any way that suggests they're a couple. By the way, do you hear something in the background? Something faint?"

"Enhancing the volume as we speak," Zorn says, looking over his glasses to the top of the screen. "The audio input is pretty solid, actually. It's only a matter of a couple of minutes. And, while waiting, I believe I can verify what Klaryssa has already stated about the Huber family."

Klaryssa gazes up at Ian before looking back at the iPad screen.

"First, there's a 95% chance that the man you see here is the man who entered the Gardner Museum the night before the infamous theft took place," Zorn continues. "Compliments of Drago, I've cross-referenced these images with our most advanced facial recognition software. Our program allots for advancing age, changes in weight, anything really. I've checked and rechecked, and it's the same man in both photos, period. And there's a 100% chance that the man we're speaking of, the one with the painfully thin out-of-date facial hair, is indeed Matthias Huber."

"One hundred percent?" Ian asks.

"One hundred percent," Zorn answers back, with a slow nod.

"And your confidence extends from…" Klaryssa says, arching an eyebrow.

Zorn adjusts the drone's viewing eye, which pans across the first floor of the cottage, an endless view of the sea visible through every window. Zorn then focuses on a pile of mail sitting on top of a small table in the living room, zooming in on a *L.L. Bean* catalog. The catalog's mailing label reads:

Mr. Matthias Huber
13 Ocean Bluff Road
Truro, MA 02666

"The United States Postal Service," Zorn answers back, "forever the font of this man's confidence."

"You win this round, Zorny," Ian says, shaking his head. "Now, what can Drago tell us about this guy and about his family?"

Zorn again allows the drone's electronic eyes to rove through the lower level of the cottage. The layout appears as simple as anyone might expect for a beach cottage, with a spare living room, a dining room with an adjoining galley kitchen, and a large sunporch that faces southward. Ian asks Zorn to stop the camera on a closed door that faces the north side of the house.

"What's that all about?" Ian asks, pointing to the bolt locks on the door. "Why a double bolt lock on a bottom-floor room? Looking at the design plan of the house that you found, that door does not lead to the outdoors. It's either an office or a downstairs bedroom, but there might as well be a

280

sign on the door that tells you to keep your ass the hell away."

"There's more than a pair of heavy-duty locks protecting that room," Zorn says, changing the iPad screen to a control panel that shows a series of horizontally oriented squiggly lines. "Drago is picking up a monitor signal, like one you might find in a casino's eye in the sky."

"I wouldn't say bingo just yet, but I'm pretty sure that's where we need to be," Ian says, tapping repeatedly at the iPad screen. "That must be where Matthias works, and we all know what his *work* involves. I mean, why else would you have a door that—"

"I heard it again," Klaryssa interrupts, holding up her hand. "Listen, guys…do you hear that?"

"Hear what?" Ian asks, looking at Zorn, who is shrugging his shoulders. "I don't hear anything. Is it a voice? Someone talking on the phone?"

"Maybe this?" Zorn asks Klaryssa, moving Drago's eye in the direction of a large birdcage in the far corner of the living room. "Are you picking up the cry of one Psittacus erithacus, better known as the African grey parrot?"

Klaryssa lets out a quick laugh. "No, it's not him," she says. "He's been pretty quiet, because I saw him on an earlier frame, munching away on a piece of fruit. No, it's something in the background, like faint music. And, whatever it is, I'm sure I've heard it before."

"I'll pay more attention," Ian says, tapping one ear with his index finger. "Promise."

"Zorny, I gotta ask the obvious here," Ian goes on, impatiently. "These two guys we're all staring at, they're just milling around, not doing much or saying much of anything. I take it we just have to wait for them to give us some hint as to what their life is all about. Or more to the point, what their business is all about. I hate to sound like the kid sitting in the backseat, whining while his dad is pulling out of the driveway, asking if we're there yet."

"That's exactly what you sound like," Zorn answers immediately, still enhancing the drone's AV feed. "Ten percent of surveillance is patient observation, and the other 90% is drinking coffee and trying not to die of boredom. This can go on for days, my friend. Weeks, truth be told. Or, longer yet, and *don't* ask me to give you examples. Too painful to talk about.

"But believe me, we're ahead of the game here. In fact, we're way ahead. First of all, we're in the house that we want to be in. Second, the clarity of the AV is better than I expected. And last, as you astutely pointed out, something of note is going on in that downstairs room. On my flight up to Boston, I pulled a pretty hefty hack into Matthias Huber's email accounts. He's not very sophisticated when it comes to electronic communications, which is of little surprise given his age, so getting into his three different email accounts didn't take long. And there is nothing, I mean nothing, that tells of high-end art fencing or any related crimes. No code speak or fancy encryptions in any of his communiqués.

"The only remote hint of something unusual going on is the volume of calls he makes to Argentina, which he makes via a darknet application that's basically Skype. I'm sure Matthias has substantial dealings in that part of the hemisphere, and he likely does business the old-fashioned way. With paper files, that is, which must be somewhere in that house because he almost never leaves the place. So, sooner or later, he'll unlock that door and waltz in, and, when he does, he'll have winged company in tow. Unbeknownst to him, of course."

"What do we have for battery life?" Ian asks with a yawn, looking at the image of Matthias sitting alone on the living room sofa and reading.

"As circumstances dictate, we can power Drago up, and we can power Drago down," Zorn says, looking over both shoulders to check for any passing tourists. He then fishes through his shirt pocket and pulls out a mechanical insect less than half the size of Drago.

"Our little friend here can refill Drago's battery like one fighter jet refueling another. At full charge, Drago can last up to 72 hours, sometimes even 90 hours if we conserve battery life when the people inside are asleep. Now, getting our charger past the door can present its own set of challenges —"

"Stop," Klaryssa says, loud enough to startle Zorn. "No, I'm sorry, Zorn. I didn't mean it like *that*. Can you freeze that image, right now, on her, the girl?"

"Of course," Zorn says, looking nervously over the top of his glasses, eyeing a group of senior citizens marveling at the ocean view from the gallery deck at the top of the lighthouse.

"Apologies, Klaryssa, and same to you, Ian, but a healthy degree of paranoia comes with the trade. You've always gotta be certain that you're not being surveilled yourself."

"*Surveilled*?" Ian says under his breath, looking at the same group of chatting tourists that are leaning against the iron rail of the lighthouse's gallery deck.

"Understood," Klaryssa says to Zorn without taking her eyes off the screen. "You can probably see half the world from the top of that lighthouse, but I don't think octogenarians searching for the camera button on their iPhones pose much of a threat to us. Can you replay the frames previous to this one?"

"Sure thing," Zorn says in a low voice. "I'll rewind slowly here."

Klaryssa and Ian watch the iPad screen as Zorn rewinds the recorded images in slow motion for several seconds. He then slowly moves the frames forward, and then back again, and then forward again. The forward images show Matthias walking out onto the outside deck while simultaneously showing Marta, who is wearing a light blue floral dress, her hair tied back in a long French braid, walking from the kitchen into the living room. Zorn repeats the backwards and forwards sequence several times.

"Think she has a boyfriend?" Ian asks, while Marta walks from one room to the other.

"Keep it in your pants, dude," Zorn says as he enhances the image. "Klaryssa, what's got your attention here? I just don't see anything unusual or suspect in these images."

"Neither do I," Klaryssa says quietly. "But I hear it. Yeah, I definitely hear something."

Zorn plugs a set of earbuds into the iPad, inserts them into his ears, and squeezes his eyes shut.

"Yeah, yeah, now I can hear it," he says, changing the iPad screen back to a live feed of Marta moving in and out of the living room. "There's music. Very low, but there's music somewhere in the background. How on earth did you ever hear that?"

"*Gagauziya, hosluum, cok sevin, koru dostluu,*" Klaryssa sings, her voice barely above a whisper. "*Gagauziya, hosluum, cok sevin, koru dostluu.*"

Ian and Zorn both look at each other and then look at Klaryssa, watching a sad smile spread across her face.

"She's singing," Klaryssa says, her eyes glassy. "This girl, whoever she is, is singing

286

"Tarafim," which is the national anthem of Gagauzia. I just can't...I can't believe I'm hearing this. And listen to her voice—it's exquisite. Tell me you can hear what I'm hearing."

"I can now, with the volume maxed out," Ian says after a long pause. "But help me out here, KD. What exactly am I listening to? What exactly are we all listening to? You're saying this is the national anthem of where?"

"Gagauzia," Klaryssa answers, still looking at the screen, straining to hear Marta sing. "Gagauzia is an autonomous territory in the southeastern part of Moldova. The Gagauz people are believed to be descendants of the Seljuk Turks who settled along the coast of the Black Sea in the 13th century. This girl is singing "Tarafim" in the native language, which is known as Gagauz."

"She's singing an 800-year-old song while she's prancing around this beach house doing... doing *whatever*? And how in God's name do you know this song? Don't tell me this Gag-whatever is another language you've mastered."

"I wouldn't say 'mastered,'" Klaryssa says in between refrains of "Tarafim," "but I get by pretty well. Gagauzia borders the south-central portion of Ukraine, which is the ancestral home of

287

my mother's side of the family. My mother spoke the language fluently, so we all learned it along the way when we were little. And the anthem, believe it or not, was composed in the 1990s, although the verses have their roots in ancient ballads and folksongs.

"Gagauzia, my happy motherland," Klaryssa sings in English. *"The obstacles didn't stop you, nor time did entangle you. God protect our land: Gagauzia, my native land..."*

"So this girl was born in Moldova?" Zorn asks. "Only possible explanation, right? I mean, how else would she know the lyrics to such an esoteric song? And in the native tongue, no less."

"Gagauzia, my joy," Klaryssa sings softly, *"You are my precious people."*

"This should be a piece of cake now," Zorn says, letting the audio feed of Marta singing "Tarafim" run while he switches the iPad screen to a 3D rendering of Marta's face and neck. After Zorn activates his facial recognition software, Marta's image begins to slowly revolve 360 degrees in a counterclockwise direction. Thousands of multicolored points of intersect flicker on and off across the screen. After no more than two or three minutes, a list of demographics appears on the right side of the image.

"My friends, meet one Marta Cebotari, age 27," Zorn says, the screen now showing multiple images of Marta's profile. "Marta emigrated from the city of Chadyr-Lunga in southern Moldova five years ago to attend college, but I have no verification of her ever graduating. She was employed as a domestic elsewhere on Cape Cod until four months ago, which is when she was hired by Matthias Huber to work in the same capacity. No known contacts, no known address, and no criminal record."

"I believe you've nailed it, Zorn," Klaryssa says, her eyes still fixed on the screen. "And I believe that makes Marta Cebotari more than just the native daughter of a people that share a border with my homeland.

"You are so beautiful, my native land," Klaryssa sings, a hint of a break in her voice.

"It makes her an ally."

Chapter 20
Truro, Massachusetts

Klaryssa, Ian, and Zorn find that they need a place to hole up while they spy on Matthias and Stephan Huber, and thanks to the collapse of the Soviet Union over 25 years earlier, they have no problem finding one.

The North Truro Air Force Station, used by the Air Defense Command as a warning and intercept outpost during the Cold War, is located immediately south of the Cape Cod Lighthouse and less than half a mile from Matthias Huber's home. After the fall of the Berlin Wall and the crumble of the empire once helmed by Lenin and Stalin, the Department of Defense mothballed the radar station and sold the property to the National Park Service. Renamed the Highland Center, the 100-plus-acre oceanfront parcel of land has been transformed, however slowly, into a science, arts, and education center. With a retro '70s music and fashion fair set to get underway later in the week, Ian pays upfront to secure a kiosk at the exhibit, making all the necessary arrangements to ensure delivery of the vintage items he just purchased on eBay. Ian is also able to rent out two small rooms in the abandoned ramshackle military barracks located along the north edge of the property.

Their plan is simple: Ian and Zorn will spy on the Hubers, while Klaryssa looks for a way to make contact with Marta Cebotari.

Klaryssa must find a way to meet Marta as far away from the Huber property as possible. She changes into her running attire and begins to run back and forth along Ocean Bluff Road, hoping to catch Marta as she exits the driveway. After an hour or so, Klaryssa's run turns into a jog, and then a fast walk, then a regular walk, then a slow walk, and then, finally, she takes a seat on a stone wall that is hidden behind a row of apple trees that stand opposite the driveway entrance.

Just before darkness falls, Klaryssa ducks low when she sees Marta pull out of the driveway on a moped, heading north in the direction of Provincetown. Klaryssa sends Ian a text message telling him that Marta's on the move, and a minute later, Ian picks up Klaryssa along the side of the road. Once Ian and Klaryssa catch up with Marta, they trail her from a distance, and when they reach the center of Provincetown, Klaryssa jumps out and tracks Marta on foot until she sees her enter a boarding house using an outside set of stairs.

Klaryssa knows that there is likely no place on earth easier to wander around unnoticed than Provincetown, which has, for generations, been a hub of alternative lifestyles, its residents embracing a live-and-let-live philosophy that has yet to meet its outer limit. Klaryssa knows that she might have only one chance to connect with Marta, so, earlier, she drove to a consignment clothing shop in Hyannis and bought enough secondhand apparel and cheap jewelry to outfit her for a lifetime's worth of costume parties.

For the next couple of mornings, Klaryssa parks her car at the end of the town pier and meanders up and down the narrow streets and alleyways that surround Marta's boarding house, returning to her car and changing her clothes and accessories every couple of hours so as to look as inconspicuous as possible. Klaryssa does everything imaginable to seem oblivious to her surroundings, trudging aimlessly in and out of honky-tonk shops that specialize in tattered paperbacks, dried starfish, 40 flavors of fudge, painted seashells, foot-long hotdogs, cotton candy, and every conceivable adult entertainment apparatus.

Klaryssa eventually catches a break when she sees Marta order coffee from the Post Office, a popular café. This is all the lead that Klaryssa needs; she figures that this is Marta's regular stop before heading off to Matthias Huber's home each morning.

During the course of the day, while making small talk with the locals, Klaryssa finds out that the Post Office also serves as one of the town's busiest after-work watering holes. She stops by a little after five in the afternoon and finds a small table near the front window, hoping to get to know some of the café's staff and maybe even make conversation with a couple of the regular patrons.

When Klaryssa hears the sound of music playing out on the street, she turns and sees a white teenager with a huge afro, dressed in the garb of a medieval minstrel, doing figures of eight on a giant-wheeled unicycle while playing the trombone. Klaryssa casually orders a Sam Adams draft from one of the waitresses while she watches the star of Commercial Street's afternoon scene strut his stuff, the soloist's trombone slide pointing toward the clouds and ringing out odes to Glenn Miller. Less than a minute later, the unicyclist and his one-man band are gone, and when Klaryssa turns back around, she is met by the ice blue eyes of Marta Cebotari.

"You go to college?" Marta asks, staring straight at Klaryssa while signaling the waitress back.

"Wha...what?" Klaryssa sputters, bolting upright in her seat, her face ashen.

"Double Belvedere, iced," Marta says when the waitress arrives, still glaring at Klaryssa. "College. I asked if you went to college. You know, those four-year stints after high school but before you go out and get your ass kicked in the real world. I was just wondering if you went to college."

"Yes, yes, I did," Klaryssa responds after an uncomfortable pause, her jaw still hanging open.

"So, let me go out on a limb here," Marta says, taking a hit of the vodka the instant it arrives, "you didn't major in detective work, did you? Because, if you did, you should march into the front office and demand a refund. You couldn't have been more conspicuous if you were the twin brother of the dude in the pink wedding dress sitting behind me. See him?"

Klaryssa takes a quick glance over Marta's shoulder and nods.

"Yeah, him," Marta says, emptying her shot glass. "The queen with the full beard, not to mention enough fur on his legs to stuff a pillow. So, let me ask you: How many of those masquerade outfits did you invest in before you began your cloak-and-dagger prowl around town? How many circuits around my apartment have you made since you started this undercover op of yours? And, by the way, that guy all dolled up in pink, the one ready to waltz down the aisle—his name is Hondo, and he's a friend who's helped me keep tabs on you over the past day or two. And, just so you know, he doesn't mind being called a queen, because that just happens to be his last name."

Without turning around, Marta holds her empty shot glass in the air. Hondo, in turn, hoists up his 20-ounce beer chalice, giving Klaryssa a quick wink and a slanted grin.

Klaryssa, guzzling the rest of her beer, doesn't even try to speak. She pulls off the tie-dye headscarf she's had on all afternoon and tosses it on the table, setting down the drained pint glass with a loud thud.

"Hat on the table. That's bad luck, you know," Marta says, picking up the scarf and throwing it in Klaryssa's lap. "And, I've had plenty of that. I don't know what you're up to, lady, but take it somewhere else. If you're with the government, I've got papers, they're all legit, and you can piss off. If you're looking for someone to twist with in the hammock, it's none of your business which side of the plate I bat from, and you can still piss off. And if I can offer some unfriendly advice, the next time you try to shadow someone, get yourself a little game first, because you're about as subtle as a dead frog in a bowl of oatmeal.

"And thanks for the refreshment," Marta says, standing abruptly and swinging her jet-black French braid across her chest. "Time for me to get lost; I suggest you do the same."

Marta is out the door in no time, heading toward her parked moped. Klaryssa throws some cash on the table and follows Marta out onto the street, Hondo watching her every move.

In a voice just loud enough for Marta to hear, Klaryssa begins to sing:

Gagauzia, my joy,
Be happy and protect the friendship,
Raise your flag high,
You are my precious people.

Marta, without turning around, stops dead in her tracks when she hears Klaryssa singing in her native language.

We set our first step with you,
We called you mother,
Our love will never fade away,
Nor our sacrifice.

Still facing the street, with her back to Klaryssa, Marta reaches into her jacket and pulls out a pen, scribbling a note on a piece of scrap paper. She then turns around and hands the note to Klaryssa without saying a word.

Marta looks over at Hondo, who is watching everything from the café entranceway. "Love that dress on you, baby," she says with a wave as she starts up her moped. "That color—it's you."

A few seconds later, Marta disappears around the corner. Hondo, brushing off both sleeves of his wedding gown, flashes Klaryssa another wink before going back inside and refilling his beer chalice. Klaryssa opens the note that Marta just handed her.

Race Point Lookout
10 minutes

Chapter 21
Truro, Massachusetts

In the early 19th century, Provincetown's main newspaper published an excerpt from the journal of a renowned British poet and storied traveler. The article quoted the writer as asserting that "the most heart-stirring sight my eyes ever beheld was the sunrise over your Race Point Beach, until 12 hours later, when I witnessed the sun setting over this very same spot."

Race Point is located at the northernmost reach of Cape Cod. When the skies are clear, the morning's first light can be seen sweeping across the seemingly endless expanse of the Atlantic to the east, and, by day's end, the glow of the setting sun spreads across Cape Cod Bay to the west.

Race Point's unmatched panoramic seascape belies its treacherous shoals and shallow sandbars, which have served as a graveyard for hundreds if not thousands of ships over the course of recorded history. The first shipwreck, according to local historians, occurred in the early 11th century when the Norse explorer Thorvald Eiriksson ran aground during an October storm while sailing west toward what is now Boston Harbor.

An inrush of whalers, merchants, and other seafarers throughout the 18th and 19th centuries led Congress to mandate the construction of multiple lifesaving outposts along the shores of Cape Cod. The lifesavers manning the Race Point Station lost so many of their fellow rescuers that they tattooed their motto, "You have to go, but You don't have to come back," across their forearms.

The only building still standing on the sands of Race Point is a wooden fortress with a four-story turret, the structure serving as a lone monument to the untold number of rescuers who gave their lives in the line of duty. Lifesaving drills are still held at the station throughout the summer, and, frequently, small crowds gather to watch the rescuers recreate the valiant efforts of the men who braved hurricane-force winds and ice-cold seawater to save the lives of countless mariners over the course of more than a century.

Today, the vast majority of beachgoers have no interest in the forlorn outpost that sits in the middle of the waving dune grass, preferring instead to tan themselves, play volleyball, throw frisbees, or challenge the undertow that is the hallmark of Race Point Beach.

The Race Point Lookout, also known as the Province Lands Visitor's Center, was built on a small hilltop several hundred yards inland from the shoreline. Klaryssa stands alone on the second-story viewing platform, taking in the raw, cold salt air, the sweeping views of the Atlantic, and the rolling sand dunes that extend for miles in every direction. Klaryssa squeezes her eyes shut when a sudden onshore gust sends a small dust storm screaming across the viewing platform.

"Last time I stood up here, I spotted three humpback whales heading north, a mile or so off shore," Marta says, appearing seemingly out of nowhere as she pulls a cigarette out of a pack of Marlboro Reds.

"I take it you've mastered the art of sneaking up on people," Klaryssa says, wiping the sand from her eyes.

"I come up here all the time, and that was a first for me, seeing those whales," Marta says without breaking stride. "Usually, all I see are the beach bums who lay in the sand and fry themselves to a crisp. Most never go near the water because of all the shark sightings. Seems to me, they ought to be more worried about getting melanoma than being chewed in half by a giant fish.

"See those one-room shacks?" Marta continues, now pointing to the tiny shanties that dot the miles of undulating sand dunes to the southeast of Race Point. "There used to be a bunch of them, but most have been blown off the map. They were built over a hundred years ago to house the rescuers who manned the lifesaving stations, but now they're used by the eccentrics who can't get enough of the Provincetown scene. You know, novelists and poets and painters and all that. I've met a few of them, even dated one for a while. These artists, they're all a little off-the-grid nutty, and those shacks they live in out there all sit on shifting mounds of sands. There are no roads in or out, and there's no running water or power. Glad to know the few huts that are left actually serve a purpose besides being a place where high schoolers go to bone each other.

"Oh, and by the way, do you mind if I ask your name? I won't bother telling you mine,

303

because we both damn well know that you know what it is."

Klaryssa pauses and takes a deep breath before extending her hand and saying, "I'm Klaryssa Mahr."

"I didn't know Feds shook hands," Marta interrupts, hesitating for a brief moment before shaking Klaryssa's hand. "Aren't you supposed to flash your creds at me, or something like that? Tell me I'm here on a temporary visa and there's a problem, right? Or that I'm heading out the door because I'm a danger to this otherwise perfect world you live in?"

"No, my God, it is nothing at all like that," Klaryssa says, feeling the dimple in the center of her cheek begin to burn. "I don't work for the government. I'm a college art professor; I work at Tufts University, teaching undergrads. Please, is there a place where we can just sit and talk?"

Marta makes a show of looking around the viewing deck, which is completely empty of seats or benches of any sort. "Uh, no," she says, searching for her cigarette lighter. "Still off-season, so the Rangers haven't put out any furniture just yet, and I can't wait until the Fourth of July to hear what you have to say." Marta lights her cigarette and sends a large puff of smoke into the air. "It's off-season, like I said, so they haven't even put out the no smoking signs. So it's just you and me and the dust devils up here."

"I am *not* in law enforcement. And, yes, I know your name, and I promise I'll get to explaining that," Klaryssa begins after letting another tall dusty swirl make its way across the platform.

"This all started just a few days ago when a complete stranger approached me with a sketch she found while cleaning out the library in her family's home. It's a very old and very valuable drawing, and this person, this woman, asked if I could investigate the origin and history of this particular piece of art. It turns out—and of this I am quite certain—that this drawing is linked to a masterpiece, thought to be forever lost, that is of immeasurable significance. Digging deeper still, which I am already beginning to regret, I discovered that this missing painting may have actually been stolen many years ago by a family whose criminal enterprise has proceeded unhindered for generations.

"That family's last name is *Huber*, as in Matthias and Stephan Huber, and I think these people you work for are very dangerous. I have a close friend who's been helping me trace this stolen masterpiece, which led me to Huber's home, which led me to you. Matthias Huber may very well have been involved in the Gardner Museum heist over 25 years ago. Are you familiar with that robbery?"

Marta nods slightly, puffing smoke out the side of her mouth.

"My friend, Ian, he asked a friend of his to help us trace this stolen art. Ian's friend, Zorn, is one of these tech *wunderkinds*, and he actually planted a bug, a drone, in Huber's cottage, so we could monitor him. That led me to you, because I heard you singing "Tarafim," and, from there, I just tailed you, hoping we could somehow meet. My mother's family is from south- central Ukraine, right along the border with Gagauzia in southern Moldova. My family name is actually Marchenko; I was born in Chervonohrad and moved to the US when I was a little girl. My mother speaks fluent Gagauz, and I learned enough as a child to get by well enough.

"Look, I know this all must sound impossibly far-fetched, but I swear to you by the heritage we share that what I am telling you is the truth. I *had* to make contact with you, because I need your help. *We* need your help."

Marta sends out a row of smoke rings after taking another deep drag of her cigarette. "We being exactly *who*?" she asks.

"Myself, Ian, Zorn, the family who asked me to trace the origins of this Renaissance sketch they found, and, for that matter, the entire art world," Klaryssa says, her voice rising as she speaks. "What we're talking about is the looting of priceless artistic treasures, and there's a *very* real chance that the family you work for is directly linked to many of these robberies.

"Getting the police involved at this point won't get us anywhere. We have no solid evidence that they committed these crimes, only a bunch of pieces that have yet to come together.

"Anyway, I can introduce you to Ian and Zorn. They're staying in a rented dorm room at the old Truro radar station, watching Huber from a distance thanks to the drone Zorn planted inside the cottage."

"My name," Marta says, crushing out her cigarette and looking straight at Klaryssa for the first time of their meeting. "You haven't told me how you know my name."

"This Zorn guy—whom I barely know—has this facial recognition software. He ran your image through a database, and your bio came up in no time. It's the same software he used to match Matthias Huber to the Gardner heist. To my eyes, this is all a new universe, you know? And it's all a little scary to me because I know *nothing* about spying and sleuthing. As you know, I'm about as inconspicuous as an elephant at a circus."

Marta smiles for a quick moment before reaching to the ground and picking up her crushed cigarette butt. "There," she says, pulling out a fresh cigarette and pointing it in the direction of the lifesaving station. "That place over there, Matthias and his son Stephan, they're obsessed with it. Both of them have some connection, some very strong connection, with the rescue drills that take place all along the Outer Cape, in particular at Race Point. Mind you, they clam up whenever I'm around, but I've heard them talk about it from a distance plenty often.

"That cottage they live in is about as isolated a place as you could ever find, and they have these people come by often enough, meeting with them out on the edge of the cliff where no one can hear them. These guys they meet with—to me, they seem like a bunch of thugs, every one of them. The biggest creep of all is that cokehead Stephan. He's either high on the white stuff or zoned out on all the androgens and other shit he injects into his veins. He doesn't even *try* to hide it. I find dirty needles stashed all over his room, rolled-up dollar bills. I even found one of those tiny spoons once. Whoever decided that coke was passé these days didn't share that news with this guy. I do all I can to stay away from him, and, from what I've heard around town, he's well worth staying away from. You said 'dangerous' a minute ago; well, you don't know the half of it."

"Zorn hasn't found out much about Stephan, except that he has no criminal record," Klaryssa says, speaking in a low voice and keeping her eye on a young couple who has walked onto the viewing deck. "What do you know that we don't?"

"For certain, nothing," Marta says, twirling the unlit cigarette. "But the stuff I've heard, I'm not sure you want to know any of it. I almost wished I had never heard it myself. To start with, I'm working out there because I need the money. I came here from Moldova on a student visa to attend the University of Rhode Island, which I did for two full years. Both of my parents are teachers at a private

309

school in southern Moldova, and they had to go underground after getting tipped off that they were under suspicion of 'subversive activities' by the Russians. Fucking Putin. Anyway, I lost track of my family, and the tuition money dried up. I was working as a domestic for a really nice couple in Wellfleet, right down the road, but they moved, so I went looking and answered Matthias Huber's ad. It's a paycheck.

"Before I started working for him, Matthias had the same domestic help for a couple of years, a single girl named Liesel, who even now is barely 20 years old. Suddenly, one day, she was gone. Disappeared. Her apartment was cleaned out with no forwarding information. Liesel largely kept to herself, but she had a few friends around town, none of whom knew anything about where she went or why she left.

"But one of Liesel's friends gets a call from one of her friends—this friend works as a volunteer at an animal hospital down in Hyannis. She said she was certain that Liesel's dog was brought into their hospital, howling and scared shitless, with metal staples in its hide. A little mixed-breed mutt, and some sadist stapled a note to the side of this helpless animal. Word is that Stephan raped Liesel one night after he got really high, and, to cover his tracks and ensure she never went to the police, he or one of his goons broke into her apartment and stapled the names and addresses of her family members to the dog's fur. No doubt some of the staples *accidentally* went a little too deep. No report, no charges, and no more domestic help for Mr. Huber and family. Like I said, I really, really need the money. The only bright spot to this story is that the dog got patched up just fine."

Klaryssa feels like she might throw up. "God, they're savages," she finally says. "I can't believe *nothing* was done. Rape, gross animal abuse. This all went by like it never happened?"

"Again, rumor and the local grapevine," Marta says, shaking her head slowly. "Can't prove that this dog *was* Liesel's dog. And no police report was filed, very likely because Liesel was, and still is, scared to death of these people. The names of her family members stapled to her dog...what might they do to her sister or her mother?"

Or her daughter, if she has one, Klaryssa thinks to herself. The prospect of anyone ever presenting such a threat to Yeva sends a wave of revulsion coiling through her gut.

"I'm sure Liesel feared for all of them, as was only natural for her to do. Any one of them could have been the next victim," Marta goes on. "She was probably just glad she escaped with her dog still alive, not to mention being alive herself."

"How can you go out there every day?" Klaryssa asks, nervously tapping the knuckles of both hands on the deck railing. "I can't believe I'm hearing this."

"Like I said, m-o-n-e-y," Marta spells out slowly, lighting her cigarette. "I'll get back to school by early next year, maybe even this fall, if I get lucky. This hassle that's following my parents, it'll blow over. Things like this happen over there; you know that. This school where my mother and father teach, it's top-shelf, and it caters to foreigners living in Moldova. I got to attend the school at no cost, since they both have spent their entire careers there. There are a lot of Yank students, which is probably why I don't speak with an accent, in case you were wondering. As far as Matthias and Stephan Huber go, I'm counting the days. I won't be out there much longer.

"And this drone you've got in the cottage," Marta continues, watching trails of wind-blown sand snake between the dunes, "what exactly does it look like? And has it shown you anything besides me trying to sing?"

"It looks like, if you can believe it, a real flying grasshopper," Klaryssa says, resisting the temptation to remark on Marta's beautiful singing voice. "Just like one you might see on a stroll through the park or wherever. So far, it's shown us very little, except for Matthias spending a lot of time in one of the downstairs rooms, always with the door shut. Zorn has tried to get the insect into that room, but there's never enough time before the door slams. Matthias seems to keep the room locked whenever he leaves, which we all find a little strange. The drone *did* pick up an image of the hollowed-out book where Matthias keeps the key hidden. The book sits sideways on one of the shelves. So far, that's all we've got."

"Well, that's more than I know," Marta says. "Where he keeps the key hidden, that is. Matthias is a proper clean freak, but he won't even allow me to go into that room to tidy up. It's totally off limits."

Klaryssa nods without saying anything.

"Then we'll just have to get you in there to find out what Matthias has been up to all these years," Marta continues, blowing out another trail of smoke rings. "Should be no problem."

Klaryssa lets out a nervous laugh, still saying nothing. Marta looks over at her, pulling in another deep drag of her cigarette, the setting sun's reflection making her eyes glint an even lighter shade of blue.

"You can't possibly be serious," Klaryssa says, her eyes now meeting Marta's gaze. "It would be easier breaking into a bank vault, and Zorn's drone has identified cameras pointed directly at that locked door. Besides, we've already established that I'm the world's worst undercover operator."

"One," Marta says, holding up her index finger. "There's exactly one camera fixed on that doorway. He has a couple of mounted cameras on the side of the house, but there's only one indoors. Matthias doesn't even know that *I* know about it. He thinks I'm this lost little child without a brain, that asshole. Nah, we'll get you in there, and I have a clever little friend of my own who'll help us out."

"Who?" Klaryssa asks with a tight knit in the middle of her forehead.

"Grommet," Marta answers, a slight grin appearing across her face.

"Grommet?" Klaryssa asks, looking even more confused. "Who on earth is Grommet?"

"Truth be told, he prefers the sky to the earth," Marta says, still grinning. "And he'll be lending a wing, not a hand. Grommet is Huber's bird, an African grey. He's the one member of that family that's actually pleasant company, and I know he can help us get into that room."

"If you say so," Klaryssa says with a sigh, looking down and shaking her head. "Good Lord, what've I gotten you into?"

Both Klaryssa and Marta are distracted by a double-v-shaped flock of cormorants passing overhead. One pair of the birds veers off and lands on a high branch of a nearby pitch pine tree, pecking at each other with high-pitched squawks.

"Like your family, mine lived under the thumb of the Soviets, the Germans, and then the Soviets a second time," Marta says through a cloud of exhaled smoke, now speaking in her native Gagauz. "And if that were not bad enough, we endured the oppression of the Romanians, just as you and all of Ukraine did under the Poles. Despotic and brutal and evil. You and I can't change that history. No one can. But my world is the here and now, and I can't turn a blind eye to what you say has been going on for a very long time. Not to mention ignoring what I know, which is almost as bad as what I suspect.

"That locked room has got to be the nerve center of whatever Matthias and his family have been up to out here all these years," Marta says, now using her hand to make a broad sweep across the landscape in front of them. "If you want my help, you've got it. Besides, how can I say no to someone who's been hanging out with some dude named Zorn? You must be on the level, because if you weren't, you would have made up a more believable name than that."

"This would all be a dead end without you," Klaryssa says, also speaking in Gagauz. "I appreciate this more than you can know. I only wish I had walked up to you sooner and just been straight about all *this*."

Marta and Klaryssa walk down off the viewing deck. When they reach the parking lot, the only vehicle left besides Marta's moped and Klaryssa's Toyota sedan is a banged-up VW Beetle with two surfboards strapped to the roof. To the west, the sky above Cape Cod Bay is alive with brilliant fronds of red and orange, with the faintest wispy threads of cloud cover visible in the foreground. The water's surface is churning fast in

316

the stiff evening breeze, the last remnants of fading yellow streaks of sunlight extending from the bay's shoreline out to the horizon.

"Let's meet for some coffee tomorrow, 7:00 AM, the Post Office," Marta says, fastening on her helmet. "We'll take it on from there. It'll work; you'll see."

"I'll be there," Klaryssa says, wondering if she had actually agreed to solicit help from an African parrot, and if that was any crazier than relying on information sent from a remote-controlled metallic grasshopper.

Halfway down the winding road that leads away from Race Point, Klaryssa pulls her car over to the side of the road when she sees Marta flashing the headlight of her moped. Marta knocks on the driver's side window and flips up the shield of her helmet.

"Have to admit, there was something nagging at me from the minute I first saw you," Marta says after Klaryssa rolls down her window. "But now I know what it is. You were the girl running in the marathon that day, the one at the finish line, right? That was you, wasn't it?"

In an instant, Klaryssa feels her chest heave. The same force that has awakened her in the middle of the night a hundred times is pulling her away, spread eagle, as if there is a cable wired to her sternum, passing through her spine and moving her upward at infinite speed. As with her recurring nightmare, there is no blood, and she feels no pain. There is total silence, and, around her, nothing else is moving. All she sees is what's left behind, the world that she will never see again. All she sees is her Yeva, alone in a shrouded corner, her stark white hand reaching for her mother, frozen in time.

After letting a long moment pass, Klaryssa nods slightly.

"That man, the one whose life you saved. Did you ever hear from him? Did he ever contact you, to thank you for what you did?"

"He sent me a letter," Klaryssa says, her eyes half closed. "A very kind, thoughtful letter."

"So you never saw him again?"

"No, no, I haven't. Not yet, anyway," Klaryssa continues, shaking her head, now staring into the distance. "Maybe...maybe someday."

"*Someday*. Well, may someday get here someday," Marta says, flipping down the shield of her helmet. "You know, I *knew* that was you right from the start. And those lame getups you had on, I guess they were even lamer than I thought. Truth is, there's just no disguising you."

Chapter 22
Uco Valley, Argentina
Present Day

One by one, Luis Soto's fellow wine aficionados gasp at the breathtaking view of the grandest of all Andean peaks.

Señor Soto's annual wine-tasting gala is an affair unlike any other in the Mendoza Province. An invitation to attend is coveted by every vintner, politician, business mogul, movie starlet, and wannabe socialite in central Argentina. Soto's winery sprawls out over more than 3500 hectares, and, at an elevation of 900-meters, the air is as dry and cool as any of the guests might expect on an April afternoon. What is unexpected, to the delight of all of the invited guests, is the completely cloudless sky to the north, and from the piazza on the top floor of Soto's newly renovated granite-facade mansion, the view of Mount Aconcagua's broad snow-covered peak is dazzling. At nearly

7,000 meters above sea level, Aconcagua is the highest peak anywhere in the Western or Southern hemispheres. As guests sample the exceptional vintages from the oak casks stored in Soto's vast cellars, they swirl their crystal wine glasses and toast the sacred peak known to the indigenous Quechua people as the "Sentinel of Stone."

Once again, as if Mother Nature herself was at his beck and call, Luis Soto has outdone himself.

Amongst winemakers throughout all of Latin America, it is common knowledge that the Soto winery is one of the oldest and finest anywhere in Argentina. What is not common knowledge—what is, in fact, unknown to anyone beyond Luis and his immediate family—is that Luis's father, Bautista Soto, was a member of the Nazi intelligentsia, a man whose birth name was Royce Schreiber.

But Herr Schreiber, while a fanatically loyal member of the Nazi elite, saw the winds of defeat approaching long before any of the other leaders within Hitler's inner circle. To voice so much as a single word of his misgivings about the future of the Third Reich would have been seen as an act of ultimate treason, and the gallows that awaited all traitors would surely be his next and final stop.

Instead, he plotted and prepared, proceeding so quietly and thoroughly that no other member of the Hitler hierarchy noticed that pallets of bullion and chest-loads of flawless diamonds, all looted from the conquered nations of Western Europe, were being shipped to banks in Uruguay, Chile, Paraguay, and Argentina.

Royce Schreiber was a man of vision and guile, building a war chest of wealth across the Atlantic that he intended to be used to forge a greater, all-powerful Reich—a Reich born from the genius of Hitler himself, the divinely decreed leader who would eventually sacrifice his life in the name of a sacred cause that would never die.

In 1944, Herr Schreiber fled Nazi Germany by way of an escape route originally intended for European Catholics seeking asylum in large metropolitan areas throughout South America. Soon, this exit pathway, known as the Spanish Ratline, became so corrupted that it provided an escape route for not only Herr Royce Schreiber but also for an untold number of other Nazi luminaries, such as the overlords of concentration camps in Treblinka and Sobibor.

Schreiber's flight from his war-torn native land was facilitated by a little-known Nazi sympathizer named Felipe Soto, a vintner and wealthy landowner in northern Argentina who provided the falsified documents necessary for Schreiber's unimpeded passage across the Atlantic via the port of Barcelona, Spain. Felipe Soto shared Schreiber's belief that fascist rule in Germany faced an inevitable and humiliating military and political defeat and decided that he would further the righteous cause of the Third Reich by secreting Schreiber, along with his massive financial resources, in his Mendoza estate. Overnight, Herr Royce Schreiber became Señor Bautista Soto, the long-lost bohemian who had returned home to assist his aging cousin Felipe in overseeing operations at the Soto Winery.

Uco Valley's climate is picturesque: over 250 days of brilliant sunshine, year in, year out, along with cold, dry nights and the pristine air of the Andes. Such a climate allows for the production of robust, full-bodied wines with distinctive floral aromas. The Soto Winery vineyards originally produced the traditional pinked-skinned Cereza and Criolla grapes, but, with time, the inky, thin-skinned Malbec grape rendered an exceptional line of rich, complex red wines that acclaimed sommeliers introduced into every world market.

323

In the years following his arrival at Felipe's Mendoza estate, Bautista spent his days in the vineyards and his nights forging the documents necessary to bring other Nazi war criminals to anonymous refuge in northern and central Argentina. Every fugitive Felipe chose to harbor was a man of wealth—wealthy in either the knowledge of the whereabouts of Nazi plunder, or wealthy in Nazi plunder itself. Former Nazi dignitaries were installed as bank executives, lawyers, university professors, building contractors, wine merchants, and, ultimately, civic and regional government officials.

Whereas Bautista worked in the shadows, Felipe, with his boyish good looks, iron grip handshake, and infectious smile, was, for years, the face of the Soto family's enterprise.

However, several years after Bautista's arrival, Felipe's vitality began to wane. The elder Soto showed signs of advancing heart disease and mental deterioration. When Felipe fell into a coma and died on a hot January morning, Bautista arranged for a grand funeral procession through the rain-soaked streets of Mendoza.

Bautista fought back tears as he eulogized his cousin Felipe, all the while marveling to himself at how simple and tidy it was to expedite your relative's slow demise by adding a dash of arsenic to his nightly glass of Cabernet Sauvignon. Mendoza's recently appointed coroner, who several years earlier had been performing medical experiments on prisoners at the Dachau concentration camp, certified Felipe's death as "secondary to complications caused by cardiovascular and cerebrovascular compromise."

Luis was Bautista's only child, and, after his father's death at the age of 90 due to natural causes, Luis took complete control of both the Soto estate and his late father's vast fortune. By using any number of South American banks as conduits, Luis and other descendants of Third Reich fugitives laundered untold hundreds of million of dollars in looted gold bullion in order to add pieces to their already spectacular art collections. With access to the volumes of files his father had pilfered from the every European country conquered by Nazi Germany, Luis had a database of the location of priceless artworks in both private and publicly held collections throughout Europe and the Americas.

As did his father before him, Luis relied on the most capable and professional of thieves to furnish an inventory of unique and otherwise unobtainable pieces, and the millions he paid through offshore banks would forever finance the righteous and divinely willed cause of the Third Reich. Soto's millions would continue to funnel into the United States via the trafficking of stolen antiquities, all paid for with gold bullion and currency stolen during the Second World War, and all in support of white supremacy and the alt-right propaganda that Matthias Huber and his legion of followers cultivate throughout the free world. The Thousand-Year Reich was only in its infancy, and under the charge of its de facto leaders, Matthias Huber and Luis Soto, the Reich would flourish and grow throughout the Western Hemisphere.

But Luis Soto does not live under the single-minded philosophy that inspired and directed his father Bautista's every move. Luis's penchant for living in splendor, forever pushing beyond the bounds of simple excess, has become more evident with each passing year.

Every square foot of the 50-room granite monstrosity he calls home has been thoroughly renovated, all completed under the direction of architects, masons, and master artisans that Luis flew in from Eastern Europe and the Middle East. Through the years, Luis has purchased several thousand more hectares of land throughout the Uco Valley, paying top dollar for property that has yet to produce any of the exquisite Malbec grapes used in the production of wines that would be exported to high-end markets.

Luis, while remaining land and property rich, has, in recent years, become debt-ridden and increasingly cash poor, thanks to a series of wanton, ill-timed, and ill-conceived investments. To help pay off his debtors, Luis spends at least two weekends every month in his luxury penthouse in the resort town of Posadas, seeking to restore some of his lost fortune at any number of gaming tables, bringing a small retinue of sculpted coeds with him each and every time as a measure of good luck.

The cost of his rooftop suite pales in comparison to what Luis shells out each month for the recreational elixirs his harem craves, which is a pittance in relation to what Luis leaves behind on the dice tables most nights.

But on this glorious April afternoon in the shadow of the Andes, Luis is a man without care or angst. Like Luis, many of his guests are descendants of last century's Nazi elite, each sworn to silently carry on in the name of the cause that took the lives of their parents and grandparents.

These are the monied elite—importers, exporters, investment bankers, stockbrokers, politicians—all forever indebted to Luis's father Bautista, a man whose foresight and perseverance saved their family fortunes, and their venerable Reich, from certain ruin.

Luis's exalted guests walk through the halls of La Villa Soto, swirling their Louis XV crystal wineglasses and commenting here and there on the vintage's subtle, spicy bouquet, with Luis's brigade of tall, white-gloved manservants handing out samples of other choice vintages as often as requested.

"Señor Soto," Luis's chief butler whispers. Luis gladly turns away from a guest that he invariably finds to bc a pompous bore. "There is a call from the United States, and, while not urgent, a call back is requested at your earliest convenience."

"Gracias, Marten," Luis says, feigning annoyance and raising apologetic palms. "My friend, you must excuse me. Simply terrible timing, I'm afraid. This just cannot wait. I was so enjoying the chance to chat and catch up."

Fucking idiot, Luis thinks to himself as he gracefully backs away from the party and opens the note that Marten just handed him.

Señor Huber. He awaits your call.

Luis is anything but surprised.

"I'll take this downstairs," Luis says to Marten, walking toward his cavernous, two-story private exhibit hall. "And there will be no interruptions."

While unlocking the door to what is essentially his family's private museum, Luis is surprised from behind by a hand that reaches between his legs and offers a squeeze that is just robust enough to elicit a quick, shuddering breath.

"Luis, running *away*?" the voice purrs, Luis now feeling the gentlest clench of teeth against his ear lobe, his assailant's welcome grip showing no signs of yielding. "Would you leave me out here with no one to *play* with, hmmm?"

"Just a brief call, love," Luis says, his voice a resonant shrill as the rapacious hand clasps with a little more conviction. "Business to tend to, you know."

"Business?" she says slowly, almost phonetically. "Seems I found the business right about... *here*."

Another somewhat less than polite handclasp, followed by a slightly more audible yelp.

"Ahhh, I was right, wasn't I?" she whispers, her wine-soaked breath steamy and lustful. "I'd say it's time for you and me to, *well*, you know. But what it's really time for is you and me and…and your choice of who you'd like to have join us."

"Bring them all. The grotto, in two hours, when these stuffed shirts are all gone," Luis says with his face still pressed against the massive double doors, hastily arranging for another evening tryst in the Roman bath he had just installed below his bedroom, a private pleasure chamber where the glow from hanging torch lights reflect against the Italian porcelain floor tiles, frescoed walls, and rows of Corinthian columns.

"You know where I'm talking about," Luis says with a halting groan. She grumbles *mmmm hmmm*, and he feels the tip of her tongue trace out figures of eight against the back of his neck.

Her grip loosens, and she is gone.

Having no idea which girl had just appeared out of the darkness to clamp a hand around his manhood, Luis awkwardly unlocks the six-inch-thick solid ebony doors and flicks on the lights to what his family has for years informally referred to as the "salon." Luis locks the door behind him and walks past the rolling ladders that line every wall of the salon, each of the ladders allowing access to 15-foot-high shelves weighed down by centuries-old maps, historical texts, native pre-Columbian artifacts, and various other archeological relics that have never sparked even a flicker of Luis's interest.

At the far side of the massive room stands an Old West saloon-style bar, and, under the marble countertop, Luis finds the hidden switch that rotates an eight-foot-tall free-standing back-bar mirror 90-degrees, revealing a wrought-iron circular staircase that descends below ground level. Ceiling lights illuminate the staircase, and when Luis reaches the bottom of the stairway, the mirror swivels back into its normal position and the overhead lights automatically switch off, leaving Luis in complete darkness.

After a brief moment, glass-covered electric candle lights are activated on either side of the room, giving life to the swirls of magenta, waves of deep cyan, and fiery flares of amethyst that streak across the solid stone walls that were hewn from blocks of rare Brazilian granite.

Luis sinks into the leather chair in the middle of the room, pouring himself a glass of his finest Cabernet Sauvignon-Malbec from a bottle stored in his small wine locker. As the glow from the candle lights slowly intensifies, Luis beholds a grandeur surpassing any vista of the Andes, a sight of incomparable beauty and refinement, a sight even beyond the delusional dreams of many of history's other great men of power.

On the wall to his left, portraits by Raphael and Rubens hang, and to his right hang two Old Testament scenes by Titian, a pastel by Degas, and cityscapes by Pissarro and Canaletto. These immortal, incomparable masterpieces are the antidote to the ignominious defeat suffered by his family at he hands of the Allies years earlier, and these and other priceless antiquities shall forever be the lifeblood of the Reich that will never die.

"Señor Soto, how good of you to return my call with such dispatch," Matthias Huber says on the other end of the phone, while Luis stares at Raphael's *Portrait of a Young Man*. "I realize that this is a day of fine celebration for you, so I will not tarry and deprive your guests of their host's august presence. And I so appreciate your invitation to attend today's festivities, but travel right now for me would not be possible. I take it your fête is well attended."

"Very much so," Luis responds between sips of his favorite vintage. "Three of the provincial governors that we have installed in recent years are in attendance. In fact, one of them is presently enjoying the unclothed company of a Russian model. But, I saw no need to share the young lady's work schedule with the churchgoing leader of our province. Suffice it to say that the batteries in the ceiling video cameras where the two of them are lounging last for several hours, so we'll have an ample supply of footage should it ever prove necessary. Always employ batteries in devices like these, Matthias, as power outages can occur at the most inopportune time. But enough of that. Please, my friend, I believe it was you who was looking for me."

"Indeed," Matthias says firmly, his voice on speakerphone and echoing off the walls of Luis's subbasement art chamber. "As your thirst for diamonds seems unquenchable, we have secured a line of beyond perfect stones, and we both know exactly which diamonds I am talking about. They can all be in your hands once the transfer is completed through the usual channels."

Luis Soto has spent his entire adult life jousting and haggling with Matthias Huber. Their dialogue invariably concerns the purchase of any number of antiquities, just as Luis's father Bautista had, for years, negotiated similar purchases with both Matthias's father and grandfather. Luis knows that this diamond purchase is nothing more than Matthias's opening salvo, getting him to buy a sack of stolen rocks before Matthias starts playing hardball over transactions with a more considerable price tag. In over 30 years of dealings and conversations and posturing, Luis knows every trick Matthias has in his bag of negotiation ploys.

"I believe, if my memory serves me correctly, that, along with the diamonds, you will at last deliver a certain Degas sketch," Luis inquires, hinting at Huber's continued reticence in giving up any of the items stolen from the Gardner museum. "You may see this as a minor piece in the grand scheme, but it is not minor to me. I agreed upon the price you quoted me without even a thought of a counteroffer, and that after you turned your backside to me when it came to a certain flagpole ornament I had my eye on for all those years."

Matthias knows that despite Soto's breezy tone, inside, the man is seething. Soto had not merely had his eye on the Napoleonic Imperial Eagle finial. He had coveted the iconic Third Reich emblem since the day he learned that Matthias had it in his possession. For years, Matthias had thrown offhanded taunts in Soto's direction concerning this particular piece, asking on more than one occasion if Soto would "trade his right testicle" for the statue. "Or perhaps, instead, it is the left one you'd swap for that golden bird," Huber would add, a knife-twisting barb that stoked Soto's silent but boiling internal rage. In the end, Huber sold the statue to another party, one of the many other customers he courts throughout Latin America, Russia, and the Middle East. He didn't choose to sell the piece to one of Soto's competitors because they offered more money. He did it for another reason entirely.

He did it because he could.

"You are most correct, my friend," Matthias says, grinning to himself. "And I believe you will also recall that $3.7 million was the hammer price we agreed upon for both the spectacular stones and the Degas charcoal. This arrangement still meets with your approval?"

"Done," Luis says without blinking, knowing he has access to this level of capital, thanks to the same Colombian bankers who hold all of his chits. "Let's finalize a rendezvous date, and my envoy can connect with Stephan in the usual manner. You'll see the transfer go through simultaneously."

"Let us not linger on this," Matthias says, sipping a fresh brew of Tibetan tea that Marta brought to him just minutes earlier. "I'm sure that battleship of a yacht of yours is wandering about somewhere in the Atlantic. And I trust there will be no surprise guests on your boat launch this time, Herr Soto. That young man your crew had on board recently, bubbling like a child lined up at a Disney thrill ride—he was all enthusiasm, wasn't he? Yes. Not to mention all ears and eyes. Careless of you, Soto. Quite careless."

"Like you, my friend, our operation has many moving parts," Soto says as evenly as he can, Huber's scolding tone causing yet another surge of anger to build behind his eyes. "I took my men to the woodshed for their error, and neither you nor Stephan will see a freeloader on board again. As you know, there was no breach of secrecy, Herr Huber, as Stephan dispatched of the problem with the aid of a previously unopened bottle of fine Champagne.

"I told the lad's parents of their boy's demise myself, and how the chemicals we found in their son's quarters shocked us all, relating to them how such illicit drugs are known to cause florid hallucinations. The boy's pursuit of some distant apparition sent him straight overboard, a harrowing scene witnessed by one of our shipmates. By the time we turned the yacht around, he was gone, swallowed into the depths but blessedly free of all pain. There was no saving him, I said, barely able to contain my grief.

"The scourge of drugs amongst our young… I can only hope the boy's mother and father can overcome the mountain of guilt they are now living with. And, I assure you, there is no chance of a similar tragedy in the future."

"Excellent," Matthias says, the buoyancy in his voice fooling neither of them. "Stephan will send you potential dates and locations, with all coordinates sent via the usual channels. I need not remind either of us of the need to consummate this transaction in a timely manner. We have covert actions planned in a dozen or so states over the next few weeks, all aimed at this inequality cause and other precepts that the far-left have been fetishizing lately. You hold the purse strings, Herr Soto, and I know you will not disappoint the legion of soldiers we have up here north of the border."

"Does that legion include the bumbling idiots who were foiled in their clumsy attempt to splatter blood across that Midwest mosque?" Luis says with a renewed edge to his voice, referring to the three terrorists whose plot to blow up a Kansas mosque and incite a religious war was thwarted by the FBI. "Can't help but wonder if such misadventures are becoming emblematic of your impotence in altering the course of American politics, not to mention any attempt to undermine your perverse social structure."

Despite sensing his blood beginning to churn, Matthias remains calm. He knows that this is one of Luis's patented attempts to put him on the defensive while he gains leverage, trying vainly to secure the upper hand in their dealings. "A mere aberration, my friend," Matthias says with a hint of a snicker in his voice. "You overlook our penetration into the core of hundreds of groups throughout the free world, a world that you and I seek to make free of every noxious, alien element that pollutes our shores.   "These groups have charters, officers, bank accounts, meetings, indoctrination ceremonies, and regular retreats with enough fire to light up the sky like one of your Andean volcanoes. We have trained and paid the leaders of these organizations because of your bankroll and the bankroll of all those many deep pockets with generations of roots in our cause."

"Our paddles must move through the water in synch, Herr Huber," Luis says without missing a beat, nodding in agreement despite no one else being in the room. "We are speaking the same language here, but surely you know the source of the angst that courses through my veins every time I hear your voice."

Luis then stands and walks toward the Raphael and Rubens portraits, staring at the empty wall space that Luis has intentionally left below these two masterpieces. "You see, my artist friends here have been alone all these years, crying out for their companions, the ones whose arrival they have long anticipated. Do you hear their yearnings, Herr Huber? Surely, you know of their pain as they await the arrival of Rembrandt and Vermeer, the two missing masters who, by all rights, belong here with us in our small chamber. All these years, all these many, many years, and my gallery walls yet suffer, day and night, in abject loneliness."

339

Matthias lets the silence mount before responding, allowing Luis time to lament over having not yet taken possession of Rembrandt's *Storm on the Sea of Galilee* and Vermeer's *The Concert*, the two most treasured artworks in the collection of pieces looted from Boston's Gardner Museum in 1990.

Matthias knows that in Luis's estimation, those two masterpieces were to be his own enduring mark on the Soto family gallery—his culminating, defining stamp on this transcendent viewing chamber forged by the iron will and resilience of Luis's father Bautista in the wake of the humiliation of the Second World War. But, above all else, Matthias Huber is a man of business, and his business is the prosecution of the precepts of the Thousand-Year Reich. This ultimate charge requires a treasury that, like the coffers of any great and righteous cause, needs a perpetual source of replenishment. Nazi wealth, like Nazi thirst for history's greatest works of art, is centered in South America. Matthias Huber holds the key to the repository of priceless artwork that must fuel the Reich's activities throughout the free world. To see this through, Matthias will only sell these unique pieces at a price that reflects a significant proportion of their true value.

But, what Matthias finds most remarkable of all, to his utter amazement, is the sheer number of massive down payments Luis Soto has made on two paintings that he has never once seen. How does he know I even *have* these two masterpieces, Matthias thinks to himself whenever the two of them converse. Presupposing that I have the two paintings you so covet just because I sold that Napoleonic finial to your rival?

"Come now, Soto, this is not the hour to thrum your violin over a yet-to-be-completed transaction," Matthias says, managing a conciliatory tone that he knows will not be well-received. "We both know that the payments you've made to date are front money on the two pieces you seek, and it is you alone who will determine the date of consummation. Besides, if my sources are correct, you've been preoccupied with the acquisition of an entire valley of arable land for your vineyards. Still chasing down this dream of cornering the Malbec market, are we?"

"A mere slower-than-expected expansion," Luis says quickly, hoping that Matthias knows nothing of the land purchase loans he has secured through his less-than-reputable connections in Cali, Colombia. "And I *do* understand the virtue of patience; you need not lecture me on that point. Now, if you will excuse me, Herr Huber, I am beginning to sense my guests becoming restless. May the next Soto Estate wine tasting find you here with a stemmed glass in your hand."

With that, Luis disconnects the phone line and leans back in his leather chair, swirling his crystal wine glass and pulling in the rich bouquet of his favorite vintage. After no more than a moment or two, Luis activates a control switch that dims the candle lights while simultaneously lowering a solid oak display case across the front wall of the viewing room.

A few seconds later, the large wooden panels on either side of the display case begin to open as the room lights extinguish completely, sending the chamber into total darkness. This is a moment of pure delight in Luis's life that is like no other—a prescient moment of ecstasy that no other man could ever or will ever know. With illumination from a single light mounted overhead, Luis is in the presence of unfathomable beauty that was, for centuries, hidden from the rest of the world, a work of singular power and incalculable importance that will forever be the private possession of one and only one family.

Luis sees the warriors in Michelangelo's *Battle of Cascina* caught in the very instant of onslaught by their enemy, soldiers who, a moment earlier, were immersed in the Arno River's cool waters but who now face the glinting iron tips of the lances thrown from the hands of their assailants. This is the world's greatest unknown treasure, a work of genius that was thought to have been destroyed during the demolition of the Palazzo Vecchio in Florence over five centuries earlier.

Luis's father, Bautista, born Herr Royce Schreiber, never revealed this epic masterpiece to anyone other than his only child. Luis, however, out of necessity, has given others audience to this singular treasure, for his Colombian creditors have demanded they see Luis's means of collateral for themselves. Luis has used his entire art collection to secure loans from his financial backers in Cali, his art serving as the wellspring that endows the cause of the modern Reich. More often than not, these same creditors advance Luis only a penny or two on the dollar market value of the masterpieces he possesses, but having revealed Michelangelo's *Battle of Cascina* to the same bankers who hold the long list of his loans, Luis knows that both his leverage and his wealth remain nearly immeasurable.

Luis then looks over at the two large blank squares on the adjoining wall, the vacancies that scream of all he has yet to accomplish in his life.

"You owe me, Herr Huber." The disdain in Luis's words echoes off the granite walls.

"You owe me."

Chapter 23
Truro, Massachusetts
Present Day

"Nixon hats!" Zorn bellows, reaching into a packaging box and pulling out a Stars and Bars political convention hat and tossing it to Ian like a frisbee. "First you find us the smallest room in this entire fleabag of a dormitory, and then you order up every conceivable Me Decade piece of crap so the place can be cluttered right up to its seven-foot ceiling. In case you forgot, I'm the one stuck in here 24 hours a day keeping watch over that beach house while you're setting up your *Rocking '70s* kiosk out on the promenade.

"You've got enough LPs and 45s in here to sink a battleship," Zorn continues, thumbing through a three-foot-high stack of LPs. "The Bee Gees, Black Sabbath, Deep Purple, Stevie Wonder, Jethro Tull, Kiss…you actually think you can manage to sell some of this shit so I have enough room to work?"

Zorn and Ian are holed up in a crumbling military barracks along the edge of the now abandoned North Truro Air Force Station, ostensibly to participate in the 1970s music festival that is scheduled to take place on the property over the weekend. What they are actually doing is continuing their surveillance operation on the Huber family, whose home is located a few hundred yards to the north of the dilapidated quarters where Ian rented two 12 foot by 12 foot rooms. And although Drago's spying eye has managed to pick up some intelligence, such as the location of the hidden key to Matthias's office and several of the passwords Matthias uses on his computer, Zorn has yet to unearth anything in the way of evidence implicating the Huber family in criminal activity.

"You hear that?" Zorn asks, jabbing his thumb in the direction of the blaring music coming from the main outdoor courtyard. "Every last damn track from Queen's *A Night at the Opera*. You think they were able to sing "You're My Best Friend" any better when it was first released, when they were probably all buzzed on better hooch than they can get nowadays? You know, there's a good reason why some periods in history are lost and forgotten. I've been listening to this clamor all day, and I'm here to tell you, each rendition is more off-key than the one before it. They should all be praying that no one is recording any of this noise."

"C'mon, Zorny, they're all just having a little fun, waxing nostalgic about the days of yore," Ian says, opening a shipping box that is stuffed with vinyl jumpsuits, studded belts, lava lamps, and a rainbow assortment of knee-high socks. "Besides, some of this stuff is bona fide collectible memorabilia. You just wait and see, bucko. We'll be making some coin out there in the yard over the next couple of days."

"Let's get a couple of things straight, if I may," Zorn says, waving two fingers at Ian. "First off, there is no *we* when it comes to having a stake in this dog-and-pony fiasco. This is your shindig, remember? And second, we are here for *other* reasons, so don't start veering off course just because you're in the same playpen as girls running around in undersized space dresses with daisies in their hair."

"You saw them too, eh?" Ian says, arching one eyebrow. "Did you see the little redhead with the curls, the one who looked like she just got back

348

from visiting her family on Pluto? You know, they don't look old enough to partake in a '70s—"

"Whoa, stop," Zorn says, putting up a hand and switching Drago's camera feed to a larger laptop screen and turning up the drone's audio input volume. "It's Marta, and she's on the move."

On the laptop screen, Ian and Zorn see Marta moving about Huber's small living room, tidying up and wiping down tabletops and bookshelves. "What's this girl's plan?" Ian asks with more than a hint of doubt in his voice.

"You heard the same as me when Klaryssa got back here last night," Zorn answers as he fiddles with the video image. "Marta says she knows of a way to get Klaryssa into Matthias's private office unscathed. We've just gotta follow Marta's lead here."

"What's the deal with that outfit she's got on?" Ian asks, pointing at Marta's skintight jeans and low-cut knit shirt. "Every other day this week she wore one of those plain, matronly house dresses. She's certainly upped her game today. I mean, it's not very '70s, but I still approve."

"Maybe it's casual Friday out at Ocean Bluff," Zorn says, giving Ian a sour look. "Try to stay on task for once, will you, please? I mean, how

349

the hell is this Marta chick, who neither of us know and Klaryssa met *yesterday*, going to get us access into that office? Supposedly, Matthias only leaves for an hour, max, every morning. We don't even know where he is right now, or exactly when he'll be back."

"Sure we do," Ian says with a slow nod. "Klaryssa mentioned that Marta would walk into the living room as soon as Matthias pulls out of the driveway, so it's safe to assume that the old man is out of the house. Marta also told Klaryssa that Matthias is fanatically punctual, and he'll be back in an hour, no more, no less."

"Well that's something, at least," Zorn says approvingly, still staring at the screen. "Marta's on the stepladder now, right next to the camera that Matthias has planted on the top bookshelf. From what Marta told Klaryssa, that is the only camera hidden anywhere inside the house. She cleans the place day and night, so I guess it would be hard to sneak anything past her. I hope she's right."

"Well, it certainly looks to me like she knows what she's doing," Ian says, moving closer to the screen. "Clever girl," he says with a wink and a nod. "Very clever girl."

On the computer screen, Marta is standing on the stepladder and, by all appearances, is cleaning the top bookshelf, her plunging neckline only inches from Matthias's camera. When she is certain that her cleavage is the only image being picked up by the camera, Marta makes a slight waving motion with two fingers, and an instant later, Drago's eye picks up Klaryssa coming into the living room from the adjoining sunporch. Klaryssa locates the office door key, which is hidden on a lower bookshelf. Within a matter of seconds, she unlocks the door.

Once the door to Matthias's office is closed with Klaryssa inside, Marta moves away from the camera and wipes down the next row of bookshelves.

"If either Matthias or Stephan are tuned in, they just got themselves an eyeful," Ian says through a wide grin. "That certainly explains today's choice of apparel."

"OK, Klaryssa is in that office without Matthias being any wiser," Zorn says, using Drago's eye to scan all corners of the room. "But how's she going to get back out? She can't go out the window, because we know there is a camera mounted outside along that side of the house. And

Marta certainly can't pull off that busty front end diversion again without raising suspicion."

"I'm not so sure about that, Zorny," Ian says, pointing to the right upper edge of the screen. "Take a look up here."

Zorn shifts Drago's eye back toward the same top bookshelf that houses Matthias's camera, zeroing in on an irregular, yellow-colored clump sitting only inches from the camera lens.

"What on *earth* is that?" Zorn asks, his face twisted. "Looks like Marta might have missed something when she was cleaning a minute ago."

"She didn't miss a thing," Ian says, again moving closer to the screen. "She put it there. Those birds absolutely love tropical fruit."

***

With the door closed behind her, Klaryssa makes a quick survey of Matthias's office, unable to imagine how any enterprise, criminal or otherwise, could operate out of such a simple, spare space. The desk Matthias uses is neither any larger, nor any more glamorous, than that used by a junior high student in an average public school classroom. The desktop itself is completely clear of any of the items one expects to find in a personal workspace: no writing utensils, no paper, no computer terminal, no telephone. The office floor is covered with a shag carpet that appears to be every day of 30 years old, with a trail of wear marks between the doorway and the desk. Paint is peeling from the center of the water-stained ceiling as well as from the upper corners of all four walls. If not for the show-stopping oceanfront vista through the two cracked double-hung windows that face to the east, Klaryssa might consider this the most forlorn space she has ever happened upon.

Since Matthias apparently considers his office impenetrable, there are no locks protecting any of the desk drawers or either of the file cabinets standing along an adjacent wall. This is fortunate, because the only tool Klaryssa planned on using is her cell phone camera, as Marta's life would be imperiled should Matthias see any evidence of a break-in while Marta was minding the house. Klaryssa starts by inspecting the top drawer of one of the file cabinets, pulling out a stack of files and noticing that none of the folders have any label or header.

Klaryssa knows that she does not have nearly enough time to inspect every last record that

Matthias has stashed away in his office, so she thumbs through the first two files quickly. All they contain are stacks of folded up, partially torn floor plans, and the dust on the file jackets alone indicates that these papers have gone untouched for many years. When Klaryssa opens the third folder, however, the printed text at the top of each of the pages jumps out at her as if the words are on fire.

In the left-hand column are the addresses of public buildings, museums, libraries, and private homes in nearly every country occupied by the Nazis between 1939 and 1943. The conquered nations are listed, more or less, chronologically: Czechoslovakia, Poland, the Netherlands, Belgium, Luxembourg, France, Denmark, Yugoslavia, Norway, and finally, Italy.

The middle column lists details of the Nazi's plunder from each of the sites in each of the annexed nations. This includes gold bullion, silver, currency, ceramics, books, statuary, religious treasures, and other precious artworks, including a virtual catalog of centuries-old paintings.

The last column lists the destination of each and every looted antiquity, with dated footnotes and annotations added as new information became available concerning the final location of each of the stolen pieces. Klaryssa is fluent in German, and, although she is tempted to read some of the details, she knows that can wait until later. She takes photographs of the evidence as fast as she can, then replaces the files just as she found them.

Klaryssa receives a text message from Marta, which reads, simply, "40," indicating the number of minutes she has left to scour Matthias's office. Marta warned Klaryssa that Matthias is a man of obsessive habits and routine, and he would be away from the house for no more than an hour.

"When I say out, get out." That was Marta's one and only directive.

The next two file drawers contain papers on much the same topic, although many of these documents include photographs of the stolen antiquities. Klaryssa lays out row after row of as many of the photos as she can, taking one picture after the next, figuring she can magnify and study each one in more detail when she rejoins Ian and Zorn back at the bunkhouse.

Another text message from Marta: "26." In her head, Klaryssa hears the clock ticking.

The second cabinet contains file after file of what appear to be Nazi war memorabilia, a virtual anthology of war officers and their legions of soldiers fighting to the death in cities and towns across the war-ravaged continent. Klaryssa rifles through the pages, seeing nothing of any apparent value in front of her. The upper-left desk drawer contains paper-clipped stacks of purchase receipts, two expired passports, an assortment of CD- and DVD-burning software, and a pair of power adapters. The drawer below that one contains multiple rolls of undeveloped film, and what appears to be a broken 35mm camera.

"9."

The upper right-hand drawer is filled with neatly arranged pads of writing paper, note pads, and an assortment of felt tip and ballpoint pens. The lower right-hand drawer contains several more overstuffed file folders, and Klaryssa knows that she has nowhere near enough time to fully inspect the documents, and taking any of the originals with her is not an option.

While quickly shuffling through the papers, she sees a clear plastic envelope containing three official-looking memos written by the US Coast Guard and the Department of the Navy, all dated from the 1940s. She takes a photo of each of the memos and then places the file folders back in the desk drawer.

"Grommet, where are you?" Marta calls out, signaling to Klaryssa that Matthias's arrival back home is imminent and her time is up.

"Grommet?" Marta repeats.

On impulse, Klaryssa again opens the lower left desk drawer. She cannot begin to guess what the canisters of undeveloped film might reveal, but taking one or more of the rolls is too big a risk. She again spots the 35mm Nikon, which has a dense, spider-shaped crack running through the camera lens. Why would Matthias keep this apparent piece of junk in an otherwise perfectly tidy office? When Klaryssa pops open the back of the camera, a narrow scroll of yellowing paper falls to the ground. Klaryssa unfolds the paper, eyeing the sequence of initials on the left side and the series of numbers listed along the right-sided margin. While taking a picture of the scroll, she hears, "Grommet! There you are."

***

Zorn and Ian are both sitting motionless, their eyes glued to the computer screen.

"What's he doing?" Ian asks while looking at Grommet, noticing that the bird is perched only inches from Drago and staring intently at the mechanical insect, his head swiveling from side to side. "Marta left the bird's cage open so he would go after the dried fruit up on the top shelf near that camera. Why's he staring back at us?"

"He's not staring at us, shit-for-brains," Zorn says in a strained whisper, beads of sweat beginning to roll off his forehead. "He's staring at his lunch. That grasshopper is a two-million- dollar prototype, and he's about to become that bird's next meal. I can't believe I'm watching this! Fuck me, I'll be executed if I lose that drone."

"Can't you make the grasshopper hiss or spit or sting or something?" Ian asks, his words desperate, watching Grommet begin to peck lightly at Drago's head.

"Sorry, I never programmed the grasshopper to defend itself against an *African parrot*. Where the hell is Marta?"

"Then make him fly," Ian says, making a flapping motion with his hands. "Just get him off that shelf, out of there, anything."

"The bird will just chase him down, and he'll win, that's for damn certain. If he's enough of a predator to be interested in a grasshopper, then he'll react instantaneously to any motion around him," Zorn goes on, covering one eye with his hand as the video feed from the drone's camera begins to break up on the computer screen. "Why doesn't he go after the mango? That bird's going to rip six months of research and development right out of Drago's eye. Look at him man, he's—"

"Grommet, where are you?" Marta calls out, distracting the bird enough to make him move cautiously away from the drone.

"Grommet?" Marta repeats.

"The picture is back. Thank you, God," Zorn says, looking at the computer screen and wiping the sweat from his brow. "Nice time to learn that these birds react to sights more than smells. Klaryssa, get out of that damn office...Matthias is due back any minute."

"Grommet! There you are," Marta says, going after the bird, who is now perched on the top shelf and munching on the dried mango. These words are Marta's signal to Klaryssa that she is in position and that the camera is completely blocked, which gives Klaryssa five or so seconds to exit Matthias's office, replace the hidden key, and leave the house through the sunporch.

"She's out," Ian says, letting out a long breath after watching Klaryssa leave the office and move out onto the sunporch. "I don't know what KD found in there, but at least she's out of that office and is nearly home free. She's wearing her running shoes, so we'll see her back here in no more than ten minutes."

Ian looks over at Zorn, whose face is ghostly pale.

"What's wrong?" Ian asks.

Zorn slowly points to the upper corner of the computer screen, which still clearly shows everything Drago's camera is picking up. There is no sign of Klaryssa, who is somewhere on the sunporch. Grommet is back in his cage, and there is no sign of Marta anywhere. Just outside the porch window, barely visible and standing alone, is Stephan Huber.

"Oh shit...oh *shit*," Ian says, slamming the heel of his hand against his head. "I thought he was gone, off the grid, out on a boat somewhere."

"That would be a negative," Zorn says in a limp voice. "He can't be more than five feet away from Klaryssa. You've got to call the police, and right now."

"The *police*?" Ian asks, now frantically rummaging through a stack of unopened boxes. "Zorny, *she* is the one who just broke into that house! She's the criminal here. She's probably a felon. If we call the police, they'll arrest her and leave Stephan out there, alone, with Marta."

***

Klaryssa is sure Stephan didn't see her.

As soon as she walked out of the living room and onto the sunporch, she saw him, standing outside along the side of the house with his back to her. Stephan was so close that Klaryssa could probably reach out and touch him if the window had been open. But Stephan was facing the Atlantic with his back to Klaryssa. With the ocean surf at high tide and roaring like a passing freight train, Klaryssa hopes to God that Stephan did not hear her close the inside porch door.

But Stephan isn't moving. He's just standing there, completely still, looking off into the distance. Why is he standing frozen in place outside his own doorstep? Does he have a suspicion that something isn't right? Could he have momentarily heard an unfamiliar sound, or seen a flash of movement in the corner of his eye?

Klaryssa crouches under a small sideboard, covering herself as best she can with a tablecloth that drapes halfway down the side of the table. She can no longer see Stephan, who is standing outside the window that is directly above her. But, she can clearly see the door that leads from the sunporch outside onto the patio. There is no question that if Stephan enters through that door, she'll be caught and her fate will be in his hands—hands that she knows are capable of brutal, unbounded violence. Will she be able to scream for Marta? Will she be able to scream at all? Can she possibly get a finger into his eye socket or kick him between the legs? Any such quick hit, improbable as it may be, would at least give her a chance to run for her life.

But what about Marta? Stephan will surely ravage Marta, figuring that she is complicit in whatever was going on inside the house while he and Matthias were away. Klaryssa could use her cell phone to call the police, but what could she possibly tell them if she calls while running away from the house? *She'd* be the one in hot water, and, by the time the police arrested her and actually got around to interviewing Stephan, Marta might already be dead and her body stashed in some distant corner of the Huber property. She could send Ian an urgent text message, but he could never get there in time to help either her or Marta.

Suddenly, Klaryssa smells something sharp and pungent, an unmistakable scent in the waft of smoke that is filtering through a partially open window. She looks up and sees Stephan standing just outside the doorway, taking a deep drag of the joint he's holding, which sends a puff of marijuana exhaust downwind through the porch window. Klaryssa ducks down even lower, holding her breath and biting her lower lip, resisting the overwhelming urge to cough.

Klaryssa hears the latch of the outside porch door rattle, and then she hears the latch release. She then hears the groaning creak of the floor planks as Stephan sets foot onto the sunporch, knowing that, in the next second, she might be hauled up by her hair and pummeled mercilessly. Klaryssa squeezes her eyes shut, and, at the exact moment that she opens her mouth to let out a cough, there is a concussive blast in the sky over the sea cliff. Klaryssa opens her eyes and sees Stephan do an about-face and head back outside. He walks along the path that leads away from the house and toward the cliffside sand dunes, staring straight up toward the clouds, watching the chrysanthemum starbursts of yellow, violet, orange, and purple spread across the sky along the cliff's edge. When Klaryssa hears

363

a succession of faint whistling sounds that are followed by a cacophony of sonic booms, she bolts from the sunporch and runs down the driveway as fast as her legs can carry her, leaving Stephan alone amidst the rolling dunes to get high on Panama Red and delight in the fireworks that are shooting across the sky.

***

"Have you totally lost your mind?" Zorn hollers out, squatting in the corner of the bunk room while Ian sets off another volley of fireworks from the fire escape landing. "You told me you ordered some M-80s and a few Roman candles, not an arsenal to fire at enemy positions on Iwo Jima! Shit, Ian. This whole building could ignite. Look at these walls, they're drier than desert sand. The place is a tinder box!"

"Take a chill pill, will ya? And hand me another shell from that box," Ian says without looking at Zorn, the fire escape's rusted iron frame wobbling a little more with each discharge from the fireworks launcher. "This was my job one summer before you and I met, and if you've got a better idea about how to get Stephan away from KD, I'm all ears."

Among those on site for the 1970s music festival, the unscripted fireworks are met with whooping approval, with many of the revelers waving up to the heavens with one hand while holding onto their libation of choice in the other. A scattering of children and their parents begin to gather around the Cape Cod Lighthouse, cheering at the cannonade of lights arching through the sky.

A couple of teenage girls chase after the glowing sparkles that are cascading over the dunes, stopping at the edge of the sand cliffs to watch the plummeting trails of smoldering ash get swallowed up by the breaking surf.

"Neither of us will have any ears left if you keep this up," Zorn says, carefully picking up one of the fireworks canisters. "And just listen to yourself, asking for a 'shell.' That's exactly what this stuff is, you know. They're explosives...sulfur and charcoal and potassium nitrate and heavy metals. They're bombs that entertain, plain and simple."

"Oh, would you *stop*. I have a permit to use all this," Ian says, loading two successive aerial shells and covering his ears before firing.

"Launched from a rusted-out fire escape that's about to collapse?" Zorn asks, going back to his computer screen. "I don't think so. I guess it's a little late to bring up such details like how the fireworks you're sending off are supposed to be for tomorrow night at the festival, which, if you will recall, is…

"Wait, wait. Ian, stop," Zorn says, interrupting himself and waving his arm. "I don't see him anywhere on the screen."

"See who?" Ian asks, looking over at Zorn while loading another shell, his hand on the firing pin.

"Stephan. Who else would I mean? The Grinch? There's no sign of Stephan anywhere near the sunporch."

Ian stops what he's doing and walks over to take a quick look at Zorn's computer screen. He then grabs a pair of binoculars out of his knapsack.

"I think we pulled it off, Zorny," Ian says, looking in the direction of Huber's house with his binoculars and spotting Stephan staring up into the sky. "As far as I can tell, anyway. The dude is standing out there alone, waiting for more rockets to shoot over his head. And there's no sign of KD anywhere out there. Man alive, I just hope to heavens she found a way out of—"

Klaryssa suddenly bursts through the door, covered in sweat and too out of breath to speak. She eyes both Zorn and Ian, spotting the empty canisters and the still-smoking launcher sitting on the fire escape landing. Klaryssa collapses onto the lower bunk, her chest heaving between spasms of dry coughing.

"You know, ever since I was a little girl," Klaryssa says eventually, still struggling to pull in air, "I just loved fireworks."

Chapter 24
Truro, Massachusetts

In less than a minute Klaryssa is back on her feet, twisting open the bottle of water Ian tosses to her and downing it in a matter of seconds. She then opens the ice chest lying next to her, reaching in with both hands and splashing two handfuls of cold water across her face. After drying herself off, she unlocks her cell phone and hands the phone to Zorn, who proceeds to download all of Klaryssa's photos onto his laptop.

"I took German all through high school, but that was a few too many moons ago," Zorn says to Klaryssa, scanning through the first set of files as the pages appear on his computer screen. "Whatever it is you've got here, which looks to me like a shit load, the task of interpreting and deciphering will have to be all yours."

Klaryssa scrolls through the first set of files that appear on Zorn's laptop screen, studying the images slowly at first, but, after several silent minutes, she races through the images at the rate of one or two every few seconds.

"Whatever I expected to find in there, this is way, way over that mark," Klaryssa says between sputters of hacking cough, Matthias Huber's chronological file flashing before her wide-open eyes. "Just look at what he has here. These records are perfectly organized, first by listing every country annexed by the Germans and then by listing the cities, towns, and addresses where they found anything. According to these records, they stole from just about everywhere—libraries, museums, churches and cathedrals, private homes and country estates, along with just about every government admin building you can name. To nobody's surprise, they looted paintings that date back to every era imaginable, but they also made off with precious gems, religious icons, medieval tapestries, Roman statuary, banknotes, scientific manuscripts, ancient Greek pottery, gold pocket watches, gold necklaces, gold anything, even gold teeth. The lengths they went to in order to record this archive of looting, documenting every last article they confiscated, is just incredible."

"Why should any of that be a surprise?" Zorn says evenly, watching Klaryssa scan through frame after frame of Huber's office files. "We are, after all, talking about a dictatorship that logged every last one of the millions of murders it committed, not to mention the streams of infamous footnotes that they kept, each one referencing the most expeditious and efficient means of mass liquidation. Would you expect anything less when it came to detailing their wholesale pilfering of antiquities across all of conquered Europe?"

"And if that wasn't enough, they raped our heritage, too," Klaryssa says, her eyes glassy as she scans through another file. "The untold thousands of irreplaceable artifacts, swiped from museums and libraries throughout all of Ukraine, particularly Kiev. Some of them are catalogued right here in front of me, starting with these wooden icons carved by Carpathian monastics as early as the 11th century. They are priceless and irreplaceable, and they're entered into this register like a store clerk doing inventory."

Although Klaryssa is making every effort to sound dispassionate while reading through the documents, it becomes apparent to Ian and Zorn that deep emotions are welling up to the surface.

When Klaryssa finishes speaking, the room remains silent for a long moment. The late afternoon sing-along on the central courtyard continues to pick up steam, with a rendition of KC and the Sunshine Band's greatest hits growing loud enough to compel Zorn to close both the fire escape door and the room's only window.

"Zorn, go ahead and send off a copy of all this to Ian" Klaryssa says eventually, taking an occasional note while scanning through the files. "Then we can all peruse through this, looking for any evidence relating the Huber family to art thefts here in the US. God knows there's enough material here for each of us to look through."

"Review stacks of files penned in German?" Ian asks doubtfully. "The only German I ever learned was written on the side of a giant beer stein, and I was usually reading it upside down."

"Let me guess. You were upside down, but you somehow managed to hold the beer mug without spilling a drop?" Klaryssa says, her eyes still glued to the screen. "Just run through it, will you please? I was clicking away like a maniac in there, and I'm sure some of the documents are in English. Give it the once-over and see what tumbles out."

"What's that?" Zorn asks, pointing at a blurry image that appears on the laptop screen. "That seems to have no relation to all the other shots you've scrolled through. Any idea what this picture is all about?"

On the screen is the photo Klaryssa took of the small, rolled-up sheet of paper she found stuffed inside the broken camera that was buried in the lower drawer of Matthias Huber's desk. In the left-hand column, there is a series of handwritten three- and four-letter initials, and, in the right margin, there is a list of numbers and dashes, with each of the number sequences corresponding to a specific set of initials written on the same line.

"I haven't the foggiest notion of what this is," Klaryssa says, shaking her head. "It was jammed inside a broken camera, and, now that I think about it, I should have left this behind and taken at least one or two of the canisters of undeveloped film that were stashed in the same drawer. I doubt the old man would have ever noticed. But, at the time, I didn't want to risk it."

"Let me run this through a decoding program," Zorn says to Klaryssa, magnifying the image. "I can do that on my iPhone, so you can keep looking through the rest of the photos."

Well over an hour passes, with little conversation taking place between the three of them. Each one of them wades through the mounds of data that Klaryssa photographed. When the singing outside finally comes to an end, Zorn opens the fire escape door, letting in some cool air along with an occasional waft of smoke that drifts in from the bonfire that is being stoked near the edge of the sea cliff.

"KD, Zorny, look at this," Ian says, pointing to three photographs, side by side, on his computer screen. "From the enlistment records of the Coast Guard Reserve," Ian continues as he points to the first of the three photos, a grainy black-and-white image of a young man in a crisp new uniform who is standing at attention. "Here we have one Harold Melcher, on the day of his enlistment in 1945. In the center, you'll recognize Matthias Huber. And, in the photo on the right, you see our Aryan prince, Stephan Huber, looking regal and spiffy. In the same file as these photos, I found an old set of documents that I actually can read, because they were written by our own government in the years prior to the attack on Pearl Harbor."

Klaryssa and Zorn read through the boldface title lines of the collection of documents that Ian has displayed on his computer screen.

"You can read through the particulars if you'd like, but the message in all these documents is the same, so I'll give you the CliffsNotes version. The bottom line is that even before the attack on Pearl Harbor, the threat of an amphibious landing by either Japan on the West Coast or Germany on the East Coast was taken very seriously. In 1940, Congress took the extraordinary step of transferring the operation of the Coast Guard to the Department of the Navy, the intent being to fortify the patrol of our coastlines after the outbreak in Europe of what would soon become World War II. This move gave the Coast Guard the power, not to mention the money, necessary to recruit and train more men and women in rescue operations. This included the emergency evacuation of disabled vessels as well as coastal landings and evacuation.

"In the grand scheme of war preparations, this all may seem minuscule, but this, in fact, may be at the center of what the Huber family and company have been up to all these years. Our government, in preparation for the outbreak of war, gave the Coast Guard carte blanche power to train personnel in rescue operations."

"To be fair, I think that's what the Coast Guard is supposed to do," Zorn says, with more than a trace of cynicism in his words. "The only question is why Huber would ever see this old stack of papers as worth saving."

"That actually is a very good question," Klaryssa says, now looking directly over Ian's shoulder. "I found these documents in a separate, sealed folder. At first glance, they would seem impertinent, but, like you said, Zorn, the old man is keeping them for some good reason."

"That good reason is right before our eyes," Ian says, opening both hands in front of his computer screen. "Of *course* rescue operations are what the Coast Guard does, but that's not the point. Under normal circumstances, the Coast Guard has purview over the patrol of maritime waters, but these government documents grant near limitless empowerment to train personnel in rescue operations all along the coastline, and there's no indication anywhere that this authority was ever rescinded. These training exercises and rescue drills have been running for three generations, with no oversight of where they are carried out or what kinds of drills they run. None. They can land on any shore they choose, day and night, all under the guise of taking part in training exercises."

"So, these boys just row their way through the breaking waves, meeting up with fellow pirates on shores miles afar, with the *Mona Lisa* stashed deep in their cargo hold," Zorn says, looking directly at Ian and trying to suppress a grin. "Aren't you running away with things just a bit here? How in the world could this grand scheme you're outlining ever work?"

"That is the *exact* reason it does work, Zorny. It works because it's so simple and in plain sight that it's damn near perfect. Rescue boats launched at all hours, carrying out these supposed rescue drills, all with our government's blessing and all with, essentially, no supervision. The vast majority of these dry runs are no doubt bona fide, but others, manned by Huber and his guys, are a charade, nothing more than a vehicle to move stolen goods offshore."

Klaryssa and Zorn both shoot a doubtful stare in Ian's direction. "Have to side with Zorn on this one," Klaryssa says. "You can see the surf out there as well as I can, and, if you ask me, more often than not, it looks pretty damn merciless. As far as I know, they launch these boats straight off the beach, not from some dock or town pier. You're the one who's spent his life on the water. This scheme you're suggesting seems totally implausible. You, of all people, should see that."

"Just listen to what you've been saying!" Ian says, standing up from his seat. "They launch from neither port nor pier, right? So, let me ask you, where are inspections carried out? Where? At the seaports, big or small. That's where boats and ships are inspected. And the boats Huber uses, they aren't the racing shells my crewmates and I rowed in college. The boats you see being used for these exercises—these craft are light and strong and agile, and they're built to be launched directly from the shoreline by a crew of no more than two or three. As you might guess, they're motorized, and believe me, they can move.

"And take another look at where they've been launching from," Ian goes on, jabbing his finger at the blown-up map on his computer screen. "Race Point, right? This is where they've been launching from for all these years. This isn't some hemmed-in beach cordoned off at the edges by private property or swampy marshland. I mean, look at the size of this place. It's so big it faces

377

every direction on the compass depending on how far you wander. It's so exposed to the elements that its coastline gets rearranged periodically, with enough storm damage, at times, that parts actually become an island at high tide.

"But Huber and company, they would never launch in a storm or into a high surf. They don't have to, because the place is *theirs*. They launch whenever they want to because they have de facto authority—complete, unchecked access, with sand dunes that go on forever inland and the deep blue Atlantic on every other side. There are no eyes on them, and no logging in and out with the authorities because they *are* the authorities.

"You couldn't choreograph a better venue to make an exchange, particularly if the goods are easy to transport and the transfer of funds is done by wire," Ian goes on, now with Klaryssa and Zorn's full attention. "Huber's maps mark the location of other launching sites farther south on the Cape Cod shore and, for that matter, all along the Atlantic Coast. Since they can launch directly from shore, they can rendezvous anywhere in sight or out of sight. They can pull up and inspect any boat they choose, including a launch sent out from an ocean-going vessel, with no alarms and no police because they *are* the police. It's as simple as it is perfect, and let's face it, you can't find a branch of the military or law enforcement that hasn't had a rogue element somewhere in the mix. And, as for crimes committed offshore, just look at the modern-day pirates in East Africa, in Indonesia, in the Caribbean. Huber has got a lot of company out there in those waters."

"This all started with Harold Melcher," Klaryssa says as she pulls up a new file. "In every sense, he was one of the original Nazis next door. I ran across this a little while ago. This is Melcher's birth certificate along with his immigration papers, and I'll bet you anything it's all as phony as Monopoly money."

"It is," Zorn says quickly, pointing his pencil at the lower right corner of the image. "Phony, that is. All of it. I can tell you that already. The municipal seal on the birth certificate that Melcher presented to US Immigration Services is a forgery. Same with the federal government seal on his work affidavits. Photos of documents that have authentic seal imprints show a series of subtle indents at the upper and lower borders and a faint circular shadow, called a warp-line, along the outer edge. Melcher's papers show neither of these

379

characteristics. These seals were never actually imprinted onto Melcher's documents. They were basically pasted on after the fact. I've been staring at forgeries like these for years. They're easy to detect now, but, back then, there was no way to differentiate an authentic imprint from a bogus one.

"It's no secret that several thousand loyal members of the Nazi party immigrated to the United States in the 1940s, both during World War II and in the years that followed," Zorn says, looking at Klaryssa with a dark expression. "Through the years, offshoots of some of my investigations have unearthed documents detailing just how bright a beacon the US once was for Nazi war criminals. Instead of being found out as the progenitors of war that they actually were, countless Nazis passed as war refugees. They were seen as the victims, renouncing their maniacal past and posing as anti-Nazis who had fled the evil regime that once ruled their lives. Many, like Harold Melcher, crossed through our border using falsified documents like these," Zorn says as he points to his computer screen.

"Others—many others—came here with the aid of the American government. Some were scientists who contributed significantly to the

Allied war effort, later becoming famous for their development of rocket weaponry that helped us win the war. But, some of the most valuable assets were the Nazis who had intimate knowledge of our new, more nefarious enemy, the Communists. In the opinion of the American intelligence community, Fascism was dead well before Hitler blew out his brains all over the walls of his bunker. The far greater threats were the Soviets and that devil Stalin, and there was a long line of 'reformed' Nazi leaders, including some of the most notorious death camp overseers, who had volumes of knowledge concerning the Soviet plans for continental and, perhaps, even world domination. In the opinion of the CIA and the FBI, the aging, defanged Nazis that were allowed across the border were hardly dangerous war criminals. In fact, they were priceless assets. They were our new, most valuable intelligence officers. They were spies, friends of democracy who had more direct knowledge of the Soviets than a legion of American operatives."

"These documents pretty much prove that Harold Melcher came here under the cloak of being a war refugee," Ian says, wagging his finger at the computer screen images. "His Nazi past, whatever it consisted of, was blotted out. And, by all appearances, he was sent here to seek, steal, and secure works of art. But who was he selling these antiquities to? And why?"

Ian, Zorn, and Klaryssa exchange blank looks until Klaryssa scrolls back to a file she was looking at earlier. "Check this out," she says, squinting at the image on the screen. "This is a separate file with its entries translated into German from a bunch of other languages: Greek, French, Dutch, and I think a few others. It's an archival record from some of the largest and most renowned museums anywhere—a roadmap that leads to works of art in every corner of the world, particularly in our corner. You might think that records from art institutions are entered into some straight-line accounting ledger, but nothing could be further from the truth. Museums, even the most well-known institutions, are woefully understaffed. At times, a single collection of donated art will come with hundreds or even a couple thousand pages of haphazard historical documents, documents that can lead to other works by the same artist or in many cases works completed by a given artist's mentor or students. No institution of the arts has the personnel, or the hours, or the finances to comb through such an immense volume of records.

So, the records just sit there. Or, should I say, they just sat there.

"Enter the Nazis," Klaryssa continues, scrolling through more files. "They collated a record beyond the wildest dreams of any curator, researcher, or historian. The Nazis had entire schools and universities at their disposal, with more than enough bright, brainwashed students to scour through every line and paragraph of the archival records of the museums and private collections that they looted. From there, the Nazis were able to trace the location and provenance of hundreds of thousands of artworks scattered across the world, the vast majority of which were in the United States and Canada. We know they found ways to ship stolen antiquities out of Europe during the war, but these files show how much they knew about works of art that were already here."

"Not totally following," Ian says, pressing a thumb against each of his eye sockets. "I thought their looting was limited to the nations they conquered. Now you're telling me they did, or are still doing, the same thing right here?"

"Think about what Zorn just told us," Klaryssa goes on. "Near the end of the war, many members of the Nazi top brass knew they were going to go down in defeat. How could they not have known, right? Europe was ravaged, the Allies were gaining on all sides, and the only way the Third Reich could survive was to find a lifeline on another shore.

"With the encyclopedia of knowledge they had culled together about the world's art treasures, they landed here, where the lion's share of the artifacts were located. No question, they found ways to stash the antiquities they looted onto our shores throughout the 1940s, and, in particular, during the waning days of the war. But, you can't imagine the number of art collectors, or, for that matter, art museums and galleries, that have no idea what they actually own—misidentified signatures, canvases stashed beneath cement dust, works assigned to the wrong artist, masterpieces lying beneath some ho-hum paint-over. Huber's files show that the Nazis put together an unparalleled archival record, light years ahead of that of any historian or library. I'm talking about combing through the records from every institution they looted, which must've totaled millions of pages, which they eventually boiled down into the files Matthias Huber has in his office. Like the artwork they were trying to locate, these records had been buried for who knows how many years.

"Zorn, you said it yourself. In the waning days of World War II, our nation's collective guard was down, with our government's focus on Stalin and the Communists. Hitler and the fascists were passé. Nazis like Melcher had their past whited out, and, as an immigrant, Melcher found a way to keep the Reich's heart beating. No doubt, he had a lot of fellow refugees helping. My guess is that Matthias and Stephan Huber also have plenty of cohorts. Who's to say they don't have people stationed all along the East Coast?"

"But, KD, who was, or is, on the other end of all this?" Ian again asks in an almost pleading tone. "Harold Melcher, Matthias Huber, Stephan Huber—they led, or lead, a network of thieves that steal works of art that are eventually fenced offshore. Like I said, it's damn near perfect—no one suspects them, no one inspects. We know Huber has a perpetual free pass, but who is paying him? We still have no idea who the buyers are."

"Thaaaaaat is not *quite* true," Zorn says, his eyes fixed on the results of the program he has been running over the past couple of hours.

Chapter 25

Truro, Massachusetts

Zorn transfers the program readout from his cell phone to Ian's laptop screen, showing Ian and Klaryssa the analysis he ran on the sheet of scrap paper Klaryssa found stashed in Matthias Huber's broken camera.

"Klaryssa, I don't know what ever possessed you to take a photo of this," Zorn says, pointing at the lines of initials and number sequences on his computer screen, each line now highlighted with annotations. "That said, it looks like your friend Marta and her African bird bought you just enough time to answer the question Ian just asked."

"Each set of initials listed along the left-hand column represents the name of a given financial institution," Zorn continues. "Put simply, they're what you might call offshore banks. Some of them are upstanding, others less so. You can't recognize the banks by just looking at the initials because they're designated by what is known as a two-left/three-right code, meaning that whoever wrote this, likely Matthias Huber, used letters that were two up or three down on the alphabet. In so doing, Huber will automatically recognize which bank is which just by looking at the jumbled initials. But, a casual observer, should one ever see this list, would be clueless.

"The real pay dirt here lies in the right-hand column, with its sequences of numbers and dashes, each one corresponding to a set of initials written on the left. These represent the routing and account numbers of the offshore bank accounts. The program I ran gives the location of each of the banks, along with a history of some of their best customers."

"Let me guess," Ian says. "The customer list you're referring to, as in the one you now have, is not for public consumption."

Zorn looks up at Ian and then over at Klaryssa, nodding slowly.

"Drug lords? Gunrunners? Money launderers?" Klaryssa asks.

"All the above," Zorn says, peering over his glasses. "Not to mention human traffickers and an

387

assortment of other soulless enterprises. And all of them do the hog's share of their business in South America. And that, fine lady and gent, is where the money is. Or, should I say, where the stolen money is."

Zorn stands up and walks over to the fire escape door, eyeing the crowd encircling the bonfire, the fire's flames burning bright enough and climbing high enough to illuminate the breaking waves offshore.

"That's where all this came from," Zorn says, stepping onto the fire escape landing and pointing directly east. "The art, the fleeing Nazis, the mountains of stolen currency, the tons and tons of gold, all from war-ravaged Europe. The difference is that the loot, meaning the pilfered currency and bullion, went that way." Zorn's index finger is now pointing south.

"The customers you ask about, Ian—the other end of the deal, or other end of the fence— they're from South America, Argentina and Chile for the most part, because that's where the money is. These are the countries that served as a haven for even more Nazis than the ones that landed on our shores. The gold and currency found hidden in the Alps salt mines after the war were only a fraction of what was stolen by the Nazis, and the Nazi henchmen that escaped knew it would be far too difficult to smuggle such wealth into the US.

"South America was a different story altogether, and the Nazi leaders that ended up there had unimaginable wealth at their disposal. But, the artworks they so treasured, the priceless pieces detailed in Huber's files, are, for the most part, here. The program I just ran gives a point- by-point log of transfers from one account to the next, and the most prolific buyers are a handful of vintners from Argentina and Chile."

"Sounds like their enterprise goes beyond the fruit of the vine," Klaryssa says. "Can you follow the flow of money, a history of transactions consummated through the years?"

"Negative on that one, I'm sorry to say," Zorn says, still scanning through the program results. "But I can use GPS to determine the exact location of the buyers, meaning those who have been transferring funds to the accounts Huber holds in these various banks. It won't be hard to name names once we have the addresses of the Latin American winemakers who spend their spare time furnishing their homes with priceless artifacts that don't belong to them."

"We need a history of sealed deals, Zorny," Ian says, pulling up a chair and leaning over Zorn's shoulder. "I'm thinking along the same lines as KD. Without a record of what deals took place and when said transactions were clinched, it will be hard to ever prove what Huber was selling and what these supposed winemakers were buying."

"Hang with me for a minute or so," Zorn says, running through the data files of multiple banks. "The transaction history is likely firewalled on all sides, but there may be another way to drag more out of all this."

While Ian watches Zorn sift through a flood of data, Klaryssa again pulls up Huber's voluminous file of stolen antiquities, scrolling down to the collection of Lydian gold coins from the seventh century BCE that were pilfered from a Dutch museum in 1940, never to be seen again.

"We're close to getting in," Zorn says, hints of triumph in his voice. "More than halfway, I do believe. I can't break into the log of previous transactions, but I broke through the active-wire-wall."

Klaryssa eyes photographs of the world's first coinage, solid gold pieces minted during the reign of King Alyattes over 2600 years ago, each piece imprinted with the image of a crowned monarch on one side and the likeness of a roaring lion on the reverse.

"Broke through the *what*?" Ian asks.

"The active-wire-wall," Zorn repeats, eyeing countless data points flickering across his screen. "It means that we can now access pending transactions, if any such transactions exist. Same for the imminent transfer of funds. You know, partial payment already made with the final payment due upon delivery."

Klaryssa then sees images of the 17th-century Flemish tapestries that the Nazis looted from French chateaus throughout the Loire Valley, each one of the resplendently embroidered pieces more dazzling than the last. Likenesses of conquerors, popes, queens, kings, empresses, and sultans are woven into silk fabric with golden thread, commemorating the subject's birth in some of the works, their day of coronation in others, and in yet others still, their day of interment. Each of the tapestries stands as a singular monument to a moment in our collective human history, and Klaryssa knows that each piece has, more likely than not, permanently and tragically vanished from the public's eye.

"You make it sound like they're a bunch of wholesale loincloth merchants," Ian says, trying without success to follow Zorn's serpentine path through multiple bank wire transactions. "We're talking about the highest of high criminals here, and you're making it out to be some sterile barter deal between desert Bedouins."

Klaryssa stumbles across another set of files that further document the Nazis' theft of Italian art, a painfully detailed record of artifacts that originate from every era in that nation's history, including Etruscan pottery, Celtic bronze work, Roman frescos, and exquisitely illustrated palm-size prayer books from the Holy Roman Empire. A moment later, one finger-click away from closing the file that chronicles the loss of irreplaccable Italian treasures, Klaryssa feels her hands freeze and her mind go numb.

"This *is* commerce," Zorn says, still staring at the stream of flickering digits and symbols racing across the screen, "plain and simple. And you're right, it *is* sterile. It's sterile because it's banking, and, as such, our one and only task at this moment is to follow the money."

Klaryssa's eyes are fixed on the startled, terror-stricken Florentine soldiers in Michelangelo's masterpiece, the *Battle of Cascina*. Twenty or more warriors are emerging from the waters of the Arno River, the victims of a barbaric surprise attack by the Pisan militia. Most of the men are barely clothed, some not at all. And each of them is about to be slaughtered.

"Got it!" Zorn proclaims, throwing both hands into the air. "A yet-to-be-consummated transaction between Matthias Huber and one Luis Soto of Argentina's Uco Valley. Three million... holy shit, $3.7 million is being transferred to one of Huber's offshore accounts. This is just one deal, one trade, between the two of them, and it's worth over three and a half mill."

Then Klaryssa sees him. She sees the man in Elle Picard's charcoal sketch, the warrior with the leather headband whose head is turned sharply to one side. The man's facial features are robust and vital, and his neck muscles are thick and taut, and, as with the other soldiers depicted in the painting, his eyes are filled with fear and awe, because this warrior, like the others, is about to meet his death at the hands of his Pisan enemy. But Klaryssa knows something is not right. Elle Picard's Michelangelo sketch is indelibly imprinted in her mind, and

Klaryssa's gut and instinct are telling her that something is very wrong.

"KD, KD!" Ian says, trying without success to pull Klaryssa's attention away from the image in front of her. "We've got him. Huber, that is. We've got him. With what you pulled out of that old camera, along with Zorn's program, we've hit the mother lode. There's a deal going down for over three million. This is *plenty* enough evidence to take to the authorities. We can nail this guy."

It's the man's eyes. Klaryssa knows it now without any doubt. The artist who painted this work may have captured the eyes of a man filled with dread, but this man's eyes impart the same sense of sudden shock as the other soldiers detailed in the painting. A work of Michelangelo's hand would have an unmistakable air of capriciousness, with no two sets of eyes betraying the same impulse or sentiment. The eyes Klaryssa saw in Elle Picard's sketch were mercurial, conveying both tranquility and desolation. They belonged to a man who was a soldier to the end, a man heeding the immediate call to battle but not yet knowing that in the next instant, he would draw his last breath.

"Today," Zorn says slowly, looking up at Ian. "This queue has a maximum 24-hour window.

This deal, whatever it is, is going down today. It has to be, or we would have never uncovered this intersect between buyer and seller."

"KD, are you hearing this?" Ian implores, leaning down next to Klaryssa while pointing at Zorn's computer screen. "We did it. We've got him!"

Klaryssa's eyes are still fixed on her screen, and she knows that the painting she is looking at never, even for the briefest of time, adorned the walls of the Palazzo Vecchio in Florence. This painting is a rich, expansive, passionate rendition of a medieval battle between two Italian cities. But it is not the work of Michelangelo.

"How much did you say again?" Klaryssa asks dryly, without looking away.

"Three million seven," Zorn and Ian say in unison.

"That's a bundle," Klaryssa says with a slight nod, her full attention still on the image in front of her.

"It goes without saying that there's no reference as to what exactly is being purchased," Zorn says, a wild stream of data points reflecting off his glasses. "After all, the goods, whatever they are, are as hot as that bonfire burning out there in the courtyard."

"So, this is the lost *Battle of Cascina*?" Klaryssa says under her breath, knowing that this must be the painting hidden under the portrait that Elle Picard's grandfather purchased in Italy all those years ago. This is the work that an Italian family unknowingly owned and unknowingly sold, that Colonel Picard unknowingly bought, and that Harold Melcher mistakenly identified as a centuries-lost Michelangelo masterpiece. Melcher actually went to the inconceivable length of fixing a horse race in order to steal a painting that is nothing more than a passable, but undeniable, imitation.

"This is more than enough dirt to bury Huber," Ian says, wringing his hands. "Zorny, you know people at the FBI, right? There has to be someone you can contact that can authorize a move on this guy, once they see what we have unearthed."

But it's Elle Picard's charcoal sketch that Klaryssa cannot get out of her mind. That work is, beyond question, an authentic Michelangelo. It is a 500-year-old charcoal drawing that was unknown to the art world until it tumbled out of a dusty tome that had sat untouched on a library shelf for generations. Michelangelo drew that sketch prior to painting the *Battle of Cascina*, the epic masterpiece that briefly hung on the walls of the Palazzo Vecchio in Florence.

"Affirmative," Zorn says with a vigorous nod. "I have to make some calls, go over all we know with people I have worked investigations with in the past. But we've got more than enough to blow the whistle, that's for damn certain."

In the hand of the artist, the painting follows the sketch, and in the hand of history, the sketch follows the painting.

"Today, right?" Ian asks, looking at Zorn and then at Klaryssa.

"Colonel Picard, how many paintings did you buy when you were in Italy?" Klaryssa whispers to herself. "And, Harold Melcher, how many of them did you steal?"

"Today," Zorn responds immediately. "As in now."

"You stole every one of them, didn't you, Herr Melcher," Klaryssa says, her voice now only slightly louder. "You stole them all. Every last one of the paintings that Colonel Picard donated, you stole. But you didn't really inspect all of them after you stole them, did you? You didn't crack open every one of the frames, did you? You tore open one after the other until you found this. *This*," Klaryssa repeats, her voice now louder, pointing at the painting that is still in bright living color on her screen. "You found this, and then you stopped, that's what you did. Then you stopped.

"Then you stopped!" Klaryssa shouts out, so loud that Zorn sits bolt upright in his seat.

"Stopped what?" Ian asks, both he and Zorn looking at Klaryssa with dazed looks on their faces.

"Klaryssa, stopped what?" Ian repeats, moving in next to Klaryssa. "Who stopped what?"

"I have to make a road trip," Klaryssa says, taking one long last look at the image on her screen before looking up at Ian and Zorn. "Road trip. I'm outta here."

"Road trip?" Ian asks, stunned. "What do you mean *road trip*? We've uncovered a decades-old crime syndicate here—Melcher, the Hubers, and God knows how many scumbag associates they've pulled in over the years. We have to find the Feds or the state police or someone so we can report all this and send this guy and his psycho son away for life."

"Yes, yes, I know," Klaryssa says, clearly distracted as she gets to her feet and scrambles for her jacket and keys. "You two gents know everything there is to know about the Huber family. Report this guy, the whole ugly family, that is, to the authorities. I'll text you when I get there."

"Get there? Get *where*?" Ian pleads, following Klaryssa to the door. "KD, where in the hell are you going?"

In the next instant, Klaryssa is out the door and bounding down the stairway that leads to the exit. "Zorny, shit, I don't know what's got ahold of this girl or where she's off to," Ian says, picking up his own jacket and heading out the door. "I'll bring her back in a minute, just hold tight here."

The bunkhouse door slams shut, and Zorn hears Ian's feet pounding down the stairwell steps. A moment later, Zorn glances out the open fire escape door, spotting Ian chasing after Klaryssa through the crowded courtyard. Clueless as to what's going on with Klaryssa, Zorn goes back to his electronic rolodex, sifting through the names of any law enforcement contacts he has worked with through the years. A couple of minutes later, Zorn curses to himself when he hears a faint knock on the door, figuring that he is, once again, being interrupted by one of Ian's around-the-clock deliveries of 1970s memorabilia.

"Damn it, Ian, more shit to clutter this room," Zorn repeats to himself. "All this stuff you've got piled up in here. And who the hell pays delivery staff to come calling at this time of..."

When Zorn opens the door, he doesn't see a man in a gray corporate uniform balancing a dolly of FedEx boxes. The looming figure before him is a man dressed entirely in black silk, and when the man uncrosses his lumberjack arms, Zorn sees the tip of a .38 revolver jutting through the end of a left-sided shoulder holster. Without waiting for an invitation, the man steps inside and quietly closes the door behind him, his hulking frame seeming to fill half the room.

"I take it you're the owner of that sly little insect?" the man says, his eyes bearing down on Zorn as he crowds in closer. "Yeah, you know the one I'm talking about. It's that little detective you sent to spy on your neighbors. The one with the metallic wings, and that magic camera strapped to his back."

Chapter 26
Truro, Massachusetts

The instant Ian emerges through the bunkhouse exit, he is met by a billowing cloud of bonfire smoke that is being carried his way by a stiff onshore breeze. He tries to wave away the dense, smoggy plumes with both hands, looking for any sign of Klaryssa in the crowd of beer-bellied revelers who are dressed in various patterns of checkerboard disco attire and fluorescent-colored leisure suits. Closer to the bonfire, there are a couple of bearded men waving their shirts in the air, their sagging, faded, four-decade-old tattoos gyrating in every direction as the pair bounce up and down to Alice Cooper's "I'm Eighteen." The music is screaming out of a boombox that is perched on top of a giant ship's anchor, which also serves as a clothesline for various pieces of lady's apparel. Once Ian makes his way past the raging fire pit, he spots Klaryssa, who is standing alone along the jutting edge of the eroding sea cliff.

"See that light out there?" Klaryssa asks after Ian joins her, pointing directly southward. "The farthest one you can see, on the stern of the small boat that's moored just off shore. That's the very spot where the *Whydah Gally* sank about 300 years ago. That boat was Black Sam Bellamy's last pirate ship, right up to the night when it found its way to the sea floor in one of those vicious spring storms. That boat sank in just 16 feet of water. They called him the Prince of Pirates; he was the richest pirate the world ever saw. He captured something like 50 ships in his time, along with enough gold to, well, sink a ship."

"The richest pirate known up until now, anyway," Ian says, looking across the shoreline in the same direction. "I read about the *Whydah* when I was a kid. Something like 100 other pirates went down with old Sam, who I guess wasn't so old."

"In his late twenties," Klaryssa says, still staring at the ship's light in the distance. "There were a handful or survivors, but they were all caught, tried, and hanged."

"Tried and hanged. That's what I'd like to see happen to the two pirates we just nailed, and the same for their minions. We've got them, lock, stock, and barrel. Zorn is on the line with the FBI right now. Any minute, you're going to see a parade of blue flashers lighting up the sky."

"I hope so," Klaryssa says, looking back toward the bonfire. "We've got all the evidence we could possibly need, so let's hope the authorities know what they're doing."

"Why the hell did you sprint out of there right when we blew this case wide open?"

"This *case* is secondary to me," Klaryssa says, now looking straight at Ian. "I was charged with establishing the provenance of a work of art, and that's the task I intend to see through. That was and remains my first priority, and nothing you can say will change that."

"KD, look, this isn't just about some old drawing, no matter how valuable it might be. This is a major—massive—international crime ring we've exposed. And you—yes, you—are smack in the middle of it. The police, not to mention the Feds, are going to have a million and one questions for you, for all of us. You can't just up and leave."

"Yeah, I think I can," Klaryssa says without a moment's hesitation, the blare of '70s rock music growing ever louder. "And who are you all of a

404

sudden, Perry Mason? You're right, we've unearthed something really big and ugly. And whatever dirt we may have dragged out into the light will now be in the hands of law enforcement, which is just where it belongs. For me, this is right back to where it all started, which is finishing the job I agreed to take on. You and Zorn know everything I do about this—about Huber and his fascists and all they've stolen and sold and on and on. You don't need me here. What use am I? And besides, I'll be back tomorrow."

"Back tomorrow?" Ian asks, clapping the top of his head with both hands. "You can't be serious. My God, what on earth could be so important? Where are you going? After that last file you were eyeballing in there, you jumped up like you had seen a ghost or something. What was that all about?"

You got it right on your first guess, Klaryssa thinks to herself, but she doesn't say so to Ian.

"Art is your life, I know that," Ian continues, leaning in toward Klaryssa until she meets his gaze. "You saw it all yourself, everything Huber has in his office files. Thousands—tens of thousands—of priceless works that will one day soon be returned to their rightful owners. You made this possible, so we have to see this through."

"*Priceless*," Klaryssa repeats, again looking out across the dark sea. "Believe me, you have no idea. That is why I have to—"

"Hey, look, that's him!" Klaryssa and Ian both startle when they see a portly man in a shaggy, undersized pink tuxedo waddling toward them at full speed. "Yep, this is the guy we're after." The man is now waving his index finger toward Ian. Limping behind the squat man in the tuxedo is an even shorter man wearing a black leather Led Zeppelin jacket along with a red-and- white Arkansas Razorbacks cap. Trailing behind the two men is a gray-haired woman dressed in a Native American getup, carrying a long ebony cigarette holder in one hand and an open bottle of Jack Daniels in the other.

"Son, what a New Year's-worthy blastoff you showed us with those fireworks this afternoon," the man in the tuxedo bellows to Ian, extending his hand. "Paul Rexton, pleasure's all mine. Friends all call me Rex. And good gravy, you lit up the sky like you were rehearsin' for the next millennial celebration. Outta nowhere seems like you fired off one volley of lights after another right from that rooftop over there. Loved it, just loved it. We all did, every last one of us.

"Drove here from Austin, Texas," Rex says, both Ian and Klaryssa now noticing the electric yellow top hat the man is carrying in one hand. "And for every last road mile between here and there, I was seated in the pilot's chair of that ultra-fine VW Bus parked out near the entrance, and, being a bettin' man, I'm laying odds you saw that baby on your way in here today. Yessir, I am readin' your mind. Vintage 1964 model, and your eyes will never see a finer specimen. Restored it myself, including the waving American flag you see painted along the length on both flanks. And shit damn, where are my manners? En route to this historic celebration, I picked up my dear friends here, Donny D. from Little Rock and Lily from Chattanooga."

While Ian and Klaryssa shake hands with the other two partiers, Rex puts on his top hat and places a firm hand on Ian's shoulder.

"My friend," Rex says, "we could surely use some help. See, well, on the way up here along Interstate 95, my chums and I made a not-so-quick stop at South of the Border to load up on all the pyrotechnics we might need for our grand finale,

407

which just happens to be tomorrow night. You know, bottle rockets and Roman candles and M-80s and the like. But as luck would have it, while poking around down there in South Carolina, I ran into a pal of mine from high school. Tried to get him up here to Truro, as he too is a child of the '70s, but his work is in full swing and it's prime time for him to make hay and all. Anyway, after a couple of shots of that moonshine he brews up in the hills near his brother's home, he sold me some *real* fireworks. Packed them up nice 'n tight and all before we hit the road. And don't you worry yourself, these goods are stashed a far cry from that conflagration we've got burnin' right behind us.

"When it comes to these things," Rex whispers, Ian picking up the distinct stinging breeze of stale whiskey as Rex pulls in closer, "it's always safety first.

"Anyway," Rex says as he steps back and tips his hat in Ian's direction, "let me be the first to admit, in front of all of you, friends both old and new, that I have no working familiarity with these devices or the chemistry of the compounds contained within. So, on behalf of all members of our festival, we would be honored if you could walk us through the particulars of the operation and discharge of these pyrotechnics, as our closing celebration will commence in less than 24 hours."

"Give us just a moment or two," Ian says, turning away from Rex and putting his arm around Klaryssa. "I just need a word with my friend here."

"Holy shit, KD," Ian says, speaking just loud enough for Klaryssa to hear him above another blast of wind funneling over the sand dunes. "These people are all looney. They're downing moonshine and Kentucky Straight and God knows what else, and they want to know how to *detonate* the *explosives* they purchased in South Carolina."

Klaryssa, having not spoken a word while Rex was carrying on, takes her eyes away from the bonfire and looks back at Ian.

"Look," Ian continues, "give me 10 minutes, 15 max. I'll take a look at the fireworks they have stashed and see if I can talk them out of this harebrained grand finale they have slated for tomorrow night. Maybe I can just buy the fireworks from them and we can avert the mass annihilation these nitwits might set off. Please, just stay here, because we have to talk this out. Don't move; I'm begging you. I'll be back in a flash. Sorry, forget I said that. I'll be right back."

Klaryssa watches Ian hurry off with the buzzing partiers, the four of them disappearing one by one into the whirling clouds of bonfire smoke. Klaryssa looks back out across the dark sea, eyeing the scattering of ship lights reflecting off the water line to the north and the lone stern light flickering at the *Whydah*'s wreck site along the shoreline to the south.

All Klaryssa wants to do is leave. She has an obligation to Elle Picard and no one else—not to Ian or Zorn or the Feds or even to any of the owners of this trove of art the Nazis stole. If she leaves now, there will be little to no traffic on the highway, and, once she nears Saratoga, she can sleep at a rest stop for a couple of hours and be at the front door of the museum the minute it opens. After she meets with the museum's director and calls Elle Picard, she can be back on the road that same morning. She'll return to Truro by tomorrow afternoon and assist the authorities in any and all ways necessary.

"Hey m'lady, the party's over here," says the young man walking Klaryssa's way in a seesaw pattern, having apparently wandered away from the crowd encircling the bonfire. "There isn't anything happening way over there on the edge," the man

410

says, Klaryssa noticing the man's gait suddenly righting itself as he nears.

"We have everything that flows back at the big blaze, and the vibe is getting better by the minute," the man goes on. Klaryssa is now wondering why such a young person would be attending a festival where the next youngest participant is likely in their early fifties. Suddenly, Klaryssa hears the drag of footsteps just behind her, and a lone figure emerges from the sand pathway that leads away from the cliff's edge. When she tries to run, Klaryssa is stopped in her tracks by a rock-hard hand that reaches around and covers her entire face. In an instant, she is suffocating, unable to let out a breath or a scream. She feels a piercing sting in the back of her arm, and the last thing Klaryssa sees before her world goes dark is the blackened, sweat-soaked face of Stephan Huber.

Chapter 27

Truro, Massachusetts

Stephan switches on the rescue raft's bilge pump and fires a gush of saltwater across Klaryssa's face. She jolts awake from her drug-induced stupor with a spasm of coughing, spitting out seawater and remnants of the ether Stephan used to subdue her before he dragged her down the steep cliff and into the raft he had moored along the shoreline. Klaryssa leans over the side of the raft and vomits violently, tasting the fire of acid and pungent gas that filled her stomach while she was frantically struggling to free herself from Stephan's iron grip just minutes earlier. She tries to sit up but can move only a few inches. She notices that Stephan has both of her arms trussed to the raft's drogue line. Stephan and a second man are strapping down a sealed tube to the floor of the raft's stern. Mercifully, the ocean surf is relatively gentle but not gentle enough to stop Klaryssa's head from spiraling as the raft rhythmically lilts from side to side. Klaryssa feels her stomach heave, and she again vomits into the frothy waves.

"Didn't care for your cocktail?" Stephan asks, walking toward Klaryssa and whipping a wet towel across her face. "Some date you're turning out to be. You know, I mixed up that concoction just for *you*. See, my buddy Earl and I, we had no trouble locating you up there in that crowd of fucking idiots who're trying to hold a tune while doing the two-step around that Girl Scout campfire. Yeah, we knew you were in there somewhere. You were plenty easy to spot once you were out in the open…that hot little ass of yours in the middle of all that sagging flab. So, you really weren't all that hard to find. You still put up one hell of a fight, even with the old-time anesthetic I treated you to and the homemade tranquilizer Earl pinched under your skin. We just couldn't wait to get you down here for a little chat. You know, a two-on-one sort of thing."

Klaryssa looks over at Earl, who, like Stephan, is dressed head to toe in a jet-black wetsuit. Earl flashes Klaryssa a snarly grin before licking his upper lip.

413

"You know something, lady," Stephan continues, twisting a tuft of Klaryssa's hair, his unblinking eyes inching closer, "I have no idea who the hell you are, and that's no shit. While escorting you down that sand dune I do believe your shoulder bag tore away, so it's bye-bye wallet, along with everything else you were carrying. It's all left for the seagulls and any other varmints around to rummage through now.

"Me and Earl and a couple other buddies spent half the day looking for you, then we find you and get you down here, but still none of us have any fucking idea who the hell you are. Now ain't that just a kick in the balls?

"Like it matters," Stephan continues as he wrenches Klaryssa's hair tighter. She can no longer choke back her screams, which are quickly drowned out by the rush of the sea. "Like it fucking matters! I'm conducting business here, lady. *Business*. My guess is you already know that, with you and your two pals snooping around my private residence, acting like *my* business is any of *yours*. You think this is some sort of playground where you can mess around where you don't belong? Think this is a game, like you're back in high school, summering up here in the sun with all the

414

other sluts? You think I didn't have enough eyes in the sky to catch that whole bullshit act of yours, you and those two pantywaists you've been running around with? You have any idea what you just walked into?"

With a slow tilt of his head, Stephan twists Klaryssa's hair even tighter, tearing a tuft of it clean out of her scalp. "Then let me tell you all about it. Might as well, because this is a secret that you won't ever get to share with anyone, including those two fuckheads you call friends. See, I'm afraid I've got some sad news there, because the first one—that little geek who's been spying inside my house—he's dead. I had an associate of mine pay him a visit about half an hour ago, and he gave him an up-close look at one of these."

Without loosening his grip, Stephan uses his other hand to pull an icepick out of his back pocket.

"There are all kinds of people up there at that party, so I wasn't going to risk your nosy pal screaming like a little candy ass while my friend was encouraging him to answer a few questions," Stephan says, dangling the icepick in front of Klaryssa's face. "So, I instructed my comrade to take back all of the files that *you* stole and then send the business end of this instrument through the base of geek boy's skull."

Stephan slowly uses the tip of the icepick to make a circular outline on the back of Klaryssa's head, barely breaking the skin. "So, that's one intruder down, with minimal mess, save for the fluid covering his brain puddling onto the carpet. Nothing that can't be cleaned up. Your other friend, the tall one who struts around like he's some world-class hot shit, he is, at this moment, the luckiest bastard on two feet. Once he's clear of those three idiots he wandered off with, he'll go back to the edge of the sand dune looking for you. Once he's alone in the dark like a lost little mutt, he'll be met not by you but with a bullet between the eyes. A nine-millimeter with a silencer. We might even see him roll down the cliff and into the surf, right here in front of us. The one thing I *can* promise is that he'll be a shark snack soon enough. And that snake Marta, your backstabbing whore of a partner. Well, I'm saving her for last."

Klaryssa's arms are so tightly strapped to the drogue line that she has no sensation in either of her hands. With her hair wrapped in Stephan grip, Klaryssa's neck is twisted to such an extreme that ribbons of agonizing pain are firing down the length of her spine.

She knows that there is no one left to help her.

"So, that leaves you, whoever *you* are," Stephan says, gently dotting the center of Klaryssa's forehead with the tip of the ice pick. "And you are going to tell me everything. You are going to tell me who sent you, what they know, what you've told them, and where they are. And, in case it's not obvious, you are going to tell me right fucking now."

Whoever you are buzzes through Klaryssa's head again and again, like an echo in a cave.

These words are all that's left for Klaryssa to care about, and they are so vital and potent that they nearly deaden the pain that is racing through every inch of her body. Stephan doesn't know who she is, and, with Zorn and Ian gone, he never will know who she is or anything about her. And he will never know about Yeva. He will never know she even exists.

Yeva will be safe.

"Don't worry yourself here," Stephan says, loosening the drogue line with his free hand. "I'm not gonna do any theatrical shit, like dunking your head into the surf until you talk. I'm much more civil than that."

In the next second, Stephan yanks Klaryssa's hair in one lightning-fast motion, sending her head plunging into the surf. Klaryssa is rendered motionless, pinned against the side of the raft, a shock of icy saltwater flooding her throat. When Stephan pulls her head out of the water, Klaryssa sends a stream of salt water spewing halfway across the length of the raft, sucking in all the air she can. When her eyes open, Klaryssa sees Stephan's expressionless face staring at her, his round, vacuous eyes briefly illuminated by rays of moonlight that appear from behind the cloud cover.

"Guess I lied," Stephan says, his voice deadpan. "But right about now, I'm not much leaning toward honesty. I'm just not feeling the love."

Stephan dunks Klaryssa's head once again, this time dragging her head back and forth, her face only inches from the sea bottom. When he pulls Klaryssa back into the raft, he sends a backhand slap across her face. "What I know is that you are about to die," Stephan says, gripping Klaryssa by the neck and pulling her off the floor of the raft. "All that's left is deciding how you're going to die.

418

This isn't going to be me sitting here interrogating you, lady, with us doing a little back and forth until you cough up a few spare details about what you know and who sent you. Not happening. Tell me *now*, every last bit of what I want to know, and it will all be over in the blink of an eye. A painless exit, that's what I'll give you. But hesitate or balk, for even a moment, and I'll know you're lying."

As he speaks, Stephan keeps tracing the icepick's pointed edge down the center of Klaryssa's face. "I will use this to peel every layer of skin off that pretty little face of yours, which will send a trail of blood dripping into the wake of this vessel. And then I'll just follow the seals, because that's exactly what the sharks do. They're great whites, mostly. And even though your face will be carved down to bare bone, you will still be breathing, as alive as you are at this very moment. In unspeakable pain, but still alive. Then it's overboard, where all those pointy teeth can work on both ends of you."

Stephan hits Klaryssa across the face with another backhand, knocking her onto her knees along the raft's stern. Klaryssa does not feel the smack. She is outside of herself, defeated. "Who sent you and who are you working for?" Stephan

419

shouts before plunging Klaryssa's head into the surf once more. "Who the fuck knows about us?"

Klaryssa feels neither fear nor pain. All she feels is her daughter, in her arms and in her heart and in the pit of her gut.

"Who?!" Stephan screams, again sending Klaryssa's head into the surf. "Tell me, because one way or another, they'll be as dead as you're about to be."

You are safe, Yeva, my beauty.

"Dead, all of them, you hear me! Dea—"

Klaryssa then feels an enormous weight tumble on top of her, sending her entire body toppling out of the raft and into the surf. She is now completely submerged. When Klaryssa instinctively opens her eyes, there is enough moonlight filtering through the water to see Stephan's shock-stricken gaze directly in front of her. Klaryssa, now struggling to free herself from under Stephan's dead weight, sees a gushing river of red blood trailing away from the hole in Stephan's temple. Klaryssa cannot free the leg that is pinned under Stephan's torso. She tries with all the will she has left not to succumb to the need to draw in the deep breath that she knows will seal her fate.

Air bubbles gurgle from Stephan's open mouth, following the streaks of blood toward the water's surface. Klaryssa feels her body go limp, no longer knowing if her eyes are open or closed. The water has completely numbed her body. Darkness edges its way into the center, and there is neither sound nor motion anywhere about her.

You are safe, Yeva, my love. Safe from all this.

Klaryssa suddenly feels two hands wedge under her shoulders, and, an instant later, she is pulled to the surface and into the raft. Klaryssa gasps, her chest heaving uncontrollably, pulling in every ounce of air possible. When she opens her eyes, she sees Earl's dead body strewn across the floor of the raft, and, a moment later, she sees a gold-and-blue badge dangling from a chain that is just above her head. Through the moonlight's reflection, Klaryssa makes out the lettering on the outer circle of the badge that's emblazoned with the words UNITED STATES MARSHAL.

"Fancy meeting you here," Marta says, holstering her service weapon and wiping her brow with the back of her hand. "You know, on your next vacation, you ought to think about keeping better company."

Chapter 28

Truro, Massachusetts

"Ian, Zorn," Klaryssa says to Marta, her voice desperate between spasms of cough. "Ian and Zorn, my God, he told me they're both dead. Maybe it's not too late. Maybe…" Klaryssa struggles to get up onto her feet, but Marta eases her back down onto the floor of the raft.

"They're not dead, Klaryssa," Marta says, handing Klaryssa a dry towel. "Trust me, they're both fine. We've got two other agents up there at the bunkhouse, and less than an hour ago, we apprehended one of Huber's stooges, the one sent to knock off both of your friends. That '70s festival has everyone in a bit of a frenzy around that campfire, so we were able to whisk the would-be hitman away as if it was part of some pre-rehearsed stage act. The guy was packed to the gills, I can tell you that…outfitted with all kinds of knives and a pair of pistols. Our other agent up there is someone you might actually recognize, and you'll see him again soon enough. But, first, you need an ambulance and a complete going-over by an ER doctor."

"No, no," Klaryssa says, shaking her head. "He didn't even break my skin, except for the icepick mark that's no deeper than a mosquito bite. I don't need a doctor or a hospital. I just need to see Ian and Zorn for myself. But...wait, wait, are you actually with the US Marshals? What the hell? How come you didn't tell me that from the start, when you found me at that café in Provincetown?"

"That wasn't going to happen," Marta says flatly. "When it comes to fencing and ferrying stolen art, Huber and company are in a league of their own. They're beyond good. They leave nothing to chance, and they've proved impossible to nail because they've long managed an operation that leaves no trail and spills no secrets. Worse yet, there have, at times, been suspicions, although no proof, that they have a mole within both the FBI and the Coast Guard hierarchy. So, the Marshals Service was assigned a task force to infiltrate their operation, but truth be told, we hadn't gotten very far before you and your friends showed up.

"And, if I may ask," Marta says through a sideways grin. "All you and Ian and Zorn are doing out here is trying to track down one particular lost Renaissance painting, right?"

Klaryssa nods, thinking back to her first conversation with Elle Picard, which now seems like well over a century ago.

"I didn't know what to make of you at first," Marta says, unfastening the long, sealed, hard-shell tube that Stephan strapped down to the raft's stern. "But then, once you told me what you knew and what you and the two boys had planned, you were a godsend.

"I've never gotten anywhere near Huber's office records, and even though the bugs we use are largely untraceable, I didn't want to chance blowing my cover, so I resisted the urge to plant anything inside that beach house. Like I said, these guys are thoroughly professional and miss nothing. They're also incredibly disciplined, and they only discuss business when they're out on that cliff, where the wind and blowing sand make recordings impossible. And they're out there 12 months a year. I would know, because I deliver them their damn tea and biscuits." Marta points a thumb at Stephan's dead body, lolling in the frothy surf.

"He was going to bump off Ian and Zorn like they were flies on the wall," Marta continues. "And I'm sure the only reason he kept you alive was to pump you for information. Then he would have killed you too, no question there. When I got down here, I gave him one warning, which is one more than he deserved. He didn't listen, so I dropped him. His buddy was carrying a sidearm and drew on me, so that decision was even easier. I've got a call into my backup, and they're on their way to clean up this mess, so it's about to get real busy down here. So, again, let me get you a lift to the emergency room down in Hyannis. The ride's on me. Or, should I say, on us."

Marta taps her badge a couple of times.

Klaryssa holds up both hands, again shaking her head.

"Suit yourself," Marta says. "I'm heading up to the bunkhouse, because there's a lot of work left and a narrow window to get it all done. We've got no time to lose. It's highly irregular, but you can tag along, given your intimate knowledge of all that's been happening around here. We wouldn't be an inch closer to taking down Huber and company if you had never arrived on the scene. And once we're indoors up there, where it's reasonably dry, we can see what's in this." Marta holds up the sealed, plastic tube. "I have a pretty good idea what we're going to find."

So do I, Klaryssa thinks to herself.

"Since you just saved my life, mind if I ask how you ever found me down here with these two psychos?" Klaryssa says, feeling a surge of stinging pain across her face and trying her best not to wince. "Now two dead psychos, blessedly."

"I slid a GPS bug into your shoulder bag when we first met out here, at the Race Point lookout," Marta says as she turns around and points halfway up the immense sand dune that looms over the shoreline. "I knew there was trouble when the signal started moving down that cliff. No one ever tries to walk down a bluff like that, so I figured you weren't heading downhill on your own volition. When the signal suddenly stopped moving, I feared they may have killed you up there on that steep slope. I had no idea that you and your bag had become separated. I was heading over to the base of the sand dune with a beacon light when I heard all the commotion on the raft. I must say, that surprised me, particularly when I saw him holding your head underwater."

426

"Thank you will never come close to sufficing," Klaryssa says, biting her lower lip. "But thank you, Marta. Thank you."

Marta remains silent, staring out across the water's black surface, watching the surf gain momentum as waves begin to break over the side of the raft.

"You might want to thank those three drunks who don't know jack shit about fireworks," Marta says, still looking out into the distance. "They certainly saved Ian from a bullet to the head. And if the killers were spotted up there, they may have taken other lives along with his. And yours could have easily been one of them.

"By the way, when we get to the bunkhouse, I'll get some ice to put on that shiner that monster gave you," Marta says in her native Gagauz, seeing the bright red bruise on Klaryssa's right cheek, the swelling beginning to creep onto Klaryssa's lower eyelid. "The more I learned about that animal's history, the more I realized just how subhuman he was. And that's about the best thing I can say about him."

"He wasn't an animal," Klaryssa says, also speaking in Gagauz while looking down at Stephan's lifeless body facedown in the surf. "He

427

was a pussy. My sweet little auntie in the Catskills slapped harder than he did."

Chapter 29

Truro, Massachusetts

When Klaryssa spots Ian standing at the entrance of the bunkhouse, she runs at full speed and leaps into his arms.

"I thought…I thought…" Klaryssa says, failing to get the words out, her head buried in Ian's chest. "My God, I thought you were gone."

Ian slowly pries Klaryssa away. He's looking at the scarlet bruise spanning one side of Klaryssa's face and the swelling along her eyelid. "He…he hurt you," Ian says, his words breaking and his eyes wide with emotion. "That fucking bastard! What else did he —"

"Nothing, nothing," Klaryssa says, pulling Ian in once again. "Nothing at all. Tell me, is Zorn all right? Tell me that he's OK. Marta says…"

"Marta is right," Ian says, his eyes bloodshot and his voice shaky. "He's waiting for you."

When Klaryssa runs up the stairs and into the small room, she finds Zorn exactly where she last saw him—seated at a small makeshift desk, behind his computer screen. Zorn seems to barely take notice of anyone entering the room, but when Klaryssa wraps both arms around him from behind, she sees tears streaming down his face. They embrace for a moment, and Klaryssa finally lets go, sensing a looming presence directly behind her.

When Klaryssa turns around, she sees a mountain of a man staring down at her. She tilts her head and eyes the man up and down before looking over at Marta. Klaryssa then looks back at the man who takes up half the room.

"Hondo?" Klaryssa asks, now spotting the UNITED STATES MARSHAL badge affixed to the man's belt. "You *too*? You mean that whole scene at the café in Provincetown was just a charade, wedding dress and all?"

"No matter where he shows up, he just fits right in, doesn't he?" Marta says.

"Rather liked the way that gown fit, but the lace was a bit too garish for me," Hondo says, extending his hand to Klaryssa. "Deputy Harold Queen, at your service. It's a real pleasure to see you again, Professor Mahr."

431

"Klaryssa, please," Klaryssa says, her hand disappearing into Hondo's grip. "You both had me completely convinced with that act of yours, I can tell you that. Any more surprises up your sleeves?"

"Maybe one more," Marta says, putting on a pair of gloves and opening the sealed tube that Stephan and Earl had brought onto the raft. "You and Hondo have more in common than you might think. Hondo is the Marshals Service's resident art guru. He gets assigned to any case that involves fine art assets that are seized from this or that criminal enterprise. He can fill you in on his CV later on. Right now, we're a little pressed for time."

"You're telling me," Zorn says without moving his eyes away from his computer screen. "As far as we know, Matthias has no idea that his son's delivery route has been permanently interrupted, so he and Soto will be on a secure phone line within the next 30 to 60 seconds, consummating their deal."

"What deal?" Klaryssa asks, looking up at Hondo.

"It's about this, to start with," Marta says, carefully rolling out a small charcoal sketch that shows a pair of dancers in the upper left corner opposite a singer and a cellist on the right side of the drawing.

"Good Lord," Klaryssa says, eyeing the sketch and then looking up at Marta with a bewildered look on her face. "This is one of the Degas artworks stolen from the Gardner Museum. This is the only Gardner piece to see the light of day since the theft all those years ago."

"So, this is one of the multimillion-dollar masterpieces that we never stop hearing about?" Ian asks.

"Not really," Klaryssa answers, still stunned from seeing the work. "Normally, at auction, a work like this would probably bring only a few thousand, although a bidding war could move it a lot higher. But its significance is immense, because Huber is telling whoever this Soto person is that he's got the Gardner goods. And, my God, maybe he does. At least some of them, anyway."

"The name of the piece is *Program for an Artistic Soiree*," Hondo says, looking at Ian. "Although it's an original Degas, it's just a teaser, as Klaryssa says. It's very unlikely that Huber would be selling one of the least valuable stolen pieces last, because the buyer would likely have little interest if he already had a Rembrandt or a

433

Vermeer in his possession. Huber is trying to communicate something to his buyer, and, from the looks of it, Huber is ground zero in the Gardner heist. But he *could* be bluffing. Maybe the Degas sketch is all he's got. There's just no way to know for sure."

"Huber and Soto will likely be communicating one-on-one any moment now," Zorn says. "When I give the signal, please, everyone stay as quiet as possible, because I have no idea how good the reception will be and we want to catch every word they say. We'll be able to hear and see both of them but not vice versa, so there's no telling how clear the sound and visual will be."

"I thought you said these guys would be using a secure line," Klaryssa asks in a whisper, leaning in toward Zorn.

Zorn turns his head slowly, offering Klaryssa a slight grin. "It's secure under what you might call normal circumstances," he says. "But have you seen or heard anything normal over the past couple of days? Huber and his customers use a darknet site similar to Skype, paying out the nose for all kinds of firewalls to prevent eavesdropping. But, I caught a break, and we'll get through, so no worries; we're as good as in. We'll all be uninvited guests, as it were."

"Huber went to all this trouble to arrange a rendezvous over a picture worth only a few thousand?" Ian asks, looking at Klaryssa and Hondo. "No offense to your man Degas, but this is all about money, right? As in millions of dollars kind of money, right? It seems to me that Huber could have shown his buyer this sketch on one of his supposedly secure connection lines."

"Maybe," Marta answers, unfastening the tie that's around a black leather pouch at the bottom of the sealed plastic tube. "But Huber needs a face-to-face to close the deal on these."

Marta lets a stream of diamonds spill out onto one of the small tables, the dim light glistening off countless facet points within the flawless crystal gems. "Here are your millions, rolling around right in front of you.

"All about the money, you ask?" Marta continues, letting out a deep breath. "You better believe it. Every one of these beauties is evidence, by the way. So admire from a distance, but don't touch."

"The dashed dream of many a damsel," Ian says, leaning down and eyeing the diamonds

435

rattling around on the table top. "I can only guess what this one alone would—"

Zorn raises and then lowers both of his arms, signaling all in the room to be silent.

Chapter 30
Truro, Massachusetts

"Herr Soto, you look as spry as ever," Matthias Huber says to Luis Soto. Soto is seated in a large leather chair positioned in the middle of his private subbasement viewing chamber. "I take it the remainder of your spring fête was as brilliant as ever, with all your guests sloshing about that granite castle you call home. I so regretted not being in attendance and even more my untimely call that interrupted your afternoon under the Andean sun."

"Hearing your voice is never an interruption," Soto says in return, noticing the night sky's half moon illuminating the rising surf behind Matthias Huber, who is seated on the deck of his beach house. "And please accept my invitation for you and Stephan to attend our next gathering. It's booked for the same weekend every year, and I have no doubt that your virile son will find some of the guests in attendance as delectable as our wines.

But enough of that. The hour is growing late there and even later here, so, tell me, why have I not heard from my envoy who was due to meet Stephan on one of your desolate beaches?"

"Come now, Soto, patience," Matthias says, showing no sign of angst or concern. "If you look over my shoulder, you'll see a freshening sea, and that always slows our transactions down a bit. Rest assured that any minute now, we will both hear that familiar ping that signifies a clinched deal. Until then, let's just enjoy each other's company, shall we?"

Zorn, having broken down all firewalls and hijacked his way into Huber and Soto's supposedly airtight cyber tête-à-tête, has the full attention of everyone in the room. Marta scribbles out a handwritten note and hands it to Zorn, asking if there is any way Huber and Soto can hear them.

"Not a chance," Zorn says without a shred of doubt in his voice. "As I discussed with Hondo earlier, we can break into their conversation if we want, but unless I activate that program option we are totally invisible and silent. And, if we do choose to break in, for whatever reason, it is thoroughly untraceable. The sound clarity we are getting right now is as good as I could ask for, but I don't like the video feed on Soto's end. The picture keeps cutting in and out, but I'm working on it."

"I have more to worry over than the deal we are about to consummate, Herr Huber," Soto says, his voice raised an octave and a distinct unease in his words. "The Degas I am purchasing from you is for the back pages of my collection. You know what I am after."

Soto pans the camera on his handheld device to the wall where he has long reserved a space for Rembrandt's *The Storm on the Sea of Galilee* and Vermeer's *The Concert*.

"You think you are appeasing me by throwing me a bone with Degas's name on it?" Soto asks with an edge, standing up from his chair, the temperature in his voice rising. "I'm not looking for a mere token from your most hallowed of thefts, Herr Huber. I know what you have in your possession, and I have paid you millions, many, many millions, as an advance on two of the works you have stashed away. And you know which two I mean."

Matthias Huber is certain he will secure the high ground in his ongoing joust with Luis Soto. He almost always does. But Soto's bellicose tone is out of character, and Matthias has never heard Soto tip his hand so early in their discussions. Matthias knows that Soto is in Dutch with the wrong people —the loan sharks and the Colombian cartels who have been financing Soto's burgeoning vineyard development and his thirst for priceless works of art.

The money Soto has fronted to purchase the stolen Rembrandt and Vermeer masterpieces was secured via loans from men who require neither paperwork nor notarized documents. Matthias knows that the untold millions in debt Soto has accrued have one and only one source of collateral.

"The diamonds are a bargain, my friend," Matthias says in a glacially calm tone, stirring his tea. "I have no doubt you're within shouting distance of customers who will pay you retail, at least two or three times what I'm charging you. And wait until you see these gems glitter in that mountain sun. Two fistfuls will be in your hands in no time."

"This isn't about a pile of fucking rocks, Matthias!" Soto shouts, walking in circles around the small chamber. "You've been shaking me down for years just for first rights on those two paintings, and now it's time to let the hammer fall. How much more—"

Soto stops himself, looking up nervously at the chamber's ceiling. He begins to spin in circles, his eyes still moving nervously.

"*There*," Klaryssa says, fixing her gaze on a vague image on the wall just behind Soto, who is now standing motionless in the middle of the chamber. "Zorn, can you freeze that frame and add some light, enhancing whatever that is along the far wall?"

"Done," Zorn says, tapping in one command after another.

"Something troubling you, Luis?" Matthias asks, squinting a bit and moving closer to the screen. "Are you sure you are alone down there?"

"I thought I heard a clanging noise of some sort, for a moment or so," Soto returns, regaining his composure. "Perhaps a clap of thunder, although I saw no sign of a storm earlier. And apologies to you, my friend. When it comes to such wondrous masterpieces as the ones we are discussing, my heart simply runs wild. I only wish to complete the humble collection in my private museum. I have waited so very long, after all."

Matthias is sure Soto is lying. Should Soto ever actually take possession of the Rembrandt and the Vermeer, Matthias knows he will try to clear his colossal debt by selling at least one of the two paintings at double the money he paid. Matthias knows he has Soto on the ropes.

"My God, stop," Klaryssa says to Zorn, sounding suddenly breathless and moving to within inches of the computer screen.

"My God," Klaryssa repeats, as if she's speaking to the image on the screen.

"Perhaps you're right, Herr Soto," Matthias says, leaning back and offering Soto a kind smile. "Let us bring this larger deal to a close."

"Marta," Klaryssa says, without averting her eyes from the computer screen, "what's your play here? What else do you need to hear from these two? How much more until you crash down Huber's door?"

"That is the music I have been waiting for, Herr Huber," Luis says, still somewhat distracted.

"We can't wait any longer," Marta says, punching in commands on her phone as she speaks with Klaryssa. "There's no way Huber is going to divulge where the other Gardner pieces are stashed, if he even has them. But we know, beyond any doubt, that he was intimately involved in the Gardner heist. I've just contacted the rest of the team, and we'll take Huber down within a minute or so. And we know exactly where Soto is, but putting him in irons is another matter. Getting the Argentinian authorities to move on someone as powerful as Luis Soto may take some doing, and a lot more time."

"Name your figure, my friend," Luis says, wiping his brow.

"He thinks it's authentic, doesn't he?" Hondo asks, looking at the image Klaryssa has frozen on the screen. "Soto actually thinks that painting is the real deal."

"Thinks what's real?" Marta asks, looking at Hondo and then at Klaryssa. "And what's that you two have your eyes glued on, along the far wall of that guy's cellar? The place looks like a dungeon to me."

"Shall we consider a trade, perhaps?" Huber asks, knowing that Soto desperately needs cash and will never acquiesce to a barter. Huber is confident that the mere suggestion of a trade will back Soto further into a corner.

Klaryssa and Hondo enlarge the image they have on the computer screen. Everyone in the room now sees a richly colored painting of a small group of warriors being ambushed along a riverbank. In the foreground, the hands of a mortally wounded soldier are seen sinking into the water's murky depths.

"Woah," Ian says, breaking the silence. "KD, isn't that the painting you told me about a little while back—the battle of so and so something or other? It's the painting that's not suppose to exist, right?"

"How does barter help the Reich, Herr Huber?" Luis asks, his tone defiant. "Trading your wall space for mine advances no one's cause. You need currency, and I want an art collection worthy of our forefathers. Come now, name your price."

"That's the *Battle of Cascina*," Klaryssa says, looking over at Hondo and sending him a sly grin. "Or, rather, it's a rendering of the *Battle of Cascina*. The problem for Soto, and maybe all the more the problem for Huber, is that it is not the rendering they believe it to be."

"You are so right, Herr Soto," Matthias says, taking another sip of tea. "The fathers of our Reich are, at this moment, scolding me for being nothing but a narcissistic boor, worthy only of the hangman's noose for my abandonment of priority. I'm thinking not of the Reich's lifeblood but rather of an inventory of my own possessions, which are, as we both know, not my possessions at all. It is

445

you who is to be applauded for staying grounded in our cause, Herr Soto."

"Marta, I know you're about to take down Huber. That's what you have to do," Klaryssa says quickly. "But I have to ask—can we break into this conversation between these two? If we can make Soto panic, we might be able to get a look at which masterpieces he has down in his chamber. The painting Hondo and I are looking at is *not* the masterpiece they think it is, but we'll get to that in a minute. I have to believe he has more paintings hidden down there, and, if we frighten him out of his own basement, we might get a look at what else he has hanging on the walls. It'll probably be our only chance."

"Pardon the cliché, ladies and gents," Zorn says, squeezing his headset," but we've got company. Someone else besides us is listening in, and, chances are, they're looking in on Huber and Soto just as we are. We may be hijackers, but someone's hijacking us. So, if you want to get something done, I suggest now's the time. I don't know how many other uninvited guests might join this party."

Marta looks over at Hondo and then at Klaryssa, giving her a sharp nod. With that, Zorn activates the program that breaks into the conversation line.

Chapter 31
Truro, Massachusetts

"Gentlemen, good evening," Klaryssa says to Matthias Huber and Luis Soto, her voice disguised in a bleating, cartoonish tone. "Pardon the interruption. And trust me, I will take no more of your time than is necessary."

Luis Soto bolts up out of his chair, looking up at the ceiling and spinning in a circle. "Who the hell is this? You think this is some sort of game? Think you can play a joke like this on me?"

On the other half of the screen, Matthias Huber has the appearance of a man thoroughly untroubled, raising his eyebrows only slightly and taking another small sip of his tea.

"Appears we have a visitor," Matthias says, his words almost welcoming. "Do you mind introducing yourself?"

"Screw the introduction!" Soto says, screaming into his phone. "Whoever you are, you think you can fuck with me?"

"Come now, Soto. We mustn't be so crude with our guest, albeit a guest without invitation. Please, who exactly are you and to what do we owe this, well, intrusion."

"Like you, Herr Huber, and you, Herr Soto, I am merely a connoisseur of fine antiquities," Klaryssa says, following Marta's prompt to use their real names and infuse a level of alarm and dread into the conversation.

Marta's tactic has every bit of the effect she anticipates. The next sound anyone hears is Huber's teacup shattering onto the ground, and, when he looks back into the camera, his face is an ashen, blotchy gray. Soto, who, like Huber, has gone stone silent, begins to frantically pace back and forth in the small room.

Good Lord, Klaryssa thinks to herself, seeing the images Soto's video camera is now picking up from the other three walls of his viewing chamber.

She sees Raphael, Titian, Rubens, and Pissarro. In the upper corner of one wall, she sees perhaps a second masterpiece by Rubens. These are

449

wonders of immeasurable importance, all of them. And each of them was looted from war-ravaged nations, hidden in this private cellar for generations.

"Yes, well, on the topic of fine art, I sit here in rapt admiration," Klaryssa says, still trying to make out some of the other masterpieces on the chamber walls. "And, tonight, I have seen creations that I never thought my eyes would behold. Please, Soto, can you oblige me one more time and show me the *Battle of Cascina?* I'm in total disbelief of what you have in your possession."

Although Huber and Soto remain connected, their line is totally silent. Matthias has set his phone down on the deck table, his back now turned to the camera and his silhouette visible against the waving grass along the sand dunes. Soto is still pacing in circles.

"To think, a treasure thought destroyed over five centuries ago, still alive and well and in your governing hands, Soto. The *Battle of Cascina,* the lost Michelangelo. The most epic of all lost treasures, in the possession of one man."

Huber and Soto both remain dead silent.

Klaryssa continues, her voice taking on an even higher-pitched, disembodied tone.

"Still there, Soto? I believe you are; can you be so kind as to indulge me this once? Please, zero in your keen eye to the lower right corner of your *Battle of Cascina* painting. Are you with me now? There, if you carefully inspect the butt end of the lance one of the militiamen is reaching for, you will see the initials *AS*. I know, the letters are quite small, so you might require the aid of a magnifier. In fact, I needed one myself just to see these scribbled initials.

"Well, you see, the *A* stands for Alessio and the *S* for Sartori, and, thus, we have Alessio Sartori. Ever heard of him? Well, neither had I, and I have been in this business for quite some time. It turns out that Alessio Sartori was one of Michelangelo's young apprentices, and, from what little history we have, he was a promising artist. I'm sure you would agree, Soto. After all, he painted that very work you have in your possession. The rendition of the *Battle of Cascina* hanging on your wall is a product of young Sartori's talented hand."

Huber whips around and picks up his phone, his slate gray face filling one side of the screen. The other half shows Soto on his knees, inspecting the lower-right edge of the painting.

451

"Tragic, really," Klaryssa goes on, Soto now slamming his fist on the stone floor. "Sartori, that is. The poor lad died of tuberculosis at age 20 or so. As for the painting you invested in, my guess is you would put its value in the hundreds of millions of dollars. If you'll allow me a moment of immodesty, being an authority of sorts, I would put its value in the hundreds...hundreds of thousands."

"You sold my family this piece of shit, Huber!" Soto shouts into the phone, his eyes jumbling in every direction, sweat running from every pore. "I have millions, tens of millions, even more, leveraged on this garbage canvas. I'm destroyed, do you hear me? *Destroyed.*"

"I would hardy call it garbage," Klaryssa says as she watches Matthias Huber stare straight up into the helicopter lights now hovering above him. "Show some respect, Soto; he was a fine artisan who was taken long before his prime. As for the other works you have hanging on your walls, these are indeed authentic treasures that the rest of the world thought lost. But they're not lost, are they? They're stolen, every last one of them, and, unless I'm mistaken, each is leveraged to the point of having no value to you whatsoever. Soon, I'm confident, each will be returned to its rightful owner, and their inestimable beauty will be no longer hidden from the world."

Two US Marshals wrestle Matthias Huber to the ground, placing him in handcuffs and leg irons. Soto drops his phone and runs to the only door leading out of the viewing chamber.

"I can't help but wonder why you chose to do business with a man like him," Klaryssa taunts as Soto struggles to open the cellar door. "All those millions, and no Michelangelo, no Rembrandt, no Vermeer. Huber is being detained by the authorities for further questioning, so you may have difficulty finding him and squaring the ledger you have with him. And that disturbing noise above you, seeming to move in closer with every passing minute—I regret to say that there were others besides myself listening in on your conversation with Herr Huber. I wish I could tell you the police were coming to pay a visit, but—regrettably—they're not the ones knocking at your door. No, I fear your creditors have come calling, each of them wondering how you will ever drain away that sea of red ink you're drowning in."

Chapter 32
Saratoga, New York
Two days later

At long last, the US Department of Justice announced the arrest of Matthias Huber, leader of an international crime syndicate that had hauled in hundreds of millions of dollars through the trafficking of stolen art. Since the announcement of his arrest and the press conferences that followed, the media had been unable to get enough of this tale of a generations-old powerhouse crime family that no one had ever heard of, one that operated out of a sand dune shack in a place no one had ever heard of either.

The US Attorney General himself announced the arrest of Huber from the Great Hall of the Department of Justice building, with Huber's mugshot now plastered across the front page of every newspaper and news website on six continents.

In that same announcement, the deaths of Stephan Huber and his accomplice were reported. It was stated that the killing of these two men occurred during the course of criminal activity that involved "the perpetrators brandishing weapons in the presence of law enforcement officers." The Attorney General stated that besides the apprehension of the syndicate's ringleader, no arrests had, as of yet, been made. Because federal authorities were still in the process of reviewing and verifying a mountain of new information, there was no mention by the Department of Justice of the Huber family's link to alt-right hate crimes or the Gardner Museum art heist.

Klaryssa had been questioned for hours by the FBI and the Marshals Service about the sequence of events that led her to the home of Matthias Huber. Ian and Zorn were also interviewed by these same officials, answering all the same questions before being allowed to leave at around 3:30 the next morning. All of the information Klaryssa had amassed from Huber's office files had been commandeered by the federal authorities, which, for her, was a blessing beyond measure, as she would receive no public acknowledgement and, in all likelihood, would remain anonymous in regard to Huber's arrest.

But every media outlet on the planet had descended upon Truro and Provincetown, and Klaryssa knows she is only one camera snap away from being forever linked to the unmasking of a criminal enterprise that is sending shockwaves around the world. When the federal agents had finally finished with her, it was still dark enough for Klaryssa to slip away unnoticed, but she still felt the same unease she knew in the weeks and months following her recovery from the marathon bombing.

Would she be recognized? Would people point in her direction from one of the other booths in a roadside diner? Would she again have to avoid walking down the street in broad daylight, fearing that the next passing stranger might spin around and tap her on the shoulder?

After leaving Truro, Klaryssa stops by her townhouse in Boston to pick up the piles of scrambled family archive papers that Elle Picard sent to her. She enters her building wearing an oversized hoodie, letting the wide brim of a floppy hat cover her eyes. She exits the building as soon as she stuffs the volumes of papers into a shoulder bag, and from there, she gets back in her car and heads onto I-90 toward Saratoga. Along the way, she has another detailed conference call with members of the National Museum of Racing's Board of Trustees, appraising the board members of all she has learned about the tangled history of the Picard art collection and the bizarre events that took place in the summer of 1946. All agree that it is imperative to meet with Elle Picard and her family, so the museum staff arranges a meeting for later in the day.

Klaryssa also contacts Zorn while driving along the interstate, apologizing for waking him out of a deep sleep but explaining that she has a pressing favor to ask. Klaryssa tells Zorn of the urgent meeting she has at the museum, and that she will need a specialized light filtration system known as a ZeenOx for her presentation to Elle Picard and the museum trustees. To no surprise, Zorn is very familiar with this particular instrument, known in high-tech parlance as a zinc oxide wave penetrator, which is designed to illuminate layers of paper or fabric beneath the visible outer surface, no matter how thick or durable that outer surface may be. Zorn immediately contacts a longtime colleague in

Syracuse and arranges to have a courier deliver the ZeenOx penetrator to the museum by early afternoon.

Klaryssa knows that she has to show her face in public sooner or later, so, once she arrives in Saratoga, she signs up for a tour of the Canfield Casino, a once world-renowned gaming establishment founded in the mid-19th century by a heavyweight boxing champion. The casino is located in the center of Congress Park, and Klaryssa figures the casino tour will serve as a distraction for all she has on her mind. But, once she walks through the doors of what was once the world's most elite gambling parlor, another thought comes to mind.

Klaryssa reckons that a quiet corner in this cavernous, otherwise abandoned building will afford her the solitude she needs to read through the Picard family archive. So, after queuing up last in line, she slips away from the small parade of gawking tourists and ducks under a rope that cordons off a back stairwell.

With no security cameras or locks on the doors, she finds her way into one of the gambling rooms on the casino's upper level, and, despite the room's musty air and the gloom that filters into the parlor from every window, there is enough natural light for Klaryssa to scour through every document Elle sent to her.

In the end, the Picard papers confirm what Klaryssa already knows to be true, and what she already knows to be true still seems numbingly impossible.

Klaryssa closes the stack of files and looks out across Congress Park. The park's main promenade is mostly deserted on a morning that has seen nothing but wind-driven rainstorms and temperatures only a few degrees above freezing. Klaryssa paces the length of the lavish gaming parlor, imagining, for a moment, the elegance and grandeur of an era long forgotten, when the world's wealthiest industrial tycoons and most fearless gamblers made this establishment the epicenter of a town once known as America's Monte Carlo.

She lifts up the thick, fraying tarp covering one of the dice tables, eyeing the croupier's stick that rests against the forest-green felt cushion. She wonders how many millions this instrument swept into the house's corner before that night over a century ago, when it was last used to rake the dreams of the highest of high rollers off the table. Klaryssa picks up a stack of wooden gambling

459

chips that she finds lined up along the sideboard, rolling them in her hand and, for a brief moment, imagining herself dressed in a glittering gown, wound like a cobra poised to strike, knowing that the next roll would be the only one she would ever remember, because that will be the one which will forever reverse her fortune.

But this brief diversion brings Klaryssa back to the here and now, reminding her that this trip to Saratoga is not about pursuing some phantasm held since her impoverished childhood in Ukraine. She is here for one express purpose, and that is to fulfill the promise she made to Elle Picard barely a week earlier.

Klaryssa startles slightly when a familiar number flashes across her iPhone screen.

***

"… for our PR and media staff, this has been a circus second to none," Marta says to Klaryssa on the other end of the line. "They're hanging on our every syllable, digging in every corner and stabbing at every edge, because they're so damn sure we're keeping a lid on 99% of this story. They've all heard what we've had to say, and now all they want is to hear what we haven't said."

"Ever occur to you that they're right?" Klaryssa says, taking a seat in the pit boss's chair behind a roulette wheel that is encased in protective glass. "You've only given them the barest of facts, without a word in reference to the miles of documentation concerning the Nazis' stolen art and, of course, the Degas drawing that puts Huber squarely in the crosshairs of the Gardner theft. All you've told them is that one Huber is caught, the other Huber is dead, and these were both bad boys who took things that didn't belong to them."

"All that's true, every word of it," Marta says. "But the AG doesn't want to spill out anything else just yet, particularly Huber's link to funding Neo-Nazis and other hate organizations. He wants to keep quiet on the naming of Huber's possible partners in crime, letting the Feds keep an eye on all potential accomplices. He wants to see which ones might try to run for cover, flushing out the collaborators who are most likely to cut a deal for a lighter sentence.

"Then the Feds can take down as many of Huber's cronies as possible. What happened out there in Truro is only chapter one of this saga, and the narrative released so far is all the public is going to get for now. And, believe it or not, there are no witnesses to any of what happened out there besides you and Ian and Zorn. Every news outlet on God's green earth is out on Cape Cod right now, interviewing as many of those '70s revelers as they can find. So far, not one of them knows jack about Huber or his guys."

"From what I saw at that festival, I'd be surprised if any of them can recollect their own name," Klaryssa says. "And on the topic of accomplices, any more on the fate of Luis Soto?"

"As reported by the Argentinian authorities within the last hour," Marta says, reading from a wire service on her phone, "'the human remains found in a burned-out vehicle that veered off a mountain road in the Mendoza Province are those of Señor Luis Soto, internationally renown vintner and philanthropist. Our nation mourns the death of one of its most enlightened and generous sons, and details of his planned funeral procession shall be published forthwith.'

"How do you like that crock of shit? One of our operatives down there knows on good authority that the body they found was burnt beyond recognition well before that car broke through the guardrail, so the 'deep thermal tissue damage' they found on the corpse likely occurred while Luis was still alive. The man was in deep with the wrong people."

"Marta, I have to ask something else, and tell me straight, no matter what the answer is," Klaryssa says in a low voice, eyeing the long hallway that leads to the casino's main staircase. "All the artwork in Soto's possession, the masterpieces we saw for ourselves. Is there any word—"

"There are plenty of words, and they're all the ones you've been waiting to hear," Marta says, interrupting. "All the artwork in Luis Soto's man cave has been seized and secured by the Argentinian National Police and Interpol. Every last piece that was hanging on that thieving bastard's wall."

"Please tell me there's no doubt about this, that you're certain," Klaryssa says, her voice thick with emotion. "Those masterpieces were assumed lost forever."

"Lost no more, Professor. Lost no more," Marta says. "The Colombians may have gotten Soto, but they didn't get the paintings. By the way, where are you? I'm hearing an echo in the background."

"I'm stowed away in this old casino in Saratoga," Klaryssa says in a hush, still casting a wary eye down the hall. "I joined a guided tour group, but I was really only looking for an excuse to be alone for a while. I needed time to read through Elle Picard's documents, but the truth is, I'm just plain paranoid about my face somehow showing up, linked to Huber getting busted. So, once I got inside the casino, I snuck away and found this old gambling parlor upstairs. There's no one here but me and the ghosts of losers past. The ghosts are *supposed* to be up here, but I'm not."

"Well, sneak yourself back out before you get locked in," Marta says, a squawking, guttural sound ringing out in the background. "From what you've told me, you've got a meeting with Elle in a little while that you can't miss. And your picture won't show up anywhere. And neither will your name. We have our story, and we're sticking to it."

"Thank God for that," Klaryssa says, again peering out the door nervously. "And what's that noise I'm hearing? It sounds like someone is squeezing a kid's toy or something."

"Grommet, say hi to your old friend Klaryssa," Marta says, the flapping noise becoming louder over the phone. "Here, I'll send you an African grey selfie."

"You *stole* the bird?" Klaryssa asks with a chuckle. "Isn't he considered evidence or something? How'd you get away with that?"

"Someone has to take care of him," Marta says back, Klaryssa covering the phone with her hand when Grommet sends out a string of loud chirps. "Though you are right. He was, after all, living in Huber's house, so he might be called as a witness. He'll have more to say than Matthias, that's for damn certain. Herr Huber has hired a million-dollar lawyer, and everyone in the AG's office is betting that he will never utter a sound about his family's past, not to mention his own. If he starts to tell tales for a lighter sentence, he'll end up wearing Soto's death mask, and he knows it.

"Matthias Huber will take all he knows to his grave behind the prison yard, and that doesn't bode well for finding the rest of the Gardner treasures, assuming he actually has the rest of them. But you cut this guy off at the legs, and now there's a chance to repatriate thousands of masterpieces that were pilfered during World War II. And Huber doesn't have to utter a single word to make that happen."

Chapter 33

Saratoga, New York

Funnels of bitter wind rip along the avenue that connects Congress Park to the Racing Museum, spewing tree branches and coils of fallen debris across the sidewalks and expansive lawns. To Klaryssa, the street seems absurdly wide. She wonders for a moment why a thoroughfare befitting a city on the scale of Paris or London would ever be needed in such a small town. But, in truth, the cold blasts of air and the broad, lonely avenue put Klaryssa at ease. She sees no one else along her half-mile walk to the museum. That is, until she sees a young woman standing near a lamppost at the far end of the main entrance to the museum.

The woman is wearing large, wide-rimmed eyeglasses, and she startles slightly when she spots Klaryssa approaching the museum. Despite her face being partially covered by the hood of her rain jacket, the woman manages to make eye contact with Klaryssa for the briefest of moments. Klaryssa immediately looks away and sprints inside the museum.

Oliver Rainey, the Racing Museum's director, greets Klaryssa at the door and ushers her down the main corridor to a small lecture hall. When Klaryssa enters the room, she's met by Elle Picard, who is standing next to a tall, stately gentleman dressed in a dark gray three-piece suit and a crimson bow tie. When Elle approaches Klaryssa, her bright features quickly darken as she notices the bruise across Klaryssa's cheekbone.

"As a young girl," Elle begins, grasping Klaryssa's hands, "I took to sports that were, at the time, largely confined to the men of this world. My classmates chided me so often that they would ask which was my favorite color: black or blue? But, once such diversions were put aside, I learned everything I could about the use of cosmetics to conceal the blemishes from one's injuries. And, my dear, you cannot apply enough makeup to hide your secrets from me. Now, whatever happened to you over the past few days?"

"I'll get to all that soon enough," Klaryssa says, closing her eyes and embracing Elle. "I promise I will. Now, I don't believe I've had the pleasure of meeting the gentleman accompanying you here today."

"My brother Kendrick, whom I mentioned when we first met on marathon day," Elle says.

"I take it this has been an eventful week, Dr. Mahr," Kendrick says, offering Klaryssa a slight bow. "How good of you to arrange this meeting here today. Mr. Rainey and members of the Trustees Board have already taken Elle and I on a most delightful tour of the museum galleries. I take it you have, in the past, toured the museum yourself?"

"Yes, I have," Klaryssa says. "I had a lovely visit quite recently, in fact. And, as I've mentioned to Elle and members of the museum staff, it's Klaryssa, please. Just Klaryssa."

Oliver Rainey introduces Klaryssa to Mrs. Kelly M. Nash, the president of the Museum's Board of Trustees, as well as three other senior board members who are present in the room. "Dr. Mahr, on behalf of all our Trustees, welcome back to our museum," Mrs. Nash says, her vice-like grip taking Klaryssa by surprise, given the woman's small frame and soft voice. "I regret I was not here at the time of your first visit, and I think it is safe to say that because of you, our galleries will never again be quite the same. Now, this room is called a

470

lecture hall for a reason, so please begin whenever you'd like."

With that, Mr. Rainey dims the lights, and the room goes silent.

"Good afternoon," Klaryssa begins quietly, as she looks out at the small gathering. "Elle, when we first met barely a week ago, you began by recounting some of the rich history of your grandfather, Colonel Picard, and, in particular, his penchant for collecting art from everywhere he traveled. The colonel kept quite an extensive journal of his travels and acquisitions, though his records were stored somewhat, shall we say, non-chronologically."

Kendrick looks at Elle and grins, clasping one of her hands.

"However, now we must turn back the hands of time many years, long before the exploits of Colonel Picard," Klaryssa continues, bringing up an image of the Michelangelo charcoal sketch on the screen directly behind her. "Let us begin with this work, which is the property of the Picard family and has been preserved for many years between the pages of a book found in their home library.

"Elle and Kendrick, of course, recognize this sketch, and, Elle, I must now confess that when you first showed me this work, I had suspicions about its origin that I didn't voice at the time. This charcoal sketch was drawn by Michelangelo in preparation for a commission he received in 1504 to paint a rendition of a medieval military engagement known as the Battle of Cascina, and that work was to be hung in the Palazzo Vecchio in Florence. The civic leaders of Florence were very powerful men, so powerful that they also commissioned Leonardo da Vinci to paint a separate work depicting *another* medieval battle, and this too was to be hung in the same grand chamber of the Palazzo. The very thought of a single room being adorned with a master work of art completed by each of these giants staggers the imagination.

"But these same ennobled Florentines then made a decision so egregious that it is somehow yet more staggering," Klaryssa goes on, letting the image on the screen fade to darkness. "Having other ideas about the design of their council chamber, they destroyed the room's interior and everything in it, including the two epic paintings hanging on opposite walls.

"Enter now one Bruno Abbiati, an otherwise obscure contemporary of Michelangelo, a historian and biographer who professes a different account of the Palazzo Vecchio's renovation. Abbiati tells of an eyewitness who swore under oath that the Michelangelo painting was removed from the wall of the Palazzo *prior* to the chamber's destruction and indicates that this eyewitness had some idea of where the painting was located. The problem with Abbiati's account is that his eyewitness told this sequence of events to his jailers while awaiting trial for thievery, so his recollections were possibly seen as a tall tale told to avoid prison time. This man, needless to say, was considered simply not credible.

"However, Abbiati did not stop there," Klaryssa continues, showing an image of a fortress-like building with a battlement crowning and a tall, off-center rectangular clock tower. "This is the Palazzo Vecchio as it appears today, and it still serves as the town hall of Florence. Abbiati records a particularly bright, cloudless sky on the night before the Palazzo chamber was to be ripped apart and decorated anew. This has, in fact, been verified by astronomers, as there was a supermoon, or perigee moon, visible in the sky that night. This witness he quotes says there was enough light for

473

him to see a man hurrying down the Palazzo stairs and out onto the street. And he believed this man to be an artist and an understudy of Michelangelo.

"Of course, a few hours later, with the sun high in the sky over Florence, none of this mattered. Carpenters tore down the chamber's interior and began renovations, as per the direction of Florence's overlords. Michelangelo's *Battle of Cascina*, along with the da Vinci masterpiece, were presumably lost forever.

"Again, the year was 1504, and until his death 60 years later, Michelangelo achieved a level of renown unknown before or since by any artist. Abbiati tells us, however, that throughout Michelangelo's long life, there were enemies at every gate—rival artisans, jealous patrons, common thieves, conniving politicians, and petty civic leaders. Michelangelo was, by all accounts, a contentious, quick-tempered man who found fault with all around him, including his assistants, whom he considered inept, and his superiors, whom he considered both shallow and indecisive. In fact, as a teenager, he once called out a fellow young apprentice for his lack of attention to anatomic detail, and the ensuing altercation resulted in the deformed nose you see in the surviving portraits of Michelangelo.

"Michelangelo's students and apprentices were forever aware of the internal and external forces that threatened their mentor, and they would go to any length necessary to protect Michelangelo and his works. Abbiati traced every step of Michelangelo's life that he could follow, right up until February 1564, when the great master died in Rome. And that's where we rely on the personal journal of a then 20-year-old understudy named Alessio Sartori."

Klaryssa shows an image on the exact painting Luis Soto had as the centerpiece of his clandestine collection, hidden for years in a deep recess below his South American estate.

"This is a replica of Michelangelo's epic work, the *Battle of Cascina*. It's the work of young Sartori, and one would reasonably assume Sartori had used various Michelangelo sketches to reproduce the original work done by the master himself, which had supposedly been destroyed years earlier. But, Abbiati tells us something no other historian has ever even hinted at before or since. He asserts that Michelangelo's *Battle of Cascina* had been rescued all those years earlier by

475

another apprentice. Apparently, a young artist faded into the night after he entered the Palazzo Vecchio and removed the canvas from the chamber's wall, boldly making off with the masterpiece within a couple of hours of its scheduled destruction.

"Sartori was with Michelangelo on the day he died in February 1564, and, to protect and preserve his master's work, he wrapped his rendition of the *Battle of Cascina* around the original Michelangelo canvas, placing both paintings in the hollowed-out leg of a wooden table. Abbiati died less than a year after Michelangelo's passing, and, presumably, even the faintest scent of a trail leading to this epic masterpiece perished with him.

"Presumably," Klaryssa says sharply, allowing spotlights to slowly illuminate two paintings mounted on separate easels at the front of the room. "Recall that Sartori was an art student, and, all in all, he was quite a fine painter. He might have made a solid living as an artisan had he not died of tuberculosis at the age of 22. But, in his few years, he kept a meticulous personal journal. When he died, his journal was passed on to another student and then another and then another and on and on. These young men were, without question, rivals, but they learned from each other incessantly, and they shared an undying reverence for their great master, Michelangelo.

"You might be wondering about the table with the hollowed-out leg," Klaryssa continues, eyeing each of the guests one by one. "I've had the opportunity to review an archive of personal journals largely unknown to the outside world, and there is a clear record that this simple wooden table was passed from one artist to the next and used by each of them as a work station for the next century or more. At some point, another young student, fearing that the stashed canvases might be destroyed by fire, unwrapped the two paintings and hid them behind two other paintings that hung in a distant relative's country home. This student's name has actually been lost to history, and his journal ends abruptly with an entry telling of his conscription into the Italian army. It would seem likely that this young man perished during the course of his military duty."

Klaryssa gestures to the two easels standing at the front of the room, and Mr. Rainey brightens the spotlights while dimming the overhead lights.

"Elle, as you related to me when we first met, many of the pieces from your grandfather's collection were donated to museums some years later by your father. A total of 14 paintings were brought here to the then-nascent Racing Museum, and of that grouping, these are the two oldest works. No one knows for certain the origin of these two paintings, but we do know that they were completed by different artists in the first half of the 17th century, and that the two artists very likely lived somewhere around Florence. The title of the work on the left is *Viscount Campden with Journeymen*, and although the original title of the work on the right remains unknown, its given name is *Morning Frolic Near Bisenzio*. Your grandfather purchased both of the works you see here from a family in Prato, which is along the Bisenzio River in the Tuscany region of Italy."

Each member of the small gathering inspects the two illuminated paintings. The *Viscount Campden with Journeymen* work shows three regally attired horsemen mounted on stallions, and *Morning Frolic Near Bisenzio* shows a small group of hat-waving men corralling a heard of yearlings toward a grazing pasture.

"These two works, along with a dozen others, were stolen from the Saratoga Racetrack in late August 1946," Klaryssa says, looking directly at Elle and Kendrick. "That story is well known, at least locally. But who stole these works, and why did they steal them? And how did the thieves ever get the paintings off such heavily guarded property? And why were they all returned, apparently intact, just a few days later?

"The men who stole your grandfather's art collection were members of the Nazi top brass, and they infiltrated our country during and immediately after World War II. They sought to continue their fight outside of Europe, if it came to that, and it did. To that end, they used a cache of archives stolen from across Europe to trace and track artworks held in private and public collections everywhere. The work they sought above any other was in your grandfather's collection, which at the time was, presumably, safely stored and under guard, in preparation for display in the galleries being built in this museum. They knew exactly what they wanted and exactly where it was, and they would stop at nothing to find and procure this one work of art.

"Nearly 400 years ago, in the first part of the 17th century, one of the two paintings you see before you was used to hide young Alessio Sartori's *Battle of Cascina* canvas," Klaryssa says with slow emphasis, feeling her pulse race as she again

479

gestures at the two paintings mounted on easels at the front of the room. "The young artisans who had, for many years, hidden these canvases in a hollowed-out table leg, kept journals that were preserved in university archives. During the course of World War II, all of these records, long since forgotten, were pilfered and scrutinized by the Nazis. According to these records, the *Battle of Cascina* canvas ended up in the home of a family somewhere in the city of Prato around 1701, and this family, whose name is lost to history, could not have possibly known what they had purchased. Neither did your grandfather, when he bought the collection all those many years later.

"But the Nazis did. They followed the trail of Michelangelo's *Battle of Cascina* from the moment it was whisked off the Palazzo wall, then hidden by a series of young artisans for over a hundred years, then acquired by a family in Prato and eventually sold to Colonel Picard. The Nazis were certain they knew where this unique masterpiece was hidden, so when the racetrack right across the street was reopened after World War II, a Nazi criminal named Harold Melcher presented forged papers to local officials and was hired as racing patrol judge.

"Unbeknownst to law enforcement or any of the racing officials, Melcher was a man with near limitless resources; he'd once been a member of Hitler's inner circle. Melcher was part of a criminal empire that consisted of many thousands, perhaps tens of thousands, of Nazi loyalists. They were so entrenched and their network so expansive that even the organized mob right here on our shores left them alone. Melcher was sent here for the sole purpose of stealing priceless artworks. To do so, he concocted an elaborate scheme to fix the last race on the last day of the 1946 summer season. Melcher actually orchestrated an unheard-of triple disqualification in that particular race, and the grandstand melee that followed was just the diversion he anticipated and needed. With every security officer called to the betting kiosks to keep order and prevent a riot, Melcher's men simply hot-wired the truck containing Colonel Picard's 14 paintings and drove off the premises as if nothing had ever happened."

Klaryssa again pauses, allowing time for all of this to sink in and to remind herself of the enormity of what she is laying out before the small gathering.

"What truly happened in the hours and days after this theft will never be fully known, but this much is certain," Klaryssa says, the curator now dimming the spotlight on one of the easels while keeping the other fully illuminated. "The thieves had both the stolen historical records and the stolen paintings they were after, but, in the end, what they didn't have was particularly good luck. The bandits carefully cracked open the frames of the paintings one by one until they saw a spectacular rendition of the *Battle of Cascina* hidden behind one of the works. With this presumed epic masterpiece in hand, they stopped their search. They then nailed the frames back together and stashed what they believed to be a Michelangelo masterpiece in a safe place, with the intent of fencing the work for millions of dollars. When all the stolen paintings were eventually returned safely to this museum, it appeared as if nothing at all was missing. They had pulled off the perfect crime, so perfect that the world would never know a robbery had even occurred. In the end, no one would ever know anything was pilfered, let alone a priceless Michelangelo.

"Perhaps not so perfect. In fact, if the city fathers of Florence made a mistake of immeasurable dimension many centuries ago, then Melcher and his band of thieves made perhaps the biggest gaffe in the history of crime. When they found this painting, they looked no further. Certain of what they had found, they stopped. We know this because some of the wooden frames that surround the paintings in the Picard collection have the original wooden pegs intact, while others show signs of being violated and repaired with copper nails. Many years later, Melcher fenced the painting you are looking at, Sartori's rendering of the *Battle of Cascina*, to an ex-Nazi officer living under an alias in Argentina for many times the piece's actual worth. Although this Nazi loyalist died many years ago, his son dedicated his life to his father's enterprise of supporting perpetrators of hate crimes throughout the world.

"I'm pleased to announce that this family has recently gone out of business. Permanently out of business. I needn't expound further, as pretty much every media outlet you can name will have plenty to say about these men, and their American-based co-conspirators, in the days and weeks to come. Suffice it to say that this Argentinian family had accumulated an immense amount of debt by using a painting believed to be a many-centuries-lost Michelangelo as collateral. But the stolen painting they purchased all those years ago was not from the hand of Michelangelo."

The single spotlight is extinguished, and the room goes completely dark. Klaryssa draws in all the air her lungs can hold.

"This one, however, is."

A moment later, the ZeenOx device is activated, and multiple beams of filtered light give life to an image lying beneath the *Viscount Campden with Journeymen* canvas that is sitting on an easel at the front of the room. Instead of seeing three horsemen mounted on stallions, all gathered in the small lecture hall now gaze upon the 20 warriors who a moment earlier were immersed in the cool waters of the Arno River but now face the swords and lances fired upon them by their Pisan enemies.

Elle, at first stunned by the apparition appearing in front of her, begins to look into the eyes of each of the besieged warriors. In some she sees a look of sheer terror, in others defiance, and in others somber innocence. In several of the men, there is a look of deadly fear. In one or two, Elle sees eyes that betray simple resignation. In the foreground of the painting, she sees the hands of a

484

man slain, surely the first of many to die, sinking beneath the murky waves that break onto the shoreline.

Elle and Kendrick both stand and move in closer, watching the cylinders of light mounted behind the easel penetrate through a dense matrix of zinc oxide, which produces a series of ghostly waveforms right in front of them. To each of the onlookers, it appears as if the desperate warriors momentarily emerge from the hidden canvas, seemingly in motion for a brief moment before again vanishing.

Then, through the pulsing light beam filtering through the center of the painting, Elle sees him. She sees the bearded man with sculpted facial features and taut neck muscles, his eyes simultaneously tranquil and forlorn, the tail of his leather headband trailing in the wind. Elle knows this is the man in the sketch that she found by pure happenstance, a forgotten charcoal scribble pressed between the pages of a book that no one would have otherwise ever noticed or cared about. This is the man in the sketch that she brought to Klaryssa, a simple drawing that she now knows led to the discovery of a Michelangelo masterpiece that the world has never seen.

"Is...is it?" Elle asks, cutting herself off, her bright eyes meeting Klaryssa's.

"You know that it is," Klaryssa says, grasping Elle's trembling hand. "Your grandfather purchased two paintings from a small gallery in Prato, just outside of Florence, and, for all these many years, both of these works have hung on the gallery walls of this museum, each holding a secret that no one could ever have imagined. Unknown to Colonel Picard or to anyone, the Sartori work was hidden behind one of the canvases, and behind the second is the painting you now see. This is Michelangelo's *Battle of Cascina*, Elle. His mark is everywhere. There's no doubt about it."

All gathered are now on their feet, surrounding the Michelangelo masterpiece that had been shrouded for centuries

"What I wouldn't give to have him here today," Kendrick says eventually, his voice breaking as he speaks. "The colonel, that is. To us, he was always Papa, but to the rest of the world, he was the colonel. If he ever knew what he had found, what he had held in his hands. If he ever knew what he'd brought to his home, into our home. And Elle, our father...how could he have ever known?"

486

Klaryssa feels a wave of heat rush through her.

"Elle, Kendrick," Klaryssa says, pulling a small stack of yellowed papers from her shoulder bag. "These are some of the records from the many files that you sent to me, and, to be honest, I barely gave these documents much notice at first. But, after all I learned over the last few days, I studied them a second time. Although the print on these papers is somewhat faded, they are all legible and quite detailed, and, given their content, I felt compelled to share them with Mrs. Nash and the rest of the museum board prior to your arrival. We have had a number of conversations over the past couple of days, including a rather long conference call last evening while on my way over here from Boston.

"These are the cities, and a list of their museums, where your father endowed artworks in the years following World War II," Klaryssa continues. "Elle, when we first met, you mentioned that your father went about distributing the artworks that your grandfather, Colonel Picard, had spent the latter part of his life collecting. It appears that your father started on the west coast and worked his way east, eventually finding his way to

487

Philadelphia, Manhattan, Boston, and, finally, to a few smaller cities such as Saratoga. As you know, at the time of your father's arrival here, the museum we are in right now was not yet built. Unlike the Metropolitan Museum in New York or the Museum of Fine Arts in Boston, this institution was not yet fully established. And I can only assume that your father was a thoughtful, cautious man, because when he brought 14 paintings to this nascent institution, they were not donated.

"They were loaned," Klaryssa says, the words catching in her throat as she produces another document and hands it to Elle. "Loaned for 12 years, to be exact. Twelve years from the day the pieces were first hung in the galleries of this museum, each and every one of the paintings he brought here was to be returned to your family. That's your father's signature, right next to the signatures of three members of the museum's original Board of Trustees, with all signatories agreeing on a return date of August 17, 1962."

Elle and Kendrick look over the documents, the lecture room remaining as still and as quiet as a tomb.

"It appears we've been a bit tardy in fulfilling our responsibility," Mrs. Nash says,

488

breaking the room's dead-shock silence. "On behalf of all our board members, I extend our apologies."

Elle and Kendrick look at each other before turning to look at Klaryssa, their faces pale and drawn.

"The thieves stole the wrong painting," Klaryssa says. "Members of the Nazi leadership came to our shores so they could steal precious antiquities, with the intent being to breath new life into their Reich. Along the way, they thought they had stolen a Michelangelo that the world knew nothing of. They thought they had history's greatest lost treasure in their hands, but they never did.

"What they had was a reproduction worth not a fraction of the value of the master's original. A few days after that art heist all those years ago, a man named Roscoe Fowler returned the stolen paintings. The one thing Roscoe had in common with your grandfather, your father, and the Nazi thieves, was that he had no idea what he had in his possession. But once you found the sketch of that one man, Elle, the charcoal drawing of that one warrior, all that changed. The shroud had at last been lifted.

"In the hand of the artist, the masterpiece follows the sketch, and in the hand of history, the sketch follows the masterpiece. And this masterpiece belongs to you and your family, Elle. The world awaits its chance to see the master's brilliance, but it can wait as long as you want."

Elle looks at Mrs. Nash with a frozen expression.

"But this painting's home is *here*," Elle utters. "I...we...never had the first thought of taking back any of the works my father donated."

"There is no thought here at all, Mrs. Picard," Mrs. Nash says, fighting back her emotions and offering a warm smile. "*Viscount Campden* and his friends have made a home in our gallery, and, with your permission, I suspect they would agree to stay. But what Professor Mahr has shown us, shown us all, is that the Michelangelo work will be at home when and only when it returns home with you."

"But what you're losing...the potential value of this work," Kendrick says, his hands and head shaking as he speaks. "We want to carry on the work our family began years ago, not strip your walls clean."

"Kendrick, you cannot imagine how much this institution will gain from this resolution," Klaryssa says. "The *Battle of Cascin*a belongs to

490

you, and to no one else. The museum trustees' decision not to contest ownership will be seen as an enlightened declaration, an example that all in the world of fine art will laud and perhaps even try to emulate. And Elle, when you mentioned carrying on the work your family began years ago, I know that a scholarship fund for art students was your ultimate goal. If I may ask, how many students do you aspire to grant scholarships to every year?"

"One or two," Elle says, giving her brother a quizzical look before responding. "That alone would be a success by any measure. Scholarships to four or more students per year would be a dream."

Klaryssa pauses for a long moment.

"Should you choose to place the *Battle of Cascina* on the auction block, I can tell you beyond any doubt that you can multiply the dream you have," she says eventually, looking once more at the besieged warriors along the shore of the Arno River, the image wobbling in and out of view through the penetrating beams of ionized light.

"Multiply?" Elle asks, again looking at her brother and then back to Klaryssa, her eyes searching. "Good Lord, multiply by...by what?"

Klaryssa looks at him one last time, the warrior in the center of Michelangelo's masterwork.

491

She sees the man she saw in the sketch, the man who unveiled both a depraved criminal empire and a lost epic masterpiece.

She sees the soldier who knows he has already drawn his last breath.

"By perhaps a hundred," Klaryssa says, a paralyzed stare at once appearing across the faces of both Elle and Kendrick Picard. "I would imagine a hundred times your dream, Elle."

Klaryssa then turns and quietly walks away, looking back just long enough to see Elle melt into her brother's arms.

Chapter 34
Saratoga, New York

All Klaryssa sees is the front door of the museum.
All she thinks about is Yeva and how fast her car
can get her back to Boston.

Klaryssa's cell phone pings, and she sees a
text from Ian.

Ian: We need you now! Where are
you and how soon can you get here?

Klaryssa: Museum in Saratoga.
What's the deal?

I: Zorn and me. We're still on Cape
Cod, a pub on Buzzard's Bay. We're
both getting drunk, that's the deal.
Zorn is closer than me.

K: Closer to what?

I: Getting snockered. Tho I'm gaining.

K: Attaboy

I: So…4 hours maybe? We'll be waiting.

K: No go. Yeva. That's me, pal.

I: Bring her!

K: Shelve it dude. Need her, she's all mine. Playing chef tonight.

I: KK got it. But Marta and Hondo will be here in an hour, tops. Be toasting you, lady.

K: No ice then. Only the heat.

I: Done. BTW, Marta's up for a vacay. Hondo's in too. Need to. Got to, all of us. You in? Maybe a quiet, lonely beach.

K: Game here. Need some sun. Anywhere but Race Point. Not so quiet. Not so lonely.

I: Yeah. Roger that.

***

Less than a minute later, Klaryssa walks out of the museum's front entrance, and she sees her.

It's the girl that she saw on the way in less than an hour earlier, the one standing next to the lamppost. Klaryssa pretends not to see her, turning sharply to the right and heading down the avenue in the opposite direction.

"Professor Mahr?"

For Klaryssa, just hearing those two words, hearing a stranger call out her name, borders on the tolling of a death knell. This girl must be a reporter who somehow, through someone, in some way, knows that Klaryssa was present at a crime scene that has been lighting up the marquee of every known form of mass media since the story first broke two days earlier. This lone voice is Klaryssa's worst nightmare, and she knows this same voice will end her anonymity forever.

There is no escape. Klaryssa stops and turns around.

"Hello...hello, Professor Mahr?" the young girl says, fumbling for the copy of Klaryssa's book that she has in her knapsack while pushing her thick glasses back up onto the bridge of her nose. "I wanted to get your autograph the minute I started reading your book. I've already read it twice. Twice, really."

In her gut, Klaryssa experiences a relief that's beyond measure, as if suddenly pardoned from the guillotine's blade. This girl isn't a reporter. She's a student of some sort. She has to be because she can't be a day over 17 years old and she's carrying neither a microphone nor a camera. All she has with her is a small torn knapsack and a copy of *Medici's Hand*, the book's cover jacket whistling in the squalls of cold wind that whip along the length of the avenue. The girl is tiny, not even five feet tall with her boots on. Klaryssa can barely make out the girl's facial features because of the hooded raincoat she is wearing and her round, oversized glasses that are covered with moisture from the rainstorm that just passed through.

"A friend who works here at the museum told me he spotted you a while back, and he heard a rumor that you might be coming today, to give a lecture," the girl says, a nervous twitch appearing across her face. "He picks up all the gossip, you know. I just hope you don't mind, but I had to meet you in person. I didn't want to disturb you, so I waited outside. I just wanted you to autograph my book. I mean *your* book. I mean *my* copy of *your* book."

Klaryssa pulls a pen out from her shirt pocket, feeling a bright flush sweep across the bruise on her face.

"I'm a student at Columbia, just a freshman," the girl says, opening *Medici's Hand* to the title page and handing the book to Klaryssa. "I travel upstate on weekends, to check out estate sales and small town auctions and all that. I go all over New England, too. Same thing, everywhere. There's no telling what you might find, all these old homes filled with who in the world knows what. I want to major in history, and so much of history is hidden, you know. So much.

"I bought this really old set of books a while back," the girl goes on, her voice cheery. She reaches once again into her knapsack and pulls out a thin plastic folder. "And inside one of the books…"

The girl uses both hands to unroll a sheet of thick, tattered parchment.

Klaryssa feels her blood jump.

"…I found this."

ACKNOWLEDGEMENTS

I cannot begin to express my gratitude to the man who assisted me with this work from the first page to the last, that man being award-winning essayist David Snyder. I don't know which has been more vital—David's guidance with regard to structure and editing, or the inspiration I came away with by having the privilege of reading so much of his brilliant personal work. This toast is for you, Bud.

My heartfelt thanks to those individuals whose encouragement, support, suggestions, and hours of assistance have been invaluable to me in completing this book, including Roberta Anslow, Amanda Grey, Stewart Lytle, Christina Roderick, and Gianna Buonopane.

And I double down on my appreciation for the critique and acute insights provided by Kathy Gantz. How much less my world would be without you in it.

I would like to recognize, with my sincerest thanks, the authors whose work taught me so much about the life, times, and transcendent genius of Michelangelo, including Romain Rolland, William E. Wallace, Ludwig Goldscheider, Howard

Hibbard, and in particular Bernard Lamarche-Vadel.

In writing this story, I relied on the writings of Ulrich Boser, Robert Poole, Shelley Murphy, and Stephen Kurkjian, all of whom detailed the infamous 1990 Isabella Stewart Gardner Museum art heist. I am indebted to each of you.

I would like to also acknowledge authors Scott Helman and Jenna Russell for their compelling account of the 2013 Boston Marathon terrorist attack, and Elizabeth Simpson, David Roxan, and Gerald Steinacher for their chronicle of Nazi Germany's looting of priceless art during World War II. All of these thoroughly professional writings proved invaluable to me. In particular, am I grateful to Eric Lichtblau, whose riveting book, *The Nazis Next Door*, was indispensable in completing this work.

Last but far from least, I can never adequately express my love and admiration for the two individuals who inspired me to write this book —Harry and Helen Snyder, my parents. They have made the beaches of outer Cape Cod the center of our family gatherings since before I was born, with more cherished memories than any of us, including this writer, could ever count.

DS
August 17, 2018

ABOUT THE AUTHOR

Dr. Dennis Snyder is a head and neck surgeon based in the greater Boston area. He has been on staff at Harvard and Tufts Medical Schools for over 25 year, and is one of the founders of Medical Missions for Children, a volunteer organization that provides free surgical care to children with severe congenital deformities and burn injuries. One hundred percent of the royalties from *Race Point* will be donated directly to Medical Missions for Children. Visit the organization online at www.mmfc.org.